The fiery brilliance ~~of the Zebra Hologram Heart~~
which you see on the c~~over~~
phy." This is the revolu~~tion~~
ful laser beam records li~~ght~~
*so tiny that 9,000,000 fit in a square inch. No print or
photograph can match the vibrant colors and radiant
glow of a hologram.*

*So look for the Zebra Hologram Heart whenever you
buy a historical romance. It is a shimmering reflection of
our guarantee that you'll find consistent quality between
the covers!*

DAWN OF DESIRE

Angelique looked up slowly. Whether it was from the brandy or the pleasure of Diego's company she could not be certain, but she was experiencing a luscious contentment, a warmth that grew from within and extended clear to the tips of her toes.

His touch was so light she thought at first she had imagined it, but as his mouth moved slowly down her cheek she was enveloped in sensations so overwhelming that she made no effort to resist him. His powerful body was very warm and the muscles of his chest hard as he pulled her close.

She clung to him, for until this moment the only companion Angelique had known had been loneliness. Until tonight she had never been kissed, nor held—had not even danced with a handsome partner. They would have no more than this one night to give each other pleasure and she wanted it all.

Angelique knew there was far more to making love than what he had shown her thus far, and she reached for his cuff to unbutton it. "Do you need help to undress each night, Captain?" she whispered seductively, her touch playful as she helped him remove his shirt.

When he pulled her back into his embrace again, she returned his deep kiss, then slipped from his grasp and climbed into his bed.

Tonight she belonged to Diego. At dawn she would disappear, not knowing she had captured his heart . . .

RAPTUROUS ROMANCE
by Phoebe Conn

CAPTIVE HEART   (1569, $3.95)
Celiese, the lovely slave girl, had been secretly sent in her mistress's place to wed the much-feared Mylan. The handsome warrior would teach her the secrets of passion, and forever possess her CAPTIVE HEART.

LOVE'S ELUSIVE FLAME   (1836, $3.95)
Flame was determined to find the man of her dreams, but if Joaquin wanted her completely she would have to be his only woman. He needed her, wanted her, and nothing would stop him once he was touched by LOVE'S ELUSIVE FLAME.

SAVAGE STORM   (1687, $3.95)
As a mail-order bride, Gabrielle was determined to survive the Oregon trail. But she couldn't imagine marrying any man other than the arrogant scout who stole her heart.

SAVAGE FIRE   (1397, $3.75)
Although innocent blonde Elizabeth knew it was wrong to meet the powerful Seneca warrior known as Rising Eagle, she came to him when the sky darkened, and let him teach her the wild, rapturous secrets of love.

ECSTASY'S PARADISE   (1460, $3.75)
While escorting Anna Thorson to a loveless marriage, Phillip wondered how he could deliver her to another man's bed when he wanted her to warm his own. Anna, at first angered, found he was the only man she would ever desire.

LOVING FURY

PHOEBE CONN

ZEBRA BOOKS
KENSINGTON PUBLISHING CORP.

ZEBRA BOOKS

are published by

Kensington Publishing Corp.
475 Park Avenue South
New York, NY 10016

First printing: May 1986

Printed in the United States of America

This book is lovingly dedicated to my mother,
Ruby Stanton Conn,
my most loyal and devoted fan.

Chapter I

As Angelique began to dress, a remarkable transformation occurred. She was nearly seventeen and the curves of her lissome figure were superb, but she bound her breasts tightly to give her body the angular lines of a child. Next she powdered her face lightly to cover her golden tan and give her a ghostly pallor that made her flawless skin translucent and caused her to appear frail rather than robust. Her deep blue eyes, which were framed by long, dark lashes, now provided the only bit of color her delicate features displayed.

Having completed the first step of her disguise, she reached for her gown. Slender by nature, she fit easily into the childish garments her mother insisted she wear. That morning she had chosen a pale pink cotton dress and now she quickly tied the satin sash that accented the high waistline. The taffeta underskirt rustled softly as she turned in front of the full-length mirror, but Angelique drew no pleasure from the demure image she presented. It was not so simple a matter to restrict the workings of her agile mind as it had been to confine her supple body.

When she heard the light taps of her mother's footsteps approaching, she turned toward the door. Her exquisite features were set in a savage frown, for she was seething with a bitter rage over the life she had been forced to lead.

7

Each morning Françoise went into her daughter's bedchamber to assist her as she dressed. Though the household of José Luis Aragon contained dozens of servants, she allowed none to serve her precious Angelique. She prided herself on the fact that it was her own attention to detail that had made their ruse so successful, but unfortunately her daughter was becoming more rebellious with each new day.

Now she was pleased to see that the lovely young woman was already dressed, and, satisfied that Angelique still presented the appearance everyone expected to see, Françoise reached out to touch her long, golden curls. "I really must trim your hair, my love, or it will soon sweep the floor as you walk."

Angelique clenched her fists so tightly at her sides that her carefully manicured nails made painful indentations in her creamy-smooth palms. "As you well know, Mama, it is not the length of my hair that concerns me. In two months' time I will be seventeen. Whether or not José Luis has proposed to you by then, I intend to leave this house."

Gesturing emphatically with her satin fan, Françoise began a spirited reply. "You must not threaten me. Your cooperation is vital to my plans and I'll have no more of your tantrums. Until I am José Luis's wife and mistress of this house, you will be my darling little girl and I want to hear no more of your selfish demands!"

Every bit as strong willed as her mother, Angelique refused to desist. "For almost four years I have pretended to be a twelve-year-old child. No one knows I am a woman, least of all me! I have played your game long enough, Mama. It is now time to end this ridiculous masquerade!"

Françoise's blue eyes filled with a determined gleam as she returned her beautiful daughter's hostile stare. "You are the one who is being ridiculous!" she responded fiercely. "Have you forgotten that your father was murdered by the filthy rabble screaming for our blood, indeed shrieking for the lives of any aristocrat they could seize? We were forced to flee France with few treasures other than our lives, and each morning, when I see the beauty of the sunrise, I thank God we escaped the *guillotine* where so many of our beloved relatives were slaughtered! We can never return to our homeland, but here in Spain I mean to regain all that we have lost. As a grieving widow with a young daughter, I have attracted considerable sympathy to our plight, and you have benefited as greatly as I. José Luis will propose to me soon, and after we are married I will swiftly reveal the truth of your age to him. Then you will be permitted to receive the fine suitors you deserve. But until that time you will be silent about this matter. Is that clear? I will not listen to another word of objection from you!"

Angelique's eyes were not a clear blue like her mother's but a far more vivid hue—a blue tinged with violet—and in the morning light they shone with a fiery purple glow. "After four years of begging at the feet of wealthy Spaniards, I have had enough! Unlike you, it is not a rich husband I desire but simply self-respect. I want the right to earn my own keep in a respectable profession. If you have not married José Luis in two months' time and finally told him the truth about me, I am going to seek honest employment wherever I can find it. I might be able to secure a position as a governess, or assist a *couturière* or milliner, but if you do not marry José Luis, I refuse to go to another man's home as his guest, Mama. I refuse to play a beautiful little child for whom he feels nothing but pity while he does his best to console you!"

Françoise drew back her hand and slapped her defiant child soundly. "Silence! For you to even consider seeking work is an outrageous insult, not only to me but to the memory of your father as well! We will not discuss this issue ever again. It is closed." Turning to look at the small jeweled clock upon the dressing table, she became even more enraged. "Now you have made us late for breakfast. You must hurry before José Luis grows impatient for my company and sends someone to summon us."

Angelique's fiery temper was unquenched by her mother's savage blow, but she held her tongue in order to escape a more brutal beating. She slipped her feet into the heel-less slippers she had been ordered to wear so that her height would not be so readily apparent. Then she bent down and hastily tied the ribbon laces about her ankles in dainty bows. As she rose she inquired curiously, "Why are you so terrified of telling José Luis the truth? Why should the fact that you are thirty-six rather than thirty make any difference to him?"

"It is because you have so little sense that you must trust me to know what is best!" Françoise hissed angrily. She looked into the mirror to adjust the drape of her lace *mantilla* over her stylish chignon, and, after tying back Angelique's hair at her nape with a pink ribbon, she placed the young woman's lacy veil so far forward that her delicate features were completely hidden. "Not another word of this matter must be spoken. José Luis is fond of you. Do not let him see the blackness of your mood. Smile and speak to him politely as you always do."

Angelique's long, dark lashes made shadows upon her flushed cheeks as she continued to frown. "My argument is with you, Mama, not with José Luis." Then lowering her voice to a sultry whisper, she asked pointedly, "What would happen if he were to learn my true age before you two are married? Are you afraid that he might prefer me?"

"How dare you!" Françoise exploded in a furious fit of temper. It was indeed her greatest fear that someday her strikingly beautiful daughter would become her rival. "Must I beat you senseless before you learn some manners? That is what you deserve for insulting me so rudely. I am sorely tempted to lock you in your room all day and forbid you to attend tonight's party!"

"You have already imprisoned me in the disguise of a child. That is torture enough!" Angelique replied with equal fervor.

Françoise turned on her tiny feet and marched through the door, but she neither shut nor locked it. Having decided that confining Angelique to her room would cause more comment than allowing her to sulk all day, she walked swiftly to the patio where José Luis sat enjoying an ample breakfast in the warmth of the morning sun.

Taking a deep breath in an attempt to regain her composure, she began to smile enticingly. "Good morning," she purred sweetly as she slipped into her chair beside him. "Please forgive us for not joining you more promptly, but Angelique seems to require more time to dress each day."

José Luis regarded the attractive Frenchwoman with a slow smile. "Perhaps if she were to have her own maid, she would not depend upon you so greatly, Françoise."

Again smiling warmly to entice the handsome Spaniard's mind away from thoughts of her headstrong daughter, Françoise replied softly, "The child is very shy. She simply will not accept the attentions of a maid. I have tried many times to help her overcome her reticence to have a servant, but she cries so pitifully that I dare not force one upon her."

"No, of course not," José Luis agreed readily, for he did not want to see the child upset needlessly. As Angelique approached the table and made a slight curtsy, he smiled to greet her. "There you are, my little kitten. Did you sleep well?"

"Yes, thank you." Angelique bent down to give him a light kiss upon the cheek. She considered him a very handsome man. His black hair was only lightly touched with gray at the temples, his skin was a smooth, deep bronze, and his flashing brown eyes were usually filled with merriment. Of the many men who had befriended them since their arrival in Spain, she liked José Luis Aragon the best. And his affection for her seemed so genuine that she had soon learned to return it. While he could trace his ancestry to King Ferdinand of Aragon, he much preferred his comfortable home in Barcelona to the intrigues of the court in Madrid. He was very rich, for he was the owner of a fleet of ships that supplied the colonies of Spain with necessary goods and returned with holds filled with gold and silver. He was generous and loving, but though he had been a widower for many years, he had showed no sign of wanting to take her mother for his wife.

As she took her place at his table, she began to wonder if perhaps she could inspire him to consider marriage, since she knew that to be her mother's goal. From time to time she had had occasion to speak with him alone and she silently vowed not to waste the next opportunity. If the idea of remarrying simply had not occurred to him, she would plant it in his mind immediately, for her own sake as well as her mother's.

José Luis was enchanted by Françoise and her sweet little daughter. Since his only son was captain of his own ship and away on a voyage to New Spain, he had been very lonely until they had come to his home for a visit. They were a sweet pair, as pleasant as they were pretty, and brought a sparkling liveliness to his home that had been lacking in Diego's absence. The mere thought of his son brought a frown to his brow, and, not wishing to appear impolite, he voiced his concern to his two feminine companions. "My son's ship, *El Diablo del Mar,* is long overdue. Though I ceased to worry about Diego's safety years ago, for he mastered the complexities of sailing as easily as a bird learns to use his wings, he has tried my patience sorely this time."

Angelique ate her meal in silence while she observed her mother bestowing upon José Luis the generous comfort the attractive woman knew how to give so well. Françoise reached out to touch the Spaniard's sleeve lightly as she encouraged him to speak of his son. They made a handsome couple, for she was very fair and he had the dashing good looks of the Spanish nobility. As usual, they made her feel uncomfortable, for she saw the spark of excitement in their glances and believed they would have preferred being alone.

"I too wish that he would return, José Luis, for I am

12

anxious to meet him. If he is anything like his father, I know I shall find him very appealing."

Françoise flattered the handsome man constantly, but, in truth, she had grown very fond of him and hoped he would not continue to disappoint her by making her wait for a marriage proposal. She was dreadfully tired of their vagabond existence and now that Angelique was becoming so troublesome, she had no more time to waste with hopeless causes.

She had told such a small lie at first, Françoise rationalized to herself. When Angelique had turned thirteen, she had not announced the fact but had continued to say that the pretty girl was twelve, for subtracting years from her daughter's age had deducted them from her own as well. Once having begun, she had found the ruse too effective to end, but she knew from their recent argument that Angelique was dangerously close to being uncontrollable. She would have no choice then but to send the high-spirited girl to a convent, for she would never allow her to disgrace the family name by going to work. Although her thoughts were in turmoil, none of the perplexing problems she faced with her daughter were apparent in the sweet expression she displayed to her handsome male companion. To him she presented a serene picture of contentment.

José Luis replied enthusiastically, "Yes, you will like Diego. All women do. It is probably a good thing he is at sea so often, for the scandals he causes here in Spain would otherwise damage the name of Aragon irreparably." Amused by that thought, he chuckled slyly as he reached into the large bowl of fruit in the center of the table, extracted an orange, and began to peel it.

"Scandals of what sort?" Angelique inquired softly, for she could not imagine what he meant. She never spoke in her natural voice around José Luis but used the wispy tone of a child instead.

"Merely good-natured pranks, kitten. Nothing so dire

13

that he need fear I will disown him." He cast a knowing glance toward Françoise then, certain she would understand why his answer to her child had been so vague.

Unfortunately, Angelique had also seen that glance and was saddened that he would not tell her the truth. Her appetite disappeared in a wave of disappointment, for she realized that she was again being excluded from a discussion because she was considered a child rather than an adult.

Knowing they would not miss her, she asked to be excused to return to her room to attend to her studies. Since coming to Spain, she had had no tutors other than her mother, but she had mastered all the instruction Françoise could present several years prior. That she supposedly spent each morning studying was simply part of their hoax, but it provided time for her to be by herself with her own thoughts and she was grateful for that. Needing a new book to read, she stopped by the library of the spacious home. José Luis had a large selection from which to choose and she perused the shelves for several minutes before removing a slender volume of poetry.

As she turned to leave the room, she noticed the small portrait of Diego upon his father's desk. She had often stopped to admire it, for José Luis spoke frequently of his son. The small painting showed so serious a young man that she found it difficult to believe he could enjoy pranks of any sort, regardless of what his father had said that morning. He appeared to be as handsome a man as his father, with well-defined classical features, glossy black hair, and brown eyes fringed with dark lashes. The Spanish were striking people, yet she was certain Diego would be considered handsome no matter where he chose to reside. She touched the gilt frame fondly, wondering what he would think of her when he finally returned home. "Will you think me as pretty a child as your father does, Diego, will you consider me unworthy of your time and simply ignore me?" Pained by that possibility since it was the more likely of the two, she left the room to return to the solitude of her own quarters.

Though José Luis often went riding or shopping with Françoise in the mornings, he spent each afternoon in his library. He enjoyed managing his business but preferred to do it from the quiet of his home rather than from the noisy offices his company maintained down at the port of Barcelona. He found the neatly penned columns of figures that filled his ledgers as intriguing as a fascinating novel and enjoyed reconciling his accounts as if it were a most amusing game.

When he glanced up and saw Angelique waiting quietly at the door, he closed the volume in which he had been working and motioned for her to come inside. "If it is another book you want, please come in and get it, child. I have never known anyone who loves to read with the passion you display. Take a dozen books back to your room if it will please you. I know you will not lose them."

Angelique came forward hesitantly and lifted her hand to cover a nervous cough before she began to speak. "Since my mother is resting in anticipation of tonight's party, she will never know I have spoken with you if you do not tell her."

José Luis rose to take the shy young girl's hand, then led her over to one of the ornately carved chairs near the fireplace. "Ah, is it a secret you wish to tell? You have my word as a gentleman that Françoise will never hear it." He flashed a charming smile, hoping to put her at ease, for truly he did like her very much and was pleased to think he had her trust. Taking the chair opposite hers, he leaned forward, eager to listen to whatever she might want to say.

Now that she had dared to approach him, Angelique's shyness was quite genuine, for she did not want to appear a fool in front of this man she had come to admire so greatly; nor did she wish to affect the flirtatious manner her mother found so effective. "José Luis," she began softly, choosing her words with great care, "you must know my mother misses my father terribly."

15

"Yes," José Luis agreed sympathetically. "That fact is apparent to all who know her, kitten, but it is not so unusual for a widow to miss a husband she loved. For that matter, I still miss my beloved Magdalena as much today as I did the day I lost her. She was a great beauty, a devoted mother, and a loving wife, but she was not strong enough to survive the birth of our second son. That the babe was lost as well only added to my sorrow, but that pain is not nearly so sharp as the one I still feel when I think of Magdalena. You must be more patient with your mother. In time she will speak of your father less often. Is that what concerns you?"

Angelique had never heard José Luis speak of his late wife. She knew he had been widowed, though the circumstances had never been explained, and she was saddened to think that Magdalena's death had involved the tragedy of a lost child as well. "Yes, I see that you do understand her feelings, but it is not the intensity of her grief that concerns me now."

"It is not?" José Luis queried skeptically. "What is it then?"

"Well, my mother seems so very lonely. I fear that someday she might make a serious error in judgment about a man. In our present modest circumstances, she would not attract men for her wealth, but there are many men who desire a woman's company simply for her beauty."

"Yes, that is true," José Luis again agreed, but he was fast becoming very confused. "Is there some particular man about whom you are worried? Perhaps a man who will be a guest here tonight?"

Angelique had not thought of that possibility, but since he seemed to think it the cause of her alarm, she readily agreed. "Yes, there are several who seem a bit too eager in their attentions, and as I said, my mother is a very lonely woman."

"And also a very lovely one." José Luis attempted to study Angelique's expression more closely, but she was looking down at her hands, which lay folded in her lap, and he could see little more than the lace *mantilla* that covered her tawny curls.

"I know she prefers you to the others, José Luis, for you have been most kind to us, but if you do not love her and other men say that they do, well then . . ."

"Ah yes, now I see your point." José Luis sat back, wondering how best to respond to such a surprising suggestion. "I enjoy your mother's company, Angelique. She is a very charming companion. But as to love, well, that is another matter entirely."

As Angelique looked up, her deep blue eyes grew bright with alarm. Her rapidly beating heart filled with dread, for she assumed instantly from the somberness of José Luis's mood that he did not love her mother at all. "Forgive me," she whispered breathlessly. "I did not mean to take advantage of your kindness and I obviously have, but it is most unfair of you to let my mother think you will someday offer marriage if truly you have no intention of doing so."

Far from being insulted by the boldness of her remark, José Luis threw back his head and laughed out loud, for he was greatly amused to have received such a lecture from a child. "You are your mother's *daughter,* Angelique, not her father, and I do not need to state my intentions to you. Now shouldn't you go and dress for the party? I have again hired the musicians you enjoyed so much the last time I entertained."

Mortified to have been laughed at, Angelique rose quickly and ran from the room, embarrassed to think how badly she had handled her mission. But she had at least found out what she had wanted to know. José Luis would not propose to her mother and so they would soon be leaving, accepting another invitation from a handsome and eligible man who was enchanted by the delightful Françoise Devereau and her lovely little daughter.

But she could no longer pretend. She would tell her mother good-bye and seek her fortune elsewhere rather than play the part of a twelve-year-old child again. She had yearned too long for others to see her as the woman she alone knew herself to be.

Françoise applied her makeup with precision, accenting the gentle upsweep of her brows lightly before tinting her lips so that they took on the enticing color of a delicate pink rose. She brushed out her honey-colored curls, and, after noting with satisfaction that they were still untouched by a single strand of gray, she styled them loosely into an attractive drape at the nape of her neck.

She had, of course, objected when José Luis had first offered to buy her a new wardrobe, but he had insisted that such a gift was proper, as she had known he would, and now she had several exquisite gowns from which to choose. The *couturière* was not nearly so fine as Rose Bertin, whom she had patronized in Paris, but the woman was skilled nevertheless and Françoise was pleased with her work.

Having saved her favorite gown for just such a special occasion, Françoise asked her maid to bring it now. Made of the softest light blue satin in the latest style, the high waistline, slender sleeves, tight bodice, and *décolleté* neckline trimmed with a frilly lace fichu displayed her graceful figure to every advantage.

She struck a variety of poses in front of her mirror in order to ascertain how best to use the splendid array of physical assets she still possessed. Looking forward to a wonderfully successful evening, she prayed that José Luis would at last be inspired to propose. Then she raised her fan to her lips and opened it coquettishly, wondering how best to sound reticent in her reply when she was so eager to accept.

Angelique had also chosen a blue gown for the party, but hers was of the same sweet juvenile style she had worn during the day. Not wanting her mother to suspect anything was amiss, she was ready when Françoise came to her room. "You look very pretty tonight, Mama," she managed to say, attempting to sound sincere.

"Why thank you," Françoise responded with some surprise, recalling that their first conversation of the day had been rather heated and they had seen little of each other since. She circled her daughter slowly, surveying her appearance with a critical eye before returning the compliment. "You look very nice too, my dearest. Now come with me for we do not want to leave José Luis alone while he waits for his guests to arrive."

As Angelique walked by her mother's side, she hoped her lack of enthusiasm for the evening's festivities would not be noticed. There were always many young people at José Luis's parties, for he enjoyed the company of Diego's friends, and it was difficult for Angelique to affect the innocent enjoyment of a child when handsome men stood all around her. The bachelors were polite, but other than remarking upon the mildness of the weather, none cared to flatter a mere child with their attentions, no matter how pretty she might be.

A few of the men were married and their wives always greeted her sweetly, yet she had no hope of developing friendships with these young women, for none among them wished to become the confidante of a child. She had found the single women most unsympathetic as well, for they were far too busy attempting to impress the bachelors to consider conversing with her.

Moreover, the worst possible torment was suffered when children were included in the invitation. Though she had been able to fool adults into believing she was only twelve, children instantly sensed a deception of some sort and were as uneasy in her company as she was in theirs. As a result, she had made no friends of any age and had led a very isolated existence since they had been forced to leave France.

They had come to Spain at the insistence of one of her mother's cousins. Her mother had accepted the offer because she knew being surrounded by relatives, no matter how distant, would help to ease her grief as she endeavored to build a new life. But she had swiftly tired of the constraints of mourning and had begun to accept invitations from wealthy Spaniards who seemed sympathetic to the loss she had suffered. That breach of etiquette had angered their Cousin Beatriz so greatly that her mother and Beatriz were no longer even on speaking terms. Angelique could recall the first of the homes in which they had stayed after leaving their Spanish cousin's, but after four years she found it difficult to remember them all. They had been living in José Luis's home for two months, but after the conversation she had had with him earlier, she feared they would not remain there much longer.

Before joining José Luis, Françoise paused to give her daughter one final bit of advice. "You must arouse absolutely no suspicion tonight, Angelique, for I feel certain that if the evening goes according to my plan, I will soon be hearing a marriage proposal."

Angelique nodded. "I understand, Mama." She watched her hurry off then, an attractive blonde in a stunning blue gown who was too anxious to remarry to give a thought to her daughter's happiness.

Angelique took a place near the musicians, for their lively tunes did much to raise her spirits and her smile was genuine as she enjoyed their music. It was not until later, when she observed her mother flirting openly with José Luis as they danced, that her apprehension returned. He was smiling at her mother as he always did, but she had seen him glance in her direction more than once and was horrified to think he might believe her mother had encouraged her to ask him about his intentions. He had promised not to reveal the subject of their conversation, but would he keep his word after several goblets of wine?

Having no wish to speak with either of them again that evening, she quickly went to her room, removed her blue dress, and scrubbed the ghostly white powder from her face. After stepping out of her lingerie and unfastening the linen band to release the fullness of her bosom, she was able to breathe deeply at last. The slender figure she now saw reflected in the mirror was most definitely that of a woman and, filled with the pain of that realization, she quickly donned her lace-trimmed nightdress and stepped out into the moonlit garden to enjoy the fragrant night air before getting into bed. She could still hear the lilting melodies being played by the musicians and, as she sat down upon a small wooden bench and hugged her knees, she imagined the merriment of the lively crowd to which she wanted so desperately to belong.

Chapter II

Juan Diego Aragon stood six feet three inches tall and weighed one hundred and eighty-five pounds dripping wet, which he had been just moments before. They had sailed into the port of Barcelona on the evening tide and, anxious to get home to report to his father on the success of his voyage, he had bathed hurriedly before donning the simple garb of an ordinary seaman. Then, with what appeared to be no more than a bag of laundry slung over his shoulder, he placed the command of *El Diablo del Mar* in the capable hands of his mate, Octavio Morales. After providing Octavio with orders as to which men should be posted as guards and which should be granted liberty, he strode down the gangplank confidently.

The evening was a balmy one and, feeling the need for exercise after so many weeks at sea, he decided to walk rather than hire a carriage as a captain of his stature might be expected to do. He was a vigorous walker and made good time, and while he walked he turned his thoughts to how best to phrase his report to his father.

His parent was a serious man, concerned with maintaining high profits but far too cautious to listen without alarm to what risks had been taken to make them. Diego, therefore, always rehearsed what it was he wanted to say so he could provide an interesting account of his voyage without revealing too much of his own recklessness. He chuckled to himself as he thought of his father, for José Luis was regarded by all as a true gentleman. Diego knew that few would pay him the same compliment.

When he reached the corner where the family home stood, he was both astonished and angered to hear the music and laughter coming from the festivities inside. It was his father he longed to see, not all their many friends who would insist he relate the tale of his voyage until he grew hoarse.

Deciding not to submit to that torture, he circled the impressive home looking for a section of the garden wall that he had discovered in his early teens to be especially well suited for scaling. The small indentations had always gone unnoticed by others, and now, in a matter of seconds, he had climbed the wall with the speed of a spider.

Once seated upon the top, he gently lowered his cumbersome bag down to the ground, but when he jumped he misjudged the distance and landed sprawled in the flower bed. And as if suffering that indignity were not enough, he heard a lilting laugh and looked up to find that his less-than-expert landing had been observed.

The full moon lit the garden with sufficient light for Angelique to recognize that the man who had appeared so suddenly was not an unwanted intruder but the long-awaited Diego Aragon. Seeing by the fury of his expression that her laughter had insulted him, she hastened to apologize, but the musical ring of amusement still filled her voice. "Forgive me for laughing. I hope you're not hurt, but wouldn't the front door have been a more logical choice for your arrival?"

Diego brushed off his hands and knees and, as he straightened up, he noticed that the shadowy figure addressing him with such unabashed impertinence was clad in a filmy, lace-trimmed nightdress. "I didn't want to interrupt the party. Tell me, do you always dress so informally when you accept my father's invitations?"

23

Glancing down at her comfortable attire, Angelique shrugged. "I was on my way to bed. The moonlight was so inviting, and I meant only to enjoy it for a moment. Naturally I did not expect anyone to leap the wall and interrupt my solitude."

Intrigued by her softly accented speech, Diego took a step forward and, finding the young woman most attractive, his mood improved instantly. Hoping to detain her for a moment longer, he asked the most obvious question. "Why would you prefer solitude to the attention you must have received at the party? Unless my friends have changed their attitudes drastically in the months I've been away, they must have been enchanted with you and gone to great lengths to impress you favorably."

His comment shocked Angelique until she realized with a slow smile that he thought her worthy of his friends' notice. Without her ghostly makeup, barefoot, and clad in a sheer nightdress, she appeared to be exactly what she was—a very beautiful young woman. Pleased by his compliment, she was nevertheless too embarrassed to reveal she had received no attention at all from the men at the party. Finally she replied in the only way she could. "Perhaps I dislike attracting attention as greatly as you do."

"Well, if that is your reason, then I understand it completely," Diego retorted with a wicked grin. His teeth were very white and sparkled against his deeply tanned skin. "We seem to be kindred souls," he added, grimly recalling several rather predatory women he had had occasion to avoid in the past. Diego considered the regard of unwanted admirers the worst of tortures. Yet he had always had a weakness for blondes and much preferred their company to that of dark-haired beauties, whose attentions he had been hard pressed to avoid recently in New Spain.

Angelique smiled in return, for Diego radiated a masculine charm she found most appealing. When he moved still closer, she did not back away but continued to regard

24

him with open curiosity. He resembled the young man in the portrait she had seen in his father's library, but he was far more handsome in person than the frozen image the artist had been able to capture in oils. There was a vitality about him, a sparkle in his dark eyes and a warmth to his smile that was absent in the small portrait. She realized she was staring most rudely and laughed again, but this time he joined in with a good-natured chuckle.

Moving to take advantage of his surpising bit of good fortune, Diego gestured toward the door leading to his room. "I have brought home some unusual souvenirs—treasures from the New World—which I think you would find far more entertaining than my father's party. Would you care to see them?"

"Why yes, I would," Angelique responded with innocent enthusiasm. She had absolutely no experience in analyzing the intentions of handsome young men and thought he meant only to display some curious mementos.

"Let's make certain none of the guests is using my room before we become too comfortable." Diego showed Angelique into his room and stopped quickly to light the candles affixed in the candalabrum upon the ornately carved dresser. Finding no luggage or any other sign that the room was presently in use, he motioned for Angelique to take a chair while he spilled the contents of his duffel bag upon the bed. "When Cortés reached the New World in 1519, he found a race of highly civilized Indians—Las Aztecas they were called. I met a man in Vera Cruz who deals in antiquities, and when he found I liked the art of Las Aztecas, he showed me some things that others had never been privileged to view. While many people consider their art grotesque, I happen to like it." He turned then to place a small jade carving in Angelique's hands.

When she rose and carried it over to the candles so that she could appreciate it more fully, his eyes swept over her hungrily. In the moonlight he had thought her appearance most attractive, but now that he could see her features more clearly he judged her a rare beauty. She was of a pleasing height—the top of her head was even with his shoulder—and her slender figure, which was barely veiled by the thin nightdress, seemed to be balanced by delightfully long legs. Her cascade of golden curls tumbled past her waist in a silken profusion, yet her brows and long, sweeping lashes were dark. Her lashes were so thick they blocked the candles' glow, casting her high cheekbones in vivid relief. She had the most perfect profile he had ever seen, for while she displayed the delicate beauty of a princess, her features were as well defined as those gracing classical Greek statuary. The mere sight of her took his breath away and he could do no more than stare as he waited for her to remark upon the jade piece in her hands.

Angelique turned the figure over slowly. It was a man whose face was emerging from a serpent's mouth. His features were clearly recognizable as those of an Indian and, in addition to an astonishing headdress, he was wearing what appeared to be a cloak of feathers. "Yes, I can see why some might not be able to appreciate this, for it is nothing like European sculpture. It is very fine, however, and I like it too. This is not simply a man in costume though, is it? Surely he must be a god of some sort."

When she turned to glance his way, Diego thought the blue of her eyes as magnificent as the Caribbean sea. He had never been so self-conscious with a woman, but he decided that with one of such astonishing beauty he would have to take a firmer hold upon himself. Focusing all his attention upon the small statue in her hands, he replied, "Yes, it is the god Quetzalcoatl, the Feathered Serpent."

"A serpent with feathers? How very strange. But of course all pagan gods are remarkable, aren't they?" Angelique asked with a mischievous smile.

"Yes, of course," Diego agreed. "This one was known as the Morning Star, the Breath of Life, and Lord of the Wind, since he could face in all directions simultaneously. He was the Precious Twin, while his opposite, Xolotl, the Evening Star, represented evil. I have one of him too. Would you like to see it?"

"Yes, I most certainly would, but he doesn't sound nearly as attractive as this little fellow."

Searching quickly for the desired object, Diego soon found it. "As you can see, he has the form of a skeleton."

Angelique set aside the plumed serpent to take the new treasure in her hands. While this figure had the detail of a skeleton, the jade was so intricately carved that it appeared to be a decorative piece rather than a gruesome idol. "The Aztecas must have been a fascinating people. Do they still exist?" she inquired.

"Yes and no," Diego replied. "There are Indians aplenty in New Spain, but they are Christian now and their old religion is no longer practiced. Since it embodied an ideology that called for constant war in order to provide the priests with victims for human sacrifice to appease their blood-thirsty gods, I think it is best that it has been eradicated. That these fantastic representations of their spirit world are also disappearing is an unfortunate consequence." Seeing her eyes grow wide with the mention of human sacrifice, Diego decided to change the subject. "If you really do like these pieces, I'll unwrap another."

"Why should I lie to you? I think these carvings are magnificent. Didn't I make my opinion clear?"

Diego had not meant to insult her, as he obviously had, but merely to enjoy a bit of teasing repartee. Seeing the fire in the lovely blonde's eyes, he apologized quickly, fearing she would swiftly leave his room if he did not. "I was merely teasing you. Forgive me, for I meant no offense."

"No, you must forgive me. I should have realized that. I'm sorry."

Thinking the young woman extraordinary in many ways, Diego marveled that she could also be so naive. He knew that a convent education often produced such demure females, and he wondered aloud about her past. "From where do you come? You are obviously not Spanish."

"I most certainly am!" Angelique responded heatedly, for her mother had warned her frequently of the danger in revealing who they really were. Even the story José Luis had been told had not been entirely the truth. "I am a resident of Spain, one of King Charles's subjects, and therefore a Spaniard."

Though dismayed by her somewhat unusual view of nationality, Diego decided against pursuing the subject further. He often relied upon his smile to impress young women and, hoping to distract this one completely, he flashed his most disarming grin. "I have some very fine brandy. Would you care to join me in a glass?"

"I have had brandy on occasion, but it is far too potent for my tastes." Angelique now realized she had spoken much too sharply to him and, regretting that rudeness, smiled now to make up for it.

Diego was pleased to see she was as easy to charm as the other women he had met and he continued in a teasing tone, "Then I will give you only a sip of this. I'm certain you will like it, for it is French and very smooth." Before she could refuse, he circled the bed and bent down beside a small chest. After he had pressed the corner, the front panel opened to reveal a secret compartment. "I no longer need to hide my brandy, but such secrecy was necessary before I was of age and now I find it a convenient habit to keep."

"Like leaping walls?" Angelique inquired with a sparkling laugh.

"Oh, definitely, but since my father still does not know about those footholds in the wall, I must ask you to keep my secret."

"I am very good at keeping secrets," Angelique responded with a bitter irony she made no attempt to keep out of her voice.

28

Setting the Xolotl aside, she gave her full attention to observing Diego. He had a powerful build, broad shoulders, a lean torso that tapered to a narrow waist, and slim hips. The folds of his shirt sleeves hid the contours of his arms, but she had no doubt they would be as well developed as the muscles of his legs, which were so handsomely defined by his close-fitting black breeches. When he came forward with the bottle of brandy and two snifters she raised her eyes to his and hoped he had not seen the direction of her glance, though she realized he must certainly know that women thought him handsome.

Diego placed the fragile glasses upon the dresser and poured no more than a swallow of the amber liquid for her before providing a far more generous amount for himself. "I'll expect your honest opinion on this, too."

Angelique watched him taste his and, after noting that he had not suffered any noticeable ill effects, she raised her snifter to her lips. She thought the aroma enticing, but when she took a small sip, the brandy burned her throat and brought tears to her eyes. "You dare to describe this . . . poison as smooth?" she asked through a sputtering cough.

Diego found even her obvious discomfort extremely appealing. He had never had such difficulty entertaining a young woman, but he was now beginning to consider this lively blonde a greater treasure than any of the Azteca carvings he had brought home and therefore worthy of his best efforts to please her. That she had such an open manner was very refreshing, for he had had his fill of the daughters of fine families who spent the entire evening flirting outrageously and then expected him to be content with a chaste kiss upon the cheek.

Despite her claim of being Spanish, he thought her most likely French and assumed her attitudes would be far more liberal than a young Spanish lady's would be. He judged her age to be close to eighteen, which was certainly old enough for her to know better than to enter a man's bedchamber in the middle of the night dressed in no more than a nightdress that was so sheer it was nearly transparent. Stepping closer, he put his hand over hers and his slim, tan fingers easily covered her delicate hand. "Take another sip, but more slowly this time. The brandy is delicious if you but give it the opportunity to please you."

Angelique's deep blue eyes took on a skeptical gleam as she looked up at the handsome young man. "Are you simply teasing me again—waiting to laugh while I choke?" she whispered softly. The expression in his dark eyes had changed somehow, she noted silently. His glance was not really mocking now, but she didn't recognize his mood for the far more dangerous one it had become.

"Of course not," Diego replied. His smile widened as he began to fathom that the fire that had begun to warm his blood was not due to the strength of the brandy but to her loveliness alone. He was a man who knew how to get what he wanted, whether it was an exquisite jade carving or an exotic beauty to share his bed for the night. At that moment he wanted her, and when she did not draw away as he inched closer, she unwittingly provided all the encouragement he required. "Come over here and sit down beside me while I unwrap the next piece. I think I can find one you'll like."

"I liked the others—truly I did," Angelique protested. Exasperated that he might be questioning her sincerity, she failed to notice that he had added another drop of brandy to her glass.

Diego swallowed the last of the brandy he had poured for himself and decided against having any more. He placed his fingertips lightly upon Angelique's back and guided her over to his bed, where he saw that she was comfortably seated. He then sorted through the bundles wrapped in linen until he found the one he wanted. Unwrapping it carefully, he explained, "This is Mictlantecihuatl, Goddess of the Land of the Dead, which, for some reason, Las Aztecas regarded as a place of music and dance. She's not made of jade, but of basalt, a heavy volcanic rock." He waited a moment for his guest to finish her brandy, then carried her snifter back to the dresser and placed it beside his own before handing her the figure to study. While she was absorbed in that task, he quite casually moved to the door leading to the hall and locked it.

"Mictlantecihuatl?" Angelique repeated, trying hard to pronounce the difficult name properly. "The Azteca names sound very strange to my ears. Do they to yours as well?"

"Yes, they most certainly do, but I asked the man from whom I bought these to write down the names so I might learn them. They are difficult to pronounce, but after a little practice you'll master them," Diego reassured her confidently.

The small female figure was kneeling and her hands were raised to shoulder height. She wore a crown and necklace of skulls, but still her expression seemed pleasant, Angelique mused, as if she were making the best of being a goddess of the underworld. Angelique thought her the most interesting of the three and turned her over to trace the incised lines that curved over her back. "I shouldn't care what anyone says about these if I were you. They are superior both in design and in execution. Anyone who says otherwise is simply too ignorant to appreciate the beauty that is plain to us."

"I knew we were kindred souls the minute I saw you," Diego confided softly. He began to gather up the linen he had tossed about the bed, and after repacking the duffel bag he carried it over to the corner to get it out of the way. He waited a moment for Angelique to complete her inspection of the goddess, but when he noticed that her grasp seemed somewhat unsteady, he reached down to take the heavy figure from her hands. "Let me put this away with the others. It has grown quite late, I'm afraid."

Angelique looked up slowly and whether it was from the brandy or the pleasure of his company she could not be certain, but she was experiencing luscious contentment, a warmth that grew from within and extended clear to the tips

31

of her fingers and toes. When he took her hands to help her rise, she wanted to tell him how much she appreciated his sharing his souvenirs with her, but as she was about to do so, he bent down to brush her brow with his lips. His touch was so light she thought at first she had imagined it, but as his mouth moved slowly down her cheek she was enveloped in sensations so overwhelming that she made no effort to resist him. Instead she stood on tiptoe to reach up and touch the dark curls at his nape. His powerful body was very warm and the muscles of his chest hard as he pulled her close.

For so tall and strong a man, he was surprisingly gentle and she relaxed against him, thinking only of how perfect the brief time she had spent with him had been. His lips found hers then, but when she readily returned his first hesitant kiss, he wound his fingers in her golden curls to hold her captive in his eager embrace. He shocked her then as his tongue passed between her lips for a deep kiss so filled with hunger she could no longer mistake his purpose as merely being to wish her an affectionate good night. Astonished that he found her as attractive as she found him, Angelique wrapped her arms around his neck to savor his brandy-flavored kiss and her initial surprise was swiftly replaced by tingles of intense pleasure.

Diego found the lissome blonde's taste more delicious than any brandy and he kissed her again and again. He scarcely allowed her the opportunity to breathe as his mouth plundered hers with a demand for the surrender she readily gave. That she was as willing to accept his affection as he was to give it filled his blood with a flame that quickly ignited an unquenchable desire.

He lowered his hand to the small of her back and pressed her hips so firmly against his own that he knew she could not fail to feel the strength of his passion. The flushed peaks of her breasts brushed against his chest, but he longed to touch the smoothness of her skin, not the softness of her nightdress. Eagerly he reached for the row of buttons that

32

began at her throat, intent upon freeing her from the garment that blocked his pleasure.

Angelique attempted to think clearly, but any coherent thought was impossible with Diego wrapping himself around her as tightly as the warmest winter cloak. Images passed through her mind in brilliant flashes, but she could find no meaning in them, for her heart was beating so rapidly she could interpret nothing but its rhythm pounding wildly in her ears.

The elegant world into which she had been born had been destroyed in the flames of the revolution, yet the heat of that fire seemed slight compared to the passion of the man who was so clearly determined to sear her very soul with the torch of his ardor. The hours she would remain in his home were now numbered, and she knew she would have to spend those as a child. Once she went out on her own, she would no longer be able to travel in his social circle and they would never meet again. That bitter realization broke her heart, for she had found Diego Aragon to be the most intelligent and exciting man she had ever met and she wanted so much more than this one brief night fate had allowed her.

She clung to him, for until this moment the only companion she had known had been loneliness. Until tonight she had never been kissed, nor held—had not even danced with a handsome partner. They would have no more than this one night to give each other pleasure and she wanted it all. The sorrow that had filled her day was swept away by his intoxicating kisses, but were she to drown in the torrent of his affection, she would consider such a sacrifice a small price to pay for the joy she had found in his arms.

Diego released the last of the tiny buttons, and, to his amazement, the lovely blonde let her nightdress slip to the floor. She moved away for an instant to turn down the covers of his bed and toss her discarded gown upon it. When she turned back to him there was not the slightest trace of coquettishness in her glance, but only a calm pride, as if she knew how greatly the sight of her nude body would please him. Her fair skin had a warm, golden sheen, a sensuous shade more tempting than that of any pagan goddess. Her full breasts were high and firm above her tiny waist, her hips narrow, and, as he had imagined, her legs were perfect, long and slender, and gave her steps a fluid grace.

He pulled her back into his arms and buried his face in the softness of her curls as he lifted her into the air with a joyous cry of exaltation. He had found in this gentle beauty more charm than he had dreamed could ever exist in so fragile a being. There was so much he longed to tell her, places he hoped to take her, adventures he wanted her to share, but as he stepped back to again place her upon her feet, he could find no words to describe the emotions that filled his heart.

Angelique knew there was far more to making love than what he had shown her and she reached for his cuff to unbutton it. "Do you need help to undress each night, Captain?" she whispered seductively, her touch playful as she helped him remove his shirt. His broad chest was covered with a thick mat of dark curls, which tapered to a thin line then disappeared beneath his belt. She unbuckled the black leather belt, not stopping to wonder if she might be acting in too forward a fashion, for he had made no secret of how desperately he wanted her and she thought her efforts to assist him would only be pleasing. When he pulled her back into his arms again, she returned his deep kiss, but then she slipped from his grasp and climbed into his bed.

Diego cast off the remainder of his clothing with such haste that he was certain he had torn it to shreds. When he joined the enticing blonde in his bed, he stretched out beside her, wanting every inch of their flesh to meet as he kissed her again. He lavished kisses upon her flushed cheeks before trailing sweet nibbles down her throat and finally reaching the pale pink crest of her breast. He was drunk for the first time in his life, not with liquor but with passion, and he savored her delicate flesh as if it tasted as sweet as honey.

Angelique had expected Diego to take her swiftly, but that he continued to shower her with such generous affection pleased her beyond measure. Surely this was all any man and woman could hope to share, she reflected, and she adored him in that instant, loved him with every bit of emotion her innocent heart could hold. She wove her slender fingers in his hair and held him close, praying this dream of devotion would never end and morning would not arrive to separate them forever.

Diego's mouth returned to hers as he shifted his position to spare her the burden of his weight, and he no longer found it possible to hold himself back from making the vibrant, golden-haired beauty his own. She stirred gracefully beneath him with a sweet yet subtle invitation, and he moved with a lithe grace to possess her fully.

As his first, forceful thrust went deep within her, he felt her whole body tremble with the jarring pain and he drew back, shocked to find that the enticing creature in his arms had been a virgin. "Why didn't you stop me?" he whispered anxiously, though how he would have found the strength to do so he didn't know.

Angelique left her hands upon his shoulders, then moved her fingertips to his nape to gently draw his mouth back to hers as she replied softly, "Because I didn't want you to stop." She slipped her tongue between his lips in a kiss that was now as expert as his and stilled any further questions he might have had. He had been her choice, she appeared to have no regrets, and he could feel the warmth of her acceptance in her lavish kiss. Such an obvious invitation ended whatever doubt had sprung into Diego's mind and he began to move within her again. Now his rhythm became far more gentle, for her pain was also his and he longed to fill her with the greatest pleasure this time.

Angelique hugged Diego tightly, luring him beyond the rapture of any fantasy with a silken caress that slid down the rippling muscles of his back and over his hips before her arms encircled his waist. She wanted to memorize the contours of his sleek body, his taste and touch, the feel of him, so she would not forget the smallest detail of his loving in the bleak years that stretched before her. There was no more than this one night in her mind, and she meant to fill it with enough memories to light the rest of her nights, when she would have to sleep alone.

She felt a new warmth within her, a heat that spread with a fire hotter than that of any candle's flame. Her joy in being his was as great as his in possessing her. His ecstasy was also hers, and she felt his rapture as it shuddered through him before bursting within her.

At last he lay still, resting in her arms, and she knew the love that overflowed her heart also filled his. She held him cradled in her embrace, not willing to release him even to the world of dreams.

Diego was not asleep, but merely too filled with contentment to stir. He had never felt so close to a woman as he did to this loving creature, and he wanted that sweet sensation to last forever. She was stroking his hair very softly, her fingertips at his temple, and he reached up to catch her hand and bring it to his lips. He had never bothered to pay pretty compliments and was sorry now to think he had no clever way to thank her for what she had given him.

Meditatively, he rose up on his elbow to gaze down at her, but her smile was so bewitching that his mind swiftly filled with thoughts more befitting a rogue than a tender poet. He wanted her again, and again—a thousand times—but as he lowered his mouth to hers she sensed without being told what it was he needed. She moved against him and her fingertips slid through the curls that covered his chest before her arms encircled his neck to lure him again into the magical spell of her love. This time his surrender was even more swift than hers.

It was nearly dawn before Angelique was certain Diego

was sleeping soundly enough for her to leave his bed. Her nightdress had served the purpose for which she had intended it, but rather than wear the stained garment back to her own room, she quickly donned his shirt, which still lay where he had flung it. She took the brandy snifter she had used, then slipped out the door into the garden and hurriedly made her way back to her own room.

The candle upon her dresser had burned down to no more than a sputtering wick, but after tossing her soiled gown into the fireplace, she used it to set the wrinkled garment aflame. The soft fabric burned quickly and soon nothing remained but the blackened buttons. These she quickly carried outside and buried. Next she removed Diego's shirt and placed it at the bottom of her laundry so the maids who did the wash would find it and think they had misplaced it themselves.

She bathed thoroughly to remove all traces of her romantic encounter, but the water that filled the pitcher beside the basin was so cold that she was soon shivering uncontrollably and hastily pulled on another nightdress. She then washed the delicate glass she had taken from Diego's room and placed it in the bottom drawer of her dresser beneath her lingerie. She would rather have taken the little Azteca goddess of the dead, but since Diego had not made her a present of it, she had had to content herself with the brandy snifter as her only souvenir.

She then climbed into bed and pulled the covers up to her chin, finally satisfied she had done all she could to destroy the evidence of where she had been that night. In the morning she would rise and dress and pretend a rapt curiosity about her mother's evening, but she would never tell a soul about the splendor of her own.

Chapter III

Diego awoke with a start and heard the beat of his heart thudding loudly in his ears. He was accustomed to the gentle rocking motion of *El Diablo* and, thinking his ship had run aground, he was badly frightened until he became aware that he was in the elegantly furnished bedchamber of his home rather than in the confines of his ship's cabin. He combed his hair out of his eyes with trembling fingers, then numbly sat staring at the row of Azteca idols that seemed to be enjoying his discomfort with wide-eyed amusement.

"Oh, my God!" he gasped, struck as if by a bolt of lightning, for the full realization of what he had done the previous evening had come flooding back to him. Having found an attractive blonde in the garden, he had simply lured her into his room and enticed her into his bed. He gave an agonized groan then, knowing his father would have him flayed alive for this unbelievable bit of folly. He had seduced a young woman who had been a guest in his home as casually as he might have contracted for the services of a prostitute.

Knowing the consequences of such ungentlemanly conduct would undoubtedly prove to be grim, he forced himself to take a deep breath and think calmly. That he had not awakened to find himself staring into the barrel of her father's pistol was a pleasant surprise, but now that he was fully awake he wanted to waste no more time before searching for the young woman who had provided him with such a marvelous glimpse of paradise. He shook his head, trying to clear his mind, but his only thought was that she had been worth whatever painful ordeal he would now have to suffer for having seduced her. He was not the type of man to brood over his misfortunes, however, and the beauty of his memory of the enchanting blonde lightened his mood considerably.

First of all, he knew he would have to strip the bed. He could not reveal to the servants that he had bedded a virgin under his father's roof, for such an enticing bit of gossip would never be forgotten. But as he stood and rolled back the covers, he discovered that his bed held not even the slightest trace of what had occurred there. He stared at the snowy white sheets and wondered how such a thing could be possible, for he was certain the fair beauty had been a virgin and he knew there should have been some trace of that fact still visible. He had heard there were countries where it was customary to hang the bedsheets from the window after a couple's wedding night to prove the bride had been a virgin, and while he thought such a custom barbaric, he knew he had not been mistaken in expecting his bed to carry the evidence of his companion's loss of innocence.

Somehow this surprising development was more perplexing than the problem of stained bedclothes would have been and he looked around the room, wondering what other bit of magic the clever blonde might have worked. His duffel bag sat in the corner where he had placed it. The carvings she had admired were still atop the dresser. The bottle of brandy was there too, but beside it there stood only one snifter.

Diego walked over to the dresser, picked up the glass, and turned it slowly in his hands as he surveyed his room for the second time. "I see," he mused quietly to himself. "I came home late, unpacked a few carvings, had a brandy, and went to sleep—alone." There was no evidence to the contrary, and he could not understand how he had been so fortunate as to

39

have found a young woman who had not gone screaming to her parents but instead had proven to be so wonderfully discreet. He had thought her a treasure, but he had not fully appreciated just how great a delight she would prove to be. He fervently hoped she had not already left his home, for he had been so fascinated with her beauty that he had neglected to ask her name. She had obviously recognized him, but he was certain they had never met.

Impatient to find her, he yanked the bellpull to summon a maid to draw him a bath, then hastily yanked on his breeches so she would not find him standing there naked. He laughed as he poured himself half a snifter of the fine brandy, pleased to think he was not going to be flayed alive after all.

The word passed quickly through the house that Diego was home, and, too impatient to wait for him to appear, José Luis went to his son's room to greet him. He found the young man standing before his mirror, his expression intense as he drew his razor up his throat. Not wanting to startle him when the result might prove fatal, the older man waited at the door.

Seeing his father's reflection in his mirror, Diego laughed at his reticence and invited him to enter. "Come on in. I will be finished in just a moment."

"I will not say I am surprised to find you here, for I am not, but what has taken you so blasted long to return home?" José Luis demanded, making himself comfortable in the same chair Angelique had chosen and waiting impatiently for Diego to respond.

"I am quite well, thank you. How have you been?" Diego asked politely in a teasing tone, rebuking his parent for greeting him so rudely.

"Forgive me," José Luis replied. "I have been very worried, Diego. Piracy is at its worst and I know you love a fight."

Diego turned to regard his father with a skeptical glance. "Are you suggesting that I turn pirate?"

"No! Only that I feared you had fallen victim to one!"

"As you can see, I have returned home safely," Diego reassured him. *"El Diablo* is far too swift for sea bandits to catch. You needn't have worried. I was delayed in Vera Cruz, not on the high seas."

José Luis threw up his hands in disgust. "A beautiful woman was the cause, no doubt!"

"No," Diego replied seriously, embarrassed to think his father knew him so well. "It was strictly business, I assure you, but since you have mentioned the subject of women, I would like to know the name of the ravishing blonde who was here last night. Since it is nearly noon, she might already be gone, but I know she spent the night here." Realizing he had revealed too much, he quickly added, "At least I think she mentioned plans for spending the night here."

José Luis frowned. "If you were here in time to speak with a guest last night, why didn't you come and speak with me?"

"It was very late and I did not want to disturb you. I chanced upon a pretty blonde in the hallway and we exchanged a few words. You must know who I mean, for she is quite the most beautiful woman I've ever seen. She had an accent, French perhaps, but she could just as easily have been Austrian or Swiss, I suppose, or maybe even Scandinavian."

"Was she dressed in pale blue satin?" José Luis asked cautiously.

Not about to reveal that the young woman had been attired in her night clothes, Diego shrugged noncommittally. "I didn't notice. But you do know her then?"

José Luis sighed with exasperation that, as always, his son's consuming interest was a woman. "You must have met Françoise, for she was the only lovely French blonde here last night. She is my houseguest. I suppose it is just as well that you did meet her, for she may soon become my wife."

"What?" As the razor slipped from Diego's hand, he missed cutting his throat by the barest of margins. He bent

41

down to retrieve the slippery instrument and, not wishing to risk injury, laid it aside while he turned to speak with his father. "You have been thinking of getting married?" he gasped hoarsely. That he might have seduced his future stepmother was too horrifying a possibility to accept calmly, even for a man as liberal in his views as Diego.

"Well, no, actually I hadn't been, but when the suggestion was presented to me recently, I found it surprisingly appealing." José Luis rose to his feet then and began to pace up and down in front of the long dresser. "I am forty-eight years old, Diego. I was only twenty when you were born and twenty-five when I lost your mother. After being alone for twenty-three years, I can no longer pretend that I am content without the comfort of a wife."

Astonished to see the sparkle of tears in his father's dark eyes, Diego turned away, pretending not to notice. He could barely remember his mother's presence in their home, but he knew how deeply his father had loved her and had never thought he would ever consider marrying again. Taking a firm grip upon himself, as well as on his razor, he completed shaving quickly, then rinsed the remaining traces of lather from his face. "If you are expecting me to raise some objection, let me assure you that I will not."

José Luis cleared his throat and hesitated a moment to compose himself before continuing. "Françoise is a young woman. Should we have children, another son . . ."

"I am a wealthy man in my own right, Father. Do you honestly think I'd resent having to share my inheritance?" Diego was in fact deeply insulted by that suggestion and his mood was reflected in his expression. "I hope you have a dozen children," he added, then turned away, sickened to think he might already have fathered the babe Françoise would present to his father as their first child.

"Resentment would be a natural reaction, Diego. I did not mean to offend you by mentioning it." José Luis regarded his son more closely. In the months they had been apart Diego had changed little, and, in many ways, he envied his son's carefree existence. At twenty-eight he had been a serious, determined widower with a small son, not a brash young man like Diego, who lived only for the excitement he found aboard *El Diablo* or in a beautiful woman's arms. "You do understand my concern, do you not? If I do remarry, it must be the best action I could take for you as well as for me. You will still be my principal heir."

Diego was not usually so on edge, but he had an excellent reason for it this morning. The last thing he wanted now was an argument with his father, so he attempted to put him at ease. "I am surprised you did not remarry years ago, and I know for a fact that there are many women who would leap at the chance to be your second wife. I assure you that whoever pleases you will also please me. Now tell me a little more about this Françoise."

He went to his dresser for a clean shirt then, and realized the one he had worn the previous evening was missing. He looked around quickly, wondering what had become of it.

José Luis stepped out of his son's way as he replied, "She is a delightful young woman. I will say no more until you meet her, for my opinion is clearly prejudiced. At this time of day she is usually out shopping, but since we were all up so late last night, I doubt that she has gone out."

Diego's hands were shaking so badly he could scarcely button his shirt, "She is blond, you say, with blue eyes?"

"Yes, she is very attractive, slender, with the most beguiling ways. Surely somewhere in your travels you must have met a Frenchwoman. They are nothing like our own. I find them much less reserved, very spontaneous and loving."

Diego simply nodded, for he was not about to admit just how loving he had found Françoise to be. No wonder the woman had been so discreet! "I need to get back to my ship to supervise the unloading of the cargo. Will you please tell Françoise I look forward to speaking with her again this evening."

"I will come with you," José Luis offered promptly. "We can talk about your cargo on the way. There are several business matters we need to discuss as well."

"Fine." Diego could not look the man in the eye. He felt ill and knew it was not due to the effects of the brandy he had foolishly consumed earlier, but to his own recklessness, which had finally landed him in the worst predicament of his entire life. But why would Françoise have climbed into his bed so eagerly if she was in love with his father? The memory of the hunger in her kiss haunted him, and for the first time he stopped to consider just who had seduced whom and why.

In the clear light of day, Angelique was not nearly as calm as she had been when she had gone to sleep. She had only to close her eyes to remember the softness in Diego's gaze as he had looked down at her. She could still feel the tingle of his touch upon her bare breasts and taste the delicious flavor of his deep kisses. She had not imagined that pleasure such as they had given each other even existed, but now she felt she knew all of love's secrets. Diego had been so considerate, so tender.

She raised her fingertips to her lips, not daring to hope they would ever feel the touch of his again, and tears suddenly welled up in her eyes and escaped her thick lashes to slowly slip down her cheeks. Knowing she would soon have to face her mother's prying eyes, however, she realized she had no time to give in to such a display of emotion. She quickly rinsed away her tears and began to assume the role of the young girl she had perfected so beautifully. With trembling hands she powdered her face, applied the tight linen band to her bosom, and slipped on a pale yellow gown she knew made her appear even younger than twelve. She now had two reasons for producing an effective disguise; she certainly didn't want Diego to recognize her when they were introduced. To that end, she stood in front of her mirror and practiced a hesitant curtsy, praying that if she did not look up at him directly, he would see no more than the sweet child others saw.

Françoise had not even bothered to get out of bed this morning, and that was where Angelique found her, propped up against a heap of satin pillows and sipping her second cup of *café au lait*. "Ah, come in, my pet. I am merely resting. What time did you leave the party last night? I am afraid I did not notice." She patted the side of her bed to invite her daughter to join her.

Angelique sat down beside her mother and folded her hands in her lap to keep from twisting them nervously. "You seem very happy this morning, Mama. Did José Luis at last speak of marriage?" That she was already certain of the answer before she asked the question did not bother the pretty blonde. Her expression was a very curious one, as if she had no idea how her mother had fared in her quest for a proposal.

"Well, not in so many words," Françoise purred with a satisfied smile. "But his manner was very tender last night and I sensed there was something weighing heavily upon his mind when he bid me good night. I think he is waiting for a more private moment to broach the subject of marriage, and I will not pressure him to do so until he is ready."

"I see," Angelique murmured, hiding her surprise. Could her mother's impression of José Luis's intentions actually be correct? Had she misjudged his responses to her questions so badly or had she simply jolted him out of his complacency and forced him to begin considering marriage to her mother? She had not looked forward to striking out on her own—that had simply been her only choice as she had seen it—but what if José Luis did actually propose to her mother? Once they were wed, she would be presented to Spanish society as a marriageable young woman and Diego would need no more than one glance at her to know exactly who she was. What a terrible scene that would be, and she would certainly never be allowed to marry her stepbrother!

Noting that her daughter seemed even more pale than usual, Françoise reached out to take her hand. "This is what I want, my angel—for you to have a stepfather who will arrange the best possible match for you. Were I all alone, I would still be living with Cousin Beatriz, who thinks a widow should dress in black for the rest of her life and never go anywhere except to church. I have sought the company of wealthy men, with only your best interests in mind."

Angelique knew her mother too well to ever believe such a blatant lie, but finding her in so warm a mood, she asked a question that had long puzzled her. "You and José Luis are not lovers, are you, Mama?"

"Of course not!" Françoise denied sharply. "How often have I told you a woman's virtue is her greatest asset—far more valuable than beauty. Were I to become José Luis's mistress, he would have no reason to offer marriage, would he?"

"There must be a difference between making love to a man for whom you truly care and becoming his mistress," Angelique insisted, for in her mind there was a great distinction between the two. In one instance love was a gift; in the other, it was merely a commodity sold to the highest bidder. Preferring not to argue the point since she knew her mother was a most inflexible woman, Angelique changed the subject. "Still, I will be seventeen in two months, Mama, and if José Luis is not my stepfather by then, I do plan to leave here."

Françoise's blue eyes filled with an icy anger at her daughter's comment, "I warned you not to threaten me, Angelique. Two months' time is nothing, the bat of an eyelash. Now summon my maid. I wish to bathe."

"Yes, Mama," Angelique replied with unconcealed ire. She left her comfortable perch and pulled the bellcord before leaving the room. She was not certain of her destination. The day was warm and the garden would be pleasant, but she did not want to be found there if Diego, by some chance, were looking for her. Perhaps he was already back on board his ship, she mused, hoping this were true, for she did not want to meet him by chance before she had been introduced as her mother's sweet little daughter. The man was no fool. If she made the slightest mistake, he would become suspicious and then she would suffer for what she had done. She would not simply be leaving José Luis's home then; she would be thrown out into the street in disgrace.

Diego had hoped for some difficulty to present itself, but when none had appeared by the time his father returned for him in a carriage late that afternoon, he had no choice but to return home with him. He had paid scant attention to the man's conversation that morning and hoped he would not be expected to give any opinion as yet on the many business proposals his father had mentioned. Tired by the day's activity, he leaned back and rubbed his hand across his eyes. "You must not think me rude if I excuse myself early this evening, Father. It has been a long day."

"You are due for a vacation, Diego. I will not fault you for beginning it tonight. Do try and impress Françoise favorably though, won't you? She is so very charming, and I promise you will not have to exert yourself to do it," he offered with a chuckle.

Diego tried to smile but wasn't certain his lips had moved. This was surely going to be the very worst evening of his life and he only hoped to live through it.

By the time he had again bathed and dressed, he had become even more depressed, something he had not thought possible—but as he stood in front of his mirror regarding his appearance with a critical eye, the blackness of his mood was readily apparent. He adjusted the fit of his dark blue coat,

47

and, satisfied he was at least dressed as the gentleman he most assuredly was not, he resigned himself to his fate.

He then attempted to display an expression so confident he would be able to meet Françoise without creating a regrettable scene. "How do you do, *Mademoiselle,*" he uttered softly, lifting his brow with a trace of amusement. He would have to speak with her privately at the first opportunity, for he would certainly not permit her to marry his father after the erotic escapade she had shared with him. If she thought to marry his father and then fill her bed with a succession of handsome young men, he would put a stop to her plan before she had taken it any further.

It seemed to him she had been incredibly stupid for several reasons, the first being that his father was most assuredly not so old that he would be happy with no more than polite conversation from his bride. José Luis was a trim and vigorous man and Diego had no doubt that his father could satisfy a young woman. At the very least he deserved a wife who would love him and be true to her wedding vows. The thought that Françoise had leapt into bed with her future husband's son was so appalling that he could barely contain his fury.

It would be exceedingly awkward for him to have to tell his father why he suspected Françoise's sincerity, but he would damn well do it if she did not follow the order he planned to issue, which would send her promptly on her way. Losing his father's respect would be a high price to pay, but it was certainly preferable to allowing his father to lose his own when his beautiful young wife would surely bring him nothing but disgrace.

Diego's reflection took on a determined frown, for he loved his father far too much to allow him to suffer for any reason, and most certainly not for one as silly as the love of a woman. Disgusted by the knowledge that the blond beauty he had found so charming had the heart of a viper, Diego wanted only to get the wretched evening over with promptly.

With squared shoulders he left his room swiftly to join his father and the delectable, but devious, Françoise.

Angelique was so nervous she could barely sit still. Her mother and José Luis were conversing in hushed tones about how successful the party had been, but she had taken no part in the discussion. Both had taken care to dress more formally for dinner than usual, while she had remained in the pale yellow dress she despised. When Diego came to the door of the parlor, she pulled her *mantilla* further forward before risking a glance at the young man.

He had been casually dressed the previous evening, but in more formal wear his dark good looks were simply splendid. He wore highly polished black leather boots, and well-cut breeches of a pale pearl gray, which were set off by an embroidered waistcoat in a deeper charcoal shade. The snowy whiteness of his ruffled shirt contrasted handsomely with his dark tan, while his deep blue frock coat fit his broad shoulders superbly, then narrowed at the waist to emphasize his trim build. She had not realized he was so tall and imposing a figure, yet his mere presence seemed to fill the room with a charge of excitement that brought a bright blush to her cheeks. She thought him quite the handsomest man she had ever seen, but as she glanced over at her mother her heart fell, for, plainly, Françoise did too.

Diego strode through the door with the resolve of a matador about to plunge his sword into the shoulder blades of a ferocious bull, but he came to an abrupt halt when his eyes met those of the delicate blonde seated at his father's side. While she was extremely attractive, she was most definitely not the woman with whom he had spent the night and he was so elated by that astonishing fact that it took him a full second to recover his momentum. He was simply ecstatic to discover that he had not seduced the woman his father wished to wed, and as he continued across the room, his contrived smile became a rakish grin.

José Luis had seen that predatory smile far too often and hoped his son would not embarrass him by flirting openly with the woman he had clearly announced he planned to keep for himself. But in an instant, Diego's expression changed to a far more respectful one and he relaxed as he introduced his son. "Françoise, may I present my son, Juan Diego. I know I have spoken of him so frequently that he will not seem a stranger to you." When the lovely woman extended her hand for Diego to kiss, José Luis continued, "This is *Madame* Devereau's daughter, Angelique, a young lady of whom I am very fond."

Diego could barely contain the blessed feeling of relief that swept through him. "How do you do, *Mademoiselle.*" He brought Angelique's hand to his lips as he had her mother's, but he could see little of her face through the cloud of lace that enveloped her. If only his father had mentioned that morning that Françoise was a widow with a child, he would not have had to spend the entire day filled with the agony of remorse for the night he had spent. Adding to his delight was the fact that, wherever the bewitching blonde he had met might be, he would not have to fight his father for her affection. He knew in his heart that she was his alone to claim and all he needed now was her name. Once he learned that, he would waste no more time before finding her.

Angelique pulled her hand swiftly from Diego's, but not before the warmth of his touch had sent a rush of heat through her whole body, leaving her so weak she had no breath to reply to his greeting. When a few moments later he extended his arm to escort her into dinner, she had no choice but to accept, though she was afraid he could feel her fingers trembling through the soft wool of his coat. When he spoke to her as he helped her to her seat, she was so startled she did not immediately respond, and he repeated himself as though he thought she had not heard.

"I did not realize my father had been enjoying the

company of two beautiful women. I am certain he keeps your mother entertained, but have you friends to invite here to play?"

"Friends?" Angelique finally managed to mumble breathlessly. "Well, no, actually, I have none."

"What? So pretty a little girl as you has no friends? How can that be possible?" Diego teased her with a ready grin. Because he could not see beyond the white lace of her veil, he had no idea whether or not she was attractive, but he assumed it was likely since her mother was so pretty.

"My daughter is very shy, Diego, and I have found it best not to force her to endure the company of other children when they are often very cruel and tease her for being so quiet." Françoise thought Diego as handsome as his father, too handsome in fact, for if Angelique were to fall in love with him it would only add a further complication to their lives. She vowed to do her best to see that the interest he was showing in her daughter was squelched immediately. Polite conversation was one thing, but devoted attention was far too dangerous to permit, and she would not let it begin.

Diego nodded, understanding exactly what Françoise meant by the cruelty of children. He then leaned closer to the little girl at his side and whispered, "Forgive me if I seemed rude, but surely we can locate a polite companion for you in one of the homes nearby. What do you do with yourself all day? Do you have dolls you like to dress or . . ."

Angelique could not believe Diego actually planned to chat with her during dinner as though he greatly enjoyed having a child for his partner. Regardless of her surprise, however, she had to respond politely or she would make him suspicious, which was a risk she wanted to avoid. "I prefer to read, Captain, rather than play with dolls," she answered primly.

"I love to read too," Diego responded warmly. "Perhaps you also like to ride? If so, I will take you with me some morning."

51

Overhearing that invitation, Françoise interrupted before Angelique could respond for herself. "You must thank Diego, dear, but since you are terrified of horses, I'm certain you'd not wish to accept his invitation." She smiled sweetly at the young man, as astonished as Angelique that he seemed so interested in her.

"We have a mare or two I'm sure would not frighten you, Angelique. Let me know when you can spare the time and I will teach you how to ride, since you've not had the opportunity to learn."

"Thank you, Captain. You are very kind—" Angelique began.

"My daughter does not know the first thing about riding, Diego. I must insist that you withdraw your invitation," Françoise interrupted quickly, uncertain as to the response Angelique had been about to give.

Puzzled, Diego studied Françoise's expression, for he could not see Angelique's. "I was once a child here, *Madame,* and I think I know how long the days can be without friends and play to fill them. If you will grant me permission, I will be happy to teach your daughter to ride and I can guarantee that she will come to no harm."

Françoise was in an extremely difficult position, for she did not want to lose José Luis's respect by arguing openly with his son on his first night home. She had hoped Diego's arrival would enhance her chances of marrying his father, not ruin them. Attempting to sound more gracious, she spoke again. "That is so very kind of you, but I really must insist that I alone be responsible for my daughter. She can ride in a carriage wherever she wishes to go."

Seeing his father's warning glance, Diego simply nodded, but he could not understand Françoise's attitude. When they had been served their soup and she again turned to speak with his father, he whispered to the child at his side, "I am sorry, but I'll keep after her until she relents. If you'd like me to, that is."

That Diego would be so kind as to offer to give her riding lessons brought tears to Angelique's eyes, but she shook her head in a quick warning. "No, please, you must not upset my mother by questioning her judgment."

"I will do my best not to, my dear," Diego vowed sincerely, but he had interpreted her remark to mean that she would indeed like to go riding with him. Despite the fact that he considered Françoise to be an overly protective parent, he noted that her affection for his father seemed sincere, and Diego found himself favorably impressed with her and hoped she would like him as well. Perhaps she would make a fine wife for his father, and then she could not object to his efforts to amuse his new sister. He rather liked the idea of having a sister and leaned over to whisper to Angelique again. "What sorts of books do you like to read?"

As Angelique took a sip of water, her hand shook so badly she nearly dropped the delicate crystal goblet. It seemed to her the most horrible of tortures to be near Diego and not be able to reach out and touch him or give him any clue as to who she truly was. When she again trusted herself to speak, she responded, "I like poetry, but novels as well."

"What sorts of novels—exciting adventures or the sweet, romantic type?" Diego inquired softly.

"I enjoy them both," Angelique replied, wondering if Diego would never run out of questions.

"Good, then maybe I can recommend a book or two you haven't read."

Françoise was growing increasingly suspicious of Diego's interest in her daughter. Such an association would be impossible and so she again interrupted their conversation. "Please give me whatever books you'd like Angelique to have, Diego. I will read them first to be certain they are suitable for the child."

Exasperated by Françoise's continued interference in his attempts to be sweet to her child, Diego frowned angrily as he responded, "I'd not give your daughter novels of too stimulating a nature, *Madame.* You needn't censor my gifts!"

José Luis grew alarmed at the change in his son's tone and sought to end the argument developing at his table before it grew any more heated. "Diego, must I remind you that Angelique is Françoise's responsibility? It is only proper that she have such a keen interest in her daughter's welfare, and I insist you apologize to her immediately for speaking to her so rudely."

Diego opened his mouth to tell his father to mind his own business, but then he thought better of it. "Forgive me, *Madame,* if I seemed rude. I meant no offense."

"We have suffered a great many tragedies in the last few years, Diego. My daughter and I are very close as a result. You must not think ill of me for loving her so dearly." Françoise brought her lace-edged handkerchief to her eyes, as though his harsh tone had caused her real pain, and, as she knew he would, Diego instantly grew contrite.

"Let me assure you again, *Madame,* I mean only the best for you both." Diego felt like a fool now, for he had not thought the woman would weep over his words. Hoping the mood of the conversation would lighten, he waited for his father to offer some harmless topic. When he did not, Diego changed the subject himself. "I purchased some carvings you might be interested in seeing. I'll fetch them later when we return to the parlor."

"What sorts of carvings?" Françoise asked hesitantly, pleased that the young man had proven easy to manipulate. That José Luis had taken her side against his son was also a point that brought her a great deal of pleasure, and all traces of the tears that had appeared on her lashes completely disappeared.

"They are from one of the indigenous peoples of New Spain. The man from whom I purchased them claims to know more about these Indians than they did about themselves. He also tried to interest me in reopening a gold mine he swore would rival any in the world, but I was only interested in his stone relics, not his tales."

"A gold mine?" José Luis scoffed. "I suppose he wanted to sell you a tattered map that would lead you right to it."

Diego laughed too. "I did not ask to see the map, so I've no idea whether or not it was tattered. I simply said I had no interest in gold. They have silver in abundance there—half the world's production—but tales of gold have all proven to be fanciful ones from what I've heard."

"But what if he were telling the truth?" Angelique asked curiously, for, in her opinion, a man who would collect the remarkable statues she had seen might well have all sorts of other information that could be genuine.

"What?" Diego had been so surprised to hear her speak that he had not understood her question. "I beg your pardon?"

"Really, Angelique. Diego doesn't want to be bothered with your silly questions," Françoise admonished her daughter sternly.

"Of course I want to hear your questions, and I'm certain none are silly," Diego replied with a bitter glance at the older woman. He was disgusted that Françoise would describe her daughter as being painfully shy and then order her to be silent when she finally did gather the courage to speak. "What did you wish to know, Angelique?"

"I merely suggested the possibility that an accurate map to a gold mine might exist," Angelique replied firmly, having had more than enough of her mother's incessant domination for one night.

Diego found that question a most challenging one and chuckled as he answered it truthfully. "Then I was a great fool to walk out of the man's shop without it. I'll definitely ask him to tell me more about this mysterious mine when next I'm in Vera Cruz."

José Luis shook his head reproachfully, "Your initial reaction was the correct one, Diego. If this man actually has a map, which I doubt, then it will lead to no more than an empty cave."

Diego winked at the lace-clad figure by his side, "Should I discover the location of a gold mine, *Mademoiselle,* you will be my partner."

"Diego really!" Françoise interjected, then hastened to caution, "You must not fill my daughter's mind with such foolishness."

"I am not teasing her, *Madame.* Should I be so fortunate as to become the owner of a gold mine, Angelique will most definitely be my partner." When he extended his hand, the child grasped it with surprising firmness. "We will be partners then," he vowed seriously, hoping the little girl was smiling even though he could not see her face clearly.

Françoise turned to José Luis with a petulant frown. "Is your son always so impetuous?"

"Yes, I am afraid that he is," José Luis admitted with a rueful smile. "We are nothing alike, you see. I am very cautious, perhaps too conservative, while he actively seeks the thrill of danger."

Diego could only laugh at those words, for he had come much too close to disaster that day to dispute them. He made a serious attempt to be charming for the rest of the meal and they finished eating in what he thought was extremely good humor. When they were ready to leave the dining room, he excused himself to go and fetch his Azteca treasures, then rejoined the others in the parlor.

Angelique was surprised to hear Diego now describe the Azteca gods in the briefest of terms. He made no mention of the brutality of the Indians' religion but stressed instead the artistic beauty of the idols he had purchased. But when she asked to hold the basalt carving of the goddess of the land of the dead, her mother objected strenuously.

"Angelique, I'd prefer you did not touch those hideous creatures. Just leave them alone." Françoise raised her fan to hide her expression, which was one of total revulsion.

Ignoring her mother's command, Angelique reached for the little goddess. "Her costume is strange, that is true. But I think she is attractive nonetheless, and certainly not hideous."

"You may be excused, Angelique. I will speak with you in the morning about this," Françoise commanded in an icy whisper.

Diego took the idol from Angelique's hands to save her any further criticism. "I'm sorry," he whispered so softly that only she could hear.

"I agree with Françoise. Those evil creatures are bound to bring bad luck." José Luis sat forward, eyeing the small statues with a deep frown. "Get rid of them, Diego. I don't want them in my house."

"You're not serious?" Diego cried out in disbelief. "These are no more than rocks with fanciful designs. They can't bring any sort of luck—good or bad."

José Luis rose to his feet in order to make his command more readily understood. Diego was a good two inches taller, but that difference did not matter between father and son. "I said to remove those grotesque carvings from my house immediately, and that is what you will do."

"Since when have you become so superstitious?" Diego scoffed.

"This is a Catholic home and I will not have pagan idols within the walls. It is not a matter of superstition but of faith," José Luis explained through clenched teeth.

Françoise felt the tension between the two men mounting to a dangerous level and motioned frantically for Angelique to leave the room. She then placed her hand on José Luis's sleeve in hopes of lightening his mood. "I did not mean to begin an argument between you two."

As Angelique rose to leave, Diego gathered up the three idols and prepared to follow. "I would have sworn this was my home too, rather than simply yours. Perhaps it is time I built my own house to store my souvenirs, and I think I'll construct it in Vera Cruz!"

"Diego," José Luis called sternly, "come back here at once!"

Diego left the room without looking back. He quickly overtook Angelique in the hall and gave her a sharp command. "Come with me." He walked into his room and placed the stone gods on his dresser. "Well, come in. I need to ask you something important."

Angelique remained in the shadows of the hall, for she had no intention of allowing him to come close enough to recognize her. "It wouldn't be proper for me to enter your room, Captain. You must know that."

Diego began to curse, then caught himself. "Of course. You are female, even though a young one, and no gentleman lures a lady into his room for any purpose other than a dishonorable one, does he?"

"I am not questioning your honor, sir, but my mother is very strict. There is no need to upset her when, if you wish to speak with me, we could converse in the library without drawing any criticism."

"The library?" Diego thought Angelique the most unusual child he had ever met. She had a very mature outlook for one so young, and since her suggestion was a good one, he agreed. "To the library then." He followed her down the hall, apologizing as he went. "My father and I argue constantly. It is an unfortunate situation, but one I feel he creates. We are too close in age for him to speak to me as though he possessed the wisdom of the centuries, and I can't help but argue. I will apologize to him in the morning and he knows it, but I hope I did not upset you and your mother needlessly tonight."

"You'll not build a house in Vera Cruz then?" Angelique slipped through the library door and moved as far away as possible from the candles that lit the room.

"No, that I just may do." Diego walked over to the desk and leaned back against it. "You attended last night's party, didn't you?"

"Yes," Angelique admitted reluctantly.

"Then I hope you can help me. I chanced to meet one of the guests, and, like a fool, I was so taken with her beauty that I forgot to ask her name so that I might call at her home. I believe she was a Frenchwoman, so I think you must know her. She has golden-blond hair and blue eyes fringed with the longest lashes I've ever seen. Can you tell me her name?"

"A blonde?" Angelique pretended to scan the titles of the books on the shelf by her side. "It was a very large party, but your father must know who she is since he issued all the invitations. Why don't you ask him?"

"I did, but he could name only your mother, and thank Heaven it was not she!"

Angelique dared not look at him then, for she understood exactly what he meant and was as appalled as he. She tried to think calmly in order to give him some logical suggestion. "I am sorry, but if your father does not know the young woman's name, perhaps one of the other guests might. Since many were your friends, they would have noticed so pretty a young woman too, wouldn't they?"

"Yes, of course," Diego agreed, sorry that he had not thought of so obvious an idea himself. "Frankly, my father seems so taken with your mother that I doubt he saw anyone last night but her."

"Your father has been very kind to us." Angelique moved quickly to the door, not wanting to risk a longer conversation with the attractive young captain. "I am sorry I can be of no help to you."

"But you have." Diego smiled warmly, still trying to make out Angelique's face beneath the lacy *mantilla*. "I meant what I said. I'd like to teach you to ride if you'd like to learn."

Hesitating just a moment in the doorway, Angelique again refused his kind offer. "I know my mother seems unreasonable to you, but I am all she has. She does not want me to take riding lessons, and so I will not. I thank you for your offer though, for it was very thoughtful of you. I hope you find that young woman for whom you are looking."

"I will," Diego promised confidently. "And soon." He followed the primly dressed child out into the hall and watched until she had disappeared into her own room. She was so graceful she seemed to float rather than walk, and for an instant a memory flashed in his mind with such clarity that he was stunned. But then the image was gone and he could not imagine of whom the little girl had reminded him. "Remarkable child," he mused softly and, since he had gotten so little sleep the previous night, he went straight to his room. But without the company of the enchanting blonde who had set his blood aflame with desire, he found his bed cold and most uninviting.

Chapter IV

Françoise's blue eyes blazed with fury as she stormed into Angelique's bedchamber the next morning. "You are never to dispute my word in front of José Luis ever again, Angelique. If I tell you to be quiet, or not to touch something, or simply to go to bed, you will do so without question! I will tolerate no more of your willfulness. That Diego is so disrespectful is a disgrace, but I'll not have you behave in the same fashion!"

Angelique felt a curious sense of detachment as she returned her mother's hostile stare. "If you are concerned that I will disgrace you, then I will be happy to leave here this very morning," she offered calmly.

Infuriated by the taunt, Françoise shrieked, "You will go nowhere until I have married José Luis! Did you not hear him remark upon his fondness for you last night? He is the perfect man for me, and I will not allow you to ruin the plan I have so carefully laid to become his wife."

"If you love him, Mama, why must you lay a trap? Why can't you simply be honest about your feelings? For that matter, why not be honest with the man about everything, including our ages?"

Françoise stamped her tiny foot repeatedly. "Does nothing I say reach you? The very last quality a man desires in a woman is honesty! Like all men, José Luis prefers the sweet sound of flattering lies to the harsh reality of truth, and that's all he will hear from my lips. Now enough of this ridiculous argument. You must promise me you will not create another awkward scene like the one through which we all suffered last night. I forbid it."

Angelique tied back her hair and donned her lacy veil. She certainly did not believe she had caused a scene by admiring Diego's carvings. Her remarks had been sincere and spoken politely. In her opinion, it was José Luis and her mother who had caused all the problems.

Watching her daughter's gaze grow distant, Françoise drew near. "It is unfortunate that Diego has proven to be such a brash young man. You must avoid him whenever possible. Under no circumstances are you to be alone with him."

Angelique had no intention of ever revealing she had already been alone with the handsome young man and that her mother's worst fears were more than justified. "I thought him very nice, but you needn't worry. I doubt he'll seek out the company of a child in his free hours."

"Who knows what such a rascal might choose for a diversion. Your answer, however, must always be an emphatic no!" Françoise insisted harshly.

"Did you have to tell him I was terrified of horses? You know I love to ride," Angelique retorted bitterly as she moved toward the door, neatly dressed and ready to join José Luis for breakfast.

"You will not go riding with him, Angelique. The suggestion was absurd, so what difference does it make what excuse I gave?"

"You could have told him I have no clothes for riding now." Angelique hoped her mother would accept that excuse and smiled slightly when she did.

Delighted with so clever an idea, Françoise's expression lit with triumph. "Of course! We will tell him you have no suitable riding habit and he will extend no further invitations. Now, let us hurry before José Luis leaves his table in disgust!"

Adjusting her *mantilla* to cover her brow, Angelique followed her mother down the long corridor and out into the sunshine, but she did not draw a deep breath until she saw that Diego was not seated with his father.

For several days Diego had been occupied with unloading his cargo and had had no opportunity to seek out his relatives and friends to question them about the attractive blond guest who had attended the party at his home. When at last he found time one afternoon to call at the home of his cousin, Miguel Rivera, he had to listen impatiently to all the young man had to say about the career he was pursuing in banking before he had a chance to reveal the true reason for his visit.

"You are not only my cousin, but my close friend as well," Diego began, "and I know your tastes in women are similar to mine." He was certain of Miguel's friendship and found it easy to confide in him.

Miguel laughed ruefully at his cousin's remark, for while he admired Diego greatly, he made no effort to match his prowess in any area, especially not in the field of romance. "Thank you. I am flattered you think so," he managed to reply, though he knew his experience with women was insignificant compared to his dashing cousin's.

Diego questioned the young man briefly about the night of his father's party and after assuring himself that Miguel had been there until long past midnight, he pursued his true goal. "Unfortunately, I arrived home too late to join the party, but I did chance to meet a very beautiful young woman. We exchanged no more than greetings in passing and now I wish to learn her name since I neglected to ask for it then. I believe she is French, but I know for a fact that she is the loveliest female creature ever born. She is blond, with eyes more blue than the summer sky. She has the figure of a goddess and Venus herself could not possess more grace and charm than she does. You must have met her, Miguel, and learned her name."

Miguel spread his hands in a gesture of puzzlement. "Diego, your description is superb and I can well appreciate your interest in such a beauty, but I did not meet this remarkable young woman at your home. I only wish that I had."

"But you must have!" Diego insisted sharply. "She might have been one of the first to leave the party, but she was there. I am certain of it!"

Miguel frowned as he made an effort to recall the names of all the young women with whom he had danced. "There was not a single young woman there whom you do not know, Diego. The three Vargas sisters, Elena Morales, Linda de la Vega, Cristina Martinez, Rosalina and Maria Ventura . . ." He went on to name several more, but all were brunettes with sparkling dark eyes and many were also cousins, though more distantly related than he and Diego.

Diego fought back his temper unsuccessfully. "Yes, of course. They are like sisters to me, Miguel. But there is no way you could have missed such a striking blonde in such company!"

Miguel rose to his feet slowly, trying to think what else to suggest. He was lean of build like Diego but not nearly as muscular. Though his hair was also dark and his eyes were brown, he resembled his cousin only slightly, for he was merely pleasant in appearance, while Diego was strikingly handsome. "Let me go ask my mother if she recalls meeting a fair-haired Frenchwoman. As you know, little escapes her notice."

"Yes, by all means consult whomever you please, but I must learn her name." Diego poured himself another goblet of wine and drank it in one long swallow. When his cousin returned with his Aunt Margarita, he rose quickly to greet her with a warm embrace and a light kiss. She was petite and still pretty, despite the fact that she was several years older than his father. The silver in her hair only made her clear brown eyes sparkle more brightly, and the compliments Diego paid her were sincere. She had been like a second mother to him when he had lost his own, and he never failed to visit her whenever he was in Barcelona.

They exchanged the usual pleasantries until he could no longer contain his curiosity. "Did Miguel tell you that I am looking for a young woman you might have met at our home the other night?"

"Yes, but I am afraid that other than your father's beautiful friend, *Madame* Devereau, there were no blondes at the party."

Diego disagreed emphatically with her statement. "No, that's not correct. There was another blonde—much younger than Françoise—and it's imperative that I learn her name. If she escaped your notice, then I will just have to ask the other guests until I find someone who was also fortunate enough to have met her."

Margarita gave her nephew a knowing glance. "Diego, I did not ever think I would see you succumb to a woman's charms. This blonde must be a ravishing beauty indeed! What do you plan to do when you finally locate her?"

Diego gave his aunt an innocent smile. He was not about to admit that he had taken his attraction for the elusive blonde to its limit upon one occasion and planned to do so again. "I will introduce myself to her father, of course, and ask his permission to call upon her. I am a gentleman— hasn't Miguel assured you of that?"

Both Miguel and his mother laughed, knowing that the words had been spoken in jest. "I do hope you find this woman soon, Diego, for if she is as exquisite a beauty as you claim, she will have many suitors, and you might find the competition for her affection very keen," the kindly woman noted wisely.

With a wicked grin, Diego disagreed. "She is a very modest young woman who dislikes attention, so I doubt I'll have many men with whom to compete. Now, if you'll excuse me, it has been a great pleasure to see you both again, but I must return to my ship."

Margarita accepted his kiss and gave him a warm hug in return. "Will we see you this weekend, Diego? The de la Vega's are having a party and you must be on the guest list."

Diego shrugged. "Perhaps, but if I do not see you then, I will return as soon as I locate the blonde. I want you to meet her, since you both missed that pleasure when she was a guest in my home."

"I will look forward to it," Miguel replied with good humor as he watched Diego take his leave. When his cousin had departed, he turned to his mother and commented, "I find it remarkable that Diego plans to take the time to pay calls at a respectable young woman's home."

Margarita frowned slightly, worried about her brother's son. "Is Diego truly as wild as all say he is?"

Miguel gave his mother a sly wink. "He is no more wild than many of your nephews."

"You did not answer me, Miguel!" Margarita pointed out promptly.

"Oh yes, I did." The young man gave his dear mother a kiss and changed the subject, knowing there was no point in revealing what a hellion Diego truly was when she loved him so.

The next afternoon, Diego went to the Vargas home, thinking that at least one of the three attractive daughters would have met his blonde, but aside from exhibiting obvious disappointment that he had not actually come to see them, they could tell him nothing. Attempting to appear interested in them for courtesy's sake, Diego remained far longer than he had intended. Finally, after paying them effusive compliments, he gave up for the day and returned to

El Diablo to devise a more effective plan to find the woman who had enchanted him so completely.

As the week progressed, Angelique found each successive dinner with Diego at the table more difficult to endure. He had great charm, but frequently his comments started arguments, for his ideas were far more progressive than those of either his father or her mother. After a week, the cheerful mood that once had brightened their evenings had deteriorated into a series of bitter confrontations, for her mother had begun to take exception to every word Diego spoke in an attempt to show José Luis she supported his views. Now the four sat at the table uncomfortably as Diego tried to defend his position.

"It is not that I condone violence, *Madame*. On the contrary, I abhor it. I merely stated that living conditions for the Indians in New Spain are as appalling as those of the peasants here or those that existed in France prior to the outbreak of the Revolution. Poverty in the provinces of Aragon, Castile, and La Mancha is severe and absentee landlords are the cause. Too much of the land belongs to the nobles or to the church and not enough to the common man who tills it. It is no wonder the dream of equality that swept the American colonies to independence from the British finds such admiration here as well."

"Diego," José Luis cautioned sternly, "must I again beg you to find some more pleasant topic of conversation? The ladies most certainly are not interested in the problems of the Indians in the New World or those of the peasants here in Spain."

After a moment of strained silence, Angelique found the courage to contradict her host. "We are not unsympathetic to their problems. My father was a tireless worker, not one of the absentee landlords to whom you just referred."

Impressed, Diego leaned forward in an attempt to look

directly at the little girl, but before he could compliment her, Françoise spoke.

"Yes, that is true. Jean Paul was exactly like you, Diego. He admired the ideals of equality, denounced the excesses of the King, and sought land reform. But when the madness erupted, he was one of the first to die. The peasants cared little for his politics. It was only his blood they were after!"

Diego was stunned by the hatred that lit the attractive woman's eyes. She had obviously been incensed by his remarks, though he had meant no offense. She seemed to blame her husband's death on the ideals of equality rather than on the abysmal economic conditions that made such values appealing, and he had no desire to debate the ridiculousness of that opinion with her. "Let me assure you I did not mean to reopen old wounds, but merely to comment upon the situation in New Spain. The society there is even more artificial than ours, for Spaniards born there are not considered equal in status to those born here, which makes no sense at all to me. Their blood is exactly the same as ours, but their destiny is determined the day they are born on foreign soil."

Intrigued by Diego's statement, Angelique inquired curiously, "Do you think a man can create his own destiny?" She dared not ask for his opinion concerning the destiny of a woman, though that was the question that was truly on her mind.

"I know he can if society does not erect insurmountable barriers in his path," Diego responded, then finished the remainder of his meal in silence. Though Angelique had been sympathetic to his views, he knew from bitter experience that her mother would send her to bed if he encouraged her to voice her opinions. It was a sorry situation indeed when he found that a pretty child was the only agreeable companion at his father's table. When she excused herself to retire for the evening, he quickly left his father and Françoise, and overtook her in the hall.

"I have a present for you in the library," he whispered softly and was pleased when she followed him into the paneled room. Taking a small book from the desk drawer, he handed it to her with a courtly bow. "I have already inscribed it to you. Since it is a book of poetry written by Sister Inez, a greatly admired nun who lived in New Spain nearly one hundred years ago, I am certain your mother will not object to it." At least he hoped she would not, though Françoise was often so unreasonable in her views that he was not certain she would not confiscate the small volume.

Angelique accepted the book shyly, for she was touched by his thoughtfulness. "Thank you, Diego. I know I will enjoy reading her poems."

"I hope that you do, and now I wish to ask a favor in return."

Angelique dared not lift her eyes to his, despite her curiosity. The room was dimly lit, but still she could not risk his recognizing her. "What favor could I possibly perform for you?" she asked hesitantly.

"I've followed your suggestion and have asked several of my friends, but I've been unable to find the young woman I told you about. It occurred to me that she might patronize the same dressmaker as you and your mother. Would you take me there tomorrow?"

"Oh no, I couldn't do that!" Angelique protested sharply, disappointed to find that his gift had only been a bribe.

"Why not? I'll take you in a carriage, and you need do no more than come inside with me while I explain I am trying to locate a young Frenchwoman who may be one of her customers. I would ask your mother to accompany me, but I know she'd refuse such a request, so I'll not embarrass either of us by asking her."

"You want me to introduce you? That is all?"

"Yes. You'll be a character reference for me, won't you? I'll buy you whatever you like while we're there," Diego promised with a warm smile.

Angelique hurried toward the door. "My mother patronizes a shop called La Belle Mode, but I have never been there, nor do I have any idea where it is located. Your father can go with you though. He's the one who recommended the *couturière* to my mother."

Diego crossed the room in one swift stride and turned to block the door. "Wait a moment. Where does your mother purchase your clothing if it does not come from the same shop as her own?"

"Oh, but my dresses are made by La Belle Mode too, but my mother gives them my measurements so I do not have to go to any tiresome fittings," Angelique explained breathlessly, hoping he would step aside and permit her to leave.

"My father believes that I am entirely too preoccupied with women as it is. He'll not help me, but I was certain you would. Now please say you will." He waited a long moment, hoping he would not have to beg the little girl to help him, though he was determined to do even that if he had to. Such a humiliation would be a small price to pay if there were a chance he might learn his blonde's name at the dressmaker's. A sharp knock rattled the library door in the next instant, but he did not turn to respond. "Well, will you agree?" he now demanded in a fierce tone.

"I think you should open the door—and right now!" Angelique whispered firmly.

That such a delicate child would defy him made Diego ashamed of what he had tried to do. "I wanted you to have that book. You mustn't think that—"

"Open the door!" Angelique stamped her foot as she had seen her mother do so often. "I will go with you, if you will just open that door!"

Diego flashed a delighted grin as he reached for the gleaming brass door handle, then he stepped back into the shadows so it would appear that Angelique was alone in the room.

The maid held several candles, and when the door swung

70

open she apologized quickly. "Forgive me, *Mademoiselle.* I meant only to replace the candles. I did not mean to disturb you."

Angelique took the long, white tapers and dismissed the servant politely. "You did not. I'll take care of the candles myself before I leave the room. Good night."

The maid made a slight curtsy and left. After closing the door, Angelique carried the new candles to the desk and began to replace the old ones, which had burned down to short stubs. "At least it was not my mother, but you must go before someone else comes."

"Your mother is a very difficult woman to please, it seems. I'm surprised my father is so willing to take on such a challenge."

Hastening to her mother's defense, Angelique explained softly, "I beg you not to think ill of her, for she is coping as best she can with the misfortune that has befallen us. She admires your father greatly and gives him none of the problems she gives us. Now please go."

Diego hesitated to leave, for he found the little girl such delightful company that he wanted to remain and discuss the matter of their parents more fully. But she seemed so nervous about their being discovered together that he did not wish to upset her any further. "I will go since you asked me so sweetly, but I'll expect you to be ready the minute your mother leaves the house in the morning. Do not keep me waiting."

"I gave you my word." Angelique extinguished the candles but did not light the new ones. She waited for several minutes after Diego left, then, still shaking with fright she went to her room. The maid had seen nothing, but her mother would have marched right into the library, taken one look at Diego, and demanded to know what the two of them were discussing. Angelique knew she would have been punished severely for having disobeyed her mother's order to avoid the young man.

71

Though she had escaped that disaster, her masquerade was daily growing more impossible to continue. Diego's plan to question the most fashionable dressmaker was a logical one, but how could she possibly help him when the woman for whom he was searching was she? Deciding that such a dilemma was too difficult to contemplate so late in the evening, she opened the book of Sister Inez's poems and read the pretty verses until she finally drifted off to sleep.

The next morning Angelique yawned repeatedly at breakfast, but each time she glanced in Diego's direction he grinned and winked at her as though they were conspirators in some hilarious plot. She seemed to feel worse by the minute and excused herself as soon as possible. Once back in her room she paced anxiously in front of her mirror, certain that in the close confines of a carriage Diego would recognize her. To enhance her disguise she pulled her hair into a tight bun atop her head so none of her blonde curls were visible beneath her *mantilla*. Her pale green dress was one of her prettiest and the most juvenile in style, but she decided anxiously that perhaps she should wear another. After searching through her wardrobe, discarding first one garment and then another, she forced herself to think more calmly and gave up the effort to find another gown. It was not her selection of apparel that was causing her panic; it was her situation. She felt cornered, trapped by her promise to accompany Diego, and when he rapped lightly at the door, she had to summon all her courage to open it.

"Are you ready? I complimented your mother upon the attractiveness of her wardrobe and she gave me the location of La Belle Mode, thinking I meant to purchase a present." Diego reached out for Angelique's hand and led her outside to the carriage at a near run. "We've got to hurry. They won't be out riding for more than an hour or so." He gave the driver directions, then helped Angelique into the highly polished black vehicle and took the seat opposite hers. "You don't know how much I hope this strategy works."

Angelique could scarcely offer encouragement, for she knew his plan was certain to fail. Since she could not say that, however, she tried to prepare him for the inevitable disappointment. "Aren't there many fine shops in Barcelona? Perhaps you will have to visit others."

Diego frowned slightly, for he did not want to admit that her observation might prove correct. "There must be a dozen competent dressmakers here, but this young woman was so great a beauty that I am certain she would wear only the finest fashions, as your mother does. Because she is French, I feel certain she would patronize the shop of a country-woman."

"Yes, of course she would." Angelique had no choice but to agree, but the thought of how disappointed Diego would be at the lack of information he would receive at La Belle Mode pained her greatly. To distract herself from the guilt she knew she deserved to feel, she moved closer to the window in order to view the passing street more closely. She seldom left the Aragon home, and, despite her worries about Diego, she found the brief excursion exciting and her mood showed clearly in her eager pose.

"My father tells me you study your lessons all morning and then you must rest in the afternoon. Do you never leave our home?"

"I have been to the cathedral—La Seu, I believe you call it—and to the Plaza del Rey. Oh yes, and once I went to the Calle del Rech to see the palaces. Even though they are three or four hundred years old, they are very pretty, don't you think?"

"Well yes, of course, but is that all you have seen of Barcelona?" Diego asked incredulously.

"I am very busy with my studies," Angelique insisted, hoping he would not press her on the matter.

"We will take the long way back then, since you leave my home so seldom. Would you like to see my ship, too?"

"Yes, very much, if it is not out of the way." Since the

question was relevant, she inquired curiously, "Why did you name the ship for the devil?"

Diego laughed at her confusion. "It is not named for the devil but for the devilfish. It is a ray—very flat—and uses the sides of its body like wings, so it looks rather like a bat in flight. I will draw you a picture of one when we get home. It sails through the water so effortlessly that I could not help but name a sailing ship for it."

"Oh, yes, I see." Angelique tried to imagine a swimming bat and decided to wait for his drawing instead.

"Good, now I want you to think of something I might purchase for you as a present. As long as we are visiting a dressmaker's, I see no reason not to buy a few things for you."

"No, really, I have all I require," Angelique insisted primly, for she could think of no way to explain to her mother that Diego had presented her with gifts.

"A lady never has too many clothes. Surely your mother would not refuse my offer." Diego studied the fidgeting child closely, for he had never seen her so nervous and felt certain their errand was the cause. Finally, he reached out to pat her knee lightly. "If you'd rather we go straight home, we will. I am used to living dangerously and this ploy involves no risk to me, but I did not mean to terrify you so severely."

Angelique watched Diego's hand move across her knee and shivered involuntarily. "I want to help you," she assured him. "Please don't think I'm afraid to be your friend."

"Let us hope my lady is known at La Belle Mode," Diego replied, smiling warmly to reassure the shy child. "If she is not, then I will visit every other dressmaker in Barcelona on my own until I find where her garments are made. While I'm busy doing that, I'll accept every invitation I receive. If she attended our party, she will attend others."

"Yes, that is undoubtedly true," Angelique agreed readily. She continued to gaze out at the city with rapt interest, for she had not realized until Diego had questioned her that her days were truly spent in isolation from the world. She found the city filled with sunlight and flowers most beautiful, and she enjoyed the ride enormously despite the peril involved.

"You go to parties, don't you?" Diego inquired politely.

"Oh no! I do not even wish to attend parties," Angelique replied honestly.

Diego shook his head impatiently. "I know you are shy, my little angel, but how will you ever overcome your fears if you never leave my home?" When he saw that his question had only upset her, Diego moved swiftly to her side and lifted her easily upon his lap so that he could give her a warm hug. He had meant only to reassure her, to provide affection in a brotherly fashion to the dear little thing. But when he found her slender body as warm and seductively perfumed as the most attractive young woman's, he was ashamed of the surge of desire that flooded his loins and prayed she was too innocent to realize the affect she had had upon him. He knew there were men who enjoyed making love to such pretty children, but until that very instant he had not understood why they craved girls too young to be truly called women. Shocked to think he might possess such a despicable weakness, he could barely catch his breath as he slid her back into her place. "Now I insist you attend all the parties to which the Aragons are invited," he mumbled hoarsely.

Angelique lifted her hand to cover a feigned cough. She had been so flustered by Diego's unexpected embrace that she could not readily find her voice to reply. When the carriage suddenly rolled to a stop in front of La Belle Mode, she leapt out as soon as the footman had opened the door and lowered the step. Then she rushed into the elegant establishment and asked to speak with the proprietress in so firm yet polite a tone that the clerk had sent for her before Diego had come through the door.

Madame Larouche recognized Angelique's gown as one of her own creations and greeted her warmly. "You must be *Mademoiselle* Devereau!" she exclaimed with delighted surprise. "And you, *Monsieur?*"

Diego reached for the attractive woman's hand and brought it to his lips. "I am Juan Diego Aragon, *Madame,* and since you dress Angelique and her mother so beautifully, I have come to inquire if your shop is patronized by a young woman I hope to meet."

Recognizing the handsome man as the son of José Luis Aragon, one of her most influential clients, *Madame* Larouche smiled even more warmly. "Ah, so it is a matter of romance that brings you here, *Monsieur* Aragon. If you are as charming a man as your father, you should captivate this young woman easily."

Though he flashed a wicked grin, Diego did not reveal just how deeply he wished to captivate her or how often. "I must locate her first, *Madame*. Will you help me find her?" Before she could refuse his request, he described the astonishing beauty he sought with the most precise detail he could provide. The mental picture he painted was so vivid and so very accurate that Angelique began to blush and moved away, pretending a rapt interest in the samples of fine fabrics the *couturière* had on display.

Madame Larouche pursed her lips thoughtfully and replied, "Your request is a difficult one, for many of my customers are Frenchwomen who fled our homeland when I did. Nearly all are very beautiful, but few are as blond as *Madame* Devereau and her daughter. But you know Françoise well, do you not?"

"Yes." Diego glanced toward Angelique, wondering what she had found to be so interesting at the far end of the shop. "I know Angelique's mother, and it is not she I seek, but a much younger woman—eighteen or nineteen, I believe."

His manner was so sincere that the *couturière* summoned her clerks for a quick conference. In a matter of minutes she returned smiling brightly. "There is one young woman; Monique LeGrand is her name. She has only recently arrived in Barcelona and perhaps she is the one you are seeking."

Diego took the woman's hand in a grateful clasp, and as soon as he had *Mademoiselle* LeGrand's address tucked away in his waistcoat pocket, he called to Angelique. "Is there not something I might buy for you?" He was so happy to have Monique's name that he felt most generous.

"No, thank you, Diego." Angelique hurried him toward the door before *Madame* Larouche had an opportunity to study her appearance. "Thank you, but no."

Diego laughed as he bid the helpful *couturière* good day and promised, "If Monique is my blond enchantress, I will return for an armload of presents, for I know she will not refuse my generosity as Angelique has." He helped the pretty child into his father's carriage, then sat back, making no effort to hide his joy that their search had been so fruitful. "I knew I was not crazy, Angelique. I did speak with a young woman with the appearance of an angel the night of the party at my home. If only I had had more sense, I would have asked her name and address then. How I could have been such a great fool I'll never know."

"I believe you said you were distracted by her beauty, did you not?" Angelique remarked softly. Her heart was beating as rapidly as Diego's but for a far different reason. Who was this Monique LeGrand, and would she be so lovely that Diego would give up his search for the woman he could not find? she wondered desperately.

"Completely!" Diego admitted with a rueful laugh. "Now I just pray *Madame* Larouche has given me the correct name."

Since Angelique knew that this was not the case, she made no reply. She had not thought it possible that she could become more miserable than she had been that morning, but now she was despondent. Surely Monique LeGrand would like Diego when first they met, but if he liked her as well, she

77

would have no hope of being able to go to him someday with the truth. Such a wretched thought brought tears to her eyes and she lowered her head to hide them.

Diego had asked the driver to go by his ship, but as they reached the docks, Angelique seemed so preoccupied that he wondered if providing a tour of *El Diablo* would be worth his trouble. "There is my ship just ahead," he remarked with obvious pride. "I trust you can see that the vessel is the finest in the harbor."

Angelique moved closer to the window to get a better view and readily agreed. "Why yes, it is indeed a beauty."

"She is classified as a bark, and, were the sails unfurled, you could readily see that she is square-rigged on the foremast and fore-and-aft rigged on the mainmast and mizzenmast." Without leaving the carriage, Diego continued to point out what he thought was pertinent information, but his impatience to depart was so evident that Angelique swiftly interrupted him.

"I know you must want to call at Monique's home. Why don't you take me back to your house, for I must be there when my mother returns."

Delighted by her suggestion since it saved him the trouble of making an excuse for not taking her on board, Diego was tempted to hug her but caught himself before again making such a grave error. "As you wish, though I'll not go to *Mademoiselle* LeGrand's home, but to the de la Vega's. If they have not invited Monique to their party this weekend, then I will see that an invitation is sent to her home within the hour."

"Can you make such a request of the de la Vegas?" Angelique wondered aloud.

"Yes, of course. They are my friends and will be sure to help me just as you have. Thank you again for coming with me today, Angelique. If I have to wait until Christmas to buy you gifts to repay your kindness, I will, but I wish you had let me purchase something for you today."

"I am your friend, Diego, and true friendship is something that can't be bought with pretty gifts," Angelique reminded him sweetly and noted with relief that the carriage had come to a halt in front of the Aragon residence.

Diego chuckled at her serious tone. He knew there were many ways to make friends and even more reasons to have them, but he would not spoil her innocent view of the world. He thought her sweetness very charming and hoped she would remain that way for many years to come. "Then I will ask you to accept my thanks graciously, since that is all you will permit me to give."

"You are most welcome," Angelique replied as she alighted from the carriage and hurried inside. Once she entered her room she was no longer forced to maintain her composure and promptly became ill. She had been certain Diego would sense something wrong the instant he took her upon his knee, but strangely enough he had made no comment upon the way she had felt in his arms. She had thought her heart would burst with fright in that moment, but the interlude had been so brief that it had been over almost before it had begun. Apparently he had not felt the surge of emotion that had nearly paralyzed her.

She bathed her face with cool water, then lay down upon her bed and wondered how she could bear to go on living if Diego were to fall in love with Monique LeGrand.

Chapter V

Despite Angelique's protests to the contrary, Diego knew it would be good for her to attend the party at the de la Vega's and, after making careful preparations, he raised the subject during breakfast Saturday morning. "I am looking forward to the party tonight. It has been so long since I've seen many of my friends. When I spoke with Carmen earlier in the week, she mentioned that you and my father would be there tonight, Françoise, but don't you think Angelique should be allowed to come with us?"

Before Angelique could offer an excuse, her mother provided one. "That you have taken such an interest in my daughter pleases me greatly, Diego, but she is far too frail to keep such late hours. The night air is unhealthful and I never permit her to go out when she is so likely to fall ill as a result."

Diego waved aside her objections. "You needn't worry. Carmen assured me she would be delighted to have Angelique spend the night at her home. The child needn't stay up too late, or be exposed to the night air. I will go and bring her home in the morning. Since there is no danger to her health if she attends under those conditions, I think the opportunity she'll have to make friends is too good to miss."

He offered his plan with a ready smile, certain Françoise would now have to permit Angelique to attend the party, which was certain to be most festive and enjoyable.

Angelique saw her mother's posture stiffen and entered the discussion on her own behalf. "Diego, please," she implored him, "it is so sweet of you to have made special arrangements for me, but I find noisy gatherings much too taxing and I truly do not wish to attend. Will you thank Carmen de la Vega for me, and explain that though I am unable to accept her hospitality, I do appreciate it."

"You see, Angelique knows what is best," Françoise purred softly, pleased that her willful daughter had chosen to be so sensible in this matter.

Diego laid his knife and fork upon his plate and, shoving away his half-eaten breakfast, he left the table before he was tempted to give his true opinion of the way Françoise was raising her daughter. He could not believe that Angelique really did not want to go with them that night. Children always had such a good time at parties because there was so much for them to enjoy. There was music and the fun of dancing, delicious treats and, of course, the excitement of staying up until nearly dawn. That Angelique would have none of those delightful memories to brighten the lonely hours of her days pained him greatly despite his own anticipation of what the evening would bring.

"Monique LeGrand," he whispered to himself and, beginning to concentrate upon his own dreams, he gave Angelique's dreary life no further contemplation, for, he reasoned, he had done his best to help her escape the prison in which her mother was keeping her and she had refused to accept his kindness. .

After the others had left for the party that night, Angelique simply sat in her room, too depressed to read or to stroll in the garden. She did not even bother to prepare for bed, but sat in the shadows of her room, trying not to give in to the flood of tears that lurked just behind her long sweep of dark lashes. She knew Diego was angry with her for refusing to attend the party, but she could not have borne being surrounded by happy children while watching him dance with Monique LeGrand. As she sat alone in the darkness, her fear that the beautiful young woman would be free to love Diego grew to an unbearable terror.

All at once she heard footsteps coming down the hall and she wondered why José Luis and her mother had returned home so early. Fearing one of them had fallen ill, she ran to open her door.

Diego halted in midstride, startled by Angelique's sudden appearance. "My goodness, aren't you up way past your bedtime?" he inquired sarcastically, then leaned back against the wall as his dark glance swept over her prim figure slowly. She was dressed as she had been that morning, an exquisite doll so wrapped in lace she seemed as fragile as a porcelain figurine.

Angelique studied Diego's face with amazement, for he had wonderfully expressive features. Frequently he conveyed his mood with no more than a slightly raised brow or a smile that barely touched his lips yet was delightfully charming. But tonight she saw something she had not seen before and could only guess at its cause. "Are you drunk?" she asked innocently.

"Very." Diego shifted his weight and nearly lost his balance, though he managed to catch himself before he fell. "Yes, indeed, I am quite drunk," he admitted with a devilish chuckle, seemingly very pleased with himself.

"But why?" Angelique wanted to know. "Was Monique not all you expected her to be?" She was so happy to see him home she could scarcely contain herself. And the fact that he was drunk concerned her not at all.

"No, she was blond and pretty, but unfortunately not my lady."

As his deep voice trailed off to a hoarse whisper, Angelique stepped forward to take his arm. "Well, that is most disheartening news, but you should not have done this to yourself. Let me help you to your room."

Diego tried to focus his eyes, but Angelique seemed to be floating in a dreamlike mist. "Stupid of me, wasn't it?" he mumbled, letting her lead him down the hall and into his room. When she pushed him toward his bed, he uttered no complaint, though he fell more than sat down upon the edge. He managed to look astonished, however, when she knelt at his feet and began to pull off his boots. "I can do that," he protested, but she paid him no mind and yanked off one of the highly polished boots and then the other.

"Your coat is too handsome to sleep in, Diego. Here, give me your hand." Angelique laughed as he tried to help, for he was so dizzy he had to lean against her while he pulled his arms from the sleeves. She left him for a moment to place the coat upon the chair, then debated how much more of his clothing to remove. "Do you do this often at parties, Diego?" she asked as she moved back to his side and unbuttoned his cuffs before reaching for the buttons on his brocade waistcoat.

"Never," he chuckled. "Absolutely never."

"You don't know how happy I am to hear that," Angelique retorted and soon had his waistcoat and shirt unbuttoned. She hesitated as she was about to unfasten his belt buckle to free the shirt tail. "Can you stand up for a moment?" she asked hopefully, thinking he might be able to prepare for bed himself.

"No," Diego admitted with a hearty laugh, then collapsed across the bed, closed his eyes, and, with a deep sigh, fell sound asleep.

Angelique put her hands on her hips, exasperated to have lost his cooperation. "Well, my beloved, I've undressed you before and I do not mind in the least doing it again, but what will you say to me in the morning?" Thinking it unlikely he would even recall speaking with her, Angelique reached for his belt, swiftly removed his breeches, then tossed his waistcoat and shirt aside so it would look as though he had undressed quite carelessly. She pulled the covers up to his broad chest to prevent his becoming chilled, then could not resist leaning down to brush his lips with a light good-night kiss. She extinguished the candles upon the low dresser and left his room to return to her own, where she found the world of dreams far more comforting than she had dared hope it would be.

When Diego next had an opportunity to speak alone with Angelique, he asked her pointedly, "What happened the night of the party?"

"I am certain I could not say, Diego, for I was not there."

"I know that!" he exploded impatiently as he raked his fingers through his unruly hair. "I mean after I came home!" His memory of her was very dim, but he knew something had happened between them and he wanted to know exactly what had transpired.

"Now let me see." Angelique appeared to be giving his question deep concentration. "I spoke with you in the hall, but I am sorry to say you had obviously had too much to drink and told me only that Monique was not the blonde for whom you're looking. You then staggered off to your room. There is nothing more to tell."

Diego frowned sullenly, certain he recalled her being in his room, even though such a possibility seemed preposterous. "I am sorry if I disturbed you," he responded contritely.

"You did not," she assured him. "I was very curious about Monique and therefore glad I did not have to wait until morning to hear about her," Angelique explained truthfully.

"Well, the next time I hear of a stunning blonde, I will not be so optimistic until I see for myself the extent of her charms. But if I have to call at every home in Barcelona to find the woman I met here, I will do so."

He was so determined, Angelique felt extremely guilty to be the woman he sought and yet be unable to tell him so. "You obviously consider her worth such an extensive search.

I hope you find her swiftly," she finally managed to say.

Diego shook his head sadly. "It cannot be too swift for me, since I—" He paused then, seeing Françoise coming toward them. "You must excuse me, please. I have something to do." He gave her a sly wink as he raised her hand to his lips, then left, bidding Françoise a pleasant good day as he passed by.

The elegantly clad Frenchwoman turned to stare at the young man. "What did Diego want?"

"Why nothing, Mama. He said no more than good day and asked how I was," Angelique replied. She thought it ironic that the very skills her mother had taught her to employ in assuming the attitude of a child could be used so effectively to lie to her as well. "He is very nice to me, and that should help you with José Luis, don't you think?"

"Yes, of course, but I do not like him speaking with you when I am not present. He is a very charming young man and—"

"Mother, please. Diego must have dozens of women to court. He speaks with me only as a courtesy to his father, I am certain."

Françoise was not entirely convinced this was so, but she let the matter drop. José Luis had continued to be attentive, but he had not yet issued a proposal and her patience was growing very thin. "Perhaps you are right. Diego is nice to you because he knows his father is fond of you. What other reason could there possibly be?"

"Why none, Mama." Angelique picked up her embroidery and was grateful when her mother made no further mention of Diego but instead discussed her hopes of marrying José Luis.

Diego made the rounds of fashionable dressmakers, attended more parties than he could count, and spent endless hours riding through town hoping to catch a glimpse of his blonde while she was out shopping. His friends' curiosity had been sparked at first, but all soon grew weary of his relentless pursuit of a woman none of them had ever seen. Finally, one night, he decided he had attended one party too many and when his father and Françoise left, he remained at home, too depressed even to challenge Angelique to a game of cards or chess. "I am sorry to be such poor company, but I can't seem to think of anything anymore but the woman I cannot find but can't forget."

They were seated in the parlor and the hour was growing late. Angelique knew she should excuse herself, yet she wanted to stay up with him for as long as she could. She had watched him grow more unhappy each day, but there was no way she could reveal her identity and her pain was every bit as deep as his. "This young woman knows you are Diego Aragon, doesn't she?"

"Yes," he replied, dismissing her question promptly. "She knows exactly who I am, but what help is that to me?"

"I was thinking only that perhaps she has left town, gone to visit relatives or friends, and will return in time. It might be the reason you cannot locate her."

"That is a most comforting thought, Angelique, that she could be anywhere in Spain—anywhere in Europe!" he responded sarcastically. "You expect me to wait, to simply be patient until she again appears upon my doorstep? What if she has left Barcelona to be married? Did that possibility not occur to you?" Diego swallowed the last drop of his brandy but saw no point in getting drunk again. He had done it too many times of late and was tired of waking up sick the next morning. "She could have married another man by now," he added morosely.

"I doubt it," Angelique whispered softly. She longed to go to Diego, to put her arms around him and cover his face with tender kisses, but that would end any hope her mother had of marrying his father. Her birthday was swiftly approaching and she had vowed to leave then. She would have to

86

persuade Diego to wait a few weeks more, she realized. Slowly an idea began to take shape in her mind, a plan that would allow her to see him, and not within the walls of his father's house. "What have you been doing with your days, Diego? Do you still go to your ship?" she inquired in what she hoped seemed a casual manner.

"Yes, there is a great deal of maintenance to be done between voyages and if I am not there, the work progresses much too slowly." Just thinking of *El Diablo* brightened his mood for the moment and he added, "I have yet to give you that tour, as I promised."

"Perhaps when all the work is completed you'd like to show me the ship." Angelique rose from her chair and went over to him. "If I bring you some paper and a pen, will you draw that picture of the devilfish for me? I am still very curious about it."

"Yes, of course. I'd forgotten all about that."

When she returned, Diego drew the ray with a few quick strokes. "There. Do you understand now? It has a triangular shape with a long tail. Some are as large as twenty feet across."

Angelique thought him a fine artist and said so. "I'm certain your sketch is perfect. May I keep it please?" she entreated. When he handed it to her without argument she leaned down to give him a light kiss upon the cheek as she bid him good night. "I must go to bed, but I would like to hear more about your ship another day."

"Yes, I will be happy to bore you with my tales," Diego promised with a rueful laugh.

"You never bore me, Diego. Never."

When the little girl was gone, Diego again reflected upon how unusual a creature she was. She was very bright but seemed content to live a life he found unbearably restrictive though he never heard her voice a single complaint. Such a shy girl would surely choose the church over a husband but that was not a choice he wanted to see her make. Despite her mother's constant worry, he did not think Angelique was all that frail, only too sheltered for her own good. He would have to speak with his father again about his plans, since apparently the older man had not yet mentioned marriage to Françoise.

For a long time he sat by himself, lost in thought. He considered his father a very fortunate man to have the woman he admired so close at hand. Eventually his mind wandered to the lovely young woman he longed to see again, and he grew cold with the fear that after no more than one night of love he had lost her forever.

One morning soon after, Françoise announced that she would be away shopping for several hours. Angelique merely nodded, but the moment her mother left the house with José Luis, she ran into her parent's room and searched through the gowns in her wardrobe. Much to her delight, she found a black dress, which she knew her mother no longer wore.

Carrying the severely tailored garment to her own room, she quickly scrubbed her face clean, brushed out her gleaming curls, then tried on the somber gown. Though it was too snug in the bosom, she had no choice but to wear it anyway. After donning a black lace *mantilla,* she slipped out the front door unseen and started down the walk with a hurried step.

She had paid close attention the morning Diego had taken her to La Belle Mode, and in less than an hour she had reached the docks and had found his ship. She walked to the foot of the gangplank and after waiting a moment and seeing no one about, she walked up to the deck and called to the first man she saw.

"Can you tell me if your captain is aboard?" she asked sweetly. Now that she had come all this way, she prayed that he was.

Octavio Morales stared wide-eyed at the slender young woman dressed in black, but he soon recovered from the shock of having such a visitor and rushed to her side. *"Señorita,* Captain Aragon is indeed aboard, but surely he does not expect you to come here!"

"Perhaps not, but I must speak with him. Will you please tell him that I have come to discuss Las Aztecas? He will know who I am."

Octavio knew Diego liked the company of pretty women, but he had never seen one so bold as to follow the captain to his ship. Since she was dressed in mourning and appeared to be a well-bred lady, he stifled the impulse to send her on her way and went instead to Diego's cabin to ask what should be done.

Diego was busily sorting through his maps when Octavio came to his door. "Yes, what is it?" he asked impatiently, not pleased to be interrupted.

"There is a young woman here who mentioned Las Aztecas and—"

"What!" Diego dashed past his mate with such speed that he left the man gaping in wonder, but he was too excited to walk, for he had been given reason to believe that this might be the woman of his dreams.

Angelique smiled as Diego approached, but when he swung her up into his arms she whispered softly in his ear, "Could we not go to your cabin, where we might speak in private?"

Diego gave the pretty blonde another affectionate squeeze, then placed her gently upon her feet and took her hand. "Yes, of course. Come with me." As they passed Octavio, he clapped the man soundly upon the back and directed him to see that they were not disturbed. Once inside his cabin he gave his quarters a worried glance and apologized. "I have been cleaning and—"

"I came only to see you, Diego. The neatness of our surroundings does not concern me." She let her *mantilla* fall

89

back upon her shoulders to reveal her blond curls as she spoke. "I know you have been searching for me, but I must beg you to cease such efforts. It is imperative that I remain in seclusion for the time being."

In the clear light of the sun flooding his cabin, the blonde's delicate coloring was so lovely that Diego could do little but stare. Her skin was flawless, the blue of her eyes as brilliant as sapphires, and her golden tresses so thick and shiny that he could not help but reach out to draw a strand of the honey-colored hair to his lips. His glance swept hungrily over her figure and he wondered aloud at her choice of costume. "Has someone died, is that it? There has been a death in your family?"

To say yes would be to invite such tragedy, and Angelique could not bring herself to do that. "No, there is no significance to my apparel, none whatsoever. But you did not answer me. You must search for me no further, Diego. I will return to you as soon as I can and you must be content with that promise for another few weeks."

Exasperated, Diego refused. "I shall never be content until I know your whereabouts each hour of the day!"

Angelique raised her fingertips to his lips in an attempt to quell his anger and he kissed her palm hungrily. "I want only to be with you," he moaned softly, then slipped his arms around her waist to draw her near. Her lips were tinged with a tempting pink sheen and eagerly he bent his head to capture her mouth beneath his own. His tongue caressed hers playfully at first, but soon he gave in to the passion she aroused so easily within him. He wanted her too urgently for loving games and pressed her closer as his hand slid down her back to her hip. When she tried to draw away, he would not let her go; instead he deepened his kiss until she ceased to struggle in his arms.

Angelique had not expected so intense a welcome. She had meant only to reassure Diego of her love, not to give herself to him again. Nevertheless, she relaxed in his embrace and drank in the warmth and affection she had missed so greatly as she tried to find the words to make him understand her plight.

When at last Diego lifted his head, it was to whisper softly, "I want to make love to you. It will be better for you now—much better."

"No." Angelique laid her head upon his chest. "No, I must go. If my absence is discovered, I will suffer greatly."

"You are not beaten?" Diego asked incredulously, for he could not believe the lovely lady in his arms could inspire any emotion other than devotion.

"Sometimes," Angelique admitted. "That is why I have no time to tarry. I came only to beg you to be patient, for I shall be free of my family obligations shortly and I will come straight to you."

"I can wait no longer," Diego cried hoarsely. "Come away with me now."

"No! That is impossible," Angelique announced firmly. "There are others who are depending upon me, and I cannot betray their trust. If only you will be patient . . ."

Diego stepped back and his expression grew stormy. "If you understood how greatly I have suffered, how desperately I have missed you, you would not ask this of me."

"Do you not care enough to wait a few weeks?" Angelique asked sweetly. "I would wait forever for you."

Diego refused to give in. "I will call at your home, speak with your father this very day. Surely when the man sees how sincere I am, he will allow me to see you."

"That is impossible. My father is dead and I am staying with . . . with relatives," Angelique added quickly.

"Then to whom must I speak? I will simply escort you home and see them this very afternoon!"

Angelique turned away, confused by his demands. "I meant only to see you once again, to ask you—beg you—to

91

cease looking for me until I can invite your attentions and return them openly."

Diego watched in fascination as the graceful blonde began to pace slowly in front of him with a step as light as a dancer's. "If your relatives need money, I have it. Do not be too proud to ask for a loan, if it would mean we could be together."

"Money is not the problem," Angelique explained. "I can tell you no more than that my situation is a most desperate one, but the difficulty will be resolved shortly and then I will be able to come and go as I please, to see you whenever you desire. Do not ask me to explain now, however, for I can provide no answers as yet."

"What is it you want me to do?" Diego finally asked.

"Why, nothing," Angelique replied. "You need do nothing except believe me when I say I will return to see you when I have my life in order. It will not be long, I can promise you that."

"You can at least tell me your name," Diego ordered firmly.

Angelique knew she could lie, could pick any name and it would satisfy him for the moment, but when he learned what she had done, he would be hurt more deeply than he already had been by her seeming disappearance from Barcelona society. "No, I cannot tell you my name, and I will not lie either. Don't we know each other well enough to overlook such formalities?"

Diego found the enchanting blonde's words far too puzzling. "Are you married? Is that it?"

Blushing deeply, Angelique shook her head emphatically. "You know that I am not."

"How would I know that? I know only that I thought you a virgin, but perhaps you were not. Or, if you were, you could have been married against your will to a man too old and feeble to consummate the union. Are you waiting for him to die so you'll be free?"

Angelique was sickened by his ghoulish suggestion. "I have been with no man but you, which I thought you understood. Were I married to another, no matter what the state of his health I'd not have made love to you. Can't you accept the simple explanation I've given you as the truth? I have problems within my family that must be resolved before I can be free, but they have nothing to do with a husband, for I do not have one."

"I have a vivid imagination, my love, and if you do not provide me with the details of your dilemma, then my mind will naturally furnish them. The circumstances of our initial meeting were mysterious to say the least, and now, when I had almost given up hope of ever finding you, you come to me with a sad tale I am supposed to accept without argument. Did you think I would be so easily placated?"

"I would not have come if I had known how difficult this would prove to be," Angelique admitted frankly. "I thought that since you were searching for me so diligently you would be relieved to learn I knew of your efforts and wished to spare you any further grief. I did not dream you would believe I was toying with you."

Diego studied his beautiful guest's manner closely, for she reminded him of someone he had met but whose identity he could not quite recall. He decided it might be a family resemblance he was seeing and, if he could just keep her talking, a name would surely occur to him, a name that would lead him to the truth. "If your family is new to Barcelona, if there is something they need other than money, then—"

"You are very generous, and so kind, but no, our problems are very personal ones that cannot be solved by outsiders."

"Do you really consider me that—an outsider?" Diego asked, obviously insulted by the term.

"No, of course not, but the others do. Now please, I have been away too long and must go. Will you kiss me good-bye?" she asked, then adjusted her *mantilla* to cover her curls before stepping forward shyly.

"I will be happy to kiss you a thousand times, but you are not leaving here just yet," Diego vowed with a slow smile. "You've given me no more to believe in than I had before, and if you are sincere in your promise to return, then you will let me make love to you again before you go."

Angelique's breath caught in her throat. "But I have explained that there is no time . . . I will be missed and—"

"You are a clever young woman, and you will think of something to tell them. Do you never go shopping, or simply out for a walk to enjoy the freshness of the new day? Have you no friends with whom you could have been visiting? Mightn't you have found a stray kitten and been searching for its owner? I am certain you will be able to think of at least a dozen excuses on your way home. Now come here. I am nowhere near ready to kiss you good-bye."

Angelique chewed her lower lip nervously. She had made a dreadful mistake in coming here. This was plain to her now, for what he asked was so underhanded a suggestion that she could not accept it. "My word is good. Isn't yours?"

"If it is my word you want, then I will give it gladly. But I won't allow you to leave until you've shown me the depth of your devotion in a way I can fully understand. I have found that the words of beautiful women can be astonishingly empty. It is not you I distrust, but your kind."

"I thought you were a gentleman!" Angelique whispered in disbelief. "I thought you were kind and good, but if you would treat me so inconsiderately, then—"

"Then what? You will not return as you've promised?" Diego inquired sarcastically. "A gentleman backs his word with his deeds. I am only asking you to do the same. Show me you mean to return by issuing a promise that I'll know is more than a softly whispered lie."

94

"How dare you!" Angelique demanded, wanting to scream, so frustrated was she by his cool indifference.

"You do not trust me with your name, so I'll not trust you to return," he retorted. Then, as if his words were not insult enough, Diego's dark glance swept over her in a silent challenge he knew she would not dare refuse.

Chapter VI

Angelique felt the same sense of helpless rage she continually suffered under her mother's tyrannical domination. Her love had been a gift, not a commodity she would now use to barter for his trust and the very idea made her so angry she could barely see through the fiery red mist that had descended upon her vision.

Diego gathered his maps and nonchalantly straightened his desk while he awaited her decision. "It is a small price to pay for my patience and, as you well know, a most enjoyable one."

Angelique continued to fume with bitter frustration. "Your demand is despicable, Diego Aragon—utterly despicable!"

"It is your choice, my dear," Diego remarked slyly. "But since I bedded you on the night we met, you cannot possibly consider me either a gentleman or the patient sort."

His taunt was spoken in a teasing manner, yet Angelique understood instantly that his feelings were much like her own. She had wanted the affection he had given so lavishly and had made no move to resist him or to leave his room once he had begun kissing her. Considering the abandon she had displayed that night, she realized that his demand was reasonable and her anger, therefore, without justification.

She sighed sadly then, knowing she really had no choice at all. "Obviously, I am no lady, nor do I possess patience in abundance either," she admitted softly.

Angelique looked down at the dull fabric of her dress, now thinking it the perfect choice for her visit. Her mother had hated this particular gown because it had been a gift from Beatriz, who had insisted she wear it long past the time she had ceased to mourn for her husband in her heart. The heavy black cotton was stiff, the dreary garment uncomfortable to wear, and Angelique's hands shook as she tried unsuccessfully to unbutton the tiny hooks at the bodice.

Diego opened his mouth to argue, for he did not want his lovely guest to think ill of herself, but when he realized she had begun to disrobe, he was too astonished to speak and could only watch in rapt fascination. And as he observed her movements, one thought tugged at the edge of his consciousness with maddening persistency. This pretty creature was related to someone he knew! But who could it be? The grace of her motions, her proud carriage, the sparkle of her wit were all so familiar to him that he could predict her actions before she took them. How was that possible, he wondered, when they had spent so few hours together?

He stepped quickly to her side and, placing his hands upon her waist, he turned her toward him. "That gown is not yours, is it?" he asked, reaching for the hooks that seemed so difficult for her to manage and unfastening them with a deft touch. "You are a mysterious beauty who comes to me in a borrowed dress, and I do not even know what name to call you."

Angelique took his hands in hers and brought them to her lips. *"Chéri* is enough," she stated simply.

Diego found the sweetness of her manner so enchanting that he wanted only to hold her, to press her dear body close to his own as he enjoyed the delicate fragrance of her golden curls. *"Ma chéri,"* he replied, his deep voice filled with desire.

Angelique relaxed against him and was swept along by the very same tide of passion that had swirled about her with his very first kiss. She lifted her arms to encircle his neck and hugged him so tightly that he began to laugh. After returning her enthusiastic hug, he quickly helped her out of the cumbersome mourning dress. Then he gathered her up in his arms and carried her the short distance to his bunk.

Sitting down beside her, he removed the rest of her clothing with care, knowing she could not return home in garments he had torn to shreds in his haste to possess her. He could not recall ever having undressed a young woman with so lovely a figure and he found the task extremely pleasurable. "Your complexion is a most unusual shade, pale yet golden, as if you've been kissed by the rays of the sun. You are even more beautiful than I remembered," he whispered seductively as he leaned down to trail tender kisses along the elegant curve of her throat.

Angelique slipped her fingers through the silken curls at his nape and drew him close. "You could not be more handsome than I remembered you to be." She brushed his cheek softly with her lips as she whispered, "I have never seen a man more handsome than you. I doubt one exists."

Diego was delighted with her compliment since it was so obviously sincere, and his grin became the wicked leer his father so heartily disliked. He peeled away her lace-trimmed lingerie as he chuckled happily and replied, "Thank you. I am glad that I please you as greatly as you please me."

Angelique's hands moved down the buttons on his shirt as she retorted with mock seriousness, "You shouldn't laugh at me, Diego. That's cruel."

"I am not laughing at you," the handsome young man protested promptly. "I am simply so thrilled to have you here with me that I feel like laughing for the first time in weeks!"

The mere sight of her filled him with a heady rush of optimism and he reasoned that if she had come to him once, surely she would be able to come often now that she knew how welcome she would be. As before, there were so many things he wanted to tell her, but he could not find the words to adequately describe the rapture that filled his heart.

Giving up the effort to make sparkling conversation when the need she aroused within him was so great, he tossed his shirt aside, yanked off his boots, then rose to his feet and reached for his belt buckle, not bothering to be as careful in removing his own garments as he had been with hers.

Now completely nude, Angelique slipped under the crisp linens that covered the bunk, but Diego leaned down and ripped the top sheet from the bed. "Your beauty is far too magnificent to hide," he explained as he joined her upon the bunk. His touch was possessive now, smooth and sure, as he pulled her into his arms and buried his face in her golden curls. She welcomed him with a graceful embrace and the agony of their separation was forgotten the instant their lips met.

Diego was so excited by the luscious blonde's surprise visit that he feared he might have cracked her ribs in his enthusiastic embrace, but she made no complaint about the force of his affection and he thought no more about restraining the joy he felt. She returned his kisses as eagerly as he gave them, and soon he leaned back for a moment, wanting only to be certain he was not dreaming.

Her glance became curious then, for she was obviously puzzled by his reticence to finish what he had begun. This was proof enough to Diego that she was more than merely a lovely vision. Satisfied that the charming young woman occupying his bed was most definitely not an illusion, he kissed her once again before announcing proudly, "I want to teach you all there is to know of making love."

"I think you already have," Angelique replied sincerely, for she could not imagine what more there was to be learned now that she had given herself to him so completely.

Diego's smile widened into a mischievous grin so amused was he by her innocence. "You don't even know how unique

99

you are, do you?"

Angelique looked skeptical and the blue of her eyes took on a decidedly violet hue. Then she realized his remark was meant as a compliment and she accepted it graciously. "If you believe me to be special, then I am very flattered." She let her hands rest upon his deeply bronzed shoulders and again drew his mouth to hers to savor the taste of his kiss.

He was also unique, in her opinion, and the only man she would ever want, for he gave love in such abundance. She clung to him as his lips moved slowly down her throat with playful nibbles. His touch was light, yet endlessly pleasant, and she stretched languidly against him, pressing her slender body still closer to his. His lips strayed across her breast, and his tongue teased the pale pink tip playfully. Had she been a cat, she mused, she would have purred, his sweetness touched her so.

Diego's mood was euphoric and he saw no reason to restrain the pleasures they could share. "Your golden skin is so very lovely, warm and soft, while the scent of your perfume is more intoxicating than my brandy," he whispered. The fact that this marvelous fragrance emanated from areas other than just her throat and wrists pleased him greatly. And though she might have offered a protest if she had sensed his thoughts, he knew no woman went to see a man doused in such seductive perfume unless she wanted him to make love to her. "You are the most desirable of women, *ma chéri.*" He trailed tender kisses across the smooth flesh of her breasts as he continued to compliment her effusively. "You are more than merely beautiful; you are perfection, and so very precious to me."

Lulled by his sentimental words, Angelique made no move to escape his affection as his hands moved slowly up the insides of her slender thighs and his mouth strayed over the flatness of her stomach. She found his loving ministrations delightful and stroked his hair lightly with her fingertips until suddenly she realized what he meant to do. "Diego!" she cried hoarsely, but it was far too late for her to stop him then.

Diego hesitated no more than a second, and his dark eyes glowed with the bright flames of desire that raged within his heart. "You are mine. Every delectable inch of you is mine," he vowed hoarsely, rubbing his cheek against the taut skin of her thigh as he tightened his hands around her narrow waist so that she could not avoid his touch. Holding her securely, he began to nuzzle the soft triangle of blond curls that lured him toward his goal. His kiss was gentle at first and teased her senses as he drew her close, but he became so fascinated by the sensuousness of her lissome figure that he wanted to savor it to its very depths. The caress of his tongue grew more insistent then as he sought the ultimate intimacy, for he longed to know her as he had never known another woman, to capture her very soul as well as her heart with the power of his devotion. He knew he had been the first to make love to her, and he longed to be her only lover. He wanted her to belong solely to him. He was determined that every delicious inch of her would be his alone, forever.

Diego's prideful boast that she was his sent a jolt of rebellion through Angelique, for she could not abide being treated as no more than an attractive possession he would use for his own pleasure. She was as appalled by his roguish manner as she was shocked by the way in which he had chosen to display his affection.

But although her mind fought his domination, her body betrayed her far too swiftly to allow her to voice any protest. His touch was much too loving to bring a complaint. She had no desire to struggle for freedom from his confining grasp when his ardent kiss brought a warm rush of pleasure that slowly deepened to a rapture so profound she could not seem to think at all. Her whole body throbbed with the force of his unselfish dedication until the final ecstasy swept through her slender limbs in shattering tremors.

Content he had achieved his purpose, Diego at last drew

away. He covered Angelique's flushed cheeks with light kisses as he now moved to seek his own release in the exquisite pleasure he knew he had given her. Her graceful body welcomed his with a fluid ease that exhilarated him and he whispered softly, "I want it always to be like this for us, my beauty—always."

He kissed her lips hungrily and his mouth ravished hers with a bruising intensity. She had driven him nearly mad with desire in the weeks they had been apart and he could no longer contain the fiery passion she inspired. He sought to take all she could give, and his forceful thrusts plundered the depths of her being with an intensity barely tempered by tenderness.

When his need for her had at last been fulfilled in a blinding splendor, he could not bear to release her, but held her locked in his arms in a tight embrace. Though she was the most exciting woman he had ever known, she was also elusive, and he was afraid to let her go for fear she would disappear forever.

Stunned to the very core by the savage passion Diego had unleashed upon her, Angelique found it impossible to draw breath enough to speak. He had not hurt her, not at all, and he had given pleasure every bit as rich as that which he had taken for himself. But she had not expected making love to be as close to violence as he had shown her it could be, and she could only wonder at what else he might want to teach her. Deciding that this was a question better left unasked, she inhaled deeply and calmly told him, "I must leave you now. I should not have stayed so long."

Disappointed by her coolly issued statement, Diego did not release her, but instead looked down into her eyes with a dark expression clouding his features. "Are you sorry now that you stayed?" he asked sharply.

Not having meant to offend him, Angelique was quick to argue. "No, I am not sorry for anything that has happened between us, but while you might insist that I am yours, we both know I am not. I must go. I have no choice," she stated firmly, but still he held her body pinned beneath his own and she could not even move, let alone leave his bed.

"Tell me your name," Diego demanded once again. Then he lowered his mouth so that his lips brushed hers lightly as he cajoled, "Please tell me and I will be content with no more than your name until next we meet."

Since revealing her name was not possible, Angelique did not respond but instead wrapped her arms around his neck to draw him close, hoping her affection would be answer enough. It wasn't. Diego's response was immediate and his anger was plain in his fiery glance as he moved to possess her once again. His motions were quick and sure and his powerful body dominated her fragile frame swiftly, but this time he was not making love.

His purpose was clear to Angelique. He wanted her destiny to lie in his hands, not with the family whose problems had kept them apart. He wanted her to choose him, and he used pleasure as a weapon to gain her confidence. And pleasure her he did, but when he looked down into her blue-violet eyes and found them bright with defiance, he knew his ploy had failed and he was disgusted with himself for even thinking of it, let alone attempting it so rudely. His expression grim, he moved off the bed and dressed quickly.

As Angelique watched him gather up his clothing, she reflected that she knew his sleek body far better than she understood his perplexing moods. Though she recognized that Diego's was a complex personality, she had found no way of explaining that he was making her life extremely difficult by refusing to understand her need for discretion.

"I have missed you," Diego finally managed to offer as the apology he was certain she deserved. "Do not stay away so long ever again. Come back tomorrow if you can, or the next day."

Thinking it best to dress before he changed his mind and returned to bed, Angelique donned her lingerie with hands that shook so badly she could scarcely tie the bows to hold the pretty garments in place. Her silk stockings seemed to be tied in knots and she was nearly in tears as she replied, "I can make no promises, Diego. I've been away far too long."

Seeing that she was truly frightened, Diego quickly knelt down in front of her and smoothed out her stockings so their fit was perfect. He slipped her tiny feet into her black kid slippers and tied the ribbons into pretty bows. Then he rose to help her put on several layers of foamy silk slips and waited patiently to fasten the tiny hooks on the heavy black dress. Handing her the black lace *mantilla,* he offered the only other assistance he could. "I would be happy to go to your home with you, if you would just let me."

"No!" Angelique cried sharply. "You must never try to find me—never!" With that hasty farewell, she reached up to give him one last, lingering kiss, and then she was gone.

Diego followed her out to the deck and motioned to get his mate's attention. Octavio Morales walked quickly to his captain's side, hoping for some explanation of what the young woman's business had been, for he was too discreet to ask so direct a question. "Yes, sir," he responded politely, though his gaze followed the pretty blonde's progress as she ran down the gangplank with flying steps.

Diego made his decision instantly and gave a terse order. "Send one of the men after her. I want to know where she lives, but she mustn't suspect she's being followed."

"As you wish, sir." Octavio hastily summoned a young sailor who had been seated nearby coiling rope. Taking him to the rail, he pointed out the slender young woman clothed in black and repeated Diego's orders. The man rushed down the gangplank after her and was soon lost in the crowd near the docks.

Diego returned to his cabin where he made up his bunk and poured himself a full glass of brandy before sitting down to savor the morning's unexpected erotic turn. He had been with more women than he cared to count, yet none had ever set his very blood aflame as this exquisite blonde continually did. He had not even thought of seeking out the brightly painted female companions who usually kept him entertained when he was in Barcelona. He had not missed their ready affection, he realized suddenly, nor had he thought of them even once since the night he had found the lovely blonde in his garden.

She had become dear to him in the short time he had known her, and he was sorry now that he had kept her with him so long. She had seemed so frightened about what she would find when she returned home. At least he hoped that was what had frightened her, though the more he considered the way the morning had been passed, the more he thought that he could be the source of her fear. He should have been more careful, for she was obviously quite delicate, but he had wanted her too fiercely to exercise the restraint he now wished he had shown.

If only she had come to me sooner, he thought angrily. If only I had not had to wait so very long to make love to her again, I would have been better able to handle the passions she aroused within me—passions aroused by little more than seeing the brightness of her smile.

Furious with himself because this was the first time in his life he had found his own desires impossible to control, Diego poured himself another drink and downed it as rapidly as the first. He did not care what problems his pretty blonde's family faced. He was confident he could solve them without her ever knowing who the benefactor had been. Then he could take her as often as he wished.

But even as he calmly sat contemplating that delightful thought, he knew he would never have enough of her, no matter what her name might prove to be. The captivating French beauty had stolen his heart and he had no desire to ask her to return it.

*   *   *

Angelique attempted to walk sedately, but she was still trembling so violently that she was certain passersby would know exactly where she had been and what she had been doing for the last hour. She pulled her *mantilla* down low to obscure her features and increased her speed to a near run. She doubted she would arrive home before her mother, and despite Diego's teasing, she could think of no credible excuse for being away from the house dressed in a widow's garb.

She had expected to speak with Diego for no more than ten minutes, not spend the entire morning in his bed. Her cheeks burned with the embarrassment of that memory. She had seen a facet of the handsome young man's personality that she had not known existed, and it was a ruthless, demanding side that she hoped to avoid arousing in the future.

But her most pressing problem now was her mother, and she had little time to devote to contemplating Diego's faults. She dared not slacken her pace and continued at a breathless gait. When she finally reached the corner opposite the imposing Aragon residence, she hesitated a moment, but as she stepped out into the roadway, she saw José Luis and her mother swiftly approaching. They were laughing together, paying no attention to the passing scene and Angelique seized the only opportunity she would have to enter the house before they arrived.

She dashed across the road, sped down the wall that enclosed the garden, and searched frantically for the spot Diego had used to scale it. It was not obvious at first glance, but she tried to recall where she had been standing when he had appeared and was able to narrow down the location to an area she could search more carefully. When she discovered the indentations Diego had found so handy, she had little choice but to gather her courage and, with lithe grace, scrambled over the wall. Then she hurried through the garden and slipped into her room unseen.

When she ripped off the ugly black dress, she realized it

was saturated with her mother's perfume and that this heady fragrance was what Diego had found so entrancing. In her haste to leave the house that morning, she had not noticed that the garment simply reeked of the scent. Disgusted, she threw the offensive dress into her own wardrobe, since there was no time for her to return it to her mother's. Then she poured water from the pitcher at the washstand into the basin and scrubbed herself as best she could, removing all traces of her mother's perfume as well as Diego's purely masculine scent, which still clung to her shapely body. She applied a generous amount of her own perfume and then once again donned the pink dress she had worn at breakfast. After stretching out upon her bed she grabbed a book so that it would appear she had been reading if her mother should chance to stop by her room on her way to her own. Her heart was pounding so wildly within her chest that she doubted she would be able to speak, but at least she would look as though she had spent the whole morning reading and that was all that would matter to her mother.

Diego found the wait for the sailor's return interminable. The morning had served only to whet his appetite for the blond beauty's company, not to sate it. She was young and therefore could be forgiven for not trusting him with her problems, but he could not imagine a situation so dire as to require her to remain in seclusion when he was so desperate to see her. When he could bear the confines of his cabin no longer, he went up on deck and paced with a long, even stride as he waited for the man Octavio had sent to return. Nearly two hours elapsed before he finally appeared.

Pablo was a conscientious lad and had followed Angelique with admirable stealth, though the young woman had been so distraught that she had suspected nothing and had not even once glanced back over her shoulder to see if she were being followed. He had observed her entering the

Aragon house by a most surprising route and was astonished to think the Captain would send him to follow a woman on her way to his own home. Believing that something had to be amiss, he waited for some time to be certain she would not swiftly leave. When after a long while she did not reappear, he ran all the way back to *El Diablo* and had to catch his breath before making his report.

"She went where?" Diego shouted incredulously.

"To your home, sir. I have run errands for you before, so I know the house is yours." Pablo quickly described the residence and its location. "I saw your father arrive with an attractive riding companion just after the lady dressed in black had climbed over the wall."

"She climbed over the wall, you say?" Diego was so confused by Pablo's report that he made him repeat it several times, but the young man's account did not vary in the slightest. Taking several gold coins from his pocket, Diego rewarded the helpful sailor generously and then returned to his cabin where he slammed the door soundly and proceeded to scream every filthy curse he had ever heard in his many years at sea.

"That lying bitch!" he finally shrieked, certain now of the secretive young woman's identity, for there was only one pretty young blond residing in his household—Angelique Devereau, the dear little girl he had befriended so readily.

Pouring himself still another brandy, he tried to grasp the full import of his shocking discovery. Françoise must have become greedy and decided that one wealthy Aragon was not enough and so she had sent Angelique after him. It was all so obvious, he could not believe how he had been such a fool not to see through it in the beginning, though the clouds of lace she wore had hidden her superb figure and lovely features completely. Whenever they had spoken together in the library she had moved to the farthest corner. He had believed her to be too shy to speak to him directly, when, in fact, she was the most cunning of wenches and had kept her

108

distance purposely to fool him. He recalled that he usually saw her only at mealtimes and when she was seated it was impossible to discern her height. And her own statement that La Belle Mode made her garments without fittings showed how cleverly she and her mother had fabricated her disguise.

Remembering the ride to the dressmaker's infuriated him all the more. No wonder she had felt like a woman when he had pulled her across his lap—she was one! His blood reached a near boil as he recounted the many conversations they had had. That she used the shy voice of a child to speak with him was one more part of the ruse she had carried off so expertly. Not one thing about the diabolically fascinating Angelique was real in his estimation. She was no more than a clever actress who had played to an audience of one!

Being duped by the charming blonde into believing that she was sincere in her affections for him though she could not shirk her duty to her family maddened him totally. Every damned day the little tart had appeared at his table in the guise of a friendly child who had even had the audacity to offer suggestions as to how he might find the lovely blonde who had haunted him with the memory of the one night they had shared. If that were not enough, she had always seemed genuinely sorry that none of her ideas had produced the young woman he sought. He would make her pay for this, and not with some elaborate scheme in which he would ensnare her as she had entrapped him, but with a scathing rebuke that very night!

Believing that his honor was at stake, Diego rehearsed several truly terrifying speeches before he paused to consider what he could tell his father that would not make the older man weep in sorrow. He knew the man adored Angelique, considered her to be the daughter he had never had, and was planning to marry her mother. What would he say about this shocking turn of events?

Distressed by the pain his revelation would cause his own father, Diego sat with his head in his hands, unable to think

109

of any way to tell this man the truth about the lovely Devereau women when he knew it would surely break his heart. Angelique deserved no mercy, and neither did her mother, who was surely responsible for the totally reprehensible scheme that had cost him weeks of anguish.

He would have to be cautious, he decided. He would have to think of some way to punish them both for their evil deeds without punishing the father he loved as well.

Chapter VII

Angelique napped all afternoon, exhausted as much by the tension of her rendezvous with Diego as by the passion they had shared. She slept without waking until her mother came to see if she was dressed for dinner. She yawned sleepily then, still unrefreshed after the hours she had spent in her bed. "I am dreadfully sorry, Mama," Angelique apologized sweetly, having no wish to fight with her mother on this of all days. "Send someone with a tray for me if you do not want to wait while I dress to join you." The idea of remaining in her room this evening had great appeal, for she would not dare even to look at Diego after having made love to him again. The depth of her devotion would be so plain in her eyes that everyone would see, and she could not risk even the suspicion that she and the devilishly handsome young man were more than friends.

Françoise tapped her foot impatiently. "You are not falling ill, I hope. I have told José Luis so often that you are frail that he will not be surprised if you are sick, but I'll not have him worrying about you if there is no need."

"No," Angelique replied truthfully, for indeed she had never felt better. She was relaxed and yet still tingling with excitement. "I am quite well. If you do not mind asking José Luis to wait a moment, I will hurry and dress if you think

I should."

Françoise drew close to lay the back of her small white hand against Angelique's forehead. "You have no fever, so there's no need for you to remain in bed as though you were an invalid when it will cause unwanted attention. Wear the pink gown you had on at breakfast and come as quickly as you can."

"Yes, Mama." Angelique waited until her mother left the room before easing out of her bed. She stretched lazily and yawned again as she wondered if Diego had found making love as tiring as she had. Were he to come to the dinner table yawning too, she would not be able to contain her laughter, though he would never understand the cause of her mirth. Amused by that possibility, she prepared for dinner with haste, slipping on her pink gown, coiling her hair atop her head, then donning the frilly white *mantilla* she always wore. She hurried to the parlor, where she found José Luis and her mother talking in a relaxed fashion, but Diego was not with them and she dared not inquire as to his whereabouts.

The main course was being served when Diego finally strode into the dining room. He was neatly groomed and dressed as handsomely as always, though in a more colorful fashion than he usually assumed. His velvet coat was a deep hunter green, his waistcoat embroidered gold satin, and his breeches the color of rich cream. As always, his black leather boots shone with the high polish only diligent effort could produce.

Obviously in a fine mood, he greeted everyone warmly, pausing to give both Françoise and Angelique an affectionate kiss upon the cheek before he clapped his hand upon his father's shoulder and declared, "Forgive me for being so tardy. I am glad to see you did not bother to wait for me."

José Luis frowned, surprised by the double meaning in his son's words. "I saw no reason to wait dinner when you had not given us the courtesy of letting us know whether or not you would even be here!" he responded harshly.

Far from offended by his father's rebuke, Diego laughed agreeably. "There was no time for me to send messages of any sort today, Father. The morning was amusing enough, but it did not match the afternoon for excitement." Leaning down, he shared a confidence in a playful whisper and it brought a deep red blush to his father's dark complexion. Before the embarrassed man could reply, Diego gave him another hearty slap upon the back and took his own place beside Angelique.

Never had she expected to hear Diego dismiss the time they had been together—the time she had considered most precious despite its dangers—as no more than amusing. Hot tears of anger stung Angelique's eyes as she tried to imagine what he had done that afternoon that had surpassed in excitement what he had done with her that morning. That it had shocked his father so greatly alarmed her all the more. Since his explanation had obviously not been suitable for a lady's ears, she had no choice but to sit in stunned silence and contemplate the no-longer-appetizing meal upon her plate. José Luis employed a superb chef and Angelique knew that the *paella* he had prepared for dinner was usually delicious, but she could not even bring herself to taste the saffron-flavored seafood dish tonight. Anxiously she moved a succulent bit of scampi through the grains of rice, hoping to make it appear that she was eating, though she knew she would choke if she lifted so much as a tiny forkful to her lips.

How dare the man refer to her as amusing! she raged inwardly. It was all she could do not to scream at him to apologize for insulting her so rudely, but she knew she had to behave as the sweet-tempered child who usually sat beside him, not as the woman he had just scorned.

Diego leaned over to give Angelique an enthusiastic hug. "Why are you so quiet tonight, little one? Was your day not nearly as exciting as mine?" he asked in a boisterous tone.

"Obviously it wasn't," Angelique replied with forced calm.

"Well, it is definitely time we did something about that,"

Diego responded with his customary confidence. "Now that you know me so much better, Françoise, don't you think I might be entrusted with the task of giving your daughter riding lessons? What if the man she marries is a sportsman who expects her to ride with him daily? Do you not think it is your duty to prepare her for marriage in every way possible? Is that not rightfully a mother's task?"

Startled by Diego's barrage of impertinent questions, Françoise first took a sip of wine before replying. "I thought you understood my position on the issue of riding lessons, Diego. Angelique has no interest in riding—indeed, she has an aversion to horses. She does not even own attire that would allow her to ride in comfort, so the matter of lessons is closed."

"But you have riding habits aplenty, *Madame,* and very stylish ones too. Couldn't you lend one to your daughter?" Diego inquired persistently, his dark eyes bright with a taunting gleam.

Françoise smiled to hide her anger. "The child and I are scarcely the same size, Diego. She cannot wear my clothing."

"Then I will be happy to have La Belle Mode make her an appropriate outfit," he responded. Turning to Angelique, he continued to make plans. "Why don't we go there in the morning? It shouldn't take them too long to make you a nice habit, and then we can begin your lessons."

With deliberate nonchalance, Angelique put down the fork she had not been using. "No, thank you, Diego. It is so generous of you to wish to buy me a riding habit, but I must refuse your offer."

"But why? Your mother has never refused any gift my father has given her."

"Diego," José Luis cautioned sternly, "you may be excused!"

Diego threw back his head and laughed heartily at this order. "I am a grown man, Father, and you'll not send me away from the table for speaking the truth as you might a small boy."

Incensed by his son's defiance, José Luis was half out of his seat when Françoise's hand tightened around his wrist. "Please, let us not quarrel, I beg you. I am embarrassed that I have been reduced to taking your charity, but I cannot deny that what Diego says is true, so there's no need for an argument." While her tone was soothing, the glance she turned upon Diego was fierce.

"If I have offended you, I again apologize as I have so many times in the past, *Madame.*" Diego offered his apology in such a sincere manner and with such elaborate gestures that she had no choice but to accept it.

"You are forgiven," Françoise conceded icily.

"Good." Diego's smile was now a wicked leer. "See to clothes for the child yourself then, and I will teach her to ride as well as you do."

Infuriated that he would not let the matter drop, Françoise grew pale. "Your father, you, and I will have to discuss this at another time, Diego. We should not argue in front of Angelique."

"Oh, of course not." Diego again reached out to hug the pretty girl at his side. "I would not want anyone to raise his voice in the presence of so dear and innocent a child as your sweet little daughter."

José Luis rose to his feet as he gave an order he wanted obeyed instantly. "I can only believe you are drunk or have taken leave of your senses completely, Diego, but you'll not be welcome at my table again until you have learned some manners!" As if that threat were not enough, he offered a more forceful one. "Do not make the mistake of believing I am too old to teach you those manners either!"

Diego took another bite of *paella* and chewed it slowly while he considered his father's harshly worded demand. "I am late for an appointment as it is, so I was about to ask to be excused anyway. You needn't throw me out." He rose with an insolent grace, then inclined his head toward Françoise in

115

a mock bow. "Forgive me, *Madame*. As I said, the afternoon was a stimulating one and perhaps I did imbibe a bit too freely, but I am looking forward to a night of—"

"Get out!" José Luis shouted in an attempt to halt his son's description of an evening he was certain they could imagine quite well without his blurting out his plans in graphic detail.

Rather than leave immediately, Diego leaned down to again embrace Angelique warmly, and he was mystified to discover that the subtle traces of perfume he detected were not those of the exotic scent he had enjoyed that morning. Confused by this startling fact, he stood up abruptly and turned on his heel without bothering to bid her good night.

José Luis sank back down into his chair and sighed sadly. "I will offer no excuses for my son. Clearly he has been touring the town with companions of whom I do not approve, but that is an old argument between us and I'll not burden you with my sorrow."

"But José Luis, you must!" Françoise placed her hand lightly upon his sleeve. "You have listened to my tales of woe so frequently. How can you think I would not also be sympathetic to yours?" The eyes she turned upon him were actually bright with tears. It was a look she knew to be very effective in swaying men to her point of view.

José Luis laughed ruefully. "Your problems are over, my dearest—I have told you that often—but I had hoped, now that Diego is a grown man and captain of his own ship, that he would adopt more gentlemanly behavior."

"He is still very young," Françoise reassured him. "Young men cannot be expected to behave as coolly as more mature men do."

"I fear he will still be a hellion when I am in my grave!" José Luis admitted caustically, for he had been outraged by the boldness of his son's behavior. "Age has nothing to do with maturity, Françoise. You are little older than my son, but you are a responsible woman, not a reckless child!"

Pleased that he would consider her as youthful as she claimed to be, Françoise continued to pat his arm affectionately. "Let us finish our dinner and talk of more pleasant things. Diego has clearly been drinking and tomorrow I am certain he will be very contrite."

"I doubt it!" José Luis scoffed, but he wanted to be an agreeable host and so changed the subject to that of the fine dinner they had been served.

Angelique was afraid she was going to be ill and, at the first opportunity, asked to be excused. "I know you have many things to discuss this evening, and I wish to return to my room if I may. There is a book I am reading . . ."

Delighted that her daughter had been perceptive enough to allow her an extended opportunity to converse alone with José Luis, Françoise made no objection to Angelique's leaving them so early. "Of course, my love, but do not stay up too late. You know how important it is for you to get enough rest."

"Yes, of course, Mama." Angelique kissed her mother and José Luis lightly upon their cheeks and forced herself not to think how much the obnoxious son resembled the father. This was a difficult task, for their striking good looks were so very similar.

While Angelique was bidding her mother and his father good night, Diego was leaving the house through the front door, but rather than summoning a horse or carriage, he circled his home and scaled the garden wall. Taking more care to land upon his feet this time, he quickly went to the door of Angelique's room and, finding it unlocked, slipped inside. He had just started to search through her dresser drawers for evidence of her double life when he heard her unmistakable light step in the hall. He quickly darted behind the draperies of the windows and positioned himself so he would have a clear view of the room while being completely hidden by the thick folds of red velvet.

*   *   *

117

Angelique managed to maintain her composure until she reached her room. Once there, she allowed herself to be overwhelmed by the pain that Diego's coarsely worded comments had caused her and she threw herself across her bed and wept despondently, her heart shattered by his brutish boasts. She adored him, and he had said such sweet things to her that morning. How could he now regard the hour they had spent together as no more than amusing?

Aghast by her tears, Diego swiftly grew impatient as Angelique continued to cry pathetically. He had meant to find something—the black dress, the bottle of that unusual perfume, the brandy snifter that had disappeared from his room—some item to use as evidence when he confronted her. He was further annoyed that she had left the dining room so promptly, and he certainly was not enjoying the sight of her sobbing so wretchedly. He could scarcely confront a woman who was already hysterical and therefore remained hidden, hoping her tears would soon be spent.

Angelique wept until she was exhausted, then, having no energy left to disrobe, she sat upon the edge of her bed and nervously wrinkled her wet handkerchief while she tried to decide what to do. She had promised she would stay in the Aragon home until she was seventeen or until her mother married, whichever came first, but that vow now seemed impossible to keep, for she did not want to see Diego ever again.

She wanted to leave his home this very night but knew such a hasty flight would not only be impractical but foolhardy as well. First she would have to find a suitable position, one that paid well enough to allow her to live on her own. She would have to borrow clothing from her mother, or make it herself, in order to go out and search for work. She was known at La Belle Mode, but where else could she seek employment if *Madame* Larouche would not hire her?

Diego fidgeted nervously, not understanding what was keeping Angelique from preparing for bed. Since he had such a good vantage point, he wanted to observe her closely in order to see how she managed her disguise. That she would weep for so long and then sit immobile for an equal length of time infuriated him, but he forced himself to stand calmly, certain the wait would be well worth his while.

Yet the longer he remained behind the heavy draperies the more concerned he became about the perfume Angelique had been wearing at dinner. What if he had made some ghastly error? What if his blonde were a cousin of Françoise's, who came and went through his home whenever he and his father were occupied elsewhere? What if Angelique were no more than the dear little girl he had originally thought her? He could not leap out and accuse her of anything if she proved to be no more than the child she now appeared to be. He wished he had taken the time to stop by his own room to discard his coat and waistcoat, for he was uncomfortably warm, but that oversight was a small problem compared to the one he would face if Angelique were no more than twelve and discovered him hiding behind her drapes!

As if in answer to his prayers, she rose from the bed, slowly removed the lace *mantilla,* then loosened her hair to free a golden cascade of bright curls he recognized instantly. Her movements were graceful as she hung the pale pink gown in the wardrobe before turning toward her dresser. She then began to peel away the lace-trimmed layers of her silk lingerie, folding each one neatly before placing it in the appropriate drawer.

As each garment was removed, the true beauty of her figure became more apparent. That her loveliness would prove so distracting was disconcerting to Diego and he attempted unsuccessfully to force his heart to return to a steady beat. But still it thudded wildly within his chest and soon his whole body was demanding that he again take the exquisite blonde for his own.

She had taken out a filmy nightdress and had tossed it on

119

the bed, but when she finally removed the linen band that had kept her breasts confined and stepped out of the last of her sheer undergarments, she moved with no real haste to don the snowy white gown. Seizing the perfect moment to reveal his presence, Diego moved out into the room and greeted her warmly.

"Well, *ma chéri,* will you now give me permission to call you Angelique?"

Angelique's eyes grew wide with fear as a terror far greater than any she had ever known swept through her slender body and gripped her heart with tentacles of ice that seemed to freeze her blood solid in her veins. She gasped sharply in an attempt to catch her breath and, grabbing up her nightdress, she clutched it to her breasts to cover herself. Realizing that he had already seen all that he needed to recognize her, she whispered defiantly, "How dare you? How dare you hide in my room to spy on me like some lecherous thief?"

Diego had expected more tears and an anguished plea for forgiveness for what she had done. He had not anticipated that she would think she had a right to be angry with him. Forcing back the fury of his own temper, he spoke calmly. "I am not the one who needs to explain his actions here. I had you followed today to—"

Disregarding her state of undress, Angelique rushed forward to interrupt. "You had me followed? You had the audacity to have me followed after you had sworn not to search for me if I slept with you?" Her cheeks were bright with a furious blush and her eyes glowed with a vicious purple fire. "How could you have done such an unprincipled thing?"

Diego eyed her coldly. In the candles' warm glow her skin took on the golden sheen he had always found so attractive, but now he believed her beauty masked a most treacherous heart. "Since your actions have been beneath contempt, I'll simply ignore your insults. I had you followed because I had hoped to be able to help your family overcome whatever difficulty they had encountered. I meant to do it in an anonymous fashion, but I never expected to find you living here, within the walls of my own home!"

Angelique simply glared at him, certain now that his performance at dinner had been a well-rehearsed act, for he was obviously cold sober and clearly as enraged by her duplicity as she was by his. Turning away slightly, she pulled her sheer nightgown over her head and shook out the soft folds so that it covered her completely, unaware that the fine fabric served only to enhance the curves of her superb figure rather than hide them from his view.

Taking a deep breath, she turned back to face him. "It should be obvious now why I begged you to cease searching for me, but since you have discovered who I am, what do you plan to do about it?"

Startled that she had somehow managed to seize the initiative, Diego clasped his hands behind his back to keep from placing them around her lovely white throat, which had been his first impulse. "I am going to do nothing, but you are going to tell your viper of a mother that her scheme to marry into the Aragon family, not once, but twice, has failed. She can give my father whatever excuse she cares to fabricate for leaving so hastily, but I want both you and her gone by sundown tomorrow."

"But my mother has nothing to do with this!" Angelique protested quickly. "She has no idea that you and I have ever, well . . ."

Several coarse expressions for what they had done came to Diego's mind, but, for a reason he was unable to grasp, he could not speak in such insulting terms to her. "She knows damn well you are no twelve-year-old child, Angelique. Don't pretend she doesn't know everything else as well!"

"But truly she doesn't!" Angelique's panic increased

tenfold at the mention of her mother. "I will leave—by tomorrow. I had planned to leave here very shortly. I told you that today. If only you had been patient, I would have left here in only two weeks!" She reached out to grab his arms in a desperate attempt to gain his understanding. "You have no reason to hate me, and even less to hate my mother!"

Totally confused by Angelique's frantic insistence about her mother's innocence, Diego's dark eyes clouded with doubt. "Why would your mother dress you as a child and treat you as if you were one, if not for some evil purpose?"

Angelique swallowed nervously, then rushed to explain since he now seemed willing to listen. "I was twelve when we arrived here from France. We had lost more than you could ever imagine, and my mother knew that the only way we could live here as we had in France was for her to use every resource she had. Her beauty was what she considered her greatest asset. She wanted to appear as young as possible in order to make a good marriage, but until she met your father, none of the men who had invited us into their homes seemed fine enough gentlemen for her to marry."

"But my father is?" Diego inquired sarcastically.

"Why yes. He is a wonderful man, but you must know that." Angelique was surprised that he seemed not to understand her praise for José Luis.

"Oh, I see. Your mother has you dress as a child as additional bait to trap my father?" Diego was tempted to shake the truth from her, but he hoped that if he just kept Angelique talking she might admit all he would need to know to force her out of his father's house.

"No! I am not bait at all! But it is far easier for a woman to attract a husband when she has a twelve-year-old daughter than when she has one sixteen!"

"Dear God! You are no more than sixteen?" Diego asked incredulously, this shock being as great as the discovery of her identity.

"I will be seventeen in two weeks, and I had planned to

leave here then, whether my mother had married your father or not. I had already told her I was leaving before you came home."

Diego felt sick to his stomach and sank down upon her bed. "This beastly situation is even worse than I thought," he admitted slowly. "I thought you were eighteen at the very least and old enough to make the choice to spend the night with me, but obviously you didn't even know what you were doing."

"Of course I knew!" Angelique protested quickly, not pressing for the advantage her youth might give her in any confrontation over his actions on the night they had met. "I am not the child my mother insists that I pretend to be. I am a woman, and I knew exactly what I was doing!"

Diego looked up at her with a disgusted glance. "That you are so accomplished an actress at such an early age is remarkable. I take it you planned to seek a career upon the stage when you left here?"

Though perplexed by his continued antagonism, Angelique readily supplied the truth. "Why, no, I've never even considered it. I'd hoped *Madame* Larouche or one of the other French couturières or perhaps a milliner who fled our homeland when we did would have work for me. I meant to find honest work, Diego, not to live as my mother does on the generosity of men who like the company of beautiful women and are willing to pay for it."

"Your mother is not my father's whore, Angelique!"

"He pays for her keep and even provides her with a lavish wardrobe, as you pointed out only this evening. She longs to be his wife, but he hasn't offered marriage, so what does that make her?"

Their conversation had not taken the direction he had planned, and Diego was at a loss for words for the moment. If what Angelique said was true, he had recklessly seduced a defiant child and had not been the victim of some well-planned plot Françoise had laid to trap him into marrying

123

her daughter. He was appalled, but angry with Angelique all the same. "You needn't have been so damn helpful in your suggestions. I thought you really wanted to help me and all the while the blonde for whom I searched was no more than an arm's length away. I do not enjoy being made the fool, Angelique—not at all!"

"I wasn't making a fool of you, but merely trying to protect myself! I told you I will leave here tomorrow, but you mustn't punish my mother for what I've done. None of this is her fault," Angelique reemphasized.

"It is all her fault!" Diego argued. "If she would be so dishonest as to disguise her own daughter as a child, then Lord knows what other desperate scheme she'll try to win a marriage proposal from my father! He deserves better than that, Angelique—far better!"

"That's his choice to make, not yours!" the feisty blonde retorted swiftly. "How many women has he courted since your mother's death?"

Diego could do no more than give Angelique a sullen stare, for he knew Françoise was the only woman who had touched his father's heart in a good many years. He had no wish to hurt the older man by revealing what a conniving bitch she actually was. He needed time to think, time to devise a plan of his own to force the elegant Frenchwoman to show her true colors. Then if his father still wanted her, he would at least know exactly what sort of woman he was marrying.

Stalling for the time he needed, Diego replied simply, "This matter will be between us then." Rising slowly, he slipped off his coat and tossed it upon the chair. "If I have misunderstood your motives, it is unfortunate, but now that I know who you are, I see no reason for things to be any different between us."

"What do you mean?" Angelique queried suspiciously.

Unbuttoning his waistcoat with a ready grin, Diego explained his terms more fully. "If two weeks is all you need,

I'll give them to you. Until your birthday, continue each day to be the same sweet child you have been and I'll not say a word to my father either about you or your mother's deceit. But your nights will belong to me."

"I am to be your mistress, is that it?"

"Don't look so insulted. Just what do you think you have been?" Diego asked with an insidious chuckle.

"I thought . . ." Angelique looked down and her long lashes veiled the anguish in her eyes. She was unable to speak of love when it was clear she had lost his.

"You thought what?" he demanded to know. "What else did you expect from me?" She had hurt him deeply with the masquerade she had carried out right under his very nose and he saw no reason to treat her with any more kindness than she had shown him.

"Nothing," she finally responded sadly, her hopes of a shared future dashed by his hostile mood.

"Well, since you had no plan, you should be delighted with mine. If you and your mother have some agreement about your moving out—"

"It is not exactly an agreement, Diego. I told her I was leaving, but she doesn't really believe that I will go."

Diego now tossed his waistcoat upon the chair and sat down to remove his boots. Suddenly recalling the night he had come home from the de la Vega's party in a drunken stupor, he glanced over his shoulder to ask, "You did come into my room that night I came home drunk, didn't you?"

Angelique hesitated to admit she had lied to him on that occasion too. "Yes. I meant only to help you to your room, but then I stayed to help you undress."

"But of course you denied that the incident ever took place when I asked you about it!" Diego shook his head and would have flung his boot against the wall had he not realized the need for self-control. "Does your mother come in each night to tuck you in?" he snarled caustically.

"No, never. She stays up quite late with your father and

125

then goes straight to bed. I'll not see her until the morning." Since the purpose of his question was clear, she did not bother to ask why he wished to know.

Now eager to learn all he could, Diego took another tack. "And are you truly afraid of horses?"

"No. My father taught me to ride before I could walk, but my mother did not want us to spend any time together. She feared you would discover that I was not nearly so young as she wished you to believe."

Rising to his feet, Diego walked to her side. "Has anything you've ever said to me been the truth?"

"Yes!" Angelique insisted unhappily. "I dared not tell you my name, but I did not lie to you!"

"Your concept of lying and mine are obviously very different. Perhaps that is due to the differences between the French and Spanish views of life. Your people are the frivolous sort, while we, by nature, are far more serious."

"You needn't insult the entire population of France simply because you are angry with me!"

Surprised to find that Angelique had kept her fiery temperament as well guarded a secret as her age, Diego did no more than laugh at her outrage. "Let me finish my explanation. In two weeks' time you will leave as you'd planned, but you'll not go out on your own. You will move into the lodgings I will secure for you. There's no need for you to seek work. I will keep you both busy and amused."

Angelique refused his offer with an emphatic toss of her curls. "Absolutely not. I want to be responsible for my own expenses. I should be able to find work in the next two weeks and if the quarters I can afford are not elegant enough for you, then—"

"You will not give orders to me!" Diego pulled her into his arms, ready to teach her in any way that would prove successful just how dependent upon him he wished her to be. "I said it this morning and I'll say it again. You are mine now, Angelique, and as my woman you'll not spend your days stitching up gowns or bonnets for anyone but yourself!"

Angelique shrank back from him, sorry she had been so foolish as to have gone to him that morning. If she had not been so moved by his sorrow, she never would have taken such a risk. She had wanted to soothe his aching need, not destroy the love that had enchanted them both at their first meeting. Regardless of the demands he made, she vowed she would maintain her independence. She was going to pay her own way no matter how loudly he yelled at her for it, though she could not risk having him shout at her now, in her room, when such an argument might easily be overheard. "We must be more quiet," she cautioned him softly. "It will be no easier for you than for me if we are discovered together."

With the graceful creature again imprisoned in his embrace, Diego cared little what complaints she made and lowered his mouth to capture hers in a kiss he hoped would crush her defiance as well as her pride. But she lifted her arms to encircle his neck and hugged him tightly as if nothing had changed between them, and gradually he relaxed his pose. For a long while he did no more than kiss her, but she broke free of his confining grasp and led him toward her bed, where his affection could take a more forceful form. When she slipped out of her nightgown and tossed it aside, he hurriedly cast off the last of his clothing so she would not be alone in the comfortable bed.

He wanted to make love to her with teasing slowness, to make her weep again for what she had lost by betraying his trust, but he found his mind filling with thoughts of her beauty and warmth until his only purpose became seeking the joy she had always given so readily. The soft curves of her lissome figure begged for his caress, her sultry violent glance lured his lips to hers, and suddenly he could not remember why he had been so angry with her when she was so seductive a temptress.

His lips moved slowly down her throat, across the fullness of her breasts, then returned to her mouth for a long, deep

127

kiss as he pulled her beneath him. He felt her pulse race as his fingertips moved over her wrist to catch her hand and he wondered at the ironic twist of fate that had provided him with both the most maddening and exciting of mistresses. But his pleasure was too great to allow him to concentrate upon her deceit, and he buried his face in her glossy curls and waited for the torrent of delight now flooding his well-muscled body to begin shuddering through hers. He could feel her response throbbing deeply within her as readily as his own and drew her closer still to enjoy the blissful harmony her ruse had not destroyed. She was as magnificent a mistress as had ever been born and he could not stay angry with her when she pleased him more than any other woman ever had. "You will always be mine, Angelique. You'll never escape me now."

His words were a threat, not a promise of happiness, and Angelique shut them out of her mind and instead let her senses drink in the sheer splendor of his loving. They had argued that morning and had had a worse scene that night, but she genuinely believed that as long as they could find such unique accord in bed, she still had a chance to win his heart.

Chapter VIII

An urgent wave of nausea swept Angelique from her bed early the next morning. She had felt well the previous day, but when the dreadful bout of retching was finally over she was so weak she could scarcely stagger back to her bed. Still dizzy, she curled up amid her pillows, hoping her strength would return if she just rested calmly for a few minutes.

Diego had returned to his own room shortly before dawn. She had heard the sounds of his restless movement as he had gotten dressed, but she had pretended to be asleep rather than speak with him, for nothing she could have said would have made any sense or mattered in the least to him. He had no faith in her now, did not trust her words to be the truth, which he had promptly demonstrated by his offer to make her his mistress rather than his bride. Why had he misunderstood her motives so completely when all she wanted was to love him? Why had he limited their choices and caused her such humiliation?

As if Diego's insults had not been enough, now she had fallen ill in addition to all her other worries and this depressed Angelique terribly. Perhaps she was simply overly tired, she speculated. She had had little to eat at dinner and now she tried to convince herself that her sudden illness was the result, but a nagging doubt preyed upon her mind until she finally gave in to it.

Her mother had frequently mentioned how she had suffered from persistent nausea during the early months of her pregnancy, and Angelique's suspicion that she might already be carrying Diego's child grew to a horrible certainty as she counted the days since they had first lain together. Huge tears welled up in her eyes as she realized that the pride she should have felt in giving the man she loved a child would now be usurped by the deepest shame. But she had suffered too much anguish of late to be overwhelmed by this new tragedy. She knew she would have to be practical and would have no time to waste indulging in self-pity when it would be of absolutely no value in overcoming the desperate nature of her plight. Instead, she would turn her mind to the alternatives now left open to her.

After a brief rest, she forced herself to rise and dress so her mother would not suspect that anything was amiss. She still felt far from well and needed little of the face powder she customarily wore to appear pale. She was distraught, incredibly sad, but her original plan still seemed to be her best hope. Surely Diego would not want a pregnant mistress, so she would have to become self-sufficient quickly, before her condition became obvious. The sooner she found employment the better off she would be. Filled with resolve, she waited patiently for her mother to come for her, then abruptly reminded the beautiful woman that her seventeenth birthday was swiftly approaching.

"You think I have forgotten your ridiculous threats or have forgiven you for making them?" Françoise responded heatedly. "What is more important to you—your dear mother who has made continual sacrifices to provide for you, or your own selfish desires?"

"That is an issue we needn't debate, since your view of my situation is so clearly in opposition to mine." Having planned to speak only about her most pressing needs, Angelique continued in a calm tone, "I will need to borrow a

130

dress to wear to seek employment. I'll go out in the mornings after you leave to go riding with José Luis. That way he need not be told of my plans. In two weeks' time I will leave here and you may tell him the truth or tell him I've gone to stay with your cousin Beatriz. Make up any excuse you like, but I do intend to leave here when I am seventeen."

Françoise clenched her fists and was tempted to strike her disobedient daughter, for her temper flared to a menacing fury. "You expect me to provide a gown for you to wear to seek work? You cannot be serious! What work could you possibly find that would not disgrace us all?"

Knowing she had already brought sufficient disgrace to the name of Devereau, Angelique ignored that taunt to explain, "*Madame* Larouche employs many seamstresses and—"

"Don't be absurd!" Françoise scoffed with a high-pitched laugh. "Last night José Luis came very close to proposing to me—so close I am confident he will speak of marriage before your birthday arrives. As soon as we are married, I have promised you I'll tell him the truth about your age and I will keep my word."

"You have told me that repeatedly, Mama, but whether or not you marry, my position will be unchanged. I will still have to leave here!"

Amazed by that announcement, Françoise asked curiously, "But why? As José Luis's stepdaughter, you will have every advantage, every luxury I've hoped to give you. Why would you wish to leave us then?"

Suddenly aware she had revealed too much, Angelique turned away. "There's no time for us to argue over my plans now. José Luis expects us to share breakfast with him and we mustn't keep him waiting."

Françoise's pretty features were twisted into a perplexed frown as she left the bedroom and her mood was as dark as her daughter's. She would not waste her breath arguing with the willful girl, she decided. She would simply go to La Belle

Mode that very morning. If Angelique thought to be hired by *Madame* Larouche or any other couturière in Barcelona, she would soon find out just how wrong she was!

Diego also had definite plans for the day. He stayed aboard *El Diablo* until it was time for the shops to open, then made his way to La Belle Mode and asked to speak privately with the proprietress. Once shown into *Madame* Larouche's small office, he quickly explained his mission. "As you know, Françoise Devereau and her daughter are our houseguests. For some reason, Angelique has decided she is a burden to us and has vowed to seek employment. Should she come to you—"

Holding up her hand, the charming *couturière* interrupted with a warm smile. "You need say no more, Monsieur Aragon, for *Madame* Devereau was here no more than five minutes ago to make the very same request."

"What?" Diego gasped, shocked by this revelation.

"She told me exactly what you have—that Angelique has become obsessed with the idea of earning her own living— but it is not an option her mother will permit. That so pretty a child would unnecessarily consider working as hard as my seamstresses do is unfortunate, but I know young girls often have foolish dreams."

"I did not realize that Angelique had discussed her desire to seek work with her mother." Diego frowned slightly, uncertain of what he should do. He could not follow Françoise all over town, nor would he allow Angelique to take a job. At least she had been telling the truth about her plans to leave his father's home and that was a point in her favor. "I will have to speak with *Madame* Devereau myself later in the day, for there is no need for each of us to contact the places where Angelique might seek work. What directions did she give you?" He smiled as he encouraged the woman to confide in him, for he wanted to know what Françoise's story had been and he knew she would surely never tell him.

Madame Larouche sighed slightly, saddened by the deception she had been asked to affect. "I am merely to tell Angelique that I have no need for another seamstress, but I am not to give her any reason to suspect her mother is behind my refusal."

"Yes, of course. That is the best thing to do. Thank you for your time, and for your willingness to help us, *Madame.*" Diego rose to his feet, but as he turned toward the door, the Frenchwoman called to him.

"There was one other thing *Madame* Devereau told me."

"What was that?" Diego asked politely.

Leaving her chair behind a desk cluttered with fabric samples, the helpful woman came to his side. "It seems Angelique considers herself something of an actress and might approach me using another name. I saw the child only briefly that day she came here with you and would not recognize her if she were wearing some sort of a disguise."

"Did you tell her mother that Angelique had been here with me?" Diego realized suddenly that he wanted desperately to avoid a confrontation with Françoise over that incident.

"Why no, I didn't," the *couturière* admitted thoughtfully. "But what happened with your search for the pretty blonde? Did you find her?"

Diego could not help but laugh as he admitted that he had. "Yes, I most certainly did, and she is even more beautiful than I led you to believe. I will bring her with me when next I visit your establishment so you may judge for yourself."

"It will be a pleasure to meet her, *Monsieur.*"

Relieved to learn that Françoise did not know of Angelique's visit to La Belle Mode, Diego thanked *Madame* Larouche again for her helpfulness and went on his way, but he was thoroughly confused as to what his best course of action would be. If Françoise had visited one fashion house, would she go to others? Would she visit them all? He needed no more than a moment's contemplation to realize that

Françoise was so determined an individual that she would stop at nothing to protect her own interests. She would probably visit establishments of which he had never even heard in her quest to keep Angelique under her control.

So much the better, he thought to himself with a sly grin. Angelique would never find work, but she would not be able to blame him for her lack of success in her quest. He returned to his ship in high spirits, satisfied that his mission had been accomplished without any effort on his part.

The day progressed and Angelique's spirits rose as her health improved. If her mother would not lend her a dress, then she would wear the black one she had borrowed to visit Diego. She had not returned it to her mother's closet but had hung it in the back of her own for the time being. The garment would scarcely serve to emphasize her talents with a needle, for it did not fit her well, but it would have to do. She simply could not go anywhere in the childish outfits her mother insisted she wear.

Seated in front of her mirror, she wondered what would become of her when she tried to make a life for herself. She had no expensive jewelry to sell as her mother did when she needed cash. She had no assets at all except herself, and the beauty of her reflection provided a taunting reminder of what Diego expected her to be. Would he prove to be only the first in a long succession of rich lovers who gave everything but true love?

"No!" she cried fiercely, determined to strive for independence in an honest fashion, but as she walked into the parlor before dinner, she knew she had never felt more insecure. Her mother nodded toward her, obviously pleased that she looked so pretty, as well as so young, while Diego glanced her way only briefly before continuing a discussion with his father, a discussion so friendly that it became instantly clear he had apologized to the man for his behavior the previous evening. That he had not also apologized to her brought her a sickening awareness of her fate, but she took a seat and waited quietly for the announcement that dinner was ready to be served.

"You have not said a word to us all evening, kitten," José Luis said kindly after they had eaten. He had taken Angelique's hand to lead her to the chair beside his as they returned to the parlor. "Is it that book you were reading last night that has depressed you so?"

"I am not depressed," Angelique insisted softly. "The novel was interesting but not a tragedy." She tried to smile sweetly to allay his suspicions, but she found the kindly man's friendly gaze impossible to return. "I hope you will not think me rude simply because I am quiet."

"No, of course not, for you are never rude, my dear. But I am concerned for your welfare and do not want to see you unhappy." José Luis smiled at Françoise, as if the responsibility for her daughter was theirs to share. "Now what would bring a smile to your lips. All you need do is ask and I will provide it."

Angelique wondered what José Luis was trying to prove to her mother. Perhaps it was only that he would be a generous parent, but, whatever the reason, she did not like being the center of their attention and politely refused his offer. "You have already provided far more than I deserve. I'll ask for nothing more."

Puzzled by her response, José Luis persisted in his inquiries. "Come shopping with us tomorrow. We would enjoy your company and you must need some new things."

Since this was something she could not permit, Françoise spoke up quickly, "You know shopping exhausts the child. That is why La Belle Mode makes her fashions from her measurements. She will be fine here alone with her studies, and I'll bring her something colorful to brighten her day."

Reluctantly, José Luis agreed to Françoise's request, "I merely wanted to please the child, but you are her mother and know what is best for her."

If there was anything Angelique disliked, it was to have people talk about her as though she were not sitting right there with them. Adults did that frequently to children—though never to each other, she had noted—but she could not openly rebel and so chose an easier course and asked to be excused. "I am very tired this evening. Will you excuse me please?" She kissed José Luis and her mother good night but hesitated as she looked up at Diego's taunting smile.

"You must kiss me too, Angelique, for you've already said you do not wish to appear rude." Diego leaned down to make the task easier for her, but as she drew near, he whispered, "Do not be impatient. I'll come to you soon."

Her cheeks burning with a bright blush, Angelique rushed from the parlor, but she chose to walk out into the garden rather than remain in her bedchamber. The beauty of the evening surrounded her in its fragrant stillness, but she found no peace in the lightly scented air. The walls of the Aragon mansion had become as confining as a prison and she strolled about aimlessly, filled with a sorrow too deep to bring tears.

Diego waited more than fifteen minutes before excusing himself, and while he again went out the front door, he had no intention of leaving his home. He vaulted the garden wall with a nimble leap, then halted abruptly when he saw Angelique standing nearby. "There is no reason for you to wait for me out here. I'll always come to your room to find you."

"I had not realized how conceited you are, Diego. Truly, I was not waiting for you. The night is a pretty one and I wanted only to enjoy it." Angelique turned away, seeking the companionship of the shadows.

Pausing to make certain they were not being observed, Diego followed the lovely blonde down the walkway lined with roses. "I am not conceited, or at least no more so than any other man."

"I do not know any other men," Angelique admitted softly.

Diego reached out for her arm and pulled her back toward him as he whispered, "Nor will you ever." He drew away her lacy veil and plucked the pins from her tightly coiled hair to release her golden curls. "I cannot bear to see you dressed as a child when you are my woman."

As he lowered his mouth to hers, Angelique pulled away. "There is too great a risk of being discovered out here," she protested, then ran ahead of him with light steps and held open the door of her room so he could follow her inside.

Not amused by her words of caution, Diego quickly closed the door and caught the elusive blonde once again. "You were too quiet tonight, and I was far too agreeable. Our parents are bound to become suspicious. Tomorrow night I will give my father some excuse for being away, but I'll expect to find you here waiting for me after dinner. Enjoy the garden during the day, not when I need you."

He enfolded her slender figure in a ready embrace and his tongue teased her lips before invading her small, moist mouth in a demanding kiss. He was gentle still but dominated her body so easily that it seemed no challenge to him to sweep her up into his arms and lay her upon the bed.

His hands went quickly to the hooks that secured the bodice of her gown, though his mouth did not leave hers until he was ready to release her. "Why must you wear so many layers of lace?" he asked hoarsely, sorry he had not found her snuggled in her bed wearing little more than a smile.

Angelique slid off the high bed and turned her back toward him as she began to undress. "Why don't you see to your own clothing, Diego. Mine will soon wear out with your pawing."

"I do not paw you!" Diego insisted sharply. "I force myself to use the utmost restraint and you do not even appreciate my kindness." When she did not reply, he was confused.

"Angelique?" he called softly.

Glancing over her shoulder, Angelique responded with a sultry look in her violet eyes. "Yes?"

"Do not tease me. What we have found in each other is too precious to waste," he cautioned her sternly. "Now come here to me and I'll help you with your lingerie without causing a single tear."

Angelique hesitated a moment, then turned toward him. "Did you not plan to provide me with new clothing? I have none that is suitable for wear as your mistress."

Having no wish to argue with the volatile young beauty, Diego thought it best to agree to whatever demands she might make until it was time for her to leave his father's house. "I will be happy to dress you in whatever attire you desire, Angelique. You will find me to be as generous a man as my father."

Angelique made no reply, but her glance swept his features slowly, for she enjoyed his nearness very much. He was more than merely handsome, yet she knew every woman he met would tell him that and so she remained silent. The lightness of his touch kindled the flame within her heart and she wished he would see to his own garments while she saw to hers, so she would not be kept waiting any longer than necessary to make love to him again.

She reached out shyly to touch his hair, which glistened with a brilliant sheen in the soft glow of the candles' light. He looked up at her as if her gesture had surprised him. "I'm sorry," she mumbled softly, embarrassed now to have been so bold.

"You needn't apologize." Diego brought her hand to his lips and kissed her palm sweetly. "You may touch me as often as you wish when we are alone."

"Yes, when we are alone," Angelique repeated sadly. She led a secret life she despised and now she found that even the joy of her love could not be revealed—not even to the man she adored.

Though puzzled by her pensive mood, Diego decided to ignore it. And once he had freed her from her confining undergarments, he cast off his own clothing hurriedly and slipped beneath the covers of her bed to join her. She came into his arms readily, but still there was a difference in her manner that he found distracting. Leaning back, he regarded her subdued expression with an intense gaze as he asked pointedly, "What is wrong with you tonight?"

Rather than reply to so involved a question, Angelique lay her hands upon his shoulders and gently pulled his mouth down to hers. She needed his comfort as much as he needed hers and his response was a loving one. He filled her lithe body with pleasure so rich it lit her dreams with a radiant glow. But when she awakened the next morning he was gone, and she was violently ill once again.

A sullen pout marred the sweetness of her features as Françoise sat opposite her daughter. José Luis had just risen from the breakfast table to see to some pressing business. "Diego left the house again last night," Françoise began, "so his father and I were alone, but something is keeping him from issuing a proposal and I cannot bring him to reveal his worries to me."

Though she was in no position to give advice, Angelique tried to be a sympathetic listener. "Perhaps he is merely shy and needs time to build up his courage."

"Shy? José Luis? The man is not shy, but extremely cautious. I have given him no reason not to trust me, but still there is a part of himself he will not share."

"Is that not true of all of us?" Angelique asked, thinking that she and Diego were moving farther apart and yet she did not dare discuss this with him.

"Women must necessarily keep secrets, Angelique. It is part of our mystique. But for a man to be so reticent to share his feelings with me is unusual." Françoise lifted a well-manicured fingertip to catch a stray curl and send it back into place in her neatly coiled *chignon*. "No, I have made some dreadful mistake somehow or José Luis would already be my husband."

"Are you now thinking of leaving here too?" Angelique asked anxiously, not certain what she would do if her mother decided to move on to another man's home.

Sitting up straight to address her daughter in a stern tone, Françoise nevertheless kept her voice at a whisper. "No! If he cannot love me while I am here with him, he would never come to love me if I left! He provides security and is wonderful company, but I want marriage and I'll have to find some way to touch his heart if I haven't already."

"I still think the truth would be your best weapon," Angelique offered simply, though she knew she dared not speak the truth to Diego.

"The truth is for fools!" Françoise scoffed. "Now I am going out to shop for an hour or two. I will speak to you another time about this, since it is obvious you have learned nothing from me that will enable you to attract a wealthy husband."

Rather than argue, Angelique watched her mother walk away and then went to her own room to put on the black dress and begin her search for a position that would pay her a sufficient sum to allow her to raise a child alone. She had no illusions to which to cling, but she knew that with diligent effort she would surely find a decent job somewhere.

Diego ate dinner in a tavern near the docks, then walked home by the longest route to fill the time so he would not have to wait for Angelique to come to her room. He had been lucky that his father had not noticed him staring at her when they had eaten dinner together the previous evening. Now that he had learned the truth about the pretty child, he could not keep his eyes off her and he found it difficult to keep the secret he had discovered from showing in his glance. He still could not believe the ease with which she had tricked him, but he was certain she would not get away with such a clever deceit ever again—at least not with him she wouldn't. His mood was dark and he was not pleased to have reached her room before she did, but he stretched out across her bed and made himself comfortable while he waited.

Believing Diego would be late in arriving, Angelique had remained with her mother and José Luis for more than an hour after dinner. She had no success in her quest for employment and had decided that their witty company would be preferable to pacing her room for hours on end worrying about her future. When she opened her door and found the handsome young man glaring angrily at her, she was badly startled. "Oh, Diego, I didn't expect to find you here yet."

"Just where did you expect me to be?" he asked sullenly.

"Well, I don't know. You said you'd be out. I thought you really had someplace to go."

"I didn't," Diego admitted, instantly regretting that he had unwittingly told her how highly he prized her delightful company.

That he would be angry with her was somehow more than she could bear, and Angelique ripped off her *mantilla* and tossed it upon her dresser before walking up to face him. "It is obvious that neither of us is content with this arrangement. Let's end it now."

Diego responded with a lunge so smooth that it caught Angelique completely by surprise. He pulled her down across the wide bed and held her wrists tightly as he explained in a hoarse whisper, "I will decide when the time has come to end our alliance, not you!" He lowered his mouth to hers and his kiss was so demanding that he left her lips bruised when he drew away. "That our arrangement is so

141

ridiculous is your fault, not mine!" he reminded her with a sneer. "You are the one who insisted upon living here for two more weeks!"

Angelique's eyes were filled with awe rather than fear, for she had not meant to provoke the proud man's anger with her offer. Clearly he was furious with her, but she replied calmly, "I am sorry I kept you waiting, but you'll have to be more precise when you tell me your plans or I'll never understand them properly."

Diego knew no man gave his mistress a schedule so she would know when to expect him. She was simply supposed to be ready to please him, no matter what time he chose to call. Angelique, however, was no ordinary mistress but a young woman who was occupied most of the day with the pretense of being a child, and the absurdity of this ruse maddened him all the more. He lowered his mouth to her throat to lavish warm kisses upon her golden skin, kisses that he knew would leave clearly recognizable traces in the morning. He cared little that she would have no way to explain how she had gotten such obvious signs of his love, nor did he consider the consequences she would have to bear.

Surprised by his affection, Angelique was very pleased and snuggled against Diego, thinking his anger had been forgotten as swiftly as her own. She slipped her hands beneath his shirt and hugged him tightly, longing to again feel the sweetness he had always shown her. When he lifted his head to look down at her, she smiled, her delight in him plain. But she was practical still. "I should put this dress in the wardrobe before it becomes more wrinkled," she stated softly.

Diego let her go and used the time to discard his own apparel before she returned to her bed. It was his own weakness for her that angered him, for he had wanted to be able to control her emotions as she controlled his and he had failed miserably in his attempt. She saw that his expression was troubled when she returned to her bed, but he pulled her into his arms and held her so tightly she couldn't escape him again.

"Diego?" Angelique whispered, then relaxed against him, seeking the peace she had always found in his arms. "I am here, and I won't leave you." That he might some day tell her to go was too heartbreaking a thought to consider, and she ignored it as her kiss grew as hungry as his. She had no idea how a mistress was supposed to behave, nor would she ask, but her devotion was plain in her kiss and Diego's response was filled with the tender affection she had never been able to resist.

The following morning at breakfast, Diego again gave his father a convenient excuse for being away from home through the dinner hour. When he slipped into Angelique's room late that night, he was pleased to find her clad only in a filmy nightgown. Unfortunately, however, she was brushing her hair with furious strokes and seething with anger. He had kept her waiting on purpose, but it was not the lateness of the hour that had enraged her.

Angelique tossed the silver-handled hairbrush upon the dresser as Diego approached her. Holding her golden tresses aside, she pointed to the telltale purple blotches that marred the creamy skin of her throat. "Would you please explain why you did this to me?"

She had not noticed the marks until after breakfast when she had donned the black dress in preparation for another day of seeking employment, which had again proven fruitless. Everywhere she had gone the response had been polite, but no one had offered the slightest encouragement that work might soon be available for her. That disappointment had contributed to her depression, but it was not the only cause. "My mother often helps me dress. Had I not awakened early, she would have seen these marks before I did. Have you no consideration for your own reputation if you have none for mine?"

Diego lifted his fingertips to caress Angelique's flushed cheek softly and a slow, teasing smile curved across his lips. "I have a very passionate nature, and I knew you have so sharp a wit that I was confident you would find an explanation for any questions your mother might raise."

Angelique brushed his hand away with a fierce slap. "That's a damn lie! You did this intentionally to hurt me! You wanted to embarrass me, but why?"

Diego's expression grew cold in response to her insults. "Do not flatter yourself. I had no motive at all save passion." At least there had been none that he cared to admit to her now.

Angelique turned her back on him to hide her tears. "When you make my days impossible, how can you expect me to fill your nights with pleasure?"

The proud set of her shoulders gave Diego clear warning that he had pushed her too far. What had he meant to do? he wondered. Punishing her for the cruel way in which she had tricked him about her identity suddenly seemed childish. "Angelique?" he whispered softly in her ear as he wrapped his arms around her waist to draw her near. "I want to take you away from here—now, tonight."

"No!" the lovely blonde argued instantly. "You promised me I could have two weeks, and I mean to take them!" She put her hands over his to hold him close, for the warmth of his hard-muscled body was too comforting to ignore, no matter what problems he had caused for her.

Diego held her in his arms while he tried to think what inducement he could offer, but he soon realized he had no choice but to be patient, for he had given his word. Françoise had already ruined whatever hope Angelique had had of

144

finding the means to earn her own living. All he had to do was wait a few more days and she would truly appreciate how attractive his offer was. Taking her hand, he turned her around to face him and asked, "Shall I go out and come in again?"

"No." Angelique's smile was a slight one as she lifted her lips to his. They had wasted enough time and she could no longer pretend an indifference she did not feel whenever he was near. She unbuttoned his shirt, then stood on her tiptoes to kiss the pulse that throbbed at the base of his throat. "What excuse would you give if I were to leave your handsome bronze skin marked with the evidence of my passion?"

Diego chuckled at her question. "I'd give no excuse at all. Go ahead and do it."

Angelique closed her eyes as she lifted her arms to encircle his neck. She nuzzled his throat softly, finding his taste delicious, but he could stand no more than a minute of her lavish kiss before he picked her up and carried her over to the bed. He tore off his own clothing, then tossed her gown aside so he could cover the pale flesh of her ample breasts with light kisses before drawing her into a tight embrace. This time she offered no protest as his lips strayed across her narrow waist, and he felt her shiver of anticipation as his mouth moved lower still.

Her body was perfectly proportioned and he could not get enough of her smooth, sleek limbs and fragile curves. His tongue slid over her hungrily as he sought release from the torment she continually caused him, and her soft sigh of surrender lured him ever deeper until the ecstasy that rose within her thundered through him as well.

Drunk with the taste of her rapture, he moved his mouth to hers for a demanding kiss and she opened herself to him eagerly. The graceful motions of her hips soon responded to his forceful thrusts in perfect rhythm. Their emotions flowed with such beauty that neither dared speak of love for fear of interrupting the other's joy. They were a pair so finely matched that they continued to find endless delights in each other until the darkness of night gave way to the first pale light of dawn. When Diego reluctantly left Angelique's bed, he began counting the hours until he could again hold her in his arms and call her his own.

Chapter IX

Diego could see no way of avoiding attending the party to which his family had been invited, but the thought of spending an evening in so frivolous a fashion while Angelique sat in her room alone pained him greatly. When it was time to depart, he found her seated in the parlor and hurriedly explained his reasons for leaving her that night. "Guillermo Rosales is one of my father's principal clients. We have made a fortune transporting his goods, so when he hosts a party we have no choice but to attend and to appear as though we are enjoying ourselves immensely. Since his vineyards produce superb wines, that task is usually not an overly difficult one."

He was attired that evening in a well-tailored coat of deep rust-colored velvet, which made his dark hair shine with copper highlights. His pale gold waistcoat was of embroidered satin and his cream-colored breeches of the finest lightweight wool. As always, his black leather boots were so highly polished he could see his reflection in them. But despite the elegance of his appearance, he had given little thought to his attire. He had merely selected the clothes he had found hanging in the front of his wardrobe, yet he cut a far finer figure than many men who would have spent the entire afternoon puzzling over what to wear to the Rosales' party.

Since his tone was so serious, Angelique could not help but ask, "Don't you like going to parties? I know I certainly would if anyone were ever so polite as to invite me."

"Do you recall what happened when I made arrangements for you to attend the de la Vegas' party? You refused to go!" Diego reminded her in a harsh whisper. "Don't tell me now you feel slighted, because I will not believe you."

Angelique's intense glance swept over him slowly and the blue of her eyes seemed dark in the dim light. "That was a very sweet thing for you to do, Diego, but can't you understand now why I refused? I would not have been able to spend my time with you and that would have been the only reason I'd have wished to attend."

Diego yanked on his white gloves as he continued in a hushed voice, "Your flattery is wasted on me, Angelique, but your two weeks here are nearly up and soon I shall expect you to be charming no matter where I choose to escort you!"

"Surely you do not plan to take me to gatherings such as this one tonight?" Angelique inquired with genuine alarm.

"And why not?" Diego asked with a rakish grin, for he found her concern for propriety greatly amusing since she was such a wanton seductress in bed. "I've no plan to keep you under lock and key. Is that what you had expected?"

"No, of course not!" Angelique replied promptly, then, fearing their disagreement would swiftly become a full-blown fight, she explained her concern more fully. "I do not believe a man should escort his mistress to parties where other men bring their wives!" At least Angelique did not think Diego should. She knew little about the etiquette of such matters, but her common sense told her there would have to be some rule about keeping mistresses and wives separate.

"But I have no wife, so whom would I bring if I did not wish to attend social functions alone?" Diego found the direction of their conversation extremely diverting, though he could tell by Angelique's bright blush that she did not. In

148

her lacy white *mantilla* and little girl's dress she looked much too young to be having such a discussion, and he reminded himself that she would need new fashions immediately, for without them he could not escort her anywhere. "I will see that you have a wardrobe filled with elegant gowns and none will find fault with your beauty or your manners. You will be most welcome wherever I take you. And if there is any gossip, I will swiftly put an end to it. You have my word on that."

"If you plan to introduce me to your friends, then I will have to use a different name," Angelique suddenly realized. "I will not sully my mother's good name while I am forced to lead the life you suggest."

Ignoring this insult, Diego simply retorted, "Call yourself whatever you like. You will still belong to me." He leaned down then to give her a lingering kiss that made his claim of ownership clear. "I will not enjoy a minute of this party without you and I'll return home as swiftly as I can. Wait up for me."

Seeing her mother appear at the door, Angelique responded sweetly, "Have a nice time tonight, Diego." Rising to her feet, she walked to her mother's side and complimented her upon the soft rose color of her gown, telling her it made her fair complexion glow with a pretty blush.

Françoise did not like what she saw in Diego's dark glance, for, in her opinion, he watched her daughter with far too keen an interest, and she found the fact that he had been alone with her alarming in the extreme. If the young man were to use his considerable charm upon her little girl, she knew Angelique lacked the sophistication to see his flirting for the amusing pretense it was. He was so handsome that any young woman would admire him, but she wondered why her daughter fascinated him so when she appeared to be no more than a child. He was sure to cause problems once she married his father and revealed Angelique's true age, but then he would be her stepson and she could rightly demand that he leave his stepsister alone. "Are you ready, Diego? Your father has already summoned the carriage."

"Yes, I was merely bidding Angelique good night," the dark-eyed young man replied with a warm smile. "I still think it is a pity she is not allowed to go with us. How is she ever to learn to dance? Or to—"

Stopping him before he could embarrass her any further, Françoise put her hand upon his arm in an attempt to lead him to the front door. "Angelique is too frail to dance. She simply does not have the stamina such a pastime requires. She is far happier here at home, aren't you, dear?" She looked back at her daughter and was pleased when Angelique gave the response she desired.

"Yes, Mama. I am more than content to remain here."

Diego turned back then to give Angelique a fiery glance she did not understand, but she smiled and gave him a slight wave as though she were no more than a pretty child bidding him good night.

When they had gone, she went first to the library for something new to read, then carried the book she had selected to her room. She doubted she would be able to concentrate on it, however, for she was totally preoccupied by Diego's comments. There had been many beautiful mistresses in France, famous courtesans whose scandalous lives were a matter of public knowledge, but she had not thought the Spanish would permit such deliberate flaunting of morals. Diego was quite liberal in his views—she knew that for a fact—and his family was so prominent that he had considerable power, but she could well imagine how José Luis would react to his only son's being seen socially with a pretty young mistress. She had not considered the possibility that her mother would find out where she had gone, but if Diego were to take her to parties, her parent would swiftly discover what she had done.

She sank down across her bed and rested her cheek upon

her outstretched arm. Each new day she had fewer choices it seemed. She had found there was no hope of securing work in Barcelona and she wondered briefly if she should make her way to Madrid and attempt to find a position there. But that would mean she would never see Diego again and she could not bear to consider that. He spent a good portion of the year at sea as it was, so they would have little enough time to share even if she were forced to become his mistress. Her head ached with the grim prospects for the future, but thinking again of the beauty that she would find that night in her love's arms, she finally drifted off to sleep.

Diego found that his plans to leave the Rosaleses' home swiftly were being thwarted at every turn. The man had two daughters of marriageable age and apparently believed them to be very attractive, although Diego could not imagine why. They were petite but plump, unremarkable in appearance, and totally lacking in charm. He had dutifully danced with each of them, but that had only served to send them both into fits of blushing and giggles. He had then attempted unsuccessfully to avoid Guillermo's persistent inquiries into his personal life. He had finally announced emphatically that he had no plans to marry in the near future and excused himself, but he knew his father had been observing that brief exchange and was not pleased by it. Though José Luis had never come right out and told him to choose a wife and begin a family, he had hinted at it often enough to put his son on his guard. But Diego knew he would prefer to die a bachelor rather than consider taking either of the Rosales sisters as a wife.

Looking around the brightly illuminated ballroom, he found himself thoroughly bored with the opulently dressed young women who flirted openly with him at every turn. There were many there of whom his father would approve, but none who had caught his eye. He would not admit it even to himself now, but despite the lie in which he had caught her, his feelings for Angelique had grown deeper each day. He had never met another young woman who could be favorably compared to her. She was not only beautiful, but charming and intelligent as well. Recalling that she was at home waiting for him, he brushed those standing around him aside, quickly called for a carriage, and left the noisy party, hoping his sudden disappearance would not be noted.

Angelique was a pretty sight as she slept upon her bed, and Diego stood for a long while simply gazing down at her. She had removed her *mantilla* and loosened her curls, but since she had not bothered to undress, she still had the appearance of a young girl. That he had grown so fond of her when he had thought her a child still pained him, but he could not deny that he had liked the independence of her thoughts then, while now her defiance simply caused him additional problems.

He had looked for lodgings on numerous occasions, but nothing he had seen had seemed to provide the proper surroundings for her. He had found something wrong with every available apartment. Either they were located too far from his ship, or too close to the docks to provide a quiet residence. Some were far too small and others so elegant and large that one young woman would be lost in them. He knew time was short, but he planned to secure a suite in a respectable hotel for the present, and hoped Angelique would eventually accompany him so he would have the benefit of her opinion as to the location of her new home. He slipped off his coat as he whispered softly, "Wake up, little angel. It is very late and the night far too short as it is."

Awakened by the mellow sound of his voice, Angelique propped her chin upon her hand as she greeted him with a wide yawn. "How was the party?"

"Splendid in some respects; quite dull in others. The food was delicious, the wine plentiful as always, the musicians talented, but the women a poor lot compared to you."

Having met few of the young ladies of Barcelona, Angelique thought he was merely teasing her. "Since you object to my compliments as needless flattery, I'll thank you not to flatter me with such blatant lies."

"I don't tell lies!" Diego replied with a deep laugh. "You'll see soon enough how lacking the others are in all areas that make a woman highly prized."

"Just what is it you prize in a woman?" Angelique inquired as she lay still and watched him disrobe with undisguised admiration. She was as fascinated by his sleek body as she was by the complexities of his unique personality.

Diego gave her question no more than brief consideration before he began to reply, "Beauty of course, wit, intelligence, charm, grace, a certain elegance of manner—" He stopped abruptly then, realizing he was actually describing her. "What do you value in a man?"

Angelique's glance grew troubled as she tried to respond truthfully. "Well, intelligence and wit too, surely, but I think a man should have a good character above all things."

"I see. You like a man to be trustworthy, honest, and brave—that sort of thing?" Since she had not moved, he sat down beside her and proceeded to help her out of her tight-fitting dress.

"Yes," Angelique agreed, "but there is something more, a strength of spirit I suppose it could be called."

"You mean a belief in religion?" Diego asked skeptically, for though their home contained a small chapel, he seldom entered it.

"No, I mean a belief in himself." Seeing that he did not understand, Angelique gave him an example. "You can see the injustices that others do not, like the fact that the lot of the peasants is a wretched one and their poverty is not of their own making. Or the things you've told us about New

153

Spain and how the Indians are being oppressed. You make up your own mind about what is right and you don't care what others believe if their opinions are different from yours. Such independence of thought may trouble your father, but I admire you for it."

Diego did not know how to react to such a compliment, for clearly Angelique thought his character worthy of praise, but he did not think he deserved the faith she had obviously placed in him. The light in her pretty blue eyes was a sincere one, but he was deeply embarrassed. "Thank you" was all he could manage to reply.

Angelique saw that Diego did not seem to appreciate her compliments about his character. She could not understand why he would be offended, yet it was not like him to be so quiet. "Would you rather I simply said I like you because you are so tall and well built?" She moved off the bed for a moment to hang up her dress, then quickly tossed her lingerie upon the chair on top of his clothes. She never bothered to snuff out the candles because she liked to be able to watch his expressions as they made love. When he stretched out upon her bed, she sat down beside him and her fingertips slowly traced his muscular thigh. She leaned over him then, and her lips moved down the tangle of dark curls that grew across his broad chest. "You are irresistibly handsome, Diego. Is that what you wish to hear?" She knew his body well now but was curious still, wondering if it were possible to make love to him as he did to her. She moved her fingertips lightly over the hard muscles of his flat stomach as she asked softly, "Is there not something more you can teach me? I do so want to be able to give you all the same pleasures you give to me." She slid down beside him then, and her lips began to nibble and tease the taut flesh covering his ribs.

As her magical touch moved lower, Diego wound his fingers in her golden curls. Astonished by her question, he made no reply until it was too late and he could respond with no more than a convulsive moan. His whole body shook

154

with the splendor of her intimate kiss until he was suffocating in a sensation so delicious he could not find the breath to beg her to stop, even when he knew he could stand no more. Nothing mattered to him then but keeping her with him, and when she at last laid her head upon his shoulder, he pulled her close to his heart to savor the rapture of her loving until he regained strength enough to give the same joy to her.

Although the Rosaleses' party was an elaborate one, Françoise found it impossible to enjoy the festive atmosphere as she usually did, even though she felt comfortable with José Luis and his friends. She was preoccupied with thoughts of Angelique, for her daughter had grown increasingly distant, not overtly defiant as she had frequently been in the past, but aloof, absorbed in thoughts she would not share. The last two months had flown by and as her lovely daughter's seventeenth birthday approached, Françoise found that she looked upon the event with growing dread. All her efforts to bend her child's will to her own had met with failure. It had been a year or more since she had given any thought to sending her to a convent, for she knew the girl would undoubtedly flee at the first opportunity. Such a disappearance would only be the beginning of the embarrassment she would cause, and, realizing this, Françoise had swiftly abandoned the idea.

If only José Luis had proposed to her when she had first come to his home! But now she feared he never would. He seemed content with things the way they were, even if she was not.

Catching a glimpse of herself in a candlelit mirror, she was pleasantly surprised by the youthful countenance of the reflection, for that night she felt all of her nearly thirty-seven years and wished simply to go home. She turned to José Luis and found him observing his son. Françoise wondered what he found so interesting, for she thought the young man's behavior amazingly predictable. Though his manners could not be faulted, he was apparently expending as little energy in being charming that night as he usually did. He was a dashing figure, both in his appearance and his stylish dress, but he was so obviously bored by the affair the young women who surrounded him were so rapturously enjoying that she wondered why he had bothered to attend the party in the first place.

None of the Spanish women were as pretty as Angelique, she noted, and Françoise felt a pang of guilt that her daughter had yet to receive the attention from young men she rightly deserved. It was time to end their ruse, to move on, perhaps to Madrid, where she would find another gentleman eager to entertain them and Angelique could be proudly presented to Spanish society as befitted a young woman of her excellent breeding.

Unaware of his lady's sorrow, José Luis frowned impatiently as he watched his only son speak with their host. He could not overhear the discussion from where he stood, but Diego's expression showed his lack of attention plainly. "Damn!" he mumbled to himself, too polite to give vent to his temper in front of ladies.

Françoise moved close to her escort as she whispered, "Whatever has upset you so?"

Shaking his head, the tall Spaniard smiled apologetically. "Nothing. What could possibly upset me at a party as amusing as this?"

Hurt by his obvious lie, Françoise turned away, but not before José Luis had seen that her expression had become as pained as his own.

"Why, what is it, my dear?" He quickly offered refreshments, but Françoise had no interest in them, nor in dancing, which she usually loved. "If I have depressed you, forgive me, for I did not mean to be less than a courteous escort."

When the usually vivacious Frenchwoman's mood remained somber, he blamed himself for having displayed his

156

emotions so carelessly. But Diego's behavior had grown so objectionable that he was deeply concerned about him. Diego had been pleasant enough the few times they had dined together recently, but still he sensed that the young man was troubled about a matter upon which he dared not even speculate. He had never known his son to squander money gambling or in poor investments, so he could not help but feel that a woman was the cause of the arrogant detachment he was displaying this night. Since Diego had favored none of the young women present with more than one dance, he assumed that if his son had come to care for one she was not among those present. If he had become involved with some woman of the streets, José Luis vowed he would put a stop to it immediately, before it went any further. It was extremely unfortunate that while Diego was a fine captain he had all the vices of an ordinary seaman as well. He saw the young man leave the crowded ballroom and knew he would not return, but still José Luis could not channel his thoughts in a more pleasant direction.

When the first of the guests made ready to depart, José Luis found Françoise receptive to his suggestion that they return home as well. When their carriage arrived at the front door of the Rosales home, he spoke quickly with the driver and asked where he had taken Diego. He was amazed to learn that his son had gone straight home. Puzzled by this unexpected news, he sat in perplexed silence until they reached his house and he realized he had been very rude. "I am sorry I was not good company for you tonight, Françoise. I will attempt to do better tomorrow."

Françoise knew that José Luis would make every attempt to please her, but his best was no longer enough and her despair showed clearly in her sorrowful expression. She whispered a strained good night, but he reached out to catch her hand before she could turn away.

"Stay with me just a while longer," he urged.

Françoise was tempted to refuse, but she was too

perceptive to miss the subtle difference in José Luis's tone. "Why yes, if you'd like my company, I'll be happy to give it." When he showed her to the small loveseat in the parlor and brought her a brandy, she sipped it slowly, wondering what he wished to discuss.

"It occurred to me just now that I have been so preoccupied since Diego has been home that I've neglected you and Angelique shamefully."

Françoise leaned forward, intrigued by his remarks, for she had not considered that Diego's presence in his home could affect the quality of their relationship. Perhaps the man was not merely complacent, but instead concerned about his son. "He is rebellious, as all young men are," she stated, "but I did not realize you have been worried about him."

"Rebellious is the perfect word to describe Diego, but I had hoped by the time he reached his late twenties that his interests would more closely parallel my own."

"But they do not?" Françoise inquired softly, hoping to keep him talking for hours if need be.

"Lord knows what occupies his time now. We seldom talk without arguing and I know I am as much at fault as he is, but he is a grown man and it is time he assumed his share of the responsibility for our firm."

"Is sailing his own ship not enough?" Françoise asked sweetly. "What more should he do?"

José Luis sighed sadly. "It would be enough if only he would ask what needs to be done, but that is a question that does not even occur to him."

"Perhaps he does not realize what it is you expect of him. Have you told him?" Françoise considered the two men very similar in temperament, and wondered if perhaps they were too much the same to ever achieve the harmony José Luis obviously craved.

"No," the distraught man reluctantly admitted. "If I have to ask for his help, he will feel obligated to give it."

158

"Yes, of course he will. But if you do not ask, he will be unaware of your need for his assistance."

"That is exactly my dilemma." José Luis paused in his restless pacing as he changed the subject to what he thought would be a far more pleasant one. "Angelique must be a great comfort to you. She is such a dear child and so eager to please. Diego was never like that, not even as a small boy he wasn't."

Françoise looked away and was overwhelmed by sadness as she considered how strained her relationship truly was with her only daughter. "You are very kind, José Luis, but also very wrong."

"My dear?" José Luis set his brandy snifter upon the table before he took the place at her side. "I had no idea you found being a parent as difficult as I do."

"There are times I find being Angelique's mother more than merely difficult. It becomes simply impossible." Françoise was surprised at how easy it was to speak the truth, but she dared not reveal all of it as yet. "She wishes to leave me, to become independent, to be responsible only to herself rather than to me."

"But that is preposterous! Where did she ever get such a peculiar idea?"

"Who knows? Our lives have been in constant turmoil since we fled France. She has grown up too rapidly and has naturally become independent as well. Your home is very pleasant, but she knows as well as I do that our stay here is a temporary one." Françoise lifted her hand to brush away the tears from her long lashes, knowing that if her sadly worded confidence did not inspire José Luis to propose, nothing would.

"I have been a stupid fool!" José Luis exclaimed angrily. He put his arms around Françoise and drew her head down upon his shoulder as he covered her back with comforting pats. "You are far too young to be a mother to Diego, and at his age he no longer needs one, but I would be proud to be

159

the father Angelique so obviously needs if you will have me for your husband."

Françoise rested quietly in his arms, wondering why it had been Angelique's willfulness rather than his deepening regard for her that had prompted him to offer marriage. Indeed, he had not once spoken of love in all the time she had known him. But she was far too practical a woman to place her pride above her need for a husband, and she murmured softly, "I think you would be a wonderful husband, José Luis. Of course I want you."

Tilting her face up to his, José Luis gave her a light kiss, and when he found her lips warm and inviting, he tightened his embrace and kissed her with the passion he had kept buried deep within himself for far too long. Her graceful figure melted against him, luring his emotions to a fevered peak, and he kissed her again and again, wanting all that the beautiful creature in his arms could give.

Françoise enjoyed José Luis's deep kisses, but the hour was late, the house dark and silent, and she dared go no further with the handsome man until he had made her his wife. Drawing away, she gave him her most dazzling smile as she asked, "Please, may I go and tell Angelique of our engagement? I am so excited I will never be able to wait until the morning."

Her radiant expression was so bewitching that José Luis was ashamed to admit he had been about to suggest they celebrate their betrothal in her bed. Her delight seemed so genuine that he could not refuse her request and he forced his own unmet desires aside. "Yes, of course, go and tell her. I will awaken Diego too, and we will have a real celebration together."

"Oh yes, let's!" Françoise was ecstatic, for José Luis had every quality she desired in a husband, and, most important, he was enormously wealthy and extremely generous. She rose and leaned down to take his hands to draw him to his feet. "Angelique will be so thrilled for us. I know she will be!"

Laughing happily, José Luis hugged Françoise's slender form before they parted outside her daughter's door. Seeing her eyes aglow with such unabashed joy, he regretted not having proposed to her much sooner. Just as he had thought, he had been a great fool.

Françoise waited until José Luis had moved on down the hall toward Diego's room before she opened Angelique's door, but as she entered the spacious bedchamber, her brief happiness was shattered into a thousand painful fragments. Her lovely daughter lay sleeping soundly, her golden curls streaming across Diego's broad chest. Knowing at once that all her hopes for a secure future for herself and her only child had been dashed by that handsome young man, she began to scream hysterically. Her terrified shrieks awakened every last soul in the Aragon household, for truly she could not have been more horrified had she found the pretty girl's bed filled with a dozen slithering, poisonous vipers rather than one virile young Spaniard.

Chapter X

José Luis dashed back down the long hall, expecting at the very least to find Angelique's room engulfed in flames. He rushed through the door, then halted as abruptly as Françoise had, for he found the sight of Diego in the girl's bed as severe a jolt as it had been to her mother. He paused for no more than a split second as his gaze locked upon that of his son's.

Diego was sitting up now, obviously debating whether or not to get out of bed to dress, but José Luis made the decision for him. He crossed the room swiftly and yanked the young man to his feet, then struck him repeatedly with the full force of his fists. He had not merely been boasting when he had recently threatened to teach him some manners, for he still had most of the stamina and all of the skill he had possessed as a youth. He planned to beat his son senseless if he had to, but he would not tolerate such an outrage as he had just discovered in his house or allow it to go unpunished.

Diego made no move to resist or counter his father's vicious blows but stood still and took the brutal abuse without flinching. Blood dripping from a cut above his left eye soon clouded his vision, but he did not lift his hands to protect his face or to block the storm of powerful blows his father continued to rain upon him.

When she saw that Diego was making no move to defend himself, Angelique scrambled across the bed and grabbed José Luis from behind. "Stop it!" she shouted, completely disregarding her lack of attire in her haste to save the man she loved from a brutal beating she was positive he did not deserve. Her mother was screaming still, her voice growing hoarse and racked with sobs, but this seemed a minor distraction when José Luis appeared determined to beat his own son to death. She wrapped her arms around the older man's neck and held on tightly, finally choking him so effectively that he staggered backward and fell across the bed, pinning her slender body beneath him. She released him then, and when he rose, she hurriedly slid off the bed and yanked the top sheet free to cover herself before she went to her mother's side.

Startled back to his senses by Angelique's feisty interference, José Luis gave Diego a sharp order. "Get dressed. Then I will speak to you both!" As he wheeled around, he looked directly at Angelique for the first time and gave an astonished gasp, for the fine linen sheet she had draped around herself scarcely hid her voluptuous curves. Her tangled curls framed her flushed features with a sensuous tawny haze and the violet eyes that regarded him with a defiant stare were unmistakably those of a woman.

He turned back to look at his son and was shocked by the blood that covered his face and dripped down upon his bare chest. He had thought Diego had raped a mere child, but clearly Angelique's spirited defense showed she was no victim of an assault, and from what he could see of her figure, she was no child either.

Readily understanding his father's confused glance, Diego gestured toward Françoise, who could barely remain standing, so pathetically was she weeping. "See to her first. There's no need for her to lose her sanity over this."

"No need? My God, have you no remorse for what you've done?" José Luis did not bother to wait for his son's reply but hurriedly lifted Françoise into his arms and carried her through the group of startled servants who had gathered outside the door to witness the noisy confrontation taking place inside Angelique's room.

Angelique slammed the door after José Luis, unwilling to continue the spectacle his servants had obviously been enjoying so immensely. She lifted the ends of the trailing sheet she wore and made her way back to Diego's side. "Sit down. I'll do what I can for your face, but why didn't you make some effort to defend yourself? I can understand why you'd not want to strike your own father, but you needn't have taken such an awful beating either."

Diego had already pulled on his breeches and now sank down on the edge of the rumpled bed while she poured water from a pitcher into the basin and moistened the ends of a towel. "Why didn't you lock the door? You knew I'd be with you tonight."

"That door has never been locked, Diego. This is the first time my mother has ever entered my room after dinner, so I didn't think it was necessary."

Diego began to swear, using several extremely colorful expressions of which sailors were so fond. "How could you have been so careless?" he finally managed to ask.

Ignoring his string of violent curses, Angelique stepped between Diego's outstretched legs and took his chin in her hand to hold his head still as she attempted to stem the flow of blood from the gash above his eye. She pressed the damp towel to the wound and tried not to become ill from the gruesome sight he presented. "Oh, I see. This is entirely my fault, is it? Had the door been locked, my mother would have had to knock, and you could have slipped back to your own room before I let her in. Is that what should have happened?"

"Yes!" Diego replied through a haze of pain, for his face was badly bruised and the cut above his eye most painful. "I thought you had sense enough to lock the blasted door so this wouldn't happen to us!"

"Was the door locked the night I spent in your bedroom?" Angelique asked innocently.

Diego hesitated a moment, for he had taken care to lock his door without her observing that action. "Yes, it was locked," he finally admitted grudgingly.

Angelique stood quietly waiting for the worst of his wounds to stop oozing blood, then she used another damp towel to wipe off the traces of his injuries that still marred his bronze complexion with gore. "At least he didn't break your nose, but your eye will be black in the morning."

"I've suffered worse," Diego sneered rudely, not thanking her for taking care of his wounds so tenderly. As he bent down to reach for his boots, he grew so dizzy he nearly slid off the bed, and he had to sit back to catch his breath.

"Are you all right?" Angelique inquired anxiously.

"Yes. I just moved too quickly, that's all."

"Here, let me help you." Angelique gathered up his socks and knelt down to place them on his feet, then helped him with his boots as well before handing him his shirt. He managed to put that on himself, but she buttoned it for him. "Wait a moment while I dress and we'll go together."

"I can walk on my own," Diego boasted cockily, though he was not all that certain he could stand without fainting. His head ached with a fearful pounding and he felt so nauseous that he feared he might become ill in front of her.

"I don't want to have to face them alone. Won't you wait for me?" Angelique asked again.

"Oh, if it is simply my company you need to arouse the courage to face them, I don't object to that." Diego was grateful for the additional time to rest and stretched out upon the bed and closed his eyes while he waited for her. "Have you anything to wear that won't make you look like a twelve-year-old?"

Angelique opened her wardrobe and took out the single black garment. "Yes. There's this one dress of my mother's."

The fragrance of the exotic perfume assailed Diego's

senses with a most erotic reminder of the single occasion upon which he had seen her in it and he opened his eyes to look up at her. "That's your mother's perfume, isn't it? No wonder I didn't recognize it on you."

"Yes, this is her scent." Angelique pulled on her lingerie, then donned the uncomfortable mourning gown. "I hate this dress as much as she does, but it's all I have to wear now." She went to the mirror and brushed out her curls, then coiled them atop her head. She looked so prim she wondered if José Luis would believe he had actually found her lying nude in Diego's arms. "Your father is furious with us, and my mother is hysterical. What can we possibly say to them?"

Diego had no idea what to suggest. For some strange reason he did not feel the slightest twinge of guilt for having been caught with Angelique. It was unfortunate, but he certainly did not view it as the tragedy his father obviously did. "I want you to keep still. I'll answer whatever questions he asks, and you'll not dispute my word. Is that clear?"

Approaching the bed, Angelique argued, "I won't let you take the blame for this, Diego. It is as much my fault as yours—more really."

Diego sat up slowly and was pleased to see how proper she looked, but he was even more gratified to see that she looked seventeen at long last, rather than twelve. He held his side as he rose to his feet, certain one of his father's blows had cracked a rib. "I'll not have him calling you a whore, Angelique. Now I meant what I said. You keep still and let me handle this."

Angelique gave him a quizzical glance. "I'll be seventeen before the week is out. Since you planned to appear with me in public after that, we couldn't have kept our relationship a secret much longer."

"That is hardly a comforting thought," Diego replied sharply. "I'll not tell him about our plans and you won't either. Just keep still." Yet even as he gave that order, he knew she would be unlikely to follow it.

"Shall I help you on with your coat?"

Diego shot Angelique a warning glance, for she had not promised to let him take charge of their defense and that annoyed him. "No, I'll just go in my shirt-sleeves. Are you ready?"

"Yes. Let's get this over with quickly." When he stood up, Angelique took his arm and held on with a frantic grasp, for she was more frightened by the ordeal that lay ahead than she dared to admit. "I wonder why my mother wanted to see me at such a late hour."

"That hardly matters now, does it?"

"It might," Angelique worried aloud. "It might make a great deal of difference."

As they entered the parlor, José Luis patted Françoise's hands lightly and rose to meet them. The distraught woman was still sobbing pitifully, and her fair complexion appeared blotchy from all her tears. "I have already sent for a priest, and since my contributions to the church are quite generous, I know he'll not refuse my request that he perform a marriage ceremony tonight."

As Angelique looked up at Diego, her long lashes swept her lightly arched brows. For once she was simply dumbfounded and had no idea how to respond to such a surprising announcement. She had had no time to consider what their punishment might be, but marriage seemed a bizarre choice.

Diego showed Angelique to a chair, then leaned against it to save his strength. "Is that what Françoise wants for her daughter, a hurried wedding that is sure to cause a sensational scandal among all your friends?"

Françoise's glance was bitter as she regarded the battered young man before crying out sharply, "You raped my little girl. You can't deny that!"

"Your little girl is nearly seventeen years old, *Madame*. Have you told my father why you've kept her disguised as a child all these years?" Diego inquired, having decided they

167

might as well get to the bottom of her story now that her ruse had been exposed for the lie it was.

"I wished merely to protect her from the savagery of brutes like you!" Françoise replied angrily. "You could have had any woman you wished. Why did you have to rape my precious Angelique?"

Seeing no point in allowing what had become a bitter exchange of insults to continue, José Luis lay his hand upon Françoise's shoulder. "My dear, I think I know my son well enough to swear he doesn't rape children."

"Oh, really?" Angelique asked pointedly. "Then why did you beat him so severely?"

"Angelique!" Diego gave her a withering look. "I warned you to be silent. Now hush!"

That the young couple knew each other well was apparent in their every glance and gesture. Curious, José Luis demanded an explanation. "How long has this illicit romance of yours been going on?"

Diego shook his head. "That's really none of your business."

"The hell it isn't! When you start seducing the daughters of my houseguests, it is damn well my business!" José Luis took a threatening step forward and then thought better of moving any closer. He could see from his son's swollen features that he had already taken enough physical punishment for one night. "This wasn't the first time you've made love to Angelique, was it?"

Diego didn't reply. He stared at his father with a menacing glare, then reached down to take Angelique's hand. He gave her fingers a reassuring squeeze and wondered why the prospect of being forced to marry her caused him such little dread.

Adopting a far more sympathetic manner, José Luis addressed Angelique. "You needn't be afraid of me, or of Diego. Just tell me the truth. When did this affair of yours begin?"

Taking a deep breath, Angelique forced herself to think calmly. Since Diego had asked her to be silent, she did not speak, assuming that José Luis would be all the more outraged if he knew she had first slept with his son the night he had returned home.

Françoise wiped her eyes with her lace-trimmed handkerchief as she watched her daughter's expression grow defiant. "Isn't it obvious that Angelique didn't realize what she was doing? I didn't raise her to behave like some common slut! Now tell José Luis what he wants to know this very minute, Angelique. It is Diego who should be punished, not you!"

"No, I will not," Angelique replied firmly.

Perplexed that things were going so poorly, José Luis turned back to Françoise. "When I asked you to marry me tonight, why didn't you tell me the truth about Angelique?"

Startled to find him concerned about such a small lie when the situation seemed so desperate, Françoise nevertheless thought swiftly. "I would have told you tomorrow, if not tonight. But if you are so concerned about Angelique's age, you must also see that clearly your son seduced her. She knew nothing of men until he forced himself into her bed!"

That José Luis had finally proposed to her mother only intensified Angelique's anguish. Would he think it improper to marry her now if their children were wed? Knowing how desperately her mother had wanted to become his wife, Angelique spoke up. "Diego didn't rape me, Mama. Please don't accuse him of that, for he's not guilty."

"Oh, but he is!" Françoise rose to her feet and walked over to her daughter's chair. "I've seen the way he looks at you. Have you forgotten how he wanted to take you to parties or give you riding lessons? That could only have been an attempt to get you alone so he could seduce you! This horrible disgrace is all his fault, and he's the one who should pay for it!"

"The only disgrace here is the way you've raised Angelique," Diego interjected calmly. "You've used your daughter far more detestably than any man ever could."

As Françoise raised her hand to slap Diego's face for his insult, José Luis reached out to catch her wrist. "This argument is senseless. These two will marry and then they will be on their own. I want you to take your bride and leave my house tonight, Diego. Where you go is your own concern."

"What do you mean?" Françoise cried hoarsely.

"I mean exactly what I said," José Luis explained, his anger flaring anew. "I think you're right. My son seduced your daughter with no regard for the consequences. I don't want him living under my roof ever again, for he has clearly learned nothing from the example I've always tried to provide as to how a gentleman behaves."

Terrified by his words, Françoise ripped her wrist from his grasp. "No! Angelique deserves far more consideration than that! You can't expect her to marry your son when you'll turn them out into the street!"

"It will hardly be the street, Françoise. Diego can well afford to support a wife," José Luis explained calmly.

Françoise turned back to Angelique and she began to plead, "Tell him the truth! He'll not punish you also if you tell him what really happened!"

Still confused by José Luis's words, Angelique could not imagine what her mother wanted her to say, but she knew that if they were forced to marry so hastily and then were banished from José Luis's house, the gossip about them would never cease.

Startled by the enormity of his father's demands, Diego attempted to make him see reason. "Look, there is no need to create a scandal that will taint your reputation as well as mine. Angelique and I can announce our engagement tomorrow and marry in a month. I have no objection to living on board *El Diablo* until then and I'll provide her with a comfortable home after we are married. That should satisfy your demands for propriety without making any of us suffer needlessly."

Though Diego considered his proposal a logical solution to their dilemma, José Luis did not. "When the priest arrives, you two will be married and then leave. Is that clear?" Without waiting for a response, he left the room to see that the chapel was prepared for the ceremony.

Mortified, Françoise again collapsed upon the loveseat and wept openly, blaming the horrible men who had taken over her native France and had forced her to bring her beautiful daughter to a country where they had to suffer such cruel humiliation as they had encountered in the Aragon home. She muttered her curses in French, too distraught to speak in a language Diego could understand, while she again berated him for raping her daughter and bringing this terrible disgrace down upon them.

With her mother in no condition to be reasonable and Diego standing sullenly at her side, Angelique knew that if any action were going to be taken to salvage the evening, she would have to take it herself. "This is ridiculous!" she stated emphatically as she rose to her feet. "I'll not marry Diego simply because his father insists I must!" As her mother began to wail even louder, she left the parlor with a confident step and returned to her room, where she took out her one piece of luggage. Opening the drawers of her dresser, she began to empty the contents into the fabric bag. With her out of the house, her mother could marry José Luis and Diego could do whatever he damn well pleased, for she was not going to force a man who did not love her into a disastrous marriage just to please his father.

Diego followed Angelique and did not bother to knock at her slightly opened door before entering her room. "What do you think you're doing?" he demanded angrily.

"This is a suitcase and I am packing what little I wish to take with me. Isn't that obvious?" She picked up the brandy snifter she had taken from his room and wrapped it carefully in a nightgown before slipping it in among her lingerie. She wanted the book of poems he had given her as well, but after regarding the sickeningly sweet dresses her wardrobe contained, she took out no more than her cloak. "You needn't bother calling a carriage for me. I've learned how to move about this town on foot in the last few weeks."

Since Diego had pretended not to know what she had been doing, he thought it safe to ask, "Why would you have been walking about the city?"

Angelique paused only a moment as she gave him a hostile glance. "I've been looking for work as a seamstress so I wouldn't have to be dependent upon you. Just because I haven't been successful so far doesn't mean I won't be tomorrow, or the next day."

The defiant tilt of her chin showed her determination clearly, and for a brief instant Diego was sorry he dared not reveal her mother's extensive efforts to see that no jobs would be open to her. "I'll not let you leave this house to wander the streets alone, Angelique. I'd never allow that."

"Well, as I see it, we have little choice. We've both been dismissed from your home, and I intend to leave before I'm insulted further." Angelique knew she sounded brave, but she certainly did not feel it. The idea of going out in the dark of night terrified her, but it was a better alternative than marrying Diego, when clearly it had never occurred to him to make her his wife.

Diego turned back to close the door quietly and this time he locked it so they would not be disturbed. "If you are going to scream and cry like your mother, then get it over with now. But you are going to marry me before we leave here."

"But that's absurd!" Angelique countered with a rude laugh. "It was a mistress you wanted, not a bride!"

While the thought of marriage had never entered his mind, Diego realized now that it should have. "When I was searching the whole town for you, and you were so helpful in your assistance, what did you think I meant to do when I found you?"

Startled by his unexpected question, Angelique paused in her packing and turned to face him. "When I came to your ship, you made it abundantly clear what you wanted of me."

Approaching her slowly so she would not bolt and run, Diego reached out to draw her into a warm embrace. "I meant to ask you to marry me the moment I found out who you were. It was only my anger at the way you'd tricked me that kept me from doing it before this."

Touched by the sweetness of his declaration, Angelique felt her eyes grow bright with tears. Relaxing against him, she laid her cheek against his chest and whispered, "You see, I told you this dreadful predicament was more my fault than yours."

Diego kissed her golden curls lightly and tried to think of something else to say, for he did not believe she was ready to agree to his proposal. While he had never done it himself, he did know what a man was supposed to do when he fell in love with a lovely young woman from a fine family. "I meant to visit your home and ask your father's permission to call upon you. I thought you'd welcome my attentions. Was I wrong?"

"No," Angelique admitted softly. "But look what a mess I've made of everything. Now with our parents planning to marry—"

"Angelique," Diego warned her softly, "we'll still not truly be brother and sister, even if they do wed, but to avoid any such controversy, we should be the ones to get married first." This sounded like a plausible argument to him, and he hoped she would accept it.

Angelique stepped back slightly to look up at him. Despite his battered appearance, he was still so handsome that she could scarcely think while his expressive eyes gazed into hers. "I can understand why you were so angry with me, but still—"

She was such an exquisite beauty, and Diego gave up all thought of persuading her with words and instead pulled her close for a kiss he did not end until he felt her trembling with desire. He took her hand then and had just turned toward the door when they heard a loud knocking. "No more arguments!" he whispered sternly, and, after turning the key, he opened the door.

José Luis stared in disbelief. "I didn't think it would be necessary to tell you to stay out of Angelique's room. Was such an obvious consideration lost on you?"

"I was merely helping her pack," Diego replied with a grin he couldn't suppress. "Is the priest here yet? We're anxious to leave."

"Yes, the man is here and he has agreed to perform the ceremony without question, for which I am deeply grateful. Let's not keep him waiting." José Luis still could not adjust his thinking to allow himself to accept the stunning blonde at his son's side as Angelique. She was so completely different in appearance. He suddenly recalled his son's search for an attractive French blonde and blurted out quickly, "Was Angelique the young woman for whom you spent so much time searching?"

Seeing no point in keeping that a secret now, Diego readily admitted it. "Yes, and she was here all the time."

Angelique blushed deeply, certain José Luis would be able to unravel everything if they gave him a few more minutes to contemplate the obvious. "Is my mother already in the chapel?"

"No, she is so overcome with grief over this regrettable incident that she refuses to attend the ceremony. Do you want to speak with her yourself? Perhaps she will lend you a more suitable gown, for black is not a color that any bride willingly wears."

After assuring herself that such a delay would not upset Diego, Angelique hurried to her mother's room, where she found her stretched out upon her bed weeping with loud, racking sobs. She sat down beside her and stroked her back lightly. "Mama, please. Please don't cry so. I love Diego dearly, and while I am sorry we have hurt you so deeply, I am

174

not opposed to becoming his wife."

Rising up on one elbow, Françoise frowned harshly, unable to comprehend the true import of her daughter's words. "But he is no more than an impetuous rogue, a brash young man who prefers the brutal excitement of the sea to the responsible life his father leads ashore. He'll be no husband to you, none at all! Had we not left France, you'd already be a nobleman's bride. How could you have wasted the only treasure you had on such a rascal?"

"If you are referring to my virginity, it was not wasted," Angelique replied calmly, not accepting her mother's bitter view of Diego's character.

As though she were a marionette controlled by the pull of strings, Françoise sat up with a sudden jerk, then slapped Angelique with the back of her hand with a blow so vicious that it nearly knocked the slender girl off the bed. "How dare you say such a thing to me! I knew you hated pretending to be a child, but I never dreamed you'd give yourself to the first man who looked your way! Get out of my sight, you stupid little bitch! I never want to see you again as long as I live! Get out of here! Get out!"

Alarmed by Françoise's shrieks, José Luis rushed into her room in time to see the furious woman shove her daughter to the floor. She then drew back her foot and kicked Angelique repeatedly as she screamed at her again, calling her a string of vile names that were comprehendible from her tone despite the fact that he could not understand her French.

Horrified by such uncalled-for brutality, José Luis grabbed Françoise around the waist and lifted her off her feet. He shook her soundly as he yelled to Angelique to flee before she came to any further harm. Since Diego had gone to his own room to dress for the wedding, he did not suspect anything was amiss until he found Angelique wandering down the hall. Her tangled hair and sorrowful tears provided clear evidence of what her reception had been in her mother's room and he quickly drew her into her own.

175

"What did that bitch say to you! If she's blamed you for this I'll wring her neck!" The print of Françoise's tiny hand was plain upon Angelique's cheek and, seeing this, he led her to the bed and knelt down in front of her. "Tell me what she said!"

Angelique shook her head, ashamed to tell him of her mother's insults, for she knew she deserved them. She had given herself to the first man who had kissed her, without ever thinking what a dear price she would have to pay. She wiped her eyes on the back of her hand and tried to catch the curls that had fallen loose from her coiffure and secure them again atop her head. "You must try to understand what plans she had for me, and how bitterly I have disappointed her."

Diego was seething with rage. He had taken the beating his father had given him, but Angelique certainly did not deserve to be disowned. He remembered how he had lured her to his room after he had found her in the garden. He had given her brandy, gained her confidence, and then made love to her. She had fallen into a carefully laid trap and he couldn't bear to see her punished for it like this.

"Wash your face and find a *mantilla*. We can't keep the good priest waiting a moment longer." Diego straightened up and squared his shoulders proudly. "At least you are packed to go and I can send for my belongings in the morning." When Angelique selected the black lace veil she had worn to his ship rather than a white one, he winced inwardly but did not question her choice. He offered his arm and escorted her to the small chapel, which was ablaze with light from more than a hundred candles.

Angelique was no more religious than Diego. Her mother had lost all faith in God when France had fallen into the hands of men she considered bloodthirsty barbarians and, other than to offer prayers for her husband's memory, she had never sought the peace so many other widows had found in the ritual of the Catholic Church. Since her mother had seldom visited a church, Angelique had not either. Naturally, this had upset their cousin Beatriz terribly, for she was a most devout woman.

Glancing around the small chapel, Angelique could not help but recall the weddings she had attended as a child in the magnificent cathedral in which her parents had been wed. Realizing that the man who would become her husband was most important, and not the humbleness of the setting, she pushed aside the painful memories of those long ago days in France and tried to concentrate instead on what was to come.

José Luis was pale as he joined them. "I do not think I ever knew your mother until tonight, Angelique. Had she not already refused to attend this wedding, I would have forbidden her to come!" He whispered his remarks so the priest would not overhear them. "Here is one of your mother's rings, Diego. You can purchase another for Angelique when you have the time."

Puzzled, Diego held out his hand. The ring was a brilliant sapphire surrounded by fiery diamonds, and while he did not recall ever seeing it before, he doubted he could find a more beautiful ring for Angelique anywhere on earth. The blue of the precious stone was so close to the color of her eyes that he knew it was the perfect choice for her. "Thank you," he said emotionally and, taking the pretty blonde's arm, he led her to the altar. After introducing her to the priest, he waited for the cleric to begin the service.

Diego's head still ached, and he could barely see out of his left eye. Angelique was trembling noticeably and dressed for mourning. Each wondered what the kindly priest must think of them. Not only was the timing of this ceremony unusual, but their appearance could not have been worse. Considering these aberrations ill omens, Diego frowned, for he knew the young woman at his side would have been the most radiant of brides had the circumstances been different. He blamed himself that her memories of their wedding would be

177

such sad ones.

Perplexed by the dark expressions of those assembled before him, the priest waited a moment while the half-dozen pews filled with the household staff. To have been called so hurriedly to the home of José Luis Aragon to perform such a secretive ceremony was astonishing. He had known Diego all his life, and when he considered how seldom he was home, he realized he had not thought him the marrying type. That so tall and obviously strong a young man had been so badly beaten could only mean he had been attacked by a gang of thieves and that was a tale he could not wait to hear.

Turning his attention to the bride, he saw that she was a young lady of quality, so he could not imagine why her family had not provided her with the elaborate wedding the members of the upper class usually held. Her black gown puzzled him too, but despite the many mysteries that confronted him, he opened his book and began the wedding ceremony in the deep tones he reserved for such solemn occasions.

As José Luis watched the striking young couple exchange their vows, he recalled how earlier that same evening he had watched his son behave with a curious disdain for the lively young ladies who had sought his favor at the Rosaleses' party. That Angelique had been the cause of Diego's melancholy mood was now clear, but he wanted to know the entire story of what had transpired between them and was angry he had been able to learn so little. He had not the slightest doubt that what he was doing was the just and proper thing. Diego had to have taken advantage of her innocence, and that was a crime for which he had to pay. What sort of marriage they would have he could not predict, but he thought suddenly of his dear Magdalena and wondered what she would have thought of the man her son had become. Wiping a tear from the corner of his eye, he prayed she would have been proud of him still.

Chapter XI

Diego held Angelique's hand tightly as their carriage made its way through the deserted streets. "It's after midnight and my ship will be the best place for us to spend the rest of the night. I'd not want to walk into a hotel looking like this anyway," he confessed. As they rode along, he tried to formulate some coherent plan for announcing their marriage, but none had come to him. With his father's mood so belligerent, none of his relatives were likely to congratulate them. There would be no reception unless he hosted one himself, and that breach of etiquette would only intensify the gossip their hurried wedding would surely cause. In the past he had never cared what people had thought or said about him, but now he had to consider Angelique's feelings and found that prospect deeply troubling. His customary cavalier attitude would have to undergo a drastic change and he was not so certain that he even wanted to change. But if he continued to devote so much of his life to the sea, she would be alone more often than not, and he could not leave her all by herself in Barcelona without friends or family for comfort.

His life had been filled with confusion since the night he had met her. With each new turn of events, his future seemed to progress further beyond his control and this was not a situation he enjoyed, nor would he permit such a frustrating pattern to continue. Drawing the fragile blonde's hand to his lips, he silently vowed to be careful not to make any promises he could not keep.

The men on watch came running as Diego carried Angelique's bag up the gangplank. He introduced them to his bride, then sent them back to their posts before they had time to do more than gape at the strikingly beautiful young woman by his side. "Naturally my crew will be curious, but, fortunately, few are on board tonight and we won't be disturbed." Taking her by the hand he led her to his cabin.

As Diego lit the lamp upon the table, Angelique surveyed the room with a curious glance. It seemed smaller than she had remembered and she wondered how long they would be living here. She made no inquiry about his plans, for she doubted that he had had any time to make them. Wide awake, she perched on the edge of a chair and waited for him to speak.

Bone weary, Diego felt a sharp stab of pain in his ribs as he tried to stifle a wide yawn. Hiding his discomfort, he began to apologize. "I know this is our wedding night, and I hate to disappoint you like this, but I plan to climb into my bunk and go directly to sleep." Since they had already shared one romantic interlude that evening, he did not think she would object to merely sleeping with him, but he was astonished by her delighted expression as she leapt to her feet and came toward him.

"Why Diego, what a wonderful idea!" Angelique exclaimed. "Now why didn't I think of that?"

"Of what?" he asked warily. He laid his coat aside but hesitated to unbutton his waistcoat until he understood exactly what she meant.

Smiling brightly, Angelique hastened to explain, "It's not the fact that we've made love before that matters. If we are not intimate now, our marriage won't be a legal one, will it? We've satisfied your father's demands and left his house, but there's no reason for us to spend the rest of our lives together if we don't really wish to. Since I'm not in the least bit sleepy, I'll just sit up and read. In the morning, I'll continue my search for a job. If you'll lend me the money to pay for lodgings at an inn, I will repay the sum when I find employment. Now, isn't that the most sensible solution to our problems?"

Dumbfounded, Diego simply stared down at his animated wife for several seconds. She seemed very pleased with herself and her eyes were alight with a mischievous glow. He was totally confused by her suggestion, however, for it was so completely unexpected and, in his opinion, ridiculous in the extreme. "After we have already become man and wife, made our promises to God in front of a roomful of witnesses, you've decided you don't wish to be married?" he finally exploded in a fit of anger. "Why didn't you just say so before the ceremony began?"

"As I recall, I did just that, Diego." Angelique turned away, sorry he had not accepted her suggestion as graciously as she had offered it. "Since you didn't say a word to me on the way here, it seems plain to me you think this is all a terrible mistake. I'm merely proposing a way out of it. I did not mean to insult you."

"Well, you most certainly did!" Diego replied hotly, his fatigue now forgotten. The muscles of his powerful body were tensed, as if this argument could soon become a physical one.

"You spend a great deal of time at sea, don't you?" Angelique asked softly.

"Yes, of course, but what has that got to do with anything?" he replied, though he could see exactly where she was leading the conversation.

"It would be expensive for you to maintain a home just for me."

"I have more money than I can count, Angelique. A dozen homes would not break me. You may have

181

whatever type of house you desire. The expense will be a slight one to me." As she moved about the confines of his cabin, Diego wished she would stand still, but she seemed determined to remain aloof in both her manner and her comments.

"Why haven't you built a home of your own before this then?"

"Because I'm so seldom here, but . . ." Diego paused suddenly, realizing too late that she had led him into a trap.

"Precisely." Angelique turned slowly to face him. "You don't need a home and you most certainly don't need a wife."

While he could not argue with her logic, Diego found the prospect of letting her walk out of his life at dawn impossible to accept. The torment he had already suffered would be slight compared to not knowing where she was or with whom now that he knew her so well.

Despite her somber attire, she seemed to glow with an inner radiance that enchanted him. Stepping forward, he removed her *mantilla* and freed her bright curls, carelessly tossing her hairpins upon the floor in his haste. He slid his fingers through her gleaming tresses to draw her near as he whispered, "How can you doubt that I need you?" He kissed her very lightly at first and his lips teased hers until she began to respond. She slipped her arms around his waist then and he knew he had already won the battle she had started, but in spite of this he did not release her. Instead he deepened his kiss until they were both breathless, then he led her over to his bunk and with exaggerated care he unfastened the hooks that secured the bodice of her dress. "Tomorrow morning you will be too busy selecting new gowns to look for work, Angelique," he whispered, trailing teasing nibbles down her throat as he slipped the straps of her lingerie off her shoulders. "And in the afternoon I will keep you busier still."

Angelique's agile mind could conceive of no further arguments, for his fingertips were now moving over the smooth swell of her breasts. She wanted him too desperately to continue to insist that their marriage was ill-advised. Her fingers trembled as they moved down the buttons of his satin waistcoat and then to his soft linen shirt. She wanted no barrier between them and, sensing the urgency of her need, Diego swiftly tossed his clothing aside and joined her in the narrow bunk. He pulled her into a fierce embrace as his mouth covered hers in a lingering kiss that demanded a loyalty far greater than that promised in the vows she had spoken in his father's chapel. He wanted to lay claim to her very soul and moved with pantherlike grace to seal the promises they had made so that she could never again deny she was truly his wife. His powerful body met no resistance, but only a warm rush of delicious acceptance, and he ceased to be concerned over the haste of their wedding or the scandal it was sure to cause. He was exultant, for he had gained a fascinating and spirited beauty to enrich his nights with the magical splendor of love.

Angelique clung to Diego and her fingers gripped his broad shoulders tightly as his tantalizing kiss and forceful loving filled her graceful body with a fiery warmth so splendid she longed to savor it into eternity. The pleasure he gave was exquisite and they both found boundless joy. Later, when Angelique at last fell asleep cradled in Diego's arms, she had no more worries that their marriage would not be both happy and deeply satisfying.

His cabin was filled with sunlight when he awakened, but the dreamy sense of contentment that had lulled Diego to sleep vanished instantly as the unmistakable sound of retching reached his ears. Angelique was trying to be quiet, but the cabin was small and her illness was impossible to hide. Rather than go to her side, he pretended to be asleep still and hoped he could fool her as easily as she had been able to trick him. It was foolish to test her honesty, he supposed, yet he wanted to know if she had mended her ways. From what he knew of her, lies came to her lips far more swiftly than the truth, but he wanted to give her the chance to win his trust and this seemed like too perfect an opportunity to miss. He kept his eyes closed and his breathing even as he waited for her to return to his bed.

When the nausea finally subsided, Angelique moved slowly back to the cabin's single bunk and lay down beside her husband. She closed her eyes and, comforted by his reassuring warmth, was soon sleeping peacefully. She knew they had much to accomplish this day and hoped to feel better when she awakened for the second time.

Diego went back to sleep too, but when he again arose, he was too curious to leave Angelique undisturbed and began to nuzzle her throat with playful kisses. "It's time to wake up, my angel," he whispered softly, but as he looked down at her, he could not fail to notice how pale her creamy skin was and he grew worried. After a brief flutter of thick lashes, she opened her eyes and gave him a pretty smile. "Good morning. How do you feel?" he asked with a disarming grin. "I hope sleeping on board *El Diablo* did not prove too difficult for you."

Although she still felt somewhat queasy, Angelique saw no reason to disclose the fact. "This bunk is a trifle narrow, but the company is very nice."

"Thank you, but I am still concerned about your health. You look rather pale and I'll insist you remain in bed all day if you aren't well. After the night we had, it would not be surprising if you felt ill." He attempted to coax the truth from her but failed.

"You've never seen me first thing in the morning, Diego. How do you know whether or not I'm pale?" Angelique could not understand his persistence in the matter of her health.

Sitting up slowly, Diego grew serious. "I am your husband now, Angelique, and I expect you to tell me the truth. If you aren't well, then I want to know about it. I will send for a physician immediately if one is required."

Brushing the stray curls from her eyes, Angelique clutched

the sheet to her breasts as she sat up to face him. "I'm fine," she insisted, but her lovely complexion still held a ghostly pallor.

Diego saw no point in carrying his ruse any further. "I'm not nearly as sound a sleeper as you seem to think, my dear. I know you were sick this morning and I want to know why."

Though a bright flush flooded Angelique's pale cheeks, no possible excuse came to her mind. The truth, however, was impossible to admit and she looked away, hoping Diego would drop the matter, but he did not.

"Your mother often described you as frail. Is that the truth? Are you frequently ill?"

Angelique could barely hear his question over the wild pounding of her heart. Even if she managed to fool him this once, what would she do the next day or the one after that? she wondered fearfully. "My mother told everyone I was frail so she'd have an excuse to keep me at home. It was never the truth though. I have always enjoyed excellent health."

"Except for this morning?" Diego asked sarcastically. He knew how he felt, which was far from good, but he wanted the truth about Angelique too.

"I am sorry that I disturbed you. I didn't mean to," she apologized sincerely.

"I don't care if you disturb me, Angelique. Just don't lie to me!" As he stared at her coldly, he could think only of Françoise and how much he despised that woman. Had she raised a daughter so schooled in deceit that she would never again be the delightfully open and loving creature who had enchanted him in a moonlit garden? Which one was truly Angelique? It pained him to realize he did not really know. Frowning, he asked her once again, "Were you sick yesterday, or the day before, or is this something new?"

Angelique retreated behind a wall of silence and made no response at all. Diego's anger was frightening and she did not know what to tell him. As long as her pregnancy did not show, she considered it a secret she would have to keep.

"There's no way for you to avoid answering my questions, Angelique, because, if we must, we'll stay right here in this bunk until you're ready to reply." He meant what he said and realized now that he had been a fool not to go to her side and ask for the truth when he had first discovered she was ill. She had never seemed delicate to him before that very moment and suddenly he was frightened that she might truly have such fragile health that he would be unable to leave her for fear she would be in her grave when he returned home. Pained by that gruesome possibility, he attempted to speak in a far softer tone. "I want to take such good care of you. How can I do that if you hide things from me or lie to me? How will I ever know what you need to be happy if you do not tell me?"

Angelique tried to smile then, but her vivid blue eyes were bright with unshed tears. "I need nothing to be happy but you, Diego. That's all I'll ever want."

"Well, thank you, but I'd like to think you trust me too. I'll not plan too much today if there's a chance you'll feel ill again."

"No, I'll be fine for the rest of the day," Angelique reassured him confidently.

"How can you be so certain?" As Diego considered the words of his ravishing bride, he was appalled at how blind he had been. "You're only ill first thing in the morning, aren't you? And it's every morning, isn't it? Well, isn't it?" He put his hands upon her shoulders, ready to give her a sound shaking if she still refused to tell him the truth.

As a single tear slipped from beneath her long, dark lashes, Angelique nodded slightly, still unwilling to admit the truth aloud.

Furious with her obstinate silence, Diego tried to remember how many times he had made love to her and suddenly the truth became painfully clear. "You must have gotten pregnant the first time we were together! Isn't that when it happened, nearly two months ago?"

"Yes," Angelique admitted softly.

"Dear God in heaven! When did you plan to tell me about this?" Diego felt sick himself then, for being faced with the responsibility of a wife seemed difficult enough, but the fact that they would become parents in seven months' time was a disgrace of tremendous proportions. "Did you really think I'd let you go, as you suggested last night? Did you think I'd allow you to live in some tiny room above a noisy tavern while you worked as a seamstress and tried to raise my child alone? Is that all you thought of me?"

"Diego, please!" Angelique did not know where to begin to refute his accusations, for he actually understood very little. "Do you remember when I came here and asked you to be patient? I planned to leave your father's house and move into lodgings of my own so that I could see you as often as we wished. I didn't even realize what had happened to me then, for I'd been so terribly worried about the way I had to deceive you. It wasn't until later, after I started feeling so wretched when I awakened in the morning, that I stopped to count the days since we had first been together. Everything's been so confused. I was just miserable, seeing you everyday and not being able to tell you who I was for fear I'd ruin everything for my mother. She wants to marry your father so desperately and—"

"To hell with your mother!" Diego shouted angrily. "I was twice as miserable as you were, as you damn well know, because I didn't know if I'd ever find you. And there you were, adorable little Angelique who was always so full of sympathy. This is the worst possible way to begin a marriage, but if we are to have any hope at all of finding happiness together, I have to come first for a change!"

Confused, Angelique didn't understand what she had done wrong. "I didn't want to force you to marry me, or ask you for money so I could get out of your life!"

"You can't believe I'd have sent you away with cash and nothing else!" Diego argued. He was deeply insulted. "Was it

187

only last night that you were telling me what a wonderful man you thought I was? What's gotten into you that you can't keep your lies straight any longer? If you had truly thought my character admirable, you would have known you could have told me the truth without any fear I'd have been angry with you or that I would have simply paid you a generous sum to forget we'd ever met! What you think of me is clear and, believe me, I think as little of you!" Diego's eyes grew black with fury, for he had had such beautiful dreams of what their life would be when he had found his elusive lady that he could not bear the bitter disappointment she had dealt him. "I might as well have married your mother. You're merely a copy of that conniving bitch and I would have preferred to have an original!"

Diego slipped off the end of his bunk to avoid crawling over Angelique. He pulled on his breeches and boots, grateful the pain in his side was now no more than a faint twinge. He found a clean shirt he had left in a drawer and went to the door. "I'll bring hot water so you can bathe. Be quick about it though. I don't want to waste any more time than absolutely necessary seeing to your wardrobe."

Angelique was so stunned by Diego's bitter denunciation that she simply sat in his bed until he returned with a copper tub and several pails of hot water. He laid out soap and a towel, then glared at her as he went out the door for the last time. Only then did she get up to unpack fresh lingerie. She stepped into the tub, made herself comfortable, and waited until the water grew tepid before she reached for the bar of soap and began to wash. If her husband could treat her so callously before they had been married even twenty-four hours, she would not feel obligated to fulfill any of his requests promptly. She used no haste in dressing either, and was still brushing her hair when he returned to his cabin.

"Do you always spend so damn much time getting dressed?"

"Always," Angelique replied coldly. "However, my

mother takes at least three times as long as I do, so you should consider yourself fortunate."

Diego had seen to his own grooming elsewhere, but he had not been pleased with the sorry sight he had seen reflected in the mirror. As Angelique had predicted, his left eye was badly swollen and quite black, and not even his deeply tanned complexion could hide his numerous other bruises. Rather than hide in his cabin like some coward waiting for his attacker to return however, Diego had decided just to go on about his business regardless of how ghastly he looked. "The cook isn't on board, so I can offer you no more than tea and oranges for breakfast."

"That's more than enough, thank you. For some reason I've quite lost my appetite."

Diego set the tray that he had carried from the galley upon the table, poured two cups of steaming tea, and cut two oranges into wedges while he waited for his bride to finish coiling her curls upon her head. When she joined him, he was glad to see that some color had returned to her fair skin, but he did not compliment her on how pretty she looked. He took a sip of his tea and insisted she try hers as well. "I have no idea when we'll have time to eat lunch, so at least drink your tea, even if you don't want an orange." When Angelique picked up a slice of orange and peeled it carefully before taking a bite, he laughed. "Must you be so fastidious? We haven't the entire morning to spend eating oranges!"

"Does nothing I do please you now?" Angelique inquired caustically.

"Well, there is one thing you do exceptionally well, but we've no time for that now either," Diego responded with a taunting leer. His dark eyes sparkled with a teasing light, which made his meaning extremely clear.

Angelique wiped her fingers upon her napkin, then tossed it aside. "I am finished then. I don't want to keep you waiting, since you seem to have so much on your mind."

Simply for spite, if for no other reason, Diego sipped his

tea slowly, and after eating one orange, he began another. "These are delicious, don't you agree?"

Exasperated, Angelique took another wedge, but after eating it, she wanted no more. The tea was good as well as hot, but the hostility of Diego's mood made it impossible for her to enjoy their meager meal. He seemed to be deliberately baiting her, hoping to start another argument, but she held her temper tightly in check. "Where do you wish to go to buy my clothes?" she finally asked.

"La Belle Mode, of course. Isn't it the best place?"

"Well yes, but . . ." Angelique scarcely knew how to tell him that she would prefer to go elsewhere. "I did ask *Madame* Larouche for work. It will be awkward to return to her shop now as a customer."

Diego studied his bride's expression for a long moment and found it surprisingly troubled. "There's no need for you to be embarrassed about anything, Angelique. My wife would hardly trade at any other establishment, for La Belle Mode is the best. *Madame* Larouche won't dare say anything to you while I'm there."

Angelique swallowed nervously. "But what can you possibly say?"

Rather than discuss the possibilities, Diego merely shrugged. "I'll think of something on the way. The shop isn't too far. Would you like to walk?"

"Why yes, if you don't mind."

"Why should I mind?" Diego responded confidently, but he soon discovered that a young man with a lovely lady dressed in black upon his arm could not move through the town without causing comment. If the young man in question also had every appearance of having been badly beaten, the curiosity aroused was more than doubled. By the time they reached La Belle Mode, he had decided he would never again go anywhere with Angelique without hiring a carriage.

Madame Larouche stepped forward as she recognized

Diego, but she was too discreet to inquire about what had happened to him. She also recognized the young woman with him, although she could not recall her name. "*Bon jour.* How nice to see you both again." She smiled warmly. "What may I do for you today?"

Drawing Angelique near, Diego smiled in his most charming fashion. "I promised to return when I located the French blonde who had bewitched me so. It seems that Angelique is a most playful kitten and knew even when we first visited you that she was the young woman for whom I was searching." Without giving the charming *couturière* time to recover from his astonishing announcement, he continued, "She is now my wife and no longer cares to wear the childish garments her mother had ordered from your shop. I would like you to make her all that a lady requires, but is there any chance you have something we could take with us today? This dreary black gown is hardly becoming and it is certainly not what a new bride wishes to wear."

Although she had been warned to expect Angelique to seek employment with her, *Madame* Larouche had not recognized this stunning blonde as that sweet child when she had come in and would have hired her had she had any openings. Knowing she was staring most rudely, she quickly recovered her manners. "We shall be pleased to make as many gowns as your bride requires, but it will take some time. However, I do believe I have a charming outfit that another patron ordered and then was unable to purchase. It might be near enough to her size for us to alter it in a day or two."

"If Angelique likes it, I'm certain you can alter it this very morning," Diego insisted calmly. "Do you permit gentlemen in your fitting rooms? I'd like to help my wife select what she needs."

"Let us use my office then," *Madame* Larouche suggested, then escorted them to her private office while she sent one of her clerks to find the garment she had mentioned. She had not realized that Diego could be such a difficult man, but now she realized that he could be extremely demanding, even if he made his requests in a charming manner. "I have your measurements in my file, but I do not believe they are accurate, *Madame* Aragon."

"I know they are not," Angelique admitted promptly. Without thinking, she turned to Diego to help her remove the stiff black dress, and while he swiftly unfastened the hooks, he noted that the proprietress had lifted a quizzical eyebrow.

"Unfortunately," he explained, "I've had no time to hire a maid for my bride, so she has come to rely upon me."

Always discreet, *Madame* Larouche pretended that gentlemen undressed her customers every day, although this was the first time such a thing had ever happened in her shop. As soon as Angelique had cast her dress upon a chair, she stepped forward with her measuring tape. "I'll take your measurements again, and then whatever you order will fit you to perfection. I guarantee it."

Taking the closest chair, Diego gave his bride a wicked grin as he announced, "We hope to have a child as soon as possible. Is there not some way to fashion my wife's gowns so that the change in her figure will not be too noticeable?"

Shocked that he would mention such a personal thing, *Madame* Larouche dropped her tape and had to measure Angelique's waist a second time. "Of course. I can make her gowns to any specifications you require."

Her face bright with embarrassment, Angelique shot her husband an accusing glance. "You must forgive Diego, *Madame* Larouche, for we are so newly married that he has not had time to adjust to it fully."

Doubting that he would ever adjust to having such a defiant beauty as his wife, Diego did no more than chuckle, but his goal had been achieved. Now when Angelique returned for additional purchases, the *couturière* would not be amazed if her condition had begun to show. "We'll need to order everything, *Madame*," he continued. "Lingerie, dresses for daytime wear, as well as more formal attire for the evenings."

"All my lingerie is still new, Diego." Angelique thought him much too extravagant and was attempting to lower the cost of her new wardrobe, but he would not hear of it.

"Nonsense. A woman can never have too much lingerie, can she?"

"Certainly not, *Monsieur*." *Madame* Larouche smiled with genuine delight, for she usually found the Spanish to be far less generous husbands than their French counterparts and she was glad to see that he was an exception.

When the clerk returned with a modest but well-tailored gown in a deep blue, Diego thought it most becoming. Fortunately, it needed little alteration and *Madame* Larouche set a girl to work on it immediately. He waited patiently while Angelique looked through dozens of swatches, but each time she asked his opinion he chose the most expensive of the fabrics, clearly wanting her wardrobe to be every bit as extensive and elegant as her mother's.

When the blue gown was brought to her, Angelique slipped it on and declared that she was ready to go. "Thank you, *Madame* Larouche. This dress is so pretty that I know it will be one of my favorites. Thank you for altering it so promptly."

"I am happy to have been able to provide it, *Madame* Aragon." She had been fascinated by the beautiful young woman all morning. While she resembled her mother slightly, she had a sparkle to her sweet personality that was entirely her own. How she could have gone so swiftly from childhood into marriage was a puzzle the woman still could not solve however. "When you return at the end of the week, we will have several things ready for fittings."

"I will be glad to pay for the most rapid service possible. Do not hesitate to hire additional seamstresses if they are required to complete my wife's wardrobe." Diego gave

193

Angelique a mischievous glance, as if he thought she might apply for the job of fashioning her own wardrobe, and her ready blush made him smile.

"I promise you will be pleased, *Monsieur.*" *Madame* Larouche saw the young couple out the front door of her shop, then hurried to the back room to summon the women to begin working on the huge order.

The day was mild and Angelique felt so much better having an attractive new gown to wear. She took Diego's arm and wondered what he had planned. "Do you want to return to your ship now? As I recall, you were not anxious to spend much time on my wardrobe."

Having found it impossible to maintain his anger while watching his pretty bride pose in her lace-trimmed lingerie, Diego saw no point in pretending he was still mad at her. "No, I want to take you to meet my Aunt Margarita. If my cousin Miguel is home, then he'll be happy to meet you too."

"Can we walk to their home?" Angelique inquired with exaggerated politeness, determined to show manners as good as his.

"No, but it is possible to rent a carriage in the next block." Diego took her arm and they walked to the stable where he had occasionally hired horses. The owner, a heavy-set man with a smile as wide as his girth, took one look at him and exclaimed with real sorrow, but the young man wanted no such show of sympathy. "Yes, I know how I look, Carlos, but a few bruises will not prove fatal. Now, my wife and I will require a carriage and driver for the rest of the day. Can you supply them?"

"*Señora* Aragon!" Carlos made a low bow and his eyes widened in astonishment. "You are full of surprises today, *Señor* Aragon!"

Since Diego had found that smiling had been particularly painful that morning, he did no more than remind the inquisitive man of the purpose of their visit. "The carriage, Carlos?"

"Ah yes, of course. You will excuse me for a moment, *Señora?*"

Angelique nodded slightly and the man left to attend to their needs. "What a friendly soul he is!" she remarked in a whisper so Carlos would not overhear.

"Aren't tradesmen usually friendly with you?" Diego asked casually. He was very pleased with the dress *Madame* Larouche had provided, since the blue complimented her eyes so beautifully and the high-waisted style was perfect for the elegance of her slender figure. He knew Carlos had been sincere in the warmth of his greeting, for she was a rare beauty and it was unlikely that he saw such women frequently.

"I am not used to dealing with any tradespeople," Angelique explained readily. Indeed she had had a great deal of difficulty traversing the city looking for work because she had not known who to approach for directions. Knowing that she appeared to be an extremely young widow, she had relied upon nicely dressed women she had passed on the sidewalk and had found them usually accurate in their reports of where establishments devoted to fashion could be found.

"No, I don't suppose you are," Diego mused thoughtfully. "You'll have a lot to learn about running a home, I fear."

Angelique had never given orders to servants. Her mother had always seen to that chore. "Won't you employ a housekeeper to manage the house and servants for me?" she asked hesitantly.

Where he would find a competent housekeeper Diego could not imagine. "Perhaps my aunt can recommend someone to us. She has a large staff." When Carlos returned with the carriage, Diego gave the driver the directions to his aunt's home, then sat back to enjoy the ride while Angelique moved toward the window to gaze out. "Don't you ever tire of sightseeing?" he asked with a chuckle. "I don't believe it is considered proper for a young woman to hang out the window like that."

"I am most certainly not hanging out the window!" Angelique responded fiercely, but she made a move to strike a more discreet pose. "Barcelona is an interesting city. Why shouldn't I wish to see it?"

"Perhaps you'd like to ride beside the driver? That would provide you with an even better view," Diego teased.

"No, thank you!" Angelique turned away, happy to concentrate upon the passing scene rather than on her husband's taunting remarks. She feared he might never again treat her sweetly and was nearly in tears over that painful possibility by the time they arrived at his aunt's home.

"Margarita is a widow, and a very proper one. Perhaps we should have brought that black dress along. She might have been able to wear it."

"I doubt she'd wish to, Diego. It was far more sensible for us to leave it with *Madame* Larouche. At least she can take it apart and use the fabric for something else."

"You're probably right." Diego escorted his bride to the door of his aunt's home and bent down to whisper, "I will expect you to let me do the talking again, please."

Angelique nodded, for she had no idea what to tell the woman about her nephew's sudden marriage. She wondered how many close relatives Diego had whom he would wish to visit and prayed he had few. She was terribly nervous and certain that it would have been expected that he would wait several years before taking a bride, and then marry a young Spanish woman from a family as prominent as his own. She lifted her chin proudly, knowing that despite her current lack of resources she was as fine a bride as any he could have hoped to have. But still she was afraid she would not be welcomed into his family when his father might have already sent everyone word about her. To her immense relief, however, Margarita was so charming she beamed with pride as she welcomed them to her home.

"That Diego should have chosen to wed with such haste does not surprise me, Angelique, but what are your plans? Are you staying with José Luis?"

Diego had brushed aside her solicitous remarks about his appearance, not admitting that his own father had given him such a brutal beating. "No, we're staying on board *El Diablo* for the time being. I will need to see to a more suitable home, however, as soon as possible. Perhaps you could assist us in hiring servants. I doubt that any of my father's could be convinced to come with me."

"They know you too well, is that it?" Margarita asked perceptively. "Well, no matter. Simply let me know how many you will require and I will see that honest and industrious servants are located. Until you have your own home, though, will you not accept my hospitality? Your ship is no place for a honeymoon and this house is so large that no one will disturb you."

Diego glanced over at Angelique and sensed her reluctance to accept such an invitation, though he thought it was a splendid idea. She would be able to meet suitable friends through his aunt, and he would be able to enjoy his customary privacy on board his ship.

Rather than risk appearing too eager to accept her offer, he paused as though he were giving it careful thought. "I had no intention of asking such a favor of you, Aunt. I hope you will not think that's why we came here today."

"No, of course not. You have come simply to give me this wonderful news. I know that. I am sorry Miguel will not be home until dinner, but you will stay to see him, won't you? If I cannot convince you to bring your bride here, surely he will be able to do so."

Diego turned toward Angelique and none of the hostility that had existed between them that morning was evident as he spoke to her. "I would like very much to accept my aunt's invitation. Why don't you rest this afternoon while I go to fetch our belongings."

Angelique was suddenly suspicious that this had been Diego's intention all along. She was saddened that he had not confided in her, but she knew she could not argue with him without appearing to be most ungracious and she replied, "I am overwhelmed. I did not expect such an invitation any more than you did, Diego, but I am very happy to accept it." She smiled at Margarita but was grateful when, after the midday meal, the friendly woman showed her to a suite of rooms and left her alone to rest. Diego did not come upstairs with them but left immediately to attend to his errands.

The two adjoining bedrooms were spacious and as elegantly furnished in dark woods and opulent velvets as her room in José Luis's home had been. The decor of one room was more masculine, however, and the other sweetly feminine. For a reason Angelique could not explain, she chose what was clearly the room meant for her husband and, after removing her new gown and slips, she climbed into the high bed and went to sleep. She had become more confused as the day had progressed, but she was so tired that she slept without dreaming until Diego's warm breath awakened her. He had done no more than drop his possessions in the center of the floor before he had peeled off his clothing and joined her. He leaned down to kiss her cheeks lightly and was pleased to find she awakened quickly.

"You're a bold one, *Señora* Aragon. Is this the room you want? Or did you simply plan to share mine?" He gave her no time to answer but slipped his tongue between her lips for a kiss he continued until she raised her arms to encircle his neck. He then let his fingertips wander slowly down her superb figure, pushing aside her remaining lingerie and seeking ever greater intimacy until she could scarcely breathe in the face of the deep pleasure filling her lithe body.

She fascinated him still, and had he not found her already

in his bed, he would have put her there promptly. The brief hours they had been apart had seemed an eternity and he was drunk with desire. His need for her was desperate now and he could spend no more time rendering playful affection when he wanted so much more.

As he moved to possess her fully, she welcomed his deep thrusts with an enticing grace that swiftly drove him beyond the limits of his considerable endurance and he abandoned himself to the wave of ecstasy that swept through him with raging splendor. His bride was a wanton mistress of such exceptional skill that, when at last he could again think clearly, he propped his head on his elbow and asked, "You were either born solely to make love, or your mother taught you the art you display with such virtuosity. Which is it?"

That Diego would again mention her mother sent a bright flash of anger burning through Angelique. "You still don't believe me, do you? You think I was merely following my mother's directions when what we had was too perfect to have been planned by any hand but God's."

Diego threw back his head and laughed out loud. "Oh no! If it was not your mother, then it was the devil himself who gave you to me!"

"You bastard!" Angelique shrieked as she raised her hand to wipe the smirk from his face.

He caught her wrist in a painful grip and pulled her to him. "I am no bastard, Angelique, and due to absolutely no effort on your part, our child won't be either!" He ended her defiance with a savage kiss that left her too shaken to hurl further insults when he finally left the bed to dress for dinner.

Chapter XII

Miguel Rivera called excitedly to his mother as he rushed through the front door and strode down the wide entrance hall of their spacious home. He dashed toward the parlor, expecting to find her alone. "Wait until you hear what's happened to Diego!" he shouted, but finding his cousin and his bride seated with his mother, the young man blushed deeply with embarrassment and hastened to apologize. "Forgive me. I had no idea you two would be here."

"That is more than obvious," Margarita observed in amusement. "May I present my son, Miguel. Unfortunately he is the impetuous sort, and no amount of effort on my part has curbed that regrettable trait in the slightest." Clearly, she had a great deal of affection for her son, and her complaint was a teasing one.

Diego rose quickly to embrace his cousin and swiftly came to his defense. "Miguel is the least impulsive man I know, Aunt Margarita. Do not chastise him for being filled with enthusiasm about my marriage. I certainly am!" With his back to the ladies, he gave his young cousin a withering glance, stilling for good whatever gossip Miguel had been so anxious to relate to his mother, for he hadn't wanted Angelique to hear it.

Readily understanding Diego's unspoken command,

Miguel was only too happy to comply, though his cousin's black eye could hardly be ignored. "You look as though you were run over by a wagon. What happened?"

Diego shrugged. "A regrettable misunderstanding, which is best left forgotten. I'd much rather introduce my bride than discuss it."

Since he knew better than to pester Diego with questions he clearly wouldn't answer, Miguel approached Angelique, and, taking her hand, brought it to his lips in a greeting he believed a Frenchwoman would expect. "We met once before, but I doubt that you remember me," he told her.

"Oh, but I most certainly do remember you, Miguel," Angelique replied as she returned his inquisitive stare with a curious glance of her own. "It was at José Luis's last party, was it not?"

Enchanted by her fair beauty, Miguel held her hand a moment too long before stepping back to converse at a more acceptable distance. "Yes, it was that night, but had I known when I saw you seated near the musicians that you were such a lovely young woman rather than a pretty child, I could have danced only with you all evening."

"I don't know any of the popular dances, Miguel, so I think it is just as well you didn't invite me to be your partner."

"Then I will be delighted to provide that instruction. We could begin this very evening if you so desired," Miguel offered brightly.

Diego watched in amazement as Miguel continued his charming banter. He could scarcely believe that this was his cousin, who was usually so shy he needed hearty encouragement to say good evening to a young woman let alone invite her to dance. He also noted that Angelique was not flirting openly in response to his attention as most young ladies would. She was merely replying politely to Miguel's compliments, though her exquisite beauty was clearly intoxicating to his bashful cousin. "You had your chance to

201

amuse Angelique and missed it, Miguel. Do not make the mistake of trying to win her away from me now," he cautioned sternly.

Miguel thought his remark was surely a jest until he turned and saw that Diego's expression was deadly serious. He had had no such intention and stuttered as he made that clear, "Your . . . your bride is now my cousin too, and I was only attempting to make her feel welcome in our family."

Angelique was as astonished as Miguel by Diego's unwarranted display of jealousy. She judged Miguel to be in his early twenties, of little more than medium height, and slim rather than tall and well built. His features were even but undistinguished rather than rakishly handsome, and she doubted that he would be considered serious competition for her husband in any category, and least of all with women. She could not imagine what had inspired Diego to make such a spiteful comment and simply stared up at him, hoping he would apologize.

Sensing the mood had shifted quite unexpectedly to an uncomfortable tenseness, Margarita inquired sweetly, "Did we meet on that occasion too, Angelique? I am sorry to say I can't recall." She did remember that Françoise had had a young daughter, but she did not understand how the poised creature seated before her could ever have been mistaken for a child.

"No, I don't believe that we did. I was not with my mother and José Luis when they greeted his guests, so I met very few."

Diego's frown deepened as he wondered how Miguel had managed to be one of those fortunate few. How many of the rest of his friends had met Angelique and had thought her only a child—every last one? Finally noticing that the silence had grown strained, Diego also realized that everyone was staring at him, waiting for him to speak, but he had no idea what they expected him to say. "It is unfortunate that so few people have had the opportunity to know Angelique for the

202

remarkable young woman she truly is."

"Surely my brother must plan to see that everyone meets her now that she is your wife," Margarita suggested with a relieved smile, hoping the conversation would now turn to plans for a lavish reception.

Seeing the flash of anger that flickered in her husband's dark eyes, Angelique was remined that it was extremely unlikely that José Luis would introduce her to anyone. She wondered why he had not paid his sister a visit that day, since it would have been to his advantage to have informed her himself of his son's sudden marriage. At a loss for words, Angelique said the only acceptable thing that came to her mind. "It must be very comforting to have José Luis so near. I am an only child and I envy you, for I know I would have enjoyed having a brother."

"You still may have one, my pet, but I doubt he'll be my brother as well as yours now," Diego whispered and, seeing the color drain from his bride's cheeks, he turned to his cousin. "Have you been given any more responsibility at the bank? I know you were hoping to take over some of the commercial accounts."

Caught off guard by the question, Miguel gestured helplessly while he gathered his thoughts. "It is a far more complex business than I had anticipated, Diego. My training is not yet complete."

Angelique dug her fingernails into her palms to force back her tears. Diego's message had been clear: she was not to speak of his father even in passing. And she could see that his hatred of her mother was barely disguised. She heard little of the rest of the conversation that went on around her, and, during dinner, she concentrated solely upon eating with a steady hand so no one would notice how badly she was trembling. She did not understand what she was to do or say, for her husband had rebuked Miguel when she had spoken to him and when she had tried to make polite conversation with his aunt, he had interrupted most rudely before the woman could respond. She was hurt and angry with him, and wished they were returning to his ship rather than remaining in his aunt's home, where he apparently wished her to hide the truth about their marriage.

She glanced over at Miguel then, but looked away quickly when she saw that he was simply staring at her with rapt attention while pretending to be listening to his mother. She wondered what he had heard that he had been so anxious to reveal. José Luis's servants would be certain to gossip, but how could their tales have reached Miguel's ears so quickly?

Diego tasted no more of the meal than Angelique did, so occupied was he in keeping the topic of conversation away from their marriage. His aunt repeatedly returned to the subject of a reception and he was fast running out of diversions. He did not want his aunt to hear the reason for their hasty marriage from his father, nor did he want to give Miguel the opportunity to speak with her alone. Frustrated at every turn, he was greatly relieved when Angelique excused herself shortly after they had finished dining. He watched the graceful sweep of her skirt as she left the parlor with her usual light step and, satisfied that she would go straight to his room, he turned an accusing glance upon his cousin. "How did you hear of our marriage?"

"Your father came into the bank this morning. He took me aside and told me that you two were married. How else would I have learned of it?"

"Is that all he told you, just that we had wed?" Diego asked suspiciously.

Miguel shrugged. "What more should he have said?"

Diego tossed down the last of his brandy and rose to his feet, grateful to have an opportunity to speak more freely at last. "Françoise wove a web of lies so thick that it nearly suffocated Angelique, and I'll not let anyone else make her suffer now. There is no more to the story except to say we are married. There will be no reception, Aunt, nor do we wish one. You are bound to hear gossip. Many people might come to you seeking the details of what they will assume is the most titillating of scandals, but I want you to send them away without comment. The flaws in my character are well known. They will have to be enough to satisfy the more imaginative of our friends, for I'll make anyone who dares to insult Angelique extremely sorry he's done so."

Her eyes growing wide, Margarita gasped out sharply, "What are you threatening, Diego—to challenge men to a duel over the question of your wife's honor?"

"It would be a pleasure," Diego boasted with a wide grin, surprised to find the thought strangely exhilarating.

"Then I will see that anyone possessing so few manners as to approach me with questions about your marriage shall be sent away promptly!" the badly shaken woman promised sincerely.

When Diego glanced in his direction, Miguel nodded emphatically. "I'll not ask any questions myself; nor will I speculate upon the answers with others. You can trust us both, Diego. You must know that. But your appearance speaks for itself. Your father did that to you, didn't he?"

Diego's eyes narrowed slightly and his reluctance to respond to the question was obvious. Although the situation was a most awkward one, he again decided to simply ignore it. "I've been in plenty of fist fights in my day. With whom or over what this last one occurred doesn't matter. The only important thing is that I brought Angelique here to meet you. I hoped that at least two of my relatives would choose to defend her reputation if the need should arise. Can I depend upon you for that?"

Margarita smoothed out the soft folds of her black skirt as she rose. "I wish you had told me the truth this morning, Diego, for I do not want to appear to be taking sides against José Luis."

"We will leave in the morning then," Diego offered calmly. "I had not meant to force you to take sides against your own brother."

Because the whole matter was still deeply puzzling, Margarita decided that Diego and his bride should remain with her for the time being. "No, you are most welcome here, for were your dear mother alive, I am certain that you and Angelique would have had a most proper courtship and wedding. I will do my best to take her place now and see that appearances are as they should be."

"Were my mother alive, Aunt, Françoise would not have been living in my father's home and I would never have met Angelique." The pain of that sudden realization was so great that Diego promptly excused himself and took the wide stairs leading to the second floor two at a time, leaving his aunt and cousin alone to ponder the plethora of problems his hasty marriage would surely inflict on them all.

Angelique was still dressed in the new blue gown and was seated in his room near a lamp. Diego saw that she was reading from the book of poems by Sister Inez that he had given her. When she stood up to greet him, a sheet of paper fluttered to the floor and he reached down to retrieve it for her. Unfolding it, he was surprised to find that it was the sketch of the devilfish he had given her. "Why did you keep this?" he asked with an amused chuckle.

"I needed something to mark my place," Angelique replied coolly. She would not reveal that she treasured it because he had made the drawing for her. "I hope you don't mind my sitting in here. The light is better than in the other room."

Though perplexed by her reserved tone, Diego did not doubt that he was the cause. "It will be difficult for us to face others if we can't be honest with ourselves, Angelique."

"What is that remark supposed to mean?" Angelique retorted as she replaced the folded drawing in the small leather-bound volume, then slammed it shut. "I don't believe I heard you say a single honest word all evening!"

206

"There is a great difference between concealing the truth and telling lies. Don't ever make the mistake of calling me a liar, my dear." Diego slipped off his coat and tossed it upon the chair she had been using.

"Or what? You'll make me walk the plank?" Angelique asked defiantly.

"Hardly. It is not an effective punishment when a ship is in port. You'd be too close to shore to risk any danger other than merely getting wet." He thought her suggestion was extremely witty, however, and could not suppress his deep laughter.

"This is all some sort of hilarious joke to you, isn't it?" Angelique was careful to keep her voice low, but her tone was vicious all the same. "From what I've seen, you've lived your whole life exactly as you've pleased, and now you think you can continue in the same reckless fashion without the slightest regard for what happens to me!" She tossed the small book aside, as if she were demonstrating how casually he had treated her that evening. "Is this what I can expect from you? That you will be jealous of every man who speaks to me? That you will prevent me from carrying on even the most innocent conversation with anyone?"

The heightened color that anger gave her delicate features was so flattering that Diego was tempted to let her insult him until she grew tired of the effort, though he doubted that she ever would. "I had never seen Miguel behave in such a bold manner, and I wanted it stopped. And my father's name is the last one I want mentioned around me, as there is no way I can make any civil comments about the way he has treated us. Discuss whatever you wish with Margarita, as long as it isn't him."

"Or the reason for our marriage?"

Diego eyed her suspiciously. "Or that as well."

"Or my mother?" Angelique continued with a fiery glance.

"What could you possibly wish to say about her?" Diego

207

was growing tired of her game. He continued to undress, hoping that she would swiftly realize it was not an argument he was after.

"You understand nothing about her, Diego, absolutely nothing." Angelique took several steps away before she turned back to face him. "Did you know that the maniacs who control the government of France put to death women whose only crime was that they made the lace that adorned our clothing? The fact that my father was one of the nobles who supported the first efforts to write a constitution would not have saved our lives any more effectively than his politics saved his. If it is the truth you demand, the honesty that should exist between a man and his wife, then I'll tell you now that our name is not really Devereau. That is merely my mother's maiden name, which she adopted as a convenient alias. As my father's widow, she is still a countess, although she dares not use that title here in Spain for fear we both might be kidnapped and returned to France, where such a show of pride would surely cost us our lives.

"My father was a close relative of Louis XVI. Had my mother and I been captured as we fled the country, the crowds surrounding the *guillotine* would have worked themselves into a joyous frenzy while watching us die. Though other *émigrés* fled to Great Britain or to Germany, my mother chose to come here, where she had relatives to protect us. She hoped that here we would be able to enjoy the peace we had once known in our homeland. Were she not such a tenacious woman, or a 'conniving bitch,' as you call her, we would both be dead! I am not ashamed to be her child, but quite proud of that fact!"

That his bride had been so closely related to the royal family who had been slaughtered in the French people's fight for independence sickened Diego totally. He could not bear to think of her being in any danger whatsoever, let alone such mortal peril as she had described. Yet he could not reconcile his opinion of her mother's continually selfish behavior with the heroic view Angelique held of the woman. Knowing it would be futile to debate such an issue since it could never be settled, he extended his arms and called softly to his bride, "Come here to me, Angelique. Just come to me." When she did not argue but rushed into his arms with a strangled sob, he lifted her clear off her feet in a joyous hug. "No one will ever hurt you again, Angelique. I promise you that."

He covered her damp cheeks with sweet kisses before capturing her trembling lips in a kiss he extended until he felt the last tremor of fear leave her slender body. She was the most splendid of women. Her lush curves fit against his lean frame so perfectly that he longed to hold her in his arms forever, and yet this tender closeness was not nearly enough. Stepping back, he regarded her deep blush with a ready grin. "If you do not remove that dress at once, I am going to rip it off you and—"

"You need not say more, Diego, for I understand exactly what you mean." Angelique's eyes never left his as she peeled away her many layers of clothing, yet she moved with seductive ease, not haste. She tossed each garment playfully aside, then, completely nude, she stepped back into his arms.

Diego covered the pale skin of her throat with lavish kisses, then slowly sinking down upon his knees, he caressed the fullness of her breasts as she wound her fingers in his hair to hold him close. He pressed his cheek against the smooth flesh of her stomach and wondered when the tiny life within would make its presence known. He knew her figure would still be every bit as magnificent even when swollen with the weight of his child.

His lips went then to the enticing triangle of blonde curls and his tongue sought the delights they hid until she could no longer stand within his embrace. He swiftly carried her to his bed then, but he did not stop his tantalizing kisses until his tongue had conquered the last tremble of her resistance and he had tasted the rich, warm essence of her being.

Understanding that this exotic surrender brought her tremendous pleasure, he wanted her to enjoy it to the fullest before he took his own. He trailed playful nibbles up the tender flesh of her thighs, then lost himself again in the delicious rush that flowed from deep within her lithe body to offer a generous welcome for his.

When she opened her eyes, the thick sweep of her lashes issued a sultry invitation that he readily accepted. He slipped out of the last of his clothes and, lost in the warmth of her loving embrace, he swiftly forgot they had solved none of their problems but had only postponed them to revel in a haze of sensations that would soon lift and leave them as troubled as before. But with his delectable bride cradled in his arms, Diego no longer cared what unforeseen dilemmas the new day might bring.

Having been awakened early by her reoccurring illness, Angelique did not return to Diego's bed until she felt well. Snuggling close, she kissed the bruise on his chin, then let her lips tease his until he began to stir. She found his earlobes delicious, but as his arms tightened around her waist, she slipped free. "Do not be so impatient," she cautioned with a saucy giggle, and when her bright curls tumbled across his flat stomach, Diego grew tense with anticipation, delighted by the way she planned to have him greet the day.

She had learned swiftly how to please him with abundant affection more lavish than any he had ever known. He had met many women, some with expert techniques offered at high prices, but all lacked any hint of warmth in their touch. Angelique, however, was like a goddess compared to them, far superior in brightness of spirit and richness of beauty. Her magical touch aroused his emotions to a fevered peak before her deeply erotic kiss filled him with a radiance that outshone the brightness of the sun flooding through the windows and bathing the spacious bedroom in light.

Paradise could provide no pleasure to surpass the one she gave him, he thought exultantly, but as the rapture burst from his loins, he could only call her name, for all his other pretty compliments were swept away on a tide of ecstasy.

While Angelique knew she had showered Diego with happiness, her own need for his affection brought her real physical pain in the form of a searing flame that spread from deep within her, demanding to be quenched. She moved against him, and her gesture was far too enticing to be mistaken for anything other than the obvious desire it was. Eagerly, he pulled her slender body atop his own. He wrapped his arms around her waist and pressed her hips to his as he kissed her with a slow, easy passion that answered her unspoken plea in a fashion far more eloquent than words. He wanted her still. Again and again he wanted to share the wonders a man and woman could create within each other, with all the fascinating variations imagination could provide. It was all so new with her, so splendid, and as he began to make love to her, he moved with exaggerated tenderness, slowly penetrating the depths of her lissome body and taking great satisfaction in knowing that no other man would ever possess the treasure of her love. Only he knew the secrets hidden behind her exotic blue gaze, and he planned to keep them forever as his own.

He moved with lazy precision to draw her slowly to the edge of rapture, then lay still within her as he hesitated, his lips enjoying the softness of her breasts before he unleashed the power that carried them both aloft on wings of pleasure so graceful, he thought they might never again descend to earth. She was an enchantress who continually amazed him, not only with the beauty of her affection, but with the boundless joy he had discovered in pleasing her. They lay in his bed, too content to rise, until Diego realized he was becoming very spoiled and forced himself to sit up.

"While I would rather lie here with you into the far reaches of eternity, my pet, I do have a ship that requires a captain and various other interests that will soon prove unprofitable if I do not give them at least a few moments of my attention today."

Angelique was in far too tranquil a mood to argue, but there was one question that still weighed heavily upon her mind. "I had no opportunity to ask you this yesterday, Diego, but did you bring me here thinking we would stay with your aunt for awhile?"

"No," Diego responded truthfully. "I wanted only for my aunt and cousin to meet you, but her invitation was such a thoughtful one, I knew I'd be a fool to refuse it. You can't complain about this bed being too narrow, now can you?"

Indeed the massive four-poster bed was enormous, and Angelique began to laugh at his teasing grin. Her husband could be so wonderfully charming at times that she wished they never had to disagree on any matter, since arguments always caused them both such grief. "What did you tell your aunt after I left you last night?"

Diego moved off the bed as he replied, "No more than what you heard me tell her. We are married, and there is nothing more to say."

Angelique soon learned that he was mistaken, however, for that very afternoon his aunt had no fewer than half-a-dozen callers who, while appearing surprised to learn that Diego had married, had obviously come only to meet his bride. How they had learned where to locate her she could not guess, but she found being stared at so openly a most unsettling experience. She had no gift for making amusing conversation out of nothing, as her mother did, but clearly the friends of Margarita expected her to display some unique qualities since Diego had chosen to marry her rather than one of their daughters. She knew she was attractively dressed and groomed, and her manners could not be faulted, but when the last of the visitors had finally said good-bye, she was greatly relieved.

"I fear they were only the first of what may prove to be a

long succession of callers, Angelique," Margarita mused thoughtfully. "I should have expected such curiosity and asked my cook to bake more pastries, but I hadn't thought anyone would have learned of your marriage so soon. My brother must be doing his best to see that everyone is informed."

"Why would he wish to do that?" Angelique asked innocently.

"He can scarcely do otherwise, now can he? I think that despite Diego's insistence that there be no reception, we will be forced to have one. It would be far better to satisfy everyone's curiosity about you at one time than be faced with inquisitive visitors for months. Personally, I feel my brother showed extremely poor judgment in not insisting that you and Diego announce your engagement at a party and wait at least until the banns could be read, as is customary before getting married. This is all too confusing." Margarita was not nearly as unintelligent as she was trying to appear. She was hoping that by this ploy she could gain Angelique's confidence and learn everything that Diego was clearly loath to tell.

Angelique simply stared at the woman who had suddenly become her aunt, trying frantically to think of some reasonable explanation to give her for not having a reception, for that would surely be even more embarrassing than having a few callers each afternoon had proved to be. Finally seizing upon what she had told Diego about her mother's fears the previous evening, she leaned forward to whisper, "My mother does not wish to attract any attention whatsoever. You know we are *émigrés*. Our existence is a precarious one, and while we seem to be safe here in Spain, we may still be in grave danger."

"What?" Margarita was fascinated by this shocking news. "Surely you do not expect to be hunted down here in Spain?"

"It could happen, or we could be kidnapped and held for ransom. There is a price on our heads in France."

Coming through the door, Diego caught only the last bit of the conversation and cried out in dismay, "Whatever are you telling my aunt, Angelique?"

Angelique leapt to her feet without thinking of propriety and ran to give him a warm hug and light kiss. "I have missed you," she whispered.

"So I can see, but what is this about kidnappings?" Diego led her back to the chair and stood by her side as he awaited her response.

"Your aunt had several callers this afternoon," Angelique began.

"Several I had not seen in months," Margarita explained. "It was more than obvious that they came here to meet your bride, and I still think a formal reception would be the best idea despite the haste of your wedding. I cannot forgive your father for forgetting to attend to such an important detail."

Now understanding why Angelique had mentioned kidnapping, Diego decided it was a brilliant excuse. "My bride is correct, Aunt. Were we to host a large reception, there might be those who attended who could foolishly mention Angelique's maiden name to a casual acquaintance. We are wealthy, and her position as one of the French nobility is, unfortunately, still a vulnerable one. No, I'm afraid having a reception would be too great a risk to take."

"Well, why didn't you tell me last night?" Margarita demanded. "Then this is the reason for the secrecy that surrounded your wedding as well, isn't it?"

Angelique looked up at Diego, sorry that what had seemed a small lie had grown to such impossible proportions. He caught her glance and understood that their plight was becoming increasingly complicated. "The world is filled with danger, and while I did not mind confronting it as a bachelor, I'll not risk my wife's life for any reason."

"Yes, you are right of course, Diego." Margarita frowned in concentration. "You speak our language well, child, but everyone can see that you are not of Spanish blood. How am

I to protect you here adequately with the staff I employ? Do you think additional men should be hired?"

"No. We are all quite safe here. I am certain of it." Diego tried to steer the conversation to more pleasant matters, but he could see that his aunt was fascinated with the possibility that Angelique might be kidnapped at any moment. He felt now that he had made a grave error in accepting her hospitality, when it had only served to whet her curiosity about them rather than quell it. But he could scarcely move his bride elsewhere without causing still more gossip. When they went upstairs to their rooms to prepare for dinner, he pulled Angelique into his arms and held her close. "Is this how a small lie grows to be a large one? Despite your mother's fears, I have not heard of any *émigré* being kidnapped, Angelique. You are not really worried about such a thing happening, are you?"

"Not any more, I'm not." Angelique snuggled against him, for she needed his reassuring strength greatly. "I tried to be polite to Margarita's friends who came to call this afternoon, but they stared at me so intently and I could give them no answers that made any sense when they asked about our wedding. When your aunt suggested it would be better to face everyone at a reception, the threat of kidnapping was the only excuse I could provide to dissuade her from the idea."

"Well, it certainly is an imaginative one." Diego rested his cheek upon the top of her head and closed his eyes. "As I told you, she is a very proper lady, one who thinks the rules of polite society should be strictly observed. I just hope she has given up on the idea of hosting a party for us, as there would be a flood of questions when my father failed to attend. I doubt your mother would come either."

Angelique chewed her lower lip nervously to keep from speculating upon what her mother might do. "Do you think they'll still get married?" she finally asked in a breathless whisper.

"I don't know, and frankly I don't care. It's their business, but with the stand my father has taken, I doubt he'd invite us to the ceremony."

Angelique stepped back so she could look up at her husband. "Is this what we'll have to face, Diego? First one scandal and then another? Will all your relatives choose sides and gossip about us? Won't we be able to make any friends?"

The fear that filled his bride's eyes was far more real than that which he had seen when she had mentioned the threat of kidnapping, and Diego tried to assure her that they could survive any amount of gossip without injury. "I have always received plenty of invitations, Angelique, and I will take you everywhere you wish to go. When we have our own home, we can entertain as often as you like. When people see for themselves what a lovely lady you are, the gossip will die a quick death. It will be assumed I was simply too, well too . . ."

"Too impetuous?" Angelique teased playfully.

Diego had been tempted to admit to far more than being impetuous, but he readily agreed with her choice of words. "Yes, impetuous. They'll think I simply saw a woman I wanted and married her before any other man had the chance. Now cease to worry over what anyone thinks about us, Angelique. We know the truth." He pulled her back into his arms, where she could not fail to understand how close he wanted them to be. He had accomplished little that day, for he had found himself constantly dreaming about her, and he could wait no longer to savor the delights of her affection again. "Have you no idea why I returned here so early?" he asked with a teasing chuckle.

He was holding her hips pressed so tightly to his that Angelique had not the slightest difficulty in guessing the correct answer. Her hand slid beneath his belt with a tantalizing caress as she replied, "Why don't you just show me."

Angelique could appear first as a demure child and now as an elegant lady, while her heart was as wild as that of the most exotic seductress, and this delightful diversity was only one of the many secrets Diego planned to keep about his bride. He responded readily to her charming, if shockingly direct, invitation and carried her rapidly to the bed.

After hastily flinging off their constraining clothing, he released every bit of the fiery passion she aroused within him. This time Diego took her with a savage swiftness that left them both dazed by the intensity of the attraction existing between them, for it seemed to grow stronger each time their lips met. Each kiss, each caress, was merely the prelude to the paradise they had discovered together. Bound by pleasure, they lay nestled in the sumptuous bed, and neither dared to give voice to the joy they shared, for both knew that words could never accurately describe the glorious emotion that filled their hearts.

Chapter XIII

On Angelique's seventeenth birthday, Diego asked his aunt's cook to prepare a special dinner and dessert in her honor. When he escorted her into the dining room, she found the table set with the finest linens, silver, crystal, and china that Margarita owned. A fragrant bouquet of pink roses and a brightly wrapped present sat at her place. Thrilled by his thoughtfulness, she turned to kiss him even before she had opened his gift. "Oh, thank you, Diego. Thank you!" She hugged him tightly, delighted that he had wanted to celebrate her birthday.

"I'd not allow such an important event to go unobserved. Happy birthday, my pet. Now open my present and tell me what you think of it." Diego saw that she was seated comfortably, then took his place by her side. His aunt was smiling warmly, but he was disappointed by his cousin's woebegone expression. "Is there something the matter, Miguel?"

"No, of course not," the embarrassed young man replied. "It is only that, had I known, I would have bought Angelique a present too," he finished regretfully.

As she untied the pink ribbon bow, Angelique looked up and, distressed by his sorrowful mood, remarked brightly, "You needn't buy me presents, Miguel. This one is the only one I need." Finding what was unmistakably a jeweler's box beneath the silver paper, she paused to give her husband an inquiring glance. "I hope you were not too extravagant."

"I am always extravagant, Angelique!" Diego leaned over to give her a playful hug, but he thought her continual concern for the state of his finances highly amusing. "Now open the box so everyone may see what I bought for you."

Wanting to savor the moment, Angelique raised the lid of the rectangular wooden box slowly, as if it held some wonderful treasure. When she found a stunningly beautiful sapphire and diamond pendant with matching earrings nestled upon a white satin pillow, she nearly let the box slip from her hands. "Oh, Diego, these are exquisite, but far too expensive a gift for me."

"My cousin is rich!" Miguel scoffed in a mournful voice. "Half the money in our bank is his!"

"And the other half is my father's," Diego joked easily. "Now please accept my gifts without complaint, or I shall think you don't like them."

"I love them." Angelique's voice grew husky as she attempted to thank him properly. "It is only that I did not expect anything so marvelous. These jewels must be worth a fortune and—"

Chuckling at her worries, Diego refused to let her continue. "Would you please listen to Miguel. I really am secure financially, and if I wish to give my wife sapphires for her birthday every year I'll do it. Now put them on so I may see how they look with your eyes. If they are not precisely the right shade of blue, then I'll send them back and get others."

"Oh, you wouldn't take them back!" Angelique cried, the bright blue of her eyes becoming even more vivid in the reflection of her unshed tears.

"You do like them then?" Diego teased. He lifted the necklace from the box and when Angelique turned he draped it gently around her throat and carefully fastened the catch. He waited while she put on the earrings, but after giving the effect of the sparkling jewels his full concentration for a moment, he had to admit that on a young woman this beautiful they would probably go unnoticed. The blue of the sapphires was the perfect hue, however, and his smile widened to a rakish grin. "Fortunately, the color of the stones is perfect, so, if you like my gift, we'll keep them."

Touching the gleaming necklace with a fond caress, Angelique reassured him once again. "I love them. Thank you so much." When he leaned over, she gave his cheek a light kiss, then she returned to her pose of a very proper lady while they dined. She smiled and complimented Diego on his selections for the menu, but while the dinner was delicious and his aunt in a festive mood, she noted that Miguel continued to frown mournfully, obviously deeply distressed that he had no present to give her.

By the time they reached Diego's room that night, Angelique had grown curious about his cousin. "Is Miguel Margarita's only child?"

"No. He has three older sisters, but they do not reside here in Barcelona. He was born rather late in my aunt and uncle's marriage, so he was raised more or less as an only child, as I was."

"They must have been thrilled to have a son at last," Angelique mused thoughtfully. "He's nothing like you though, is he?"

Diego chuckled at the comparison. "No, indeed he is not. My uncle was a very conservative sort. That's what made him a success as a banker. He wouldn't risk a penny of his own money, nor any of his depositors', in poor investments. Miguel is doing his best to follow in his father's footsteps, but I don't think he has any talent for working with figures or with people, and it is difficult for him."

"Then perhaps he should pursue some other career." Angelique sat down upon the edge of Diego's bed as she removed the sparkling necklace and earrings. "He doesn't seem very happy. At least he wasn't tonight."

Diego sat down beside Angelique and pulled her into an easy embrace. "My cousin has a far more sensitive nature than I do. He's very fond of you and was sorry he didn't have a present for you, but it isn't really his place to give them. I'll speak to him in the morning before I leave, as I certainly don't want him running out to buy you anything tomorrow either."

"I think he was embarrassed enough this evening, Diego. Please don't make it any worse for him."

"Oh, I see. You do want other men to shower you with presents!" Diego stated in a teasing manner.

"No, I am more than satisfied with yours. It was sweet of you to remember my birthday."

"Sweet?" Diego laughed out loud at the term. "Don't you recall that this day had rather special significance for us?"

Confused, Angelique thought a moment, then asked hesitantly, "Do you mean because I'd promised to move out of your father's house today?"

Diego nodded and his grin was now a most satisfied one. "You would have been mine beginning today anyway, and I'd have given you those dazzling sapphires as a present. I had meant to make your life a very good one, Angelique. Truly I had."

That he would wish to recall this unflattering arrangement now that they were married hurt Angelique deeply, and she did not respond but continued to study the sparkling necklace and earrings she held in her hands. Their design was delicate, the diamonds set in platinum above the suspended sapphires, and she knew she had never seen any jewels as exquisitely mounted as these. But knowing that Diego would have given them to her as a mistress was disappointing. Obviously the fact that they were married meant nothing special to him, while it meant a great deal to her.

Diego didn't know what he had done wrong, though he could clearly see that Angelique's mood was not the

221

agreeable one he had hoped to create. He slid his fingertip down her cheek slowly, and when she turned toward him he smiled. "I'm not sorry that we're married. Are you?" he asked perceptively.

Angelique's thick sweep of dark lashes made shadows upon her cheeks as she glanced away. She was sorry he had been forced to marry her and that the idea had not been his own, but she loved him too dearly to regret that they were together, no matter what the reason. "No, I'm not sorry," she replied softly. "Not at all." She rose then and carried the jewels into her room to put them away, but she returned to his room as she did each night, and there was no hint of sorrow in her kiss as she began to thank him again for his generous present.

When it became plain that Margarita's numerous acquaintances would continue to flock to her home to meet his pretty young bride, Diego began returning from his ship in time to take her out for a ride or to do some shopping so she would not be at home when his aunt's inquisitive callers arrived. Although they received many invitations, he politely refused them all until La Belle Mode had completed the first of the many stylish gowns he had ordered for his bride. He was perplexed to discover, however, that while Angelique desperately wanted to make friends with his numerous relatives and acquaintances, she was terrified of attending the very parties where she could meet them. While he assured her that her manners and conversation could not be faulted, she had no confidence in her ability to be simply herself, since she had had so little practice.

Diego brought Angelique's hand to his lips as he winked at her. "You have mastered the steps of every dance, my dear. Now you have no reason not to enjoy the party tonight as much as all the other guests will."

At Diego's insistence, they had spent a few minutes each

evening practicing dance steps with Miguel and his mother. Margarita had not danced in years but saw no reason not to practice a few steps in her own home if it would aid Angelique's instruction. Though the lithe blonde swiftly learned the intricate patterns and performed them with both elegance and grace, she had no faith she could remember the steps if her partner were anyone other than her husband or his cousin. "Whatever shall I do if someone else should ask me to dance, Diego? I will forget everything, step on the poor man's feet, and embarrass us both dreadfully by my clumsiness."

As Diego looked down at her, his warm brown eyes filled with amusement. "We both know what's troubling you. You've spent the last five years trying to attract as little attention to yourself as possible, but you know that at the Ventura's party tonight you'll be unable to hide in the corner with the children, which I very much hope you no longer wish to do." Taking her hand, he led her over to the full-length mirror, where he hoped she would see just how lovely she truly was. Standing behind her, he smiled as he explained, "Your gown is exquisite. The deep rose shade is the perfect compliment to your blonde hair and fair complexion. The sapphires I gave you look as though God created them solely to enhance the incredible blue of your eyes. You could not be more attractive if you were to spend another hour arranging your pretty curls. Now, tell me what else you see reflected in this mirror."

Puzzled, Angelique looked up at her husband and then back at their reflection. He was wearing a coat of royal blue trimmed with gray and a waistcoat of pale silver satin. His well-tailored dove gray breeches accentuated his height and his highly polished black boots glistened handsomely. His dark hair shown with a healthy glow, and the bruises and scrapes his father had inflicted had all healed, leaving his complexion with an even, bronze hue. The cut above his eye had left only a slight scar, a faint line that would soon vanish

223

completely. She thought what she always did—that he was simply the most splendid man ever born—and she gave him an impish smile. "Is it you I'm supposed to see?"

"Precisely. I'll not leave your side, Angelique. You need not dance with anyone but me if you'd rather not. If you grow tired, or in the least bit bored, just let me know and we will come straight home." Home to bed, he had nearly said, but thought better of being so explicit with his plans when he knew she understood exactly how the evening would end without his having to say it in words. She continually amazed him, for she gave so unselfishly of her affection that he was certain that if she had not already been pregnant when they had married, she would be by now. He slipped his arms around her narrow waist and gave her a playful squeeze. "Now I'll encourage your vanity no further. Let's see if Miguel and my aunt are ready to go." He swept her out of his room and down the stairs before she had time to offer a single word of protest.

The Ventura home was an elegant structure with graceful arches and windows covered with delicate filigree reflecting Spain's Moorish past. Built around a central courtyard as José Luis's house had been, it was filled with light and laughter by the time the carriage from the Rivera home arrived. Miguel escorted his mother to the front door, but he kept looking back over his shoulder at Angelique. His admiration for her had not been diminished by the frequency with which he saw her. When he tripped and nearly fell at the entrance, Diego caught him, set him back upon his feet, and was kind enough not to laugh at him for being so distracted.

Angelique clung to Diego's arm as he introduced her to their host and hostess. She understood that the party was being given to provide their daughters, Rosalina and Maria, with the opportunity to meet suitable men, but even though

224

Diego was no longer among the ranks of the bachelors in attendance, clearly he was still welcome. After receiving an effusive greeting, which included congratulations upon their recent marriage, they walked on to meet the other guests and she whispered softly, "Does everyone like you as much as the Venturas do?"

Diego grinned at her unexpected compliment. "I certainly hope so." Seeing a small group of young men he had known all his life, he introduced them to his bride, and while their stares were very curious, none dared say anything improper. In fact, his friends were so polite that Diego was inspired to move on to another group and then another, so in less than an hour's time, Angelique had met all his friends. When the dancing began, she was swiftly surrounded by eager partners, but Diego led her out on the dance floor himself.

"You see, I knew you'd have a wonderful time here tonight." He flashed a charming grin as they drew close, but the moves of the dance gave Angelique no time to reply. She was concentrating so intently upon executing the steps properly that he doubted she had even heard his remark, though when the piece ended she surprised him by asking if they could please dance to the next tune as well. When the music began, she did not realize that this particular dance required that the women move on to new partners, but when she saw that Miguel was the next man in the line, she smiled warmly and took his hand as she bid her husband a hasty farewell. The number was a spirited one, and Diego's initial pleasure that Angelique had so swiftly overcome her reluctance to dance was soon replaced by growing frustration when he saw her swiftly surrounded by several of his friends as the dance ended. Before he could reach her side, she had accepted another man's invitation and had begun the next dance, but rather than choose a new partner himself, Diego moved to the sidelines where he watched in amazement as his shy bride smiled and laughed as if her partner's remarks were highly amusing. He thought she surely would look for him when the set was over, but this time Miguel was by her side when the music ended and he claimed her for a dance.

His cousin usually displayed little talent for dancing, but having had the benefit of having Angelique as his partner during numerous dance lessons in his home, he suddenly appeared to be one of the most proficient men on the dance floor. Not pleased by the young man's obvious infatuation with his bride, Diego found he had little alternative but to watch Miguel whirl Angelique around the room. He could only reflect that his warnings to Miguel about giving Angelique unnecessary attention at home were not being heeded at this public gathering. His stare was dark as he watched them move close to exchange whispers, and they did not once glance his way, which infuriated him all the more.

When the music ended, Angelique opened the fan she carried to cool her flushed cheeks. "Oh, that was wonderful, Miguel. It is much more fun to dance with you here than in your mother's parlor, but I'm afraid I must stop and rest for awhile."

Seeing several men eagerly heading their way, Miguel took her arm to lead her toward the doors that opened out onto the gardens. "Let's step outside just a moment. No one will miss us."

Grateful for the opportunity to rest, Angelique did not consider his suggestion an improper one. The night was clear, the heavens filled with sparkling stars, and as she looked up she took a deep breath of the cool air. "What a glorious night!" she exclaimed happily.

She seemed so delighted by the beauty surrounding them that Miguel moved closer as he blurted out a compliment that came from deep within his heart. "If only I had not been too great a fool to invite you to dance when we met at my uncle's house. You are so beautiful and—"

Angelique took a step backward to put more distance between them. "Miguel, I am flattered, but you mustn't ever

226

forget that I am Diego's wife." She turned back toward the party, sorry now that she had stepped outside with the young man, since he had moved so quickly to take advantage of the situation, but he caught her arm to draw her into a rude embrace. "Miguel!" she whispered hoarsely, averting her face as she attempted to avoid the sticky kiss that slid off her cheek. "Let me go!" Finally she succeeded in freeing herself from his grasp, but as she turned to flee, she found Diego blocking her way and had to halt abruptly.

"You should not have invited Angelique to come outside with you, Miguel. You see, she has a great fondness, not only for gardens but for whomever she might find in them. Isn't that true, my dear?"

Appalled by his uncalled-for insult, Angelique flashed her husband a look filled with both shock and pain. She tried to push past Diego, but he stepped to the side to block her way. "Will you excuse me please. I'd like to go back inside," she said nervously.

Offering his arm, Diego waited until Angelique had placed her fingertips tentatively upon his sleeve before he took the first step toward the open doorway. One dance had just ended and couples were taking their places for the next. "If you'd care to dance again, then I will be your partner," he remarked sternly, but before she could refuse his rudely worded invitation, the music had begun and he swept her along beside him, moving in perfect time to the lilting melody as though he enjoyed nothing as much as dancing with his gorgeous bride.

Angelique did not know which was worse, that Diego had assumed she had been flirting with Miguel or that Miguel had attempted to kiss her. She could scarcely deny that the incident had taken place, since Diego had obviously seen her in his cousin's arms. Nor could she place the blame upon Miguel, for her husband might lose his temper and give him such a severe beating that the slender youth might not recover for weeks. She attempted to smile, hoping to lighten Diego's mood, but the glances he gave her in return were dark and suspicious. He held her hand too tightly and danced with such cold precision that when the number ended she had no desire to dance with him ever again.

"Have you tired of dancing already?" he inquired sarcastically.

"No, I've simply tired of dancing with you," Angelique replied proudly and, when one of his friends appeared at her side, she accepted his invitation without giving her husband a second glance or considering how she would have to pay for such behavior when they got home.

Angered by her haughty display of willfulness, Diego danced first with Rosalina Ventura and then with her sister, Maria. The girls were pretty and their conversation not uninteresting, but his mind took in little other than his wife's stunning popularity. When the musicians paused for a break, one young man brought her a glass of wine. Many others came to stand beside her while she sipped it slowly, and soon he could see nothing more than the top of her glistening curls. When his aunt appeared at his elbow, he was so startled he jumped.

"Are you enjoying yourself, Diego?" she inquired politely.

"Of course," he replied sharply, his response a barely disguised snarl.

"It is nice that Angelique has been so warmly received, but you shouldn't let your friends lavish such attention upon her if you don't approve. She is, after all, your wife, but her conduct this evening has been more like that of a single woman. She is French though, and perhaps she does not realize what our expectations are." The petite woman cast a disapproving glance toward the circle of admirers surrounding the pretty blonde. "You should speak to her before the next party or I'm afraid her behavior will inspire unfortunate talk."

Diego considered his aunt's point well taken, but he had no desire to stand in line to dance with his own wife. He wanted her to excuse herself from his overly attentive friends and return to his side where she belonged. But he wanted her to do it of her own accord, not by his command.

As he looked about the room, he soon discovered he was not the only one watching Angelique. There seemed to be plenty of women who were eyeing her with what he recognized as undisguised jealousy, and he realized he had made a serious mistake in not introducing her to any of the nice young women there that night. She had wanted to make friends and he had promptly introduced her to all the single men present. Therefore she had swiftly made friends with them! How could he have been so stupid? "This is entirely my fault, Aunt Margarita. There are married couples here as well as single women she should know, and I failed to introduce her to any of them. She is a pretty young girl and she's never even had the opportunity to learn to dance until just recently. It is no wonder she is enjoying the attention she's receiving tonight."

"The time for a young woman to enjoy the attentions of single men is before she's married, Diego, not after," Margarita remarked primly, not understanding why he was allowing his wife to make such a spectacle of herself. "I thought we were teaching her to dance so she could dance with *you.*"

Diego had no desire to argue with his aunt, nor could he explain why he and Angelique had parted company after having danced together so briefly. Whatever had possessed Miguel to make such a fool of himself over Angelique? A man couldn't simply grab a young woman and kiss her! And most especially not another man's wife! he reflected angrily. It seemed that he needed to give his cousin lessons in how to make love, but then the fool would undoubtedly attempt to practice on Angelique and that would never do. He glanced around the crowded room, wondering if his father had sent his regrets. If he were to arrive late with Françoise, Diego had no idea how he should react. He fervently hoped they would not appear at all.

The heat generated by the exuberant dancing soon became unbearable for Angelique. She could not finish her wine but had nowhere to place the glass, so she simply held it, hoping not to spill any on the skirt of her new gown. The men clustered around her kept raising their voices to be heard above the din of the merriment of the party, but she still had considerable difficulty following the flow of their conversation. Their glances swept her figure hungrily and she thought them extremely bold, though what she could hear of their remarks seemed polite enough. She wanted only to sit down by herself in a quiet corner for a few minutes, but she did not know how she could escape from the animated group that surrounded her.

She wished she had not spoken so sharply to Diego, but she had found his sullen insult impossible to bear in silence. His unusual height permitted her to locate him easily, but he was standing on the far side of the room and appeared to have no interest in coming to her rescue. At the point of tears, she was overwhelmed with gratitude when a gentleman she had not met approached and whispered softly in her ear.

"Why don't you give me that wine, since you don't really want it?" When she handed it to him, he offered his arm. "Now come with me. I'm sure you'd rather sit down for awhile, wouldn't you?"

"Yes. Thank you so much. I really would." Angelique ignored the protests being raised by the talkative circle of young men as she left them to follow the stranger's lead. He opened a nearby door and ushered her into what appeared to be a small library. She took the seat he offered and quickly opened her fan to cover a wide yawn.

"You do not find the party amusing?" the man asked with a quizzical glance.

Using the fan to provide herself with a refreshing breeze, she admitted, "It is a lovely party, but had you not found this chair, I fear I soon might have fainted from the oppressive

230

heat. Thank you for being so thoughtful."

"You are most welcome. Allow me to introduce myself. I am Ramon Ortega, and I already know you are Angelique Aragon, the bride Diego has taken with a haste that has amazed all who know him."

She was certain it had not been difficult for Ramon to learn her name, but she did not appreciate his comment about the haste of her marriage. He seemed a few years older than her husband and was ruggedly handsome. His dark hair had a slight curl, while his eyes were an unusual gray, and she instinctively sensed they could cast a cold and forbidding gaze. Despite his helpfulness, she did not think she liked him. "Are you a friend of my husband's?"

"No," Ramon replied with a sly grin. He leaned back against the book-lined wall and crossed his arms over his chest. "Diego would never describe us as friends, although we've known each other for many years."

Puzzled by this apparent contradiction, Angelique asked cautiously, "Well then, are you mortal enemies or merely business rivals?"

"A bit of both," Ramon admitted. "Let me say only that we have similar tastes and interests and unfortunately they often conflict."

Though his confident manner might have been considered charming, Angelique found his direct glance unsettling. He had left the door wide open and was standing at a respectable distance, but she felt uneasy nonetheless. He had finished the wine left in her glass and had placed the empty goblet upon the table beside the door as they had come in, but she could not say that he appeared to have been drinking heavily. When the musicians began another tune, she thought that perhaps she had rested long enough and rose gracefully. "I think we'd better return to the party, Mr. Ortega."

"I insist that you call me Ramon."

"Ramon, then. The musicians have returned and I'd like to join the others." She took a step forward, but he did not

231

move aside to let her pass.

"Why Angelique, are you asking me to dance?" Ramon teased with a sardonic grin.

Angelique's fair complexion was already flushed, but she blushed deeply at his suggestion, since it would have been a great breach of etiquette. "No, that was not my intention at all."

"Pity." Ramon stood aside and gestured for her to precede him through the door, but they had taken only two steps when Diego appeared. "Ah, Diego, I've just been talking with your bride. She's a lovely child, but I'd have thought a man with such sophisticated tastes as yours would—"

Angelique saw Diego's expression turn from mere anger to fury and she rushed into his arms before he could silence Ramon Ortega with his fists. "There you are, darling," she purred sweetly. "I very nearly fainted from the heat and Mr. Ortega was kind enough to find me a quiet place to rest. Are you ready to go home? I certainly am," she chattered vivaciously as she pushed him back into the ballroom and this distraction gave Ramon time to disappear into the crowd before Diego could respond to his taunt.

"Please, Diego, can't we go home now?" Angelique pleaded, certain her quick action had prevented, by the barest margin, a fight that would have caused a terrible scene. The guests standing nearby were all staring at them now and she whispered insistently, "Let's just go home."

With a fierce scowl, Diego took Angelique's arm in a firm grip and escorted her around the edge of the dance floor to the row of chairs where his aunt was seated. "If you are ready to go home now, we can leave together," he told the older woman, "or I will send the carriage back for you and Miguel if you'd prefer."

Though startled by Diego's sudden appearance, Margarita saw that his mood was most hostile and quickly agreed to leave. "Let me tell Miguel we are leaving. If he can get a ride home with one of his friends, then our driver need not return."

Diego nodded in agreement, and while his aunt went to speak with her son, he led Angelique over to the Venturas to thank them for the invitation to their party, which, he assured them, they had greatly enjoyed and regretted having to leave so early. When Margarita joined them, they went outside to the courtyard to wait for their carriage and then rode home in strained silence. Diego stared out at the night with a sullen frown, while Margarita pretended not to notice that Angelique was fidgeting nervously, opening and closing her fan and tapping it incessantly upon her knee. She excused herself the moment they arrived at her home, discreetly leaving them to work out their problems by themselves, without any interference from her.

Angelique followed Diego up the wide staircase but hesitated to enter his room. She stood at the door and waited for him to invite her to come inside. When he did not even glance her way, she called softly to him. "If there's something you want to say to me, I wish you'd just say it now."

Diego replaced his coat in the wardrobe, then sat down upon the edge of his bed to remove his boots. "Frankly, I don't even know where to begin."

"Tell me about Ramon Ortega," Angelique prompted.

"There are no words I'd use in front of you that would adequately describe that snake. Let's talk about something else." When she didn't move from the doorway, Diego gestured impatiently. "Come in and close the door. We needn't shout across the room to each other and keep my aunt awake."

Distressed by this prospect, Angelique closed the door softly. "Do you plan to shout at me?"

"Now why would I wish to do that?" Diego snarled sarcastically. "I took you to that party so that you could meet my friends and enjoy yourself, and you obviously did!" He struggled to remove his boots, then flung them aside as he rose to his feet. "I doubt anyone there tonight had a better

233

time than you did, my dear, including the Ventura sisters!"

"If I did something of which you disapproved, it was not intentional, Diego." Angelique thought immediately of her mother's criticism that she had not learned anything that would help her attract a rich husband. She had married one though, but clearly did not know how to please him.

"If I'm supposed to take comfort in that thought, believe me, it isn't enough! Ramon deserved a quick punch in the mouth for what he said to me, and I didn't appreciate your getting in my way! I've given him a beating on more than one occasion and I wouldn't have minded in the least doing it again tonight!"

"He said you weren't friends," Angelique responded calmly.

"Is that a fact? I didn't think he ever told the truth about anything. What possessed you to sit down and chat with him as though you two were old friends?"

"I told you. I merely wanted to rest for a few moments, and he knew where to find a chair. There was nothing more to it."

"Only because I arrived when I did!" Diego spat out in disgust.

"We were already returning to the ballroom when you appeared, but I can take care of myself, Diego. I don't need you to protect me from Ramon Ortega or anyone else," Angelique announced proudly. The evening certainly had not gone the way she had hoped it would, but she did not think that it was entirely her fault.

"We could debate that question all night!" Diego retorted, stripping off the last of his garments and dousing the lamp. "I'm tired, however, and I'd rather go to sleep."

Angelique stood in the darkened room not knowing what he expected her to do. Since his mood was so foul, she could hardly cuddle up beside him and hope he would want to make love as much as she did. She knew she had disappointed him, but he had failed her as well. She wanted him to put his arms around her and tell her he loved her and trusted her, and that silly misunderstandings occurred between all newlyweds and meant nothing. But clearly he did not love anyone but himself. He was furious with her and planned to stay that way from what she could see. When after a few moments he did not speak to her again, she went into the adjoining room and put away her jewelry. She carefully hung up her gown in the wardrobe, then sat down at the dressing table to brush out her hair. She removed the hairpins securing her coiffure and combed out the golden tresses with her fingers before she began to brush them with slow, even strokes. Her head ached dreadfully, her legs were tired from standing up so long, and her feet ached, for more than one of the dance partners had stepped upon her toes. Her new slippers were scuffed from their clumsiness, and she was afraid her feet were bruised. She had wanted to impress his friends favorably, but despite their enthusiastic attentions, she did not think any had truly liked her. They had merely been curious about her, that was all. Laying her hairbrush aside, she sat dejectedly in front of her mirror, thinking she now had pretty gowns and expensive jewels, but the most important element was missing from her marriage and she did not know how to recapture the love she knew Diego had once felt for her. "If only I knew what to do!" she moaned sadly.

"About what?" Diego called softly. He had wrapped a towel around his waist and was standing at the door that connected their rooms. It had not taken him long to realize that she had far too much pride to come to him that night, and he was not so foolish as to punish himself by not going to her. The custom they had adopted was an unusual one anyway, for most men went to their wives' rooms when they wanted their company, not the other way around. "Come to bed with me, and I'll be happy to solve whatever problems you might have."

"I didn't think you'd want me in your bed tonight."

Angelique rose slowly and took a tentative step toward him. "You were so angry with me that—"

Diego raised his hand to still her. He reminded himself, as he had been doing for the last ten minutes, that he was twenty-eight years old and she was barely seventeen. Though she prided herself on being independent, she really had had very little practice at it, and he should not have been so surprised at her unconventional behavior tonight. He had made the mistake of thinking that since she pleased him so greatly in bed she would know how to please him elsewhere, but she was obviously going to have to be taught how a wife should behave and he would have to do so with the same patience he had used to teach her how to dance. "For some reason I find it impossible to remain angry with you. I should have complimented you on how beautifully you danced this evening, Angelique. You are so light upon your feet you almost float."

"Thank you, but I think that is only because you taught me. I am sorry I cannot compliment most of your friends. I'm afraid to remove my stockings for surely my poor feet will be blue from all the bruises."

"Sit down on the bed a moment and let me see." Once she was seated and had removed her slippers, Diego knelt by her feet and, after unfastening her sheer silk hose, he rolled them slowly down her calves, over her slender ankles, then tossed them aside. Taking her right foot in his hands, he kissed her toes playfully and insisted that her feet were still the same delightful pink shade they had always been. He rubbed first one tiny foot and then the other, until she could wiggle her toes without cringing in pain. "Now what about your back? Does that hurt too?"

"Yes. I'm not used to standing up for so long," Angelique admitted apologetically. "Do you like to rub backs as well?"

"Only yours. Now just stretch out here on your stomach and I'll fix your back too." Diego climbed upon the bed and knelt down, straddling her hips. He untied the bows holding

236

her camisole in place so that he could touch her bare skin, and, beginning at her nape, he gently kneaded the tension from the muscles of her shoulders then worked slowly down her vertebrae with his fingertips. Her lightly perfumed skin was as seductively soft as satin and, when he reached her hips, he leaned down to spread tender kisses along her spine.

"You have an unusual technique," Angelique whispered languidly, "but it feels wonderful."

"That's all that matters." Diego saw no reason to return to his own room when her bed was just as accommodating as his. He moved to one side and untied the bow that held together the first of her many layers of slips. "I should have thought of this first, however, as I'll bet you're far too comfortable now to want to get up and undress."

"Mmm," Angelique mumbled softly, but she turned to gaze up at him with a look that was most inviting. "Would you help me please."

"My pleasure." Diego found his bride's superb figure endlessly fascinating and he was becoming too anxious to possess her to pay much attention to the delicate lace underthings she wore. He made an effort to see that he ripped none of her lingerie, but he did not remove it with nearly as much style as he would have liked to effect. Making his task even more difficult was the fact that she had slipped her hand beneath the towel he had knotted at his hips and her teasing touch was driving him nearly mad with desire. "Lord, woman, how am I to do this when—"

Angelique sat up then, capturing his mouth in a luscious kiss as she ran her fingers through his hair. She had meant to apologize to him, to say that she knew she should have stayed with him and ignored all the other men at the party, since none were even half as good looking or as intelligent as he, but she could not make herself stop kissing him long enough to speak.

When Diego could stand no more of her enthusiastic affection, he lay down upon his back and pulled her astride him, gently guiding her hips so their bodies met smoothly when he entered her. Her eyes widened and filled with surprise, but he grinned and placed his hands upon her waist to show her how to move so their pleasure would be shared as deeply as always. He raised his hands to her breasts and caressed their flushed tips tenderly as the first tremors of rapture brought a rush of warmth to his loins. Her small hands moved over his chest so that her fingertips combed the black curls, and she tried to breathe evenly as she moved upon him with an ever-increasing rhythm. She soon found such discipline impossible to maintain. Diego knew so many ways to make love, she realized, but each had its own special excitement and she gave herself up eagerly to the pleasure of this new adventure.

Angelique grew dizzy as the bright flame of desire smoldering within her swiftly ignited a blazing ecstasy that brought a low moan of surrender to her lips. Diego's handsome features were a blur in the hot mist of her joy, but she could feel his smile as her lips sought his in a kiss that was still filled with hunger, and she knew as she fell forward into his arms that even if he had not spoken of love in words, he had shown her all of its magnificent splendor.

Chapter XIV

Diego had already left his aunt's home by the time Angelique awoke the next morning. She was uncertain as to why his mood had changed so abruptly from anger to passion after they had returned home from the party, but she certainly would never offer a complaint. Still, she believed it would be foolish of her to leave such an important question unanswered. Had it only been that she had left him alone a sufficient time for him to miss her? She had not walked out of his room for spite, but because she had felt she was unwanted. Yet she could not deny that when he had come to her he had been so sympathetic and affectionate that she had had no desire to continue their argument. Perhaps a few minutes apart had done both of them good, though still it frightened her to think how quickly Diego's temper had flared. Her own temper was difficult enough to control, and she doubted she could share the responsibility for restraining his as well. "There is far more to being your wife than I had imagined, my dearest, but I will try my best to please you," she vowed aloud. With that solemn promise, Angelique nestled down among her pillows and drifted back to sleep.

As Angelique lay snuggled in her bed, Diego was puzzling

239

over the same questions that had disturbed his wife. He was growing restless with the routine of his days, for they were not nearly as fascinating as the nights he spent with his beautiful bride. He paced his cabin with a measured stride, forcing himself to think logically instead of allowing his emotions to gain the advantage again. Ramon Ortega was an obnoxious nuisance, a pest who had plagued him for years, but it was certainly not worth his time to pursue him with a warning to stay away from Angelique. He had not lived a sheltered life and knew he should have expected not only eager friends but envious enemies to stalk his bewitching bride. Her inexperience made her vulnerable, and he had made so damn many mistakes at the Venturas' party that he was surprised she had even agreed to go home with him. He had wanted everyone to meet her, but such a large and boisterous gathering had not been the proper place to present his bride.

What they needed was a home of their own, where they could entertain couples of quality, with whom Angelique could rightly expect to associate. That a shrew like Françoise was a countess was somehow amusing, but he could well imagine Angelique having such a title. Undoubtedly, her mother had intended for her to marry into the Spanish nobility, while she herself had merely wanted the security of his father's wealth. Angered by the thought of the hateful way she had treated Angelique on the night of their wedding, Diego went out on deck and sought the salt-scented breeze to clear his mind and cool his blood.

With his hands firmly clasped upon the rail, Diego looked out over the city of Barcelona and felt the same surge of pride in his home port he always experienced. It was no wonder Cataláns considered the rest of Spain inferior, for Barcelona was built upon a remarkably picturesque site. Nestled between two hills, Tibidabo on the north and Montjuich on the west, the city had sprung to life at the dawn of history and had soon become a thriving Mediterranean port welcoming the commerce and cultures of all who cared to grace its shores. Part of the city still retained the flavor of the Middle Ages, with dark, narrow streets, which Diego avoided whenever possible. He much preferred the wide avenues and splashing fountain of the Plaza de Cataluña, where he could stroll with his friends in the sunshine and enjoy the heritage of which he was so justly proud. In his opinion, Barcelona was a magnificent city in which to raise a son and the sooner he began construction of his own home, the sooner he would have a proper residence for his bride. Giving Octavio a jaunty salute, he raced down the gangplank, eager to discuss his plans with the ravishing young woman who had inspired them.

He found her perched upon the window seat on the landing, and he sat down at her feet and slid his hand beneath the folds of her skirt to give her calf an affectionate squeeze, but her welcoming smile was a faint one. "I seldom find you without a book or some bit of embroidery in your hands. Where is my aunt this morning that you have been left here alone and in such a melancholy mood?" he queried.

Not wishing to depress him as well, Angelique attempted to smile, but the depth of her concern was still plain upon her delicate features. "She's gone to see your father, and since I was uncertain as to what my reception would be in his home, I begged to be excused, saying I wished to rest because we were out so late last night. What are we going to do, Diego? If he tells her the truth, she'll feel that we've simply used her kindness . . . accepted her hospitality when we've no right to it."

Diego took a deep breath and let it out slowly. "Margarita has been a mother to me ever since my own mother died. She would never think we had used her because she knows her affection for me is readily returned." He raised his hand and cupped Angelique's chin to draw her near for a gentle kiss before resting his forehead against hers for a moment. "She is an intelligent woman and knows that something is amiss.

241

These are perilous times for the French nobility, but Spain is at war with Revolutionary France, and she must realize you are safe here, regardless of the fiction we told her about our fearing a kidnapping. Now there is no point in your sitting here brooding about what my father might tell her. We need a home of our own, for I've no desire to make excuses to anyone, and most especially not my own aunt."

Not encouraged by his confident attitude, Angelique glanced out the window. "Have you a place in mind?" she asked absently.

"Which would you prefer first, a country estate or a house here in Barcelona? You need not worry over my resources. They are adequate for whatever you choose."

Angelique found both possibilities disturbing at this time, for she feared his true purpose was to shield her from gossip rather than to establish a comfortable home. "I know little of Barcelona and so few people here, but this would be the better place for you, wouldn't it? Don't you want to be near the port?"

Diego frowned impatiently. He had wanted to please her, but he could see that she was so distracted she was giving the matter of their home little thought, though he believed it deserved her full attention. His first impulse was to purchase an estate in a location so remote that his enchanting bride would have absolutely no distractions save him, but he knew that such a plan would undoubtedly go awry, for in the country she would be able to entertain whomever she pleased while he was at sea and he would never hear of it. While life in the city had distinct disadvantages at present, he knew she would be happier surrounded by the friends he hoped to make for her, and the demands of propriety would keep her interests centered in her home and child. He became disgusted with himself then for worrying about how to keep her faithful, for he was intelligent enough to realize that if she should wish to fool him, she had the skill to do so wherever he chose to build their home. The real challenge would be to see that she had no wish to know other men and, with that in mind, he made a greater effort to understand her mood. "Angelique," he called softly.

"Yes?" Angelique kept her eyes upon the road approaching the house, for she still anxiously awaited his aunt's return.

"The day is too pretty to waste in worrying over what my father might tell Margarita. I will take you out. Perhaps you will find something to raise your spirits. I need to buy another ring for you, and this is a good time for such an errand."

"What? Oh, I'd forgotten that this is your father's." Angelique stared at the brilliant sapphire and diamond ring as if fascinated by its fiery sparkle.

"I'll have that one copied since you seem so fond of it," he told her. His decision made, Diego sprang to his feet and offered his hand to help his bride rise. She came without argument, but once they were seated in his carriage she voiced her opinion about the ring.

"Since your father asked to have this ring returned, I know we'll have to buy another, but it seems a shame to copy this. It will be part of your inheritance and then you'll own two."

This seemed a small problem to Diego. "I'll give one to our first son for his bride. We'll begin a family tradition."

"I hope that is the only one we'll begin," she remarked wryly. Angelique thought her husband's good humor remarkable when she considered that the scandal surrounding their marriage was undoubtedly gathering momentum. Regardless of how much he loved his aunt, she was certain the woman would not be pleased by what José Luis told her. She knew the man too well to expect him to lie to his own sister, and she dreaded the confrontation that was bound to result.

Diego had considered her comment an attempt at humor until he saw that her expression contained not even a hint of levity. "I will kill any man who dares to insult us, Angelique!

243

You are my wife, and I'll not allow anyone to speculate as to why!"

Appalled by his vow, Angelique shrank away from him, for the fury in his dark gaze frightened her greatly. "You would not kill a man for speaking the truth?"

"You don't even know what the truth is, do you?" Diego drew her close and his lips stilled her protests with a torrent of kisses. The carriage bounced over the cobblestones and made their journey an uncomfortable one, but he moved with practiced ease as he drew her into his arms and bent her will to his. His fingertips slid up the silk of her stockings, along the smooth flesh of her thigh, and with a deft touch invaded the farthest recesses of her reason. Slowly and surely his teasing caress lifted her gently upon the winds of rapture to finally shower her with a sparkling cascade of pleasure, after which she lay sated in his arms, languidly enjoying his embrace. Her eyes were closed to better savor his marvelous touch, which had again made any thoughts save those of him seem unimportant. At last her breathing grew slow and it seemed as if she had fallen asleep in his arms.

Diego adjusted the fit of her silk lingerie and rearranged the folds of her skirt to restore her appearance to a more proper one, then whispered softly, "You were born to be mine. You have belonged to me since the hour we met, and I'll not allow you to think otherwise, Angelique."

Her eyes opened with a flutter and their color seemed more violet than blue as she took a deep breath, uncertain how she was to reply to so compelling an argument as he had just presented. Had she fallen in love with his portrait in his father's library, or with the man himself in the moonlit garden? The distinction was no longer clear, but she knew it mattered little and leaned forward to kiss his lips lightly. "If that is what you believe, then I will believe it too, but I beg you to ignore whatever insults you might hear, for I could not bear to lose you in some foolish argument over honor."

"It is not foolish for a man to protect his wife's reputation!" Diego insisted firmly.

That he had once planned to escort her around town as his mistress with no regard for her good name seemed to have slipped his mind, yet Angelique knew better than to remind him of that. "Protect only yourself, Diego. You are all that matters to me."

Before the brash young man could dispute her words, the carriage arrived at the jeweler's. The door was opened for them and the striking young couple entered the exclusive establishment with the sedate air of a man and his bride who had nothing more pressing to discuss than the quality of gemstones. Diego explained the purpose of their visit, but the proprietor, a slender, gray-haired man by the name of Raul Estrada, had another suggestion.

"Rather than an exact duplicate of this ring, perhaps you would like a ring fashioned in the same design as the necklace and earrings you gave your wife?"

"Oh Diego, they are so pretty, and I'm certain the same motif adapted for a ring would be just as stunning," Angelique responded enthusiastically.

Happy to see an improvement in her mood, Diego smiled widely. "Whatever pleases you, my pet. The choice is yours."

"My designer will need only your ring size, *Señora* Aragon." Raul summoned a young Frenchman who took one look at Angelique's fair curls and sweet features and greeted her in their native tongue. He kept up a steady stream of animated conversation while he ascertained her ring size and made a quick sketch so that the ring would flatter rather than overpower her delicate hand. When he finally paused for a breath, Angelique turned to her husband.

"He is the one who made the necklace and earrings and says a ring will be a simple matter to fashion for me."

"Surely that is not all he said," Diego commented brusquely. While he spoke Castilian as well as Catalán and had been forced by his tutors to study Latin and Greek, he

245

was not at all fluent in French. He had found that Catalán was similar to the dialects of Southern France rather than to the more formal French that Angelique spoke. Until that very moment he had no inclination to become proficient in French, but he vowed to himself that he soon would, for he would not like to be excluded from all of his wife's future conversations with her countrymen.

"He was merely remarking upon his delight in meeting an *émigré* who wished to purchase fine jewelry rather than sell it." Angelique thought it remarkable that Diego would be jealous of the young man, who appeared to be barely out of his teens. Although clearly devoted to his art, he had a quite ordinary appearance, and their conversation had been friendly rather than flirtatious.

"Ah yes," Raul promptly agreed. "Only this morning I purchased an exquisite amethyst and pearl ring from a lovely Frenchwoman. It is a pity you prefer sapphires, for it is quite unique."

Alarmed by his description, Angelique quickly asked, "May I see it please?" She cast a worried glance at her husband, but she could tell by his puzzled expression that such a ring meant nothing to him. Raul asked the Frenchman to bring it, and the moment he placed the pretty ring in her hand, Angelique knew from whom it had been purchased.

Diego watched his bride's expression grow troubled and asked softly, "Do you want that ring also? If so, you may have it. There are times your eyes are more violet than blue, so it would be as perfect for you as the sapphires are."

"Would you excuse us for a moment, *Señor* Estrada?" she asked softly. Taking her husband's arm, Angelique led him over to the front window, where she pretended to inspect the amethyst ring in the bright sunlight. "This is my mother's ring, Diego. If she has been forced to part with it, then it can only mean one thing."

Diego nodded perceptively. "If she needs money, she must

246

be planning to leave my father's home."

"She might already have left him, for all we know. Whatever shall we do? It is entirely my fault that she is not marrying your father as she longed to do."

Diego turned his back to the jeweler, who was still watching them, undoubtedly hoping they would take the ring. "She has only herself to blame for the situation she is in now. No one forced her to lie about your age or to take such an unforgiving attitude about us. She has orchestrated her own fate, Angelique. It may not be a happy one, but it is still the one she deserves."

Angelique knew better than to begin an argument with Diego about her mother's faults when clearly he thought she had so many. Instead, she stepped close. "Will you please buy this ring for me? I wish to return it to my mother. It was a gift from my father, and I know she would not have sold it if she had had any other choice."

"After the despicable way she treated you, you wish to do such a nice thing for her?" Diego asked in disbelief.

"She is my mother, Diego, and I will always wish to help her in any way I possibly can. You'd not turn your back on your father, would you?" she dared ask, but she swiftly regretted the question when his eyes took on the dangerous gleam she had not wanted to see ever again.

"Simply because he has turned his back on me?" Diego responded bitterly. Since he had already offered to buy the ring for her, he knew he could not go back on his word and agreed to her request with a rueful smile. "Of course I will buy it for you, and what you wish to do with it is your own business."

"Oh, thank you!" Angelique hugged him enthusiastically, forgetting they were being observed, and when she turned to find Raul and the young Frenchman watching her, she could not help but blush.

Diego paid for the amethyst ring and gave a deposit on the sapphire ring he had ordered, then he asked the driver of their carriage to take the road up Tibidabo. "I want you to see Barcelona from the hill, Angelique. There is a legend that the devil brought Christ there to tempt him with the world. The view is spectacular and perhaps it will inspire you to think about where you'd like to build our house."

Snuggling beside her handsome husband in the plush carriage, Angelique found that her mood had become decidedly happier. She glanced up at him through her thick lashes and asked in a teasing whisper, "Have you often made love in a carriage, Diego?"

"No!" he replied with a deep chuckle. "Until today I have never been inspired to, but I find your many charms difficult to resist."

Angelique moved away from him for a moment to pull down the shades at the windows to assure their privacy. "I am no more able to resist you, Diego." She unbuttoned his waistcoat and his shirt, then spread eager kisses over his broad chest before reaching for his belt. "The least I can do is repay your generous affection in kind."

Diego was too pleased by the devilish gleam in her lovely blue eyes to argue that this was neither the time nor the place for such a display of devotion. The sadness he had seen earlier that morning had left her expression and she was so very lovely that he leaned back against the leather seat and relaxed completely as he waited for her to work the same magical enchantment he always enjoyed at her touch. His breath quickened as her fingertips slid up the powerful muscles of his inner thighs, for she was moving with a teasing slowness he found wildly exciting.

It still amazed him that this gently raised young beauty had learned so swiftly how to return his loving in such a wanton fashion, but he knew better now than to wonder aloud where she had gotten her expertise, for surely she had been born with it. Her talent for bestowing pleasure seemed instinctive and he wove his fingers in her bright curls and tried to tell her how much her tantalizing kisses pleased him, but he could not seem to make his lips form the words. He heard no more than a low moan, which surprised him, for what he really wanted to do was shout with the joy she had given him. He scarcely felt the jarring ride, she had given him wings as graceful as the eagle's upon which to soar and he wanted to stay aloft forever.

No experience of his life had prepared him to expect such remarkable joy as that which he continually drew from his bride's exquisite loving. He shuddered as the rapture he could no longer contain sped through his powerful limbs with a shattering jolt and brought with it waves of pleasure as tumultuous as those upon the high seas.

When Angelique at last drew away and moved quickly to restore his clothing to order, he found it difficult to do more than smile, but finally he found his voice. "I am certain you are the most incredibly loving woman God ever created."

Angelique cared little that his mind was still so dazed with the ecstasy she had given him that his sweet words were slurred. That he loved what she did rather than who she was did not matter in the least to her, and she kissed him again and again until they were both breathless and convulsed with laughter. "I was afraid you were too suspicious of me now to ever pay me compliments, Diego. Does this mean you've forgiven me for not telling you who I was?"

"Oh I haven't forgiven you. You are the most devious female I've ever had the misfortune to meet, but I want you anyway," Diego swore amidst a flurry of sweet kisses.

Angelique tried to conceal her hurt, for more than her pride had been wounded by his teasing. "I want you to trust me, Diego. You've no reason to fear I will be deceitful ever again, nor have you any reason to be jealous of other men."

Seeing that she had become serious, Diego pulled her across his lap and hugged her tightly. "I will try to remember that the next time I see some man slowly undressing you with his eyes, but it will be difficult when each man you meet nearly drools over you."

249

"It is not my fault that I am considered attractive, Diego, and I do nothing to encourage men to think I would welcome their attentions," Angelique insisted stubbornly.

"I did not mean to make you feel guilty when you've done nothing of which to be ashamed, my pet." Diego kissed her again, this time letting his mouth linger upon hers until she had forgotten everything but how desperately he needed her. He could no more tell her not to smile, or move with such delicious grace, or hide the intelligence that made her such a charming woman with whom to converse, than he could tell her not to breathe. But he knew it would be a long while before he learned to contain the smoldering jealousy that leapt into flames each time he saw another man look her way with the hunger in his glance he was certain filled his own.

Angelique found the view from Tibidabo so exhilarating that she sat upon the hillside with Diego for the better part of the afternoon without once worrying about how his aunt would greet them when they returned to her home. Diego pointed out the most interesting features of the city and kept her entertained with amusing stories of some of his more innocent adventures with his friends in the years before he had gone to sea. They had been a lively band, and on numerous occasions their escapades had tested his father's patience sorely, before he had learned how to sneak in and out of his house without being seen.

"And that is when you discovered the place in the garden wall that has such fine footholds?" Angelique inquired with a lilting laugh.

"Yes. In those days I had need of them often, I'm afraid."

"When we build our own home, let's make certain we have such a convenient section of wall in case our son has need of it," she suggested. When she considered the fiery temperaments they each had manifested, Angelique was certain he would.

"But if we know the secret first, he'll not be able to fool us, so there would be no purpose in having a wall built to those specifications," Diego pointed out with an easy grin.

Angelique smiled shyly. "If he is as charming a lad as you, I will pretend to be fooled."

Diego thought her idea outrageous but understood her motive well. "That is a more devious plan than I've come to expect from you, my pet. I doubt any son of ours will ever be able to outsmart you." Returning his gaze to the city stretched out below them, he gestured with a wide sweep of his hand. "All of Barcelona lies at your feet. Do you see an attractive spot for our home?"

"This one has a marvelous view. Would it be possible to build a house right here?" Angelique asked eagerly.

"While the view is indeed splendid, don't you think this location is a trifle remote?"

Angelique hugged her knees tightly. "I wouldn't mind. I don't need anyone but you to be happy."

"But I will not be here all the time, Angelique, or had you forgotten that I spend far more time aboard *El Diablo* than I do here?" The instant he said the words Diego saw pain fill his bride's eyes, and he was sorry he had reminded her of their imminent separation.

"You plan to set sail again in early spring?" Angelique asked softly.

"Yes. Had I known how mild the autumn would be this year, I might have made another voyage to New Spain. It is a shame such fine weather has been wasted."

Angelique observed his expression closely and was disappointed to see that he seemed completely serious. "These last two months have been a waste, in your opinion?"

"Not entirely," Diego replied with a satisfied smirk, for he considered taking a bride and having the hope of a son sufficient accomplishments to merit two months of his time. Rising to his feet, he extended his hand to help her stand. "If you'll not select a location for a house, then I will choose one

251

myself, for there is no time to lose."

"I'll care little where the house is if you'll not be there to share it." Angelique walked back to the carriage and took her place inside, but the bleakness of her mood was unmistakable. She bit her lip savagely to force back the torrent of angry tears that lurked just behind her lashes. That the man would leave her alone to bear their first child was too great an insult to suffer in silence, but she would not beg him to stay with her if he did not truly wish to do so.

Diego chose the seat opposite hers and made little effort to conceal his displeasure over her mood. He had not really thought about leaving her until that very moment, and since he found the brief hours he spent aboard *El Diablo* each morning nearly endless, he wondered where he would find the strength to sail away on a voyage that would part them for several months. The future lay in the New World, not here in the Old, and he longed to return to the excitement of Vera Cruz, though not without her by his side. Leaning forward, he rested his hand lightly upon her knee. "The spring may never come this year. Do not hate me for leaving you before I have gone."

"I do not hate you!" Angelique insisted with an anguished cry. "I know you love the sea. I know that. But I cannot help but think what life will be like here without you."

"Desolate? Empty? Wretchedly lonely?" Diego moved swiftly to her side. "It will be the same for me, too, Angelique, but I will have to speak with my father before I can make you any promises concerning our future."

Not understanding why he would wish to see José Luis, Angelique was filled with questions. "But what can you say? How can you ask the man for his advice when he has chosen to turn us out of his house? I thought he made it very plain that we were on our own."

"I'm not certain what I'll say, or how he'll reply, but let me speak with him before we make any further plans. Now give me a kiss and don't fret another minute over what the spring

252

might bring when the present is so very promising."

Despite her husband's enticing smile, Angelique was afraid to hope for more than this one blissful afternoon.

When they returned to his aunt's home they found Margarita waiting to see them, and suddenly the pleasant hours they had spent together seemed all too brief.

"I'd like to speak with you alone, Diego. There is a matter we must discuss at once," the petite woman declared as she swept a cold glance over Angelique.

Taking his bride's hand, Diego drew her along beside him. "Angelique is my wife, Aunt Margarita, not a servant who can be dismissed with a wave of your hand. She should hear whatever it is you wish to say to me."

Though she was not pleased by her nephew's decision, Margarita did not argue. She walked with a brisk step into the parlor and, when Diego and Angelique were seated, she closed the doors so they would not be interrupted. "I went to visit José Luis today, for I thought it most unusual that he had not invited us all to his home since you two have been here." Taking the chair nearest Diego, the delicate little woman continued. "I found my brother so changed that I scarcely recognized him."

"Has he been ill?" Diego asked with alarm.

"If he has been sickened, it is only by your behavior, Diego. He did not know you had come to me after leaving his home until I told you two were my guests. I told you the night you arrived that I would not take sides against my brother, and so I must ask you to leave at once. When José Luis told you to leave his home, he never imagined you would come to mine."

"I didn't!" Diego replied angrily. "I came here so that you could meet Angelique. You are the one who invited us to stay."

Margarita rose slowly and walked toward the door. "I'll not permit you to raise your voice to me as you do to your crew, Diego. Simply pack your belongings and move

253

elsewhere, for you and your wife are no longer welcome in my home."

"Just what did my father tell you?" Diego approached his aunt with a menacing step, determined to learn exactly what had been said. It was obvious to him now that he had seriously underestimated the severity of her reaction to her visit with his father. He had thought that her affection for him would have tempered her opinion, but clearly she was going to rely on her strict moral code rather than on the love she had always shown him.

"Only that you gave yourself no choice other than to marry Angelique and that you left his home at his insistence. If there is more than that to be revealed, then you will have to tell me yourself."

Diego was so infuriated by what his father had done that he could scarcely speak. He knew his behavior had been inexcusable, but once he had found Angelique residing in his own home, he never would have been able to leave her untouched. When she came to his side, he pulled her close. "My father seems determined to ruin what little chance Angelique and I have to be accepted by polite society. You have had ample opportunity to observe us together. Do you think we deserve to be hounded from the homes of our relatives when our only crime is that we love each other?"

"Let your love sustain you then, Diego, for I will not permit you to live here in my home when my brother has forbidden you to live in his." Margarita lifted her chin proudly, certain that what she was doing was right. "I'll thank you to stay away from Miguel. He admires you greatly and it is obvious that his esteem is misplaced."

"Miguel is old enough to choose his own friends," Diego responded bitterly. "I'll not pretend we are no longer cousins."

Angelique was so mortified by his aunt's hostility that she did not blame Diego for being disrespectful, but she wanted the ghastly scene over and interjected, "It will not take us long to pack our things. I am sorry the pleasant time we've spent here in your home has come to such an abrupt and unfortunate end. When we have moved into our own home, I shall be happy to receive you and your son there any time."

Startled by an invitation she knew she would be unlikely ever to accept, Margarita stepped aside to let the young couple pass. She had found the stunning blonde's behavior above reproach until the party at the Venturas' had revealed that she apparently liked to flirt, though any true lady would surely know that such provocative behavior was bound to inspire the worst sort of gossip. That her own son had fallen under the vixen's spell was not something she would tolerate a moment longer. She shook her head sadly, sorry to think that her brother had forced Diego to marry Angelique when it would have been far better for all concerned if he had paid her a sufficient sum to send her on her way.

Chapter XV

Diego awoke when Angelique returned to his bunk. "You're still sick each morning?" He smoothed her golden curls away from her pale cheeks and kissed her forehead tenderly, sorry to find she had again been unwell.

In his aunt's home she had been able to escape into her own room to hide her illness, but his cabin offered little in the way of privacy. "Perhaps it was only the *caracoles* you fed me last night. They prepare them with too much garlic here." Angelique yawned sleepily, certain despite her excuse that it was not what they had eaten for supper that had upset her stomach.

"Your *escargot* are superior?" Diego asked with a sly chuckle.

"In every way." Angelique snuggled against her husband's warm chest, not wanting the day to begin when it was certain to be a most trying one. She clung to him, for only in his arms did she feel truly safe, but when her tears began to roll down his ribs, she could no longer hide her sorrow.

For once in his life Diego found himself unable either to fight or talk his way out of a difficult situation. He had seduced the loveliest creature it had ever been his good fortune to meet and had made her life miserable as a result. He held her tightly as she wept, searching his mind for some tender promise he would be able to keep. He knew how to make her luscious body tremble with pleasure, but not how to make her happy. His handsome features formed a hostile mask as he lay with her locked in his embrace, for he had had more than enough of his father's meddling and was determined to give his bride the best possible life, since that was what she deserved. Yet such a dream no longer seemed possible in Barcelona. When he was certain she was sound asleep, he left his bunk and dressed for the day, anxious to put into effect the plan he had conceived.

When Angelique again awoke, she found that Diego had left her breakfast upon a tray with a brief note stating that he would return before noon. Rather than wait for him in his cabin, however, she went out on deck and, after looking up and down the docks, she decided to go for a stroll. As she neared the gangplank, Octavio rushed to her side.

"*Señora* Aragon, if you wish to leave the ship for any purpose, I will go with you."

Angelique liked the mate. He was a few years older than Diego, of medium height, and solidly built. His dark hair curled in tight ringlets that seemed more suited to the role of court jester than the responsible job he held, while his bushy eyebrows gave his brown eyes a fierceness that was totally lacking in his manner. His features were too coarse to ever be considered handsome, but when he smiled he radiated a good-natured warmth that she found most appealing. "You needn't leave your duties, Octavio. I plan only to walk a short distance in either direction to look at the other ships. I'm too restless to wait for Diego in his cabin."

"I must insist, *Señora*. The docks are no place for a woman to move about alone." Octavio offered his arm, but Angelique drew away.

"I'll not go near where the men are working. I'll stay on the walk and be quite safe," Angelique assured him.

"If you leave the ship, *Señora,* I must go with you," Octavio explained in an embarrassed whisper, hoping she would not persist with the independent attitude Diego had told him to expect.

Angelique had wanted the time to be by herself, not to spend chatting with Octavio, no matter how pleasant she thought him, but she could see by his anxious expression that he had been ordered to accompany her. "Just what did my husband say? Am I forbidden to leave *El Diablo?*"

"Why no. You may come and go as you wish, but I am to escort you," the mate admitted frankly. He was acutely aware of the stares of the crew, all of whom had stopped working to observe his exchange with the captain's attractive bride. When Octavio gave orders, he expected them to be obeyed without question, and he had no idea how to deal with this slip of a girl who wanted to argue the wisdom of Diego's command.

"I see. Well, if I am to be chaperoned constantly, then I'll simply stay here where all the men may watch me." Angelique went to the rail and pretended an interest in the ship moored beside the *Diablo,* which had just begun unloading its cargo. But her features were set in a petulant frown.

Certain he had insulted the pretty young woman by following his captain's orders, Octavio threw up his hands in defeat. He was no fit companion for such a fine lady anyway and had felt foolish offering to be her escort. With a harsh glance, he saw that his crew stopped gaping at the high-spirited blonde and went about their assigned tasks.

Angelique raised her hand to cover a wide yawn and wondered where Diego had gone that he had not wanted her to go with him. If he had gone to see his father, she would be furious with him that he had not taken her along too. She had no desire to see him suffer another beating and she was terribly afraid that could happen if he paid José Luis a call. When she saw Miguel making his way through the crowd milling about the docks, she waved to him and greeted him with a light kiss upon the cheek. "If you've come to see

Diego, he'll be back soon. Would you care to wait in his cabin?"

"Yes, please." Miguel took Angelique's arm and led the way. "I have been on board the *Diablo* several times, although I've never had the opportunity to sail with Diego." Once seated in his cousin's cabin, the young man cleared his throat nervously, then began what he had come to say. "I came to apologize; that is, I wanted to tell you two that I will never forgive my mother for what she has done. It was wonderful having you live with us, and I am sorry she asked you to leave."

Angelique was pleased to have made one friend at least, but she hated to think that Miguel might have jeopardized his own position in his home by siding with them. "I don't want to be the cause of an argument between you and your mother, Miguel, and I'm certain Diego doesn't wish to be either. When we have our own home, we'll be able to invite you to come see us and to repay your hospitality. You need not feel you have lost two cousins simply because we are no longer welcome in your mother's home."

Miguel blushed deeply, uncertain what to say to the charming blonde, for he knew the love he felt for her would never be returned. "No, I do not feel that I have lost you, but it will be most awkward for me to see you now."

"Surely we will be able to converse when we meet at parties. We'll be able to dance together and to talk then," Angelique suggested hopefully.

"Oh I doubt you will be invited to any other parties." Miguel realized too late what a dreadful mistake he had made. "I'm sorry. That was very tactless of me. I'm sure there are many people who will still wish to entertain you and Diego."

When Diego stepped through the door, he saw Angelique's pained expression and Miguel's bright blush and completely misread the situation. "Miguel, if you have—"

Angelique rose quickly and crossed the cabin to her

259

husband's side. "Miguel has come to offer encouragement, nothing more. Now tell us where you have been all morning, for I'm certain it is a much more amusing story than what we can tell you."

"I have been looking for possible cargoes—hardly an amusing pastime, my pet—that's why I did not wait to take you with me."

Miguel was embarrassed by what Diego had obviously assumed to be the subject of his conversation with Angelique and, rising to his feet, he moved hastily toward the door. "Will you excuse me please? I must return to the bank without delay, but I did want you to know I am on your side."

"There'll be no battle, Miguel. You needn't take sides." Diego knew his cousin had shown considerable courage in coming to them that day and he walked with him to the gangplank. "I ask only that if you hear any gossip, you ignore it. You needn't speak in my behalf."

Squaring his shoulders proudly, Miguel disagreed. "I would be glad to help you in any way I can. I am sorry Angelique will be the one to suffer, for my mother's sudden hostility toward you is bound to cause comment among her friends. I know she will not spread rumors herself, but her silence will surely inspire them."

Diego shrugged. "If people want to talk about us, we can do little to stop them, but frankly I'll not waste my time waiting for everyone to grow bored with the topic of our marriage. The extent of the Queen's interest in Godoy always makes for lively conversation. See if you can't change the subject to them whenever anyone mentions my name."

Miguel had to agree. "Yes, that a handsome guard could be promoted to the post of Minister of Foreign Affairs and become a duke is remarkable in all respects. The King is obviously a fool!"

"You see, already you've forgotten why you came here!" Diego slapped the young man on the back and sent him on his way, but he was not pleased that Angelique had been talking with Miguel alone, for surely she must know he was in love with her. She was so very innocent in her appraisal of people's motives and he would have to caution her again about walking into situations from which she could not readily extricate herself. But before he could lecture his lovely bride on the wisdom of receiving male callers in his absence, she rushed forward to confront him.

"Why did you tell Octavio not to let me off the *Diablo* alone? Did you honestly think I'd run away? I can imagine no other reason for your giving the man such an absurd order, but such reasoning is ridiculous in the extreme!" Angelique stood in a defiant pose, her hands upon her hips as she glared up at her husband.

Diego had had no difficulty winning the respect of his crew and maintaining discipline on board his ship, and he saw no reason to allow his bride to speak to him in an obnoxious tone that he would never accept from one of his men. "No one questions my authority here, and I strongly suggest that you don't either. It never occurred to me you might wish to run away. Is the idea an especially appealing one to you?"

"No, of course not!" Angelique responded with an exasperated sigh.

"That's reassuring." Diego's smile was grim despite his attempt at humor. "I merely told Octavio to provide an escort for you—as a courtesy—not to make a prisoner of you."

Angelique was not convinced that courtesy had been his motivation when his first reaction upon finding Miguel speaking with her had clearly been a jealous one. He still did not trust her, but it seemed pointless to argue the matter any further, for nothing she said seemed to convince him she would never betray him. It would take time to win his confidence and she prayed he would change his opinion of her soon.

Recalling the purpose of his errand, she asked curiously, "Do you always arrange for cargoes so far in advance? I thought you'd be here in Barcelona for several more months. What's the necessity for securing a cargo now?"

Diego considered the wisdom of revealing his plans to her and promptly decided against it. "It is always good to be prepared for the future, Angelique. Now, let us have something to eat and then we'll pay my father a visit. That blue dress is perfect. You look like a grown woman and I want him to think of you that way."

Angelique didn't like the look in Diego's eyes. Their usual teasing sparkle had become a menacing gleam when he had mentioned his father. "Just what is the purpose of this visit? Are we merely paying a friendly call, or trying to change his mind about the way he's treated us? He's as proud a man as you are and I doubt he'll be glad to see us, no matter how we're dressed or what we might say."

"There is only one thing about which I am extremely proud, and that is you, my dearest. Since I've ordered another ring for you, we'll return his. There is also a business matter I wish to discuss. We are partners, or at least I think we still are."

"What if he says that you are not?" Angelique asked anxiously.

"Then we are not. The choice is entirely up to him. The *Diablo* is mine however, and I will continue to sail her regardless of whether or not I fly the flag of the Aragon line."

No matter what he wished to discuss, Angelique was certain their visit would not be a pleasant one, but had Margarita not warned them, José Luis's manner would have provided more of a shock than it did. He had obviously lost weight and was so tense he seemed barely able to speak without resorting to the anger the sight of his son aroused. He had always been a meticulously groomed and dressed gentleman and he appeared that afternoon in a splendid coat of dove gray and white breeches that made his dark good looks doubly handsome, but his greeting could not have been more forbidding. "What is it you wish to discuss, Diego? I am extremely busy."

They had at least been permitted to enter the house, which Diego considered a good sign, and regardless of the blackness of his father's mood, he responded with a ready smile. "I came to speak with you about transporting some of the goods stored in our warehouses. I've decided to make another voyage to Vera Cruz this year and—"

"What?" José Luis asked with an astonished gasp. "You can not possibly be seriously considering sailing at this time of year! That would be lunacy!" he declared emphatically, his hands tightening upon the arms of his chair until his knuckles were white.

Diego paused to give Angelique's hand a reassuring squeeze. He had again asked her to let him speak for the two of them, and he was delighted she had not yet interrupted. "I am leaving for Vera Cruz as soon as I can load a profitable cargo. It might as well be made up of goods we're holding for shipment."

"No. I want no part of this foolhardy scheme of yours," José Luis stressed with a forceful gesture. "The idea is preposterous."

"What do you mean?" Diego spoke softly, hoping to coax his father into responding in a more reasonable tone. "I think the good weather will hold until we reach the Caribbean, and so far south the fall is not severe. There is little danger in my proposal."

"That is a matter of opinion!" José Luis responded with a hostile sneer. "Do you actually plan to leave your new bride for a voyage that will surely end at the bottom of the sea? Is this how you plan to support Angelique, by taking even greater risks than you have in the past so that you will leave her a rich widow?"

Since Angelique had no idea what is was that Diego truly wanted from his father, she kept still, but it was difficult for

263

her to remain calm when José Luis's words terrified her. She could not bear the thought that Diego wanted to leave her so soon and the fact that he would undertake such a perilous voyage unnerved her completely.

With a rueful laugh, Diego denied his father's accusation. "Of course not. I have no intention of leaving Angelique a widow, or even of leaving her alone here in Barcelona. She is coming with me."

José Luis rose from his chair with a menacing growl, clearly tempted to strike his son with as many savage blows as would be required to bring him to his senses. "Mother of God! The *Diablo* is no place for Angelique!"

"She is quite comfortable there now." Diego stood to face his father and straightened up to his full height since he had a slight advantage in that respect. "Angelique is my wife and my responsibility, not yours. And since you've chosen to make our lives so difficult here, I've decided we'll be happier in Vera Cruz. You've often remarked upon the problems we have in directing our business affairs in New Spain. I will simply take over that responsibility, for I plan to remain there."

José Luis could barely see his son's face through the rage that consumed him. "Since you'll disregard my wishes so blatantly, find a cargo elsewhere, and if by some miracle you should actually reach Vera Cruz, I forbid you to conduct any business in my name!"

The two men stood toe to toe and the violence of the energy flowing between them seemed a tangible force that Angelique felt would swiftly suffocate them all. Leaping to her feet, she grabbed José Luis's arm and pulled him away from her husband. She had often seen her mother distract him from releasing the fury of his temper and she tried the same strategy now as she spoke in a soft, sweet tone. "We need decide nothing today. Now I would like to speak with my mother if I may. I have something to give her." She attempted to smile in the most dazzling manner possible and was relieved to see she had at least confused José Luis so greatly that his dark eyes had lost their black fire.

"She is no longer here." José Luis looked down at the young woman he had never really known and marveled again at her surprising beauty. "She has left me."

"Where has she gone?" Angelique inquired softly.

"We were no longer speaking when she left, so I have no idea where she might be found," José Luis explained simply.

"That is a damn lie!" Diego interrupted loudly. "There is not one thing that happens in Barcelona that you don't know about before the deed is half done. She left in your carriage, didn't she? You must have asked where she was taken."

Angelique was furious with her husband for interjecting his bitterness when she knew she could have persuaded José Luis to tell her everything she wished to know in a few more minutes' time. "If you did not think to ask your driver what my mother's destination was, then we can ask the man now. There is no reason to shout insults back and forth over this," she stated, glaring at Diego.

"I do not wish to know where Françoise has gone, Diego, and I have never once lied to you." Clearly José Luis was issuing a challenge, for he knew Diego had deceived him, even if he had not ever told an outright lie.

"Stop it, you two!" Angelique insisted firmly. She kept a hold upon José Luis's arm and hoped that it would be enough to keep him from striking his son for being so belligerent. "Will you please summon your driver, or, if you'd prefer, I will go out to the stables and find him myself. I think I have every right to know where my mother is, even if you don't care to know her whereabouts."

Perplexed by the turn of the conversation, José Luis remarked sadly, "It is not that I don't still care for Françoise, but nothing is the same as it once was between us. There is no way it could be."

Angelique smiled with satisfaction, knowing he had told her more than he realized. "My mother was very happy here

265

with you, José Luis, happier than she's been since we left France. If you want her back, I'm certain you possess the charm to make her return to you." Suddenly recalling that she had once asked her mother if she feared José Luis might prefer her if he knew her true age, she confided with another bewitching smile, "At least I have always thought you most charming."

Diego watched in amazement as Angelique continued to flirt openly with his father. She removed the sapphire ring from her finger and pressed it into his palm, explaining that Diego had ordered a beautiful new one for her. Still holding José Luis's hand, she moved close and her voice and manner were so enticing that Diego could barely control the urge to yank her away. What possible difference could it make to her what became of her father's romance with her mother? he wondered silently. For that matter, he still did not understand why Angelique still loved the woman who had rejected her so harshly.

Enchanted by his stunning daughter-in-law's wiles, José Luis summoned his driver, who, after a moment's reflection, recalled the location of the house to which he had taken Françoise. "That is my cousin Beatriz's home," Angelique announced with a troubled frown. "I doubt that my mother will still be there now though, for she and Beatriz found little upon which to agree."

"Do you want to go there this afternoon?" Diego asked, resigned to the fact that he would have to take her there whether he wanted to go or not, and he was not looking forward to it.

"Yes, if you will, please." Angelique gave José Luis a light kiss upon the cheek and left him blushing too deeply to realize how easily she had manipulated his mood into a cooperative one. Her husband, however, was not at all pleased by what he had seen her do.

Once they were comfortably seated in the carriage he had again rented from Carlos's stable, Diego made his point clear. "I know why you flirted so outrageously with my father today, but I swear that if I ever see you behave in such an ingratiating manner with any other man, or if you try such an appalling trick with me, you will regret it!"

"What would you have had me do? Should I have shouted insults at him as you did? Or perhaps thrown a punch or two? You'll never get your way by making your father lose his temper. He is as unreasonable as you are when he is angry, but he is the dearest of men when his mood is agreeable."

Surprised by Angelique's spirited response, Diego replied in kind. "If you think him so dear, it is unfortunate you did not marry him instead of me!"

"Believe me, I considered it!" Angelique answered without thinking, but when she saw Diego's astonishment turn to rage, she regretted her own burst of temper. "Why do you think my mother wished him to think me a child? She didn't want to have to compete with her own daughter for his love. It is not all that unusual for a man in his forties to wed a young woman of seventeen."

Diego found it difficult to catch his breath for he recalled the panic he had felt the day he had thought the beauty he had encountered in the garden was his father's fiancée. "God help me, Angelique, but if I had come home and found you married to my father, I would have done my best to take you away from him."

The anguish in his voice made anger impossible and Angelique pulled him into her arms and covered his face with tender kisses until he began to respond. "It's pointless to worry over what did not happen, Diego. I am your wife, and our marriage was meant to be."

There was no time to take his passion for her as far as he longed to, but Diego did not release the graceful beauty from his embrace. He clutched her slender body to his heart and prayed that the plan he had chosen was not as ill-conceived as his father believed. He wanted to take her away now, before she could be hurt by the vicious gossip he knew would already be circulating. He wanted her to be safe from all harm and he did not let her go until they had made their way through the narrow streets of the oldest part of the city and had finally arrived at Beatriz's door.

"She is every bit as proper a woman as your Aunt Margarita, and I will consider myself fortunate if she agrees to speak with us," Angelique whispered in Diego's ear as the maid went to announce their arrival. The entranceway of the ancient home was cold, and she shivered with the chill.

"Is the woman too poor to heat this place properly or merely too reclusive to open the windows and let the sun do it?" Diego didn't like the austere setting any more than Angelique did. If the whole house was as cold and dark as the hallway, he was certain Françoise would have made her visit brief.

"Hush! She'll hear you!" Angelique could not help but be amused by his comment though, for Beatriz was wealthy but spent little of her money on anything as foolish as firewood.

The maid returned with a hurried step to escort them to the parlor, where they found Beatriz waiting alone. Her angular figure was clothed in black. Seated upon an ornately carved chair, she displayed a stern dignity that would have become the Spanish Queen. Her age was impossible to discern, for while her fair skin held a deathly pallor, it was unlined, and the color of her hair was hidden beneath the lacy folds of her black *mantilla*. Her eyes were such a dark blue that they appeared black as she observed them with a critical stare. Although their mothers had been sisters, her resemblance to Françoise was slight. Her features were sharp rather than delicate, and she had never possessed the Frenchwoman's beauty.

The starkly furnished room was several degrees cooler than the hall and there was nothing in the woman's manner to dispel the mood of impending doom that had greeted them at her door. She lifted her right hand slowly to point at Diego and her voice was filled with contempt as she spoke.

"So you are the young man who has brought this dreadful disgrace to our family. Come closer. I want a better look at you."

Angelique felt Diego's posture stiffen, but he took a step forward and gave a slight bow. When her inspection of him seemed complete, he replied to her insulting greeting. "The name of Aragon is a proud one, and it is no disgrace that Angelique has taken it."

"That is an opinion I do not share," Beatriz remarked coolly.

Not wanting her husband to get into another unfortunate argument that afternoon, Angelique stated the purpose of their visit. "I've come to see my mother. Is she at home?"

"Yes, but she'll not see you," Beatriz announced boldly.

"Would you at least send your maid to tell her we are here? I am leaving for Vera Cruz and I wish to tell her good-bye."

Beatriz weighed her request carefully and after a brief hesitation called her maid, who swiftly returned and, blushing deeply, gave them Françoise's message. *"Madame* Devereau says she has no daughter."

"The bitch." Diego had sworn softly, but Beatriz had heard him and promptly rose to her feet.

"You are not welcome here, *Señor* Aragon. Take your bride and be gone."

"Beatriz, please," Angelique implored, "I must see my mother, if only for a minute. Is she in the same room she occupied before?"

Her dark eyes narrowed and Beatriz shook her head. "I'll not permit you to wander the house searching for her. Françoise has at last seen the error of her ways and I'll not allow her meditation to be interrupted."

Since she knew her mother had never been given to introspection of any sort, Angelique doubted she could be meditating with serious effort on any subject and persisted in her request. "I also have something to give her. It is quite valuable and I must put it into her hands myself."

269

"There are no thieves within these walls. Give the object to me and I will see that Françoise receives it." Beatriz held out a hand so thin that the blue veins at her wrist appeared to be stretched over bare bones rather than flesh.

"No, I must give it to my mother myself," Angelique insisted.

In no mood to beg or plead in his wife's behalf, Diego leaned down to whisper in Angelique's ear. "Let's give the amethyst ring to my father to return. He'll not leave your mother here with this witch."

Angelique nodded in agreement, for his idea was a good one, but she was greatly disappointed that she would not be able to see her mother. "Will you please tell my mother that I can be found on board Diego's ship and that I would like to see her before we sail? If she'll just send me an invitation, I will be happy to return. Will you please do that for me?"

"I will convey your message. Now, if you are waiting to receive my blessing, you need tarry no longer, for I will not give it."

Diego laughed as though he considered her insult ridiculous. "God has already blessed us, so we have no need of your good wishes, even if you were inclined to give them. Good-bye." He took Angelique's hand, but he would have carried her out if she had not come with him willingly. They made their way alone to the front door, which he slammed soundly behind them. Stopping to look back at the dreary dwelling, he could not help but offer a jest. "That is more a tomb than a home. Is your cousin the original owner?"

"Diego!" Angelique laughed with him. "She is very proud of the fact that she lives in one of the oldest homes in Barcelona, but she certainly didn't build it!"

"I am not convinced of that, my pet. She looks like a relic of the Inquisition to me." As he helped Angelique into their carriage, Diego glanced back over his shoulder and, seeing a face in a window on the second floor, he waved, hoping it had been Françoise. While he thought she deserved to be in such a miserable setting, he could not help but feel sorry for her for having to rely upon the hospitality of such a bitter woman. As he climbed into the carriage, he asked, "How long did you reside with Beatriz?"

Angelique folded her hands primly in her lap as she tried to recall. "About six months, I think. My mother felt safe with her cousin, and that was all she wanted for the first few months we were here. She spent most of her time crying over my father's death. Then, gradually, she began to long for the carefree life she'd always known. When Beatriz objected to her receiving male callers, my mother accepted an invitation from one and I've not seen our cousin since, although I do believe my mother called upon her from time to time."

"I cannot fault her for choosing to leave. She was young and pretty, and undoubtedly not eager for the depressing company of that hag." Diego shivered at the memory of the hostile woman, and he could well imagine Françoise's haste to leave her oppressive domination.

"Beatriz isn't truly a witch, Diego, although she certainly behaved like one today. She was widowed after only a few months of marriage and has never stopped mourning her husband."

"I am tempted to speculate upon the cause of the unfortunate man's death, but I'll refrain out of respect for you, Señora Aragon y . . . Angelique, if your name is not truly Devereau, then what is it?" Diego realized with a start that he did not know his wife's true name.

Angelique looked away for a moment, as if she were trying to recall the answer to a difficult question. "My father's name was Bourbon, but I'm certain you will agree that it is too dangerous a name to combine with yours."

Diego leaned back with an astonished sigh. "Since the reign of the house of Bourbon came to such a tragic end in France, I have to agree, but you must also be related to our King Charles as well."

"Yes, of course, but it is quite a distant relationship. I'm not a princess, Diego," Angelique told him. She decided that his amazed expression was very amusing.

Diego found her revelation astounding, for he truly believed in the worth of the common man, and the fact that his wife's bloodlines were so fine troubled him. To have married the daughter of a French count was one thing, but a cousin of the King of Spain was quite another, and he was thankful she did not behave as though she were impressed by her royal blood. "Should anyone inquire, refer to yourself as *Señora* Aragon y Devereau and let it go at that."

"Why don't you use your mother's name?"

"My parents were cousins—Aragon y Aragon," Diego revealed with a smile.

"Yes, it's pointless to be so repetitious, but it is a nice custom to give a child his mother's name as well as his father's. I am only sorry I cannot give our child my name."

"The world changes constantly, Angelique. No one can accurately predict what the political situation will be in France in a year or two."

"You mean you think someday we might be able to return to France?" Angelique sat forward with her lips slightly parted and her posture tensed in eager anticipation of his next words.

Frightened by what he interpreted as a great desire to return to her homeland, Diego spoke sternly. "It won't matter whether or not you'll be welcome in your beloved France in two years or in ten, Angelique. Your place will always be with me!"

Angelique could not imagine what she had done to inspire such a temperamental outburst from her husband, and she regarded his hostile expression with a startled glance. Rather than try to improve his mood, she waited until they were alone in his cabin. Then she placed her hands upon his chest as she explained, "Diego, I had never even danced with a man until you began to give me lessons. I'd never been held or kissed until you took me into your arms. I had no idea

272

what joy could be found in loving a man until you showed me, and were the people of France to make me their queen, I would not return to Paris unless you were by my side. Perhaps it will always be in your nature to be jealous, but I will never give you any cause. I will never want any man but you, nor will I ever wish to leave you."

In the back of his mind, Diego knew she was simply manipulating his emotions as skillfully as she had managed to control his father's, but despite his threats, he could not summon the anger to punish her when the sweep of her thick lashes veiled the striking blue-violet color of her eyes so seductively. The subtle blush in her cheeks, the slightly upturned angle of her nose, the gentle bow of her pink lips, all called to his senses with a siren's song so harmonious he could think of nothing but the pleasure he found in her arms. He began to pull the pins from her hair, spilling the bright curls upon her shoulders where he could touch them as he leaned down to give her a kiss. He knew he had been her first love, but his torment now was in his desire to keep her his forever. Yet, as she came into his arms, he knew he would be a fool to waste a minute of the present in worrying over the future when she had again turned the confines of his cabin into the shores of paradise.

Chapter XVI

When he took Angelique out for a ride the next afternoon, Diego waved with his customary friendliness to those of his father's friends they happened to pass, but he received only cool looks of disdain in return. Since Angelique was, as always, fascinated by the passing scene, he was grateful she did not observe the rudeness he had encountered. But when they arrived at La Belle Mode to pick up the last of the gowns they had ordered and he found that the Ventura sisters had also arrived for fittings, he could not control the awkward situation that ensued.

Angelique greeted the two young women warmly. "How nice to see you again. We had such a wonderful evening at your home. It was a marvelous party and I'm sorry I had so little opportunity to speak with you. Perhaps we can chat a while today."

Maria and Rosalina exchanged embarrassed glances and, after offering hurried excuses to *Madame* Larouche, they promised to return the following day and left after having spent no more than two minutes in her shop.

"Did I say something wrong, Diego?" Angelique watched the two attractive sisters begin to whisper excitedly once they reached the street, and she turned to her husband. "Didn't their behavior seem a bit odd to you?"

Knowing they would probably receive the same cool reception from nearly everyone they met, Diego nonetheless determined to shield his bride from the pain of that reality for as long as possible. "Who knows what happened? Perhaps they had forgotten to arrange payment for their bill. I'm certain their wardrobes must cost their father a small fortune."

Madame Larouche waited patiently while Diego spoke with his wife, for she found the young couple a fascinating study in contrasts. Angelique was a rare beauty who seemed totally unaware of her marvelous array of physical assets. Although fair, she had vivid coloring, as perfect as the beauties in the paintings by Leonardo da Vinci she had been privileged to view in Paris. Her eyes then lingered over Diego, for the sight of such a magnificently built male made her wish she did tailoring for men in addition to creating lovely gowns for the wealthy women of Barcelona. His thick black hair and flashing brown eyes combined with the same classical perfection of features his wife possessed, and she easily placed him among the most dashing men she had ever met.

She sighed wistfully, recalling a beau of her youth who had had the same dark good looks and passionate nature she believed Diego possessed. Her memories were as beautiful as those she hoped he would create for Angelique, but she had been as startled as they by the Venturas' hasty departure. She was privy to all the current gossip and knew that Diego's sudden marriage to a young woman whom all had believed a child had at first caused astonishment. Then unfortunately, after an inital period of curiosity, she had heard there had been outrage at what was generally assumed to be a seduction of the most scandalous sort. Being a Frenchwoman of considerable experience, however, she was not shocked by passion or by a marriage that had all the appearances of an elopement. She thought the young people's obvious love for each other enchanting and would

275

do nothing to discourage their patronage. She could not help but raise an eyebrow slightly, however, when the waistline of the last of the gowns she had created for the slender blonde proved to be too snug. She checked her measurements but was too discreet to remark upon the additional inch at Angelique's waist or to speculate as to its cause. She called a seamstress to adjust the fit promptly and, presenting the completed gown, she bid the striking couple *adieu*. She was chagrined to think that the most malicious of the gossip surrounding them had yet to begin.

In the following days, Diego spent his mornings searching for a cargo without success, but he did not let that disappointment show in his manner when he escorted his bride to the fashionable shops or popular restaurants in the afternoons. When they were snubbed as they had been by Rosalina and Maria Ventura, he pretended not to notice. He was grateful Angelique did not ask him why ladies she had met at his aunt's home pretended not to know her, or why the young men who had rushed to dance with her at the Venturas' party did no more than tip their hats as they hurried by. But he was certain she understood that, once they had been asked to leave his aunt's home, whatever slight cloak of respectability her initial blessing had given their marriage had been torn to shreds by imaginative speculation. Barcelona society adhered to a strict code and Diego knew he had broken every one of the rules. That Angelique's reputation had been irreparably damaged was the unfortunate result.

Angelique, however, pretended not to notice the hushed whispers that greeted them at every turn and gave her attention solely to her husband. She was a pleasant and charming companion and her smile was always bright when they were together. Diego prayed that she was not moved to tears when she was alone.

After refilling Angelique's wine glass, Diego sat back to enjoy the beauty of the afternoon. He had come to admire his wife's courage so greatly that he hid the anger he knew he would be foolish to express in front of her and smiled warmly despite the complexity of the problems that faced them. Earlier that day they had picked up the sapphire ring he had had made for her, and he thought again how perfect the vivid blue of the gems was for her.

While her husband sat openly admiring her, Angelique was thinking more practical thoughts. "Diego, what sort of business interests does Ramon Ortega have?"

Not pleased that she had recalled even the rascal's name, Diego shrugged. "He moves from one enterprise to another with such rapidity that I've no idea what he's doing at present. Why do you ask?"

"He's been staring at us ever since we arrived. He's sitting at the corner table with two men I've never met. One is fair haired and appears to be a gentleman, while the other is dark and looks coarse, despite his fine clothes."

"Since my back is toward him, it would be more accurate to say he's staring at you, wouldn't it?" Diego asked caustically, unable to keep the sharpness out of his voice.

Angelique regarded her husband's stern expression for a moment and decided to ignore his question rather than reply to what was surely more evidence of the jealousy she had done her best to quell. "Whatever his interest, could he secure goods for a cargo?"

"I'd rather sail with no more than rocks for ballast than do business with him. He'd just as soon fill a ship with stolen goods as he'd arrange for honest cargo, and then he'd alert the authorities and collect a reward when they'd confiscated the very merchandise he'd provided. He is lower than the belly of a lizard, and I'll thank you not to mention his name to me again."

"As you wish, but he's getting up and it looks to me as though he's coming our way." Angelique neither smiled nor frowned, but returned the man's effusive greeting with a slight nod.

Despite the fact that he had received no such invitation, Ramon pulled up a chair to join them, then came straight to the point. "I hear you wish to sail to Vera Cruz. Since you have been unable to find a cargo, I would like to supply one."

"My plans are no concern of yours, Ortega, so I'll not detain you." Diego tossed down the last of his wine, ready to leave even if the ill-mannered man was not.

"I have a friend whose financial situation is most desperate," Ramon began.

"Then he should see my cousin, Miguel Rivera. He is the banker, not I."

"He is too proud to go begging to bankers, since he has already received several loans and would undoubtedly be refused. When I told him you planned to sail, he was most anxious that I contact you about transporting his wines. Since the making of wine is forbidden by law in Spanish colonies, you know as well as I do that such a cargo would bring high profits."

Diego's eyes narrowed and his dislike for Ramon was readily apparent in the darkness of his glance. "That is certainly true, so why should any man who produces fine wines be in need of money? Or for that matter, come to you for assistance? Does he share your passion for gambling?"

Ramon turned then to Angelique. "Your husband is a clever man, *Señora* Aragon, but gambling was at one time his passion as well as mine."

Angelique looked at her husband with undisguised alarm, for she had not thought him one so foolish as to risk the money he worked so hard to earn in such a frivolous fashion. Her father had had many friends whose addiction to games of chance had nearly cost them their estates, and while she was not certain just what Diego did own, despite his boasts of being wealthy, she could not bear the thought that he might gamble excessively.

"You needn't look so worried, my pet. You are my only passion now." Diego rose to his feet and reached for his bride's hand. "I am not interested in any business venture you might arrange, Ortega. Tell your friend to come directly to me if he wants to do business."

Ramon leapt to his feet, as insulted by his remark as Diego had meant him to be. "He wishes me to handle all the arrangements in the interest of discretion."

"For a considerable commission, of course," Diego remarked slyly.

"If I were to arrange for a cargo for you and a profit for him, then I would deserve the commission I'd charge!" Ramon exclaimed in his own defense.

"What did you ask, Ortega—your usual twenty-five percent, or more?" Without waiting for a reply, Diego escorted his bride out into the sunshine and helped her into their waiting carriage.

Since her husband was nearly shaking with rage, Angelique waited a moment before making a suggestion. "Your family is a respected one, or at least it was until quite recently, Diego. You must know every man who makes wine and should be able to determine which one would be likely to mention his need for money to Ortega."

Not seeing her point, Diego shrugged. "I know of several men who might be forced to consider such a regrettable alliance. I'm certain my father is behind my inability to find a cargo, so they'd know they couldn't go through him to place goods on the *Diablo* as they usually do. Why?"

"Wine is a good cargo though, isn't it?" Angelique asked thoughtfully.

"Excellent," Diego admitted. "It is easy to load, transport, and sell."

"Then all you'll have to do is go to the men you think might need to ship their wines and arrange for the cargo yourself. Wouldn't this man who is supposedly desperate be happy to avoid paying Ortega such an exorbitant commission? Twenty-five percent is outrageous!"

For a moment Diego stared in wonder, then he pulled his clever bride into his arms and flashed a devilish grin. "How I have managed to be a successful businessman without you I will never know! Your idea is more unscrupulous than any Ortega is likely to devise. Let's stop to see Miguel before I make any calls upon my father's friends. He will undoubtedly know which man is most heavily in debt."

"Revealing such information would be unethical, wouldn't it?" Angelique inquired suspiciously.

"If the client makes a good profit, he will be able to repay what he owes to the bank. Both he and Miguel will be happy and what's unethical about that?"

Angelique frowned. "I will give it some thought, but I'm certain a banker should not reveal the financial status of his clients. It just isn't right."

Miguel Rivera agreed with Angelique in principle, but he trusted Diego not to reveal his source of information. "Since you know the man well, I'd go first to Guillermo Rosales; then if he does not wish to ship goods with you, I'll suggest another name. I will consider this referral a service to my customers, since I know you will be discreet."

Angelique looked away, unable to hide her smile, for had Diego been more discreet they would be facing an entirely different set of difficulties than they were facing at present. After a short discussion of his own financial affairs, Diego thanked Miguel, then took his bride back to the *Diablo*.

"I'll call upon Rosales within the hour. If he's desperate for cash, I'll pay him a fair sum and load the wine tonight. The more I think about it, the more I am convinced that he is in some sort of financial difficulty. When I attended a party at his home recently, he kept pestering me for details of my personal affairs. At the time, I thought he wanted only to find a wealthy husband for one of his daughters, but his intentions might have been entirely different. He might have simply wanted a loan."

"When was that party?" Angelique inquired curiously. "I recall the man's name, but not when you went to his home."

"It was the same night we were married, my pet"—Diego leaned down to kiss the pretty blush that filled her cheeks—"nearly a month ago. Now I must hurry. There's no time to lose."

"If you can load the wine tonight, when will we sail?" Angelique followed him to the door of his cabin, anxious to know when they would be leaving.

"On the morning tide. Most of our provisions are already stored and I'll send Octavio for the last of them now. The crew is as anxious to sail as I am, and the longer I delay the more time Ortega will have to get furious over losing a large commission and come after me."

Angelique grabbed her husband's arm. "He would not harm you!"

"Not that coward. But he'd hire others to cause me grief. Now cease your worry over it. Give me the amethyst ring and I'll drop it off with my father on the way back."

Angelique pulled it from her hand slowly. "You will tell him how important it is that he place it in my mother's hand himself, won't you? I don't want him just to leave it with Beatriz."

"I will insist he does this favor for you, Angelique. I am sorry we've heard nothing from your mother. I know you wanted to tell her good-bye."

"You must hurry, Diego. We've no time to dwell upon my mother's neglect now." Angelique paced the cabin slowly, forcing herself not to weep over her mother's obvious lack of concern for her. Then she realized that if Octavio was away purchasing the last of their provisions, she would be able to leave the ship and make one last attempt to see her mother. Perhaps Beatriz had not relayed her message after all. Maybe her mother had no idea where she was or how to reach her. Grabbing her cloak, Angelique made her way out on deck, and when she found all the men occupied at the bow, she sprinted down the gangplank and hurried away through the crowd of peddlers and sailors who always seemed to have business on the docks.

Beatriz's home was close to the waterfront, in the original part of the city, and she made her way carefully through the narrow maze of streets that apparently never fully enjoyed the warmth and light of the sun, certain she could find her cousin's home within the hour. But it was nearly dark when she at last arrived at the forbidding edifice. She rapped loudly with the wrought iron knocker and after a long delay, the maid appeared at the door.

"You needn't bother Beatriz. Please go straight to my mother and tell her I have come to say good-bye." Angelique stamped her feet nervously as she waited for the maid to reappear. She had to get back to the *Diablo* before Diego returned or he would worry about her needlessly and she knew he had more than enough on his mind without her adding to his problems.

After an interminable wait, the diminutive maid again entered the hall. "*Madame* Devereau still insists she has no daughter. I must ask you to leave."

Not about to admit defeat, Angelique pushed past the servant, but she had gotten no further than halfway up the narrow staircase before she heard Beatriz shriek her name, and in the next instant she was overtaken by a burly groom who wrapped his arms around her waist and lifted her into the air. "Put me down, you oaf! I want to see my mother!" Angelique beat on his fists, struggling to break free of his confining grasp, but he was too strong for her to escape him. When they reached the foot of the stairs, Beatriz was waiting for them, her proud posture rigid, her stare dark and menacing.

"You may toss this strumpet out in the street, Felipe, for she seems to be unable to comprehend the simple truth that she is unwelcome here."

The haughty woman ignored Angelique's angry protestations that she be allowed to see her mother, and after flinging open the front door, Felipe followed his mistress's instructions and hurled the defiant blonde out onto the cobblestones, where she landed sprawled upon her left hip.

Angelique heard the door slam shut as she got slowly to her feet, then moved gingerly to be certain she had not been badly hurt. Her whole left side felt numb and she had cut her left palm trying to break her fall, but she had no choice other than to try to walk back to the *Diablo*. She limped badly and had taken no more than half a dozen steps before she remembered the baby. Terrified that she might suffer a miscarriage as the result of the shocking abuse she had just suffered, she sank down upon the curb to try to catch her breath. Having no desire to be out after dark in such a dismal section of town, she soon forced herself to rise and with slow, shuffling steps she began to make her way in the direction whence she had come. When she heard the sounds of a carriage approaching, she drew back into a doorway in order to escape being splattered with mud as a climax to the other indignities she had suffered that afternoon. Huddled in the shadows, she waited until the vehicle had passed by, then continued on her way. She had to stop more than once to rest, for the initial numbness she had felt had gradually been replaced by a bone-jarring pain. When the next carriage rolled by, she lacked the energy to step into a doorway and was astonished when the vehicle came to a stop at her side.

Diego threw open the door, yelling angrily as he leapt out of the carriage. "Where have you been? We traversed this same street half an hour ago and didn't see you!" Seeing the trace of tears on her long lashes, he was instantly ashamed of himself for being so angry with her and lifted her into his arms to place her gently upon a seat inside the rented carriage. "When I returned to the *Diablo* and found you gone, I knew there was only one place you might be, but

283

Beatriz's maid refused to give me any information. Were you able to see your mother?"

"No." Thoroughly miserable, Angelique nonetheless lifted her chin proudly as she recounted the unfortunate result of her visit. "Beatriz called me a strumpet and had one of her servants toss me out into the street."

"What?" Diego grabbed his wife's shoulders and made her repeat what she had said, certain he could not possibly have understood the statements she had uttered between the sobs she tried so valiantly to stifle. "I'll not allow anyone to treat you so harshly, Angelique. If there's anyone who deserves to be thrown out of that house, it's that witch, Beatriz, and I'm tempted to use a window on the third floor to do it!"

"No, please, don't go back there. I want only to go to the *Diablo* and lie down. I'm afraid I'm going to be sick." She did not resist as he pulled her across his lap but instead snuggled in his embrace and wept softly while he uttered the worst string of curses she had ever heard. She could not fault him for his anger, however, and made no comment on the vile terms he had used. Yet she knew that if she had become his mistress rather than his wife she truly could have been considered a strumpet and that made her mood all the more bleak.

The carriage rambled on through the narrow streets, but they were still several blocks from their destination when they heard an angry shout and the sound of their driver's response as he fought to keep the horses under control when they were pulled to a jarring halt. Wanting to investigate the cause of the commotion, Diego placed Angelique by his side and moved toward the door, but before he could reach the handle, the door was yanked open by a masked man brandishing a pistol.

"Climb out, Aragon, and be quick about it or I won't be nearly so polite to that sweet little wife of yours," the bandit ordered in a threatening whisper.

Diego stood as if he would follow the brigand's order, but

as he came to the doorway he grabbed hold and struck out with both feet. He caught the felon full in the face with a savage kick and the heels of his boots found their mark as well. Sent flying by the force of the unexpected blow, the man hit the back of his head against a nearby wall, then slumped to the walk, where he lay unconscious with blood gushing profusely from his broken nose. With their leader so severely injured, the two men who had grabbed the team's reins lacked the courage to carry out their mission and bolted. The sounds of their running feet echoed off the deserted cobblestones as they disappeared rapidly into the darkness.

"Are you all right, sir?" the driver called out anxiously.

"Yes. Give me a minute to see who this fool is and we'll be on our way."

Angelique grabbed her husband's arm and gripped it frantically. "What if there are more men waiting out there?"

With a delighted grin, Diego drew a knife from his belt and promised, "Then I'll kill them." He stepped out of the carriage and once satisfied that no one else was lurking about, he replaced his knife in its sheath. He bent down beside the injured man and untied the scarf he had used as a disguise. The lanterns upon the carriage provided sufficient illumination for him to recognize a man he knew to be in Ramon Ortega's employ. He wasn't surprised when Angelique peered out the carriage window and called to him excitedly.

"That's the dark-haired man who was seated with Ortega in the restaurant this afternoon! Is he dead?"

"Not yet he isn't." Since the fellow was unconscious, Diego stuffed his limp body into the luggage compartment at the rear of the carriage and gave their driver Ortega's address.

"We'll make a slight detour on the way to the *Diablo*. I don't want that man to go without medical attention and I'm certain it should be Ortega who provides it."

285

"You don't mean we're taking that bandit to his house!" Angelique gasped in fright. "Isn't that too dangerous? If he'd send men out to get you, what would he do if you were to fling one of them upon his doorstep?"

Placing the pistol he had just confiscated at his side, Diego leaned over to give her a reassuring kiss. "I imagine he'll be dreadfully embarrassed and hire more-experienced rogues next time. But he'll not be able to do anything else tonight, and tomorrow we shall be gone."

Angelique shivered despite his show of confidence and she dared not draw a deep breath, for she saw that her husband was courting disaster and apparently relishing that thrill.

When they reached Ramon Ortega's home, he deposited the injured man at the front door and rapped the knocker soundly. When a servant responded, he gestured casually toward the unfortunate victim of the foiled attack.

"Will you please tell *Señor* Ortega that Diego Aragon has returned one of his men? He will require the attentions of a physician and a good, long rest, but the next man he sends to annoy me will be returned in a coffin. Now I want you to repeat that message to me before you call your master."

The terrified man mumbled Diego's threat in a high-pitched whine before dashing off to call Ramon without bothering to first drag inside the poor soul who lay sprawled before the door. Not about to correct this oversight himself, Diego turned on his heel and strode to the carriage.

Angelique leaned out the window to observe what would happen next, but their driver wasted no time in returning to the road and she lost sight of the Ortega home before anyone appeared. Sitting back in her seat, she glanced at her husband's satisfied smirk and shook her head in disbelief. "I hope he has the good sense not to pursue us tonight, but what if he does?"

"He'd regret it for the rest of his life, Angelique, and I can guarantee that that wouldn't be more than an hour." Pulling her across his lap once more, he hugged her tightly. "Now cease your worry over him. I am more concerned about you. Do you still feel ill?"

"I am too frightened to accurately assess how I feel. That man did not expect you to kick him in the face any more than I did. How did you think of such a clever trick?"

"Why? Do you plan to use it?" Diego asked with a chuckle.

"I hope I shall never need to, but it was most effective," Angelique confided with obvious admiration.

"The fool was standing too close. The street was so narrow he had little choice, but such an error was his undoing and I merely took advantage of it. Now let's forget that the incident ever occurred." He held her tenderly as he kissed the salty trails her tears had made upon her cheeks and, when they reached the *Diablo*, he carried her into his cabin and laid her tenderly upon his bunk. "I'm sending for a physician. You're still trembling, undoubtedly badly bruised, and I want to make certain you're all right before we sail."

Angelique made her choice quickly. She had been appalled to hear her husband laugh in the face of death and feared that if they were to delay their departure any longer, Ramon Ortega would try some other method of harming him. "Being thrown out of Beatriz's house was a slight discomfort compared to being stopped by men whose purpose I shudder to imagine. Since the man called your name and we recognized him as one of Ortega's men, how far do you think they meant to go? Would they have been satisfied to rob you, or would they have given you a beating? What do you suppose he meant about being polite to me?"

Distracted by her barrage of questions, Diego sat down upon the edge of the bunk. "They probably had orders to rob us and rough me up a bit, but not even Ortega is low enough to try to reach me by harming you." At least Diego believed he was not, but he had no intention of remaining in Barcelona long enough to find out. Angelique seemed so alert that he hesitated a moment before saying, "I still think I

287

should call a physician."

"That's not necessary for a few bruises, Diego." Angelique hoped he would believe her, for she knew she would never be able to admit to a doctor that she was pregnant and that would be the most important thing for him to know. "If you'll just bring me warm water to bathe, I promise to rest and I'll be fine."

"You're certain?" Diego wasn't entirely convinced.

"Of course." Angelique leaned forward to give him an enticing kiss, hoping to distract him. Her ploy worked.

"The men are already loading the barrels of wine and making the last of our preparations to sail. Do you truly think I have time to carry water for my wife's bath?" Diego laughed as he went to the door. "I will never live this down."

"If it's too much trouble . . ." Angelique began sweetly.

"No trouble at all." Diego waved as he went out the door, but it was not until he reached the galley that he realized that the real danger to Angelique lay not in bruises, but in the risk of a miscarriage. He sent Pablo to bring a physician who lived nearby while he returned with the water for her bath.

He waited until after she had bathed and was dressed in a nightgown and resting comfortably to tell her the doctor had arrived. He thought it only fair to warn her, so she would not take out her anger on the young man.

"Diego!" Angelique was tempted to use some of the curses she had heard him speak earlier that evening. "I won't see him. I refuse!"

Diego looked down at her, reminding himself as he frequently did that she was little more than a pretty child who made a courageous effort to portray his wife. "This man is remarkably discreet, Angelique, and I doubt his examination will require more than a few minutes of your time. Humor me. The voyage will take several weeks, and I can't spend all my time worrying about your health."

Angelique's features were set in an angry frown as she responded tersely, "Since I have no choice then, let's get this ordeal over with quickly."

Doctor Delgado smiled nervously as he was introduced, for he had had far more experience treating the injuries and diseases of sailors than those of fine ladies. He knew Diego Aragon well, but he had never expected to be called to treat his wife. "I understand you had a bad fall, *Señora* Aragon. If I may be permitted to, that is to . . ."

Since the young man was obviously more embarrassed than she was, Angelique saw no reason to be secretive. "I did not fall. I was dropped by a brute who is totally lacking in manners. I have a few bruises, which aren't particularly severe, but if you'd like to see them, come closer and I will be glad to show you." Tossing back the covers, she slowly began to draw up the hem of her gown, and, to her amazement, the doctor began to blush. She glanced over at Diego, wondering where he had found such a self-conscious physician, but his attention was also focused upon her left leg. She wanted to maintain some degree of modesty but could not think how to do so, for the ugly purple bruises extended all the way from her knee to her waist. The doctor stepped close to the edge of the bunk, but she could tell from his breathless whisper that his mind was most certainly not on her injuries.

"Would you please just turn toward your right a bit?" he requested nervously, for he realized that the long, slender leg she had just exposed was the most perfect he had ever seen. His eyes swept hungrily from the tiny foot to the dainty ankle, up the gentle swell of her calf to the smooth fullness of her thigh, and he found concentrating upon her injuries extremely difficult when her beauty affected him so strongly. When he reached out to touch her, his hand moved slowly down her hip in an appreciative caress. "Can you bend your knee without discomfort?" he finally asked hoarsely.

Angelique sat up straight before she bent her knee, jamming her nightgown between her legs so as not to display any more of herself than she already had. Her muscles screamed in protest, but she did not admit it. "See, my knee is fine," she said with an innocent smile.

Straightening up, the physician coughed to hide his embarrassment. "Well then, you don't seem to be badly hurt but merely bruised. That is undoubtedly because you are so fair. Just relax for a few days and soak in a warm tub if your hip gives you any pain." He turned then to look up at Diego, hoping he would be satisfied with the treatment he had prescribed.

"Angelique is nearly three months pregnant. If she were going to suffer a miscarriage as a result of this unfortunate accident, would it have already begun?" Diego asked with studied nonchalance.

Angelique wanted to pull the covers over her head and hide, for she was deeply mortified by Diego's question. She hoped the young doctor had no idea when they had been married, but she could see by his astonished look that he knew all about them. "Will you leave me without a shred of pride, Diego?"

"Pride has nothing to do with this." Diego dismissed her complaint as trivial. "Well Delgado, what's your opinion? I'd planned to sail at dawn, but if there's a chance Angelique will require additional medical attention, I'll delay our voyage until you think she can travel safely."

Since the physician had no experience treating pregnant women, he shrugged helplessly. "I really don't know what to recommend, but I think your wife would be in pain now if a miscarriage were imminent."

Diego frowned, not satisfied with his reply. "Is there any way to avoid such a tragedy?"

"Not that I know of. Miscarriages simply happen. But if your wife remains in bed for a few days, it will undoubtedly be helpful."

"Of course." Diego looked down at Angelique. "You haven't felt even the slightest twinge of pain that could be the first sign of a miscarriage?"

Angelique shook her head, too embarrassed to reply aloud. Her husband was treating her as a child again, and she did not like it at all. As soon as the physician bid them good night, she turned her anger loose. "You should have told me it was the baby you were worried about rather than me."

"What?" Diego walked back to his bunk and stared down at her. "What is the difference? You are the one who will suffer if you lose the child. There was no point in keeping your pregnancy a secret when Delgado might have been able to offer some valuable advice."

"Which he didn't!" Angelique pointed out angrily. She did not want Diego to discover how badly frightened she really was about what might happen to her and she was successful, for he completely misunderstood her true concern.

Diego began to smile, a slow, sad grin that played across his lips as he tried to reassure her. "Delgado will not tell anyone anything, so you needn't fear that the next rumor about us will be that I had to marry you."

"But you did!" Angelique protested. "Your father gave you no choice! What you wanted was to make me your mistress. Then I would have been open to even worse slander and would have had no way to deny it!" She clenched her fists tightly in her lap. She was hurt, angry, and so embarrassed at the way he had talked with the doctor—as if she had not even been there—that she did not know what to do.

"I'll not dignify that insult with a response. I've got too much to do tonight to worry about your mental state as well as your health. I'll send your supper on a tray. Stay in bed to eat it!" With that command, Diego turned on his heel and left her alone with only her terrible fears for company.

Chapter XVII

It was after midnight when Diego returned to his cabin. He took care that his footsteps did not make the slightest sound and he closed the door quietly, but as he turned toward his bunk he discovered that such precautions had been unnecessary, for Angelique was wide awake. She was curled up in a seductive pose, but her deep blue gaze held none of the enthusiastic sparkle with which she usually greeted him after they had been parted for a few hours, and he knew instantly that her mood had not improved. "I thought you'd be asleep." He held his breath, praying she had not begun to feel ill, though she certainly did not appear to be in any pain, he noted.

"I don't feel tired," Angelique explained softly. There were many words to describe how she did feel at the end of such an exciting day: disappointed that she had failed in her attempt to see her mother, unsure both of her own and her husband's feelings, and apprehensive about the type of life that awaited them in Vera Cruz. She had had far too much on her mind to grow tired.

Diego started to peel off his clothes, but his eyes never left his bride's hauntingly beautiful face, for the complexity of her fascinating personality was vividly reflected in her subdued expression. He had believed she possessed a serious nature when he had thought her a child, and recalling this first impression, he decided that perhaps her mood was understandable after all. He had not expected her to be awake though, and had not planned any clever greeting to regain her favor after having walked out on her. "Would you rather I slept elsewhere?" he finally thought to offer.

"Is that what you really want to do?"

Diego shook his head. "Not unless I have to, but it might be the best thing for you tonight." The mere sight of her golden curls fanned out upon the pillows had brought a surge of heat to his loins that seemed most improper considering the rough treatment she had suffered. He could not expect her to want to make love, and while he could justify the need for restraint on several counts, his body ignored his mind's command and continued to torment him with ever-increasing desire.

Angelique licked her lips slowly, not wanting to have to beg for his company if he would not give it willingly. Suddenly seeing a way to make his presence seem imperative, she swiftly used it. "I'd rather not be alone tonight."

"I understand." Diego smiled to himself, satisfied that her excuse had not cost either of them his pride. He doused the lamp before removing the last of his clothes to prevent her from being shocked by the effect she had upon him. Then he climbed over the end of the bunk to position himself so that she would be able to sleep on the outside. This would reduce the risk that he would inadvertently brush against her bruised hip. The bunk seemed impossibly narrow however, and he could not find a comfortable position where the soft tips of her breasts, which were scarcely contained by her sheer nightgown, were not pressing against his arm or bare chest in an invitation he knew he should ignore.

When her husband ceased his nervous tossing and turning, Angelique asked in a hushed whisper, "I know you're tired but could you please put your arms around me?"

293

Since her request was made so sweetly, Diego did not see how he could refuse to grant it and, turning upon his left side, he placed his right arm across her waist in a brotherly hug.

Angelique turned toward him, resting her left arm upon his arm and lightly touching the soft curls at his temple. "I did not mean to behave like such a shrew. I know you would never intentionally do anything to harm me. But I don't like being treated like a child. When you knew I didn't wish to see a physician, why did you call one anyway?"

Diego sighed wearily. "I'll not fight with you about that again, Angelique. It was merely a precaution I thought I'd be foolish not to take. That isn't treating you as a child, but simply taking care of you as I know I should." The subtle scent of her perfume made coherent thought nearly impossible for him then, for he regarded that sweet fragrance as the prelude to love and not as a stimulus for clearheaded discussion. As her fingertips strayed to his nape, he closed his eyes in a futile attempt to shut out the craving her slightest touch created within his heart.

He thought again of the night they had met, for there had been no shyness in her manner even then, and he began to wonder if perhaps it might not be wrong to seek release from the hunger she had aroused with no more than her enchanting presence. He began to kiss her with the lightest caress of his mouth moving slowly down her cheek to her lips. When she returned his first, hesitant kiss with a saucy nibble, he ceased to worry over her fragile health and slid his tongue between her lips for a kiss he deepened until he could feel that the tremors of delight flooding through him were being echoed along the length of her shapely form. She slipped her arm under his then so her hand might move slowly down the taut muscles of his stomach to invite an intimacy of a far more erotic sort. Her touch was tantalizing and gave him such abundant pleasure that he had to force himself to draw away. After taking a deep breath, he asked her to tell him the truth. "If I cause you the slightest bit of discomfort, please stop me. Promise me that."

Angelique smiled, even though she knew he could not see her expression in the darkness enveloping the cozy cabin. "I promise," she vowed with unmistakable sincerity, though she had no intention of stopping him unless she began to suffer unbearable pain.

"We can make love lying side by side. It's really very pleasant this way." Moving closer still, Diego kissed her once again before asking, "Can you rest your leg upon my hip?"

"Like this?" Angelique could not help but wonder where and with whom Diego had learned so many fascinating variations for making love, but she knew this would be an extremely inappropriate time to inquire about the source of his expertise. His fingertips slid between her legs to provide the most delicious sensations, and when his mouth returned to hers, she no longer had the means or the desire to speak. His magical caress moved down to tease the flesh of her inner thigh for a moment, then strayed back up to the spot where his smooth, rhythmic touch drew her emotions to a shattering peak. He slid lower in the bunk then, and with a swift upward thrust he entered her and began moving with long, slow strokes to bring them both to the brink of ecstasy. He paused then for what seemed to her an eternity and lay motionless within her. His tongue continued to dominate her mouth, silencing all protest to such teasing until he could no longer hold back. With a quick, staccato rhythm he led her through the golden portal to paradise and, after feeling her whole body shudder with that exquisite joy, he filled her with the fiery splendor of his love.

Their arms and legs still entwined, they lay exchanging unhurried kisses until sleep at last overtook them. Because they were filled with the warmth of such deep contentment, their dreams were sweet, but before dawn Diego left his bunk to again assume his duties as captain of the *Diablo*.

The gentle rocking motion the ship had maintained when moored to the dock changed abruptly to a far more vigorous rolling once she headed out into the Mediterranean. Angelique was rudely jarred from her slumbers then, and the nausea she usually experienced upon waking was compounded by the pitch and sway of the graceful ship. She sat up slowly, remembering her bruised hip too late to save herself from a jolt of pain when her feet touched the floor. Her left leg felt stiff and sore, and the constant motion of the *Diablo* made walking extremely difficult. She soon gave up the effort to dress and returned to the bunk. There she pulled the covers up to her chin and closed her eyes tightly, hoping to stop the dizziness that tormented her, though this measure brought her only partial relief.

Diego was in such a fine mood that he was whistling merrily as he brought Angelique her breakfast. "Ah, I'm pleased to see you've taken the doctor's advise and decided to remain in bed. The view of the coast is interesting, but perhaps by the time we reach Gibraltar you'll be able to come up on deck."

Angelique dared not open more than one eye. "Do you never get seasick, Diego?"

"We are moving through the water with an amazing smoothness today, Angelique. Don't tell me you think you're seasick!" Diego laughed at such an absurdity. "Wait until we hit rough water and then you'll find out what seasickness really is."

"You're teasing me, aren't you?" Angelique asked hopefully, for she could not imagine feeling any worse than she already did.

Diego sat down beside her and smoothed her glossy curls away from her pale cheek. "The best place for you is right where you are, my pet. In a few days, when you can safely get up, you'll be much more comfortable on deck. The fresh air will make you feel ever so much better. You'll see."

Angelique tried to smile. "I'm certain I will, but how long

will this voyage take?"

Diego chuckled at her question. "Do you plan to start marking off the days now? In two to three weeks we'll stop in the Canary Islands, where you can put your pretty little feet upon the ground once again while we buy fresh provisions. Then it will be approximately a month more before we reach Vera Cruz."

"Nearly two months in all?" Angelique murmured with obvious distress.

"No, not if we're lucky. Our time depends greatly upon the weather and we might make the voyage in six weeks if all goes well."

"I'll pray for good weather," Angelique vowed solemnly.

Diego continued to chuckle happily. "Well, at least this is keeping you in bed. I'd no idea how I was going to force you to follow the doctor's advice."

Despite her queasiness, Angelique gave him a seductive smile. "You wouldn't have to force me. All you would have to do is stay here with me and I'd never want to get up."

Diego leaned down to kiss her tenderly before he shook his head. "That is a delightful idea, but unfortunately not possible. As captain of this vessel I do have several duties that would make remaining in bed difficult, and then our voyage would only be delayed."

"Then by all means see to your tasks, Diego. I don't want this trip extended one minute past the record time." She sat up slowly then to sip the tea he had brought her and picked up a biscuit, but she had taken no more than two bites when she asked him to take the tray away. "That's all I can eat now. Maybe later."

"All right. I'll come back as often as I can to see if you need anything. Go back to sleep."

Recalling his remarks about his crew, Angelique reached out to touch his sleeve. "Diego? Your men aren't teasing you about me, are they? You do bring the water for my baths yourself, and now if you bring me my meals, will they all tease you unmercifully?"

"They wouldn't dare, Angelique, but there are quite a few who aren't pleased that there's a woman on board. Old superstitions die hard, it seems."

"Women are considered back luck, aren't they?" Angelique thought such a notion silly. "Speaking of superstitions, where are the little Azteca gods? Did you bring them along?"

"Of course. They've been on board since the night my father told me to remove them from his house." Diego got to his feet and moved toward the door. "I'll get them out for you later if you'd like to see them again."

"Would you please?" Angelique tried once more to smile and hoped she did not look as ghastly as she felt. "I really would like to see them."

"I won't forget." Diego returned the tray to the galley, where the cook gave him a skeptical glance.

"*Señora* Aragon seems to have little appetite. Does she find my biscuits unappealing?" Eduardo Ortiz was a portly man who sampled his own cooking liberally.

"No, not at all. She is simply not as used to the sea as we are and doesn't feel like eating. Your biscuits are the pride of this ship. You know that," Diego teased, then slapped him on the back, for both were aware that the entire crew complained that his biscuits were only slightly less difficult to eat than stones.

By the time Diego had finished eating his own supper much later, he had managed to coax Angelique into taking only three bites. "I know this sounds preposterous, but eating will make you feel better, Angelique. If you don't eat, you'll become ill simply from that, and then what will I do with you? I am no physician, so you must help me take the best care of you I can."

Angelique opened her mouth dutifully, but her stomach lurched the moment she swallowed the bite of chicken. She raised her hand to plead, "Please, Diego. I'll try to eat, but

298

give me just a little more time."

"I will sit here beside you all night if I must, my pet, but you are going to eat your supper." Diego's grin was a teasing one. He knew she was not hungry, but he was certain he must convince her that she would have to eat anyway. When she closed her eyes and leaned back against her pillows to rest, he simply waited until she opened her eyes again. It took a long while, but at least he was satisfied that she had consumed enough nourishment to remain healthy. Taking the tray over to the table, he wiped his hands and then went to the drawer where he had placed the three Azteca figures. "I've not shown these to anyone on board, for I told you sailors are a superstitious breed. You like the little lady of the dead best, don't you?"

"How did you know that?" Angelique's pale cheeks took on a bit of color as she sat up straight to take the little goddess in her hands.

"I thought so when I first showed her to you, and then the next night you went ahead and touched her after your mother had forbidden you to do it. I should have known then who you were." Diego again took his place on the edge of the bunk. "Do you still think her charming?"

Angelique looked up for a moment to study his expression and she was so pleased to find that he did not seem in the least bit bitter about the way she had fooled him that she did not comment upon the nobility of her motives. "Yes, I think she's very appealing, but I like Quetzalcoatl too. *Lord of the Wind* would make an impressive name for a ship, wouldn't it?"

"Superb," Diego agreed. Then his expression grew troubled, "If I ever have need of an additional vessel, I'll name it that just for you."

"Did you mean what you said about staying in Vera Cruz forever?" Angelique kept her eyes focused upon the carving, not daring to look directly at her husband when his mood seemed so dark. She did not want him to make such an important decision simply for her, if it were not the best possible choice for him as well.

"Forever is a damn long time, Angelique. We'll have to wait and see what we find there before we make our final plans. Perhaps you'd like to go on to California. It is reputed to be spectacular in both scenery and weather."

"How would we reach it, another voyage?" Angelique inquired with a pained expression.

"No, it is possible to go overland," Diego assured her. "One trip at a time though, my dearest. You'll like the Canary Islands. They are very pretty in themselves."

Angelique handed Diego the little stone goddess and covered a sleepy yawn. "I don't know how I can be tired when I've been in bed all day, but I am."

"Would you like me to play you a lullaby? I never had an opportunity to serenade you, but I do play the guitar passably well."

"Do you really?" Angelique's smile was a delighted one. "Well then, by all means, play something for me."

First Diego returned the Azteca goddess to the drawer where she had been stored with the other carvings and then he excused himself briefly to borrow a guitar from one of his men. "I had my own instrument at one time, but I mislaid it somewhere and didn't think to purchase another before we sailed."

"Mislaid it?" Angelique thought that unlikely. "Are you certain you didn't serenade some lovely young woman and then leave it beneath her balcony when you climbed up to her bedroom?"

Since she seemed well enough now to tease him, Diego did not want to spoil her playful mood. "Well, if I did, it must have been in Vera Cruz, for I've not even looked at another woman since I met you."

"I think you'd better just play your melodies for me and save the flattery for another time. I've no reason to be jealous now, since I'm the only woman on board." Angelique found that thought very amusing and began to giggle mischievously.

Diego thought his bride such a charming creature that he laughed with her, and several moments passed before he grew serious enough to begin to play. He first picked out one pretty tune and then another. He had mastered the guitar with the same ease with which he had learned to sail, and it did not surprise him that his playing pleased Angelique.

"You're very good, Diego. Really good. Do you know any other songs you could play for me?" Yawning again, Angelique snuggled down beneath the covers to get more comfortable while she listened.

"A few. Just close your eyes and rest while I play what I can recall." Diego soon became so involved in the harmonies he was producing that he began to devise his own tunes when he had exhausted all the ones he had memorized. When he glanced over at Angelique, he was surprised to find her sound asleep and wondered how long he had been playing solely to amuse himself. He leaned down to kiss her cheek before returning the guitar to its owner. He remained on deck afterward, and stood at the rail, fascinated as always by the play of the moonlight upon the water.

Seeing the captain standing alone, Octavio approached him. "Your wife is feeling better tonight?"

"Yes, but she's still far from well," Diego revealed with a sad smile. "I hope she'll be better in a day or two though."

"I will look forward to seeing her again, for she is a very pretty girl," Octavio remarked truthfully.

"Girl?" That word conjured up memories Diego wanted only to suppress. "Angelique is a woman, despite her years— one whose courage any man would respect."

"I meant no disrespect by saying she is pretty!" Octavio insisted.

Diego's expression grew stern. "I was not insulted by your compliment, and she would not be either, but do not forget that she is my wife and I expect the entire crew to

301

treat her politely."

"I will make certain that they do." Octavio had not realized Diego had become such a jealous husband and resolved not to provoke his anger again. There was enough talk about the wisdom of having such a beauty on board, and he did not want to make the situation more difficult than it already was for any of them.

The two men shared an uncomfortable silence until Diego finally moved away to return to his cabin. He found his emotions were surprisingly tender rather than erotic that night. He joined Angelique in the narrow bunk, drew her into a warm embrace, and, content simply to hold her graceful form in his arms, he went to sleep.

As they neared the Canary Islands, Diego grew accustomed to dividing his hours between the command of his ship and the gentle care Angelique still required. She had not become used to the constant roll of the *Diablo* as he had hoped she would, but still continued to be bothered by motion sickness whenever she was awake. She had not complained but only begged his forgiveness that she had proved to be such a poor sailor. She was dreadfully embarrassed to have caused him so much trouble, and that was the sole cause of the depression she kept hidden from him as best she could. When he returned to his cabin unexpectedly one afternoon and found her in tears, he rushed to her side.

"What is wrong, Angelique? Tell me at once." He pulled her trembling body into his arms and patted her back soothingly. "I'm sorry I must leave you alone so much of the day. Are you simply bored, or is something else troubling you?"

Angelique attempted to dry her tears upon the back of her hand. "I have never been ill, Diego, *never,* and I cannot bear to be such a burden to you."

Diego was tempted to shake the usually feisty blonde for being so foolish, but he restrained himself. He had never treated women roughly and would not begin with her. "You are no burden to me, Angelique, none whatsoever. If I were ill, would you not wish to take care of me?"

"Yes, of course, but that would be different," Angelique insisted with a mournful sigh.

"In what way? A husband and wife should care for each other, and don't you dare tell me I am not your husband by choice. You say that again to me and I'll walk out of here and let Octavio bring your meals!" He kissed the sweet curve of her throat hungrily then, as if to emphasize just how much she would be missing.

Angelique relaxed against his broad chest, enjoying his affection greatly despite his obvious purpose. "I'll not say that, since it hurts you, but you must admit I have made a great difference in the way you live your life, and I fear it's not been an improvement."

Her eyes, which seemed more violet than blue, were dark with tears, and Diego kissed her lashes tenderly before he replied, "I live my life as I please, Angelique, and you are not to give my happiness another thought." With that command, he lifted her into his arms. "Now, it's time you came out on deck, if only for a minute or two. It is no wonder you have become so tired of this cabin."

"But Diego, I'm not dressed!" Angelique was so embarrassed by the prospect of being put on display in her nightgown that she insisted she at least be allowed to don her cloak. Diego quickly wrapped her in it, not wanting to waste a minute of what remained of the afternoon sun.

Once on deck, Angelique found herself imprisoned in her husband's arms. He sat down upon an overturned barrel and kept her perched upon his knee as he pointed out the various tasks in which his men were engaged. The wind was brisk and their progress swift, and he hoped to reach the Canary Islands the next day.

"Tomorrow you think?" Angelique squealed with delight, for she was thrilled by the prospect of walking on solid ground again.

"With luck, yes." Diego loved the pretty creature in his arms so dearly that he leaned forward to kiss her. He cared little what his men would think of such obvious devotion, and when he heard the whistles and catcalls, he merely laughed and did not take offense. "You see, when all on board know I am your slave, how can you regard yourself as a burden?"

Angelique blushed deeply. She did not care either how many pairs of eyes might be observing them. She saw only her husband's wicked grin. "You are a devil, Diego Aragon, but I love you."

"Perhaps simply because I am a devil, my angel." Diego winked slyly and gave her waist a playful squeeze. He leaned forward then to whisper a most enticing invitation in her ear, and when she smiled in return he carried her back to his cabin and remained there to share the single bunk for a blissful hour.

The prospect of going ashore lifted Angelique's spirits considerably. She dressed and styled her hair attractively instead of allowing it to fall in loose curls, and by the time Diego brought her breakfast, she was eager to go out on deck. "Why are these islands called the Canaries. Are there many of the tiny yellow birds here?"

"Actually it is the other way around." Diego peeled an orange for his wife and divided it into sections as he spoke. "Apparently in ancient times sailors found large dogs on the islands and the name 'Canary' comes from the Latin word for dog, *canis*. The little birds were then named for the islands."

"Really?" As always, Angelique found that Diego could answer her questions with the most fascinating information.

"Since I had no time to study the islands, what more can you tell me about them? Are there many of them? Are they large?"

"No, they are neither many nor large, but very beautiful. The seven main islands are volcanic mountain peaks and, while rugged in appearance, they provide spectacular scenery. We'll be stopping at the port of Santa Cruz de Tenerife, which is on the largest island, and you can see the highest of the peaks, Pico de Teyde, then."

"These volcanoes . . . they are not active ones, are they?" Angelique did not see how any trade could be conducted upon an island if it were constantly spewing lava, but she wanted to know what to expect.

"No, the volcanoes have been dormant for centuries. We can go for a walk if you like while Octavio manages the provisions. The islands' soil is volcanic ash and very rich. We'll be able to buy bananas, tomatoes, potatoes, and onions, in addition to fresh meat. We'll need to replenish our supply of fresh water and then we'll be ready to sail again. I'm sorry we can't remain here longer, but I want to reach Vera Cruz as swiftly as possible."

"I will be grateful for today, Diego." Angelique reached for his hand and they both laughed because their fingers were sticky from the oranges they had been eating. After washing her hands, Angelique nearly skipped out on deck. Her hip had ceased to trouble her, although the last traces of the deep purple bruises she had received were still faintly visible on her fair skin. She had walked up and down in the cabin for exercise, restlessly pacing while she tried to compensate for the roll of the ship, and she could scarcely wait to go ashore where she would be able to walk without feeling the constant motion of the sea beneath her feet. Diego wasted no time that morning bringing the *Diablo* into port, then left the tasks that needed to be accomplished in Octavio's capable hands.

"There is a hotel of sorts. Would you like to stay there

tonight?" Diego knew without asking that Angelique would, but he wanted to make it appear that the choice had been hers.

"Oh, could we? They would have real beds there, wouldn't they?" Angelique's eyes lit with an entrancing sparkle. "I mean . . ."

"I know exactly what you mean. We'll stop by the hotel first and reserve a room, then we can just explore the island until you're tired."

"How can I possibly grow tired when I've done nothing except rest for so many days?" Angelique waited outside while Diego stepped into the hotel lobby. She found the sounds and sights of the busy port fascinating and did not want to miss a second of her time there by foolishly remaining indoors when the sunshine felt so glorious upon her fair skin. It did not require much time for her to realize that there were few women about, however, and when Diego joined her again, she quickly took his arm. Santa Cruz de Tenerife was, after all, a port city and filled with transients. The women she saw were either peddling produce or so brightly painted and costumed that she had no trouble guessing their profession.

Diego led Angelique past the busy port to the edge of the lush vegetation that gave the islands their beauty. "These islands have belonged to Spain for nearly four hundred years, but they look very different from Barcelona, don't they?"

"Barcelona is not the only city in Spain," Angelique reminded him playfully.

"In my opinion it is." Diego laced her fingers in his and matched his long stride to hers. "You will like New Spain. It is immense in size and while much of it is arid, the Yucatan is a rain forest, tropical in nature like this paradise."

They walked at an easy pace for a long while and neither felt it necessary to converse, for the surroundings continuously filled their senses with its verdant beauty. Diego finally thought to ask Angelique if she would like to stop and rest, and she found that she had not even realized she was tired until she sat down. They were seated upon a small rise with the majestic sea stretched out before them and the volcano, Pico de Teyde, at their backs. Angelique covered a wide yawn and then lay back to gaze up at the cloudless sky. "It would be a simple matter in a place as lovely as this to forget that the rest of the world exists."

Diego stretched out on his back beside her and propped his head upon his hands. "I would enjoy this peaceful atmosphere for perhaps two days, and then I'd be down at the port looking for a ship to take me away. We're not far from the coast of Africa. It might be interesting to go there."

Because she felt better that day than she had at any time since they had left Barcelona, Angelique could appreciate the spirit of wanderlust that filled her husband. "Have you been to Africa? It must be a fascinating place."

"No, not yet. The world is filled with interesting places, Angelique, but I've decided to concentrate upon the New World rather than the Old."

"Oh, have you now?" Angelique smiled prettily. "Am I to remain at home rocking a cradle while you have all these adventures?"

Giving her a sly wink, Diego promised, "I'll bring you home nice presents."

"Thank you," Angelique replied with mock enthusiasm. "Had I not found living on board a ship so difficult, I'd want to go with you. Unfortunately, I think I would be better off at home, although I know I'll miss you terribly."

Taking her hand, Diego brought it to his lips, "Since we'll not be parted for a good many months, my pet, don't worry over it now."

Frowning slightly, Angelique wondered out loud, "Do you think your father went to see my mother as you asked him to?"

Not pleased to be reminded of Françoise on such a lovely

day, Diego waited a moment before replying and then did so without revealing his true thoughts. "Your mother can be a very charming woman when she wants to be. I know my father would not have taken that amethyst ring from me if he had not wanted an excuse to visit her. I'm certain he could get past Beatriz, even if you couldn't, so it doesn't take too much imagination to predict what happened or soon will."

"I would like both of them to be happy and if it can be with each other, so much the better," Angelique commented wistfully.

"I still think it is remarkable that you do not despise the woman." Diego sat up then, resting his arms across his knees. "Thank God you are nothing like her."

Angelique was too wise to remind her husband that quite recently he had thought her and her mother cut from the same cloth. "I did not see the husband I adored murdered before my very eyes either. I wish you would try to remember what she has suffered and not judge her so harshly."

Disgusted, Diego looked away. Françoise was still a malevolent bitch in his opinion, and he did not care what horrible tragedies she had survived. She had no excuse for turning her back on her own daughter and he would never forgive her for it. "Just don't ask me to allow you to name any of our daughters Françoise, because I'll never agree."

"Well, if you're off sailing around the world, you won't be able to control what I do, will you?" Angelique was only teasing him, but she had not understood the depth of Diego's rage.

With speed that would have shocked a cobra, Diego grabbed Angelique's shoulders and yanked her up so their eyes were level. "Then I'll forbid it right now. Is that plain enough for you? You are not to name any child of mine for that despicable creature you still call your mother!"

Angelique was so shocked by her husband's wrath that she simply stared at him wide-eyed, unable to comprehend what sort of reply he expected. Since she had not meant to anger him, she said so. "Diego, you needn't yell at me. I'd not ever disregard your wishes so flagrantly as that. If you'll not be with me when our baby is born, then all you need do is tell me how you wish the child named and I will follow your instructions."

Angelique was so sincere in her manner that Diego felt very foolish and relaxed his grip upon her. "I will be with you when each of our children is born and not because I'd worry about what you'd name them, but because I'll be concerned about you. I'll not let anyone shut me out of the bedroom either. I mean to stay with you. I think it is barbaric not to allow fathers to witness the births of their children. I'll not simply get too drunk to hear your screams. I'll stay with you."

"Screams?" Angelique licked her lips nervously. "Do women actually scream when they give birth?" That prospect frightened her considerably. Other than remarking about morning sickness, her mother had told her nothing about her pregnancy. Like all wellborn young ladies, she had been carefully shielded from the harsh realities of life and understood little of what she would eventually have to face.

Diego's dark eyes swept her expression rapidly. He had realized too late that she lacked all practical knowledge of childbirth. He pulled her into his arms and hugged her tightly, unable to bear the thought that he had needlessly frightened her. "I was being overly dramatic. Forgive me. Having children cannot be so very difficult or there would not be so many of them in the world."

Angelique was not convinced. "Well, I am no coward and I shall not scream, no matter how badly it hurts," she declared proudly, though her eyes were bright with unshed tears.

"Let's walk a bit further. As I recall, there was a man living nearby who made elaborate cages for canaries." Diego leapt to his feet and offered Angelique his hand, hoping to distract her from the wretched turn their conversation had taken. He was furious with himself for not being more thoughtful and laced her fingers protectively in his as they moved back to the path. The house was a good distance away, they found, but the man remembered Diego and displayed his wares proudly.

The cages were as delicate as the creatures they were fashioned to contain, and Diego explained that he had once bought several of the wooden cages, filled them with the charming birds, and had given them away as gifts when he had reached Barcelona.

"You did not keep one for yourself?" She thought the dear little birds very sweet, but had not seen one in his home.

"No, I gave them all away," Diego confessed.

"To women, no doubt?" Angelique asked coyly.

"Every single one."

"And you still can't recall where you left your guitar?"

Diego laughed out loud at her question. "No, but I'm still certain it was not left beneath some young woman's balcony."

They chatted a while longer with the craftsman and then Angelique asked if Diego would buy her one of the cages so she could take a canary with her to Vera Cruz. "Surely the bird can eat no more than a handful of seeds each day and the cage would not take up much room in your cabin."

"There is nothing I would rather do than please you, my pet, but keeping birds on board ship is more difficult than you might imagine. Several died on my way home from here, and when you consider that we have the major portion of our journey yet to make, we would have to buy half-a-dozen birds to be certain one would survive the voyage. They have to be kept out on deck, for they throw their seeds all around, and keeping the area they occupy clean is an additional chore none of us needs. If you will be patient, when we reach Vera Cruz I will buy you a parrot and you can amuse yourself by teaching him to speak."

Since the little yellow birds were obviously delicate,

Angelique was easily convinced that Diego was correct in refusing to risk transporting them. "Yes, I can understand why their care might be too difficult to manage, but if we make a return trip to Spain, will you buy me one then?"

"I promise." Diego tipped the craftsman handsomely for sharing his wares with them and promised to buy several cages if he returned to Spain by a route that took him through the Canary Islands. Again taking Angelique's hand, he started back for town, but when they reached the outskirts, he suggested they go to the hotel. "It will be nice to bathe in a larger tub for a change, and you might like to rest before supper. I'll drop you off at our room and then go back to the *Diablo* to get whatever you'll require for the evening."

Angelique knew her husband well enough to know he had far more in mind than merely bathing and readily agreed to his suggestion, for the long walk had quite exhausted her. "I would be delighted to rest in the hotel this afternoon, and soaking in a real bath would be wonderful."

"I had a feeling you'd enjoy spending the night at the hotel," Diego replied with a smile. He led her through the crowded street and up the side stairs of the two-story hotel. Taking the key from his pocket, he unlocked the door and ushered his bride inside, but he was as shocked as she was to find the room already occupied.

A raven-haired beauty with luminous black eyes lay nude upon the bed. She regarded Angelique with a curious glance and then greeted Diego warmly. "When I saw the *Diablo* dock this morning, I didn't realize you'd have a woman with you. Well, no matter. We can have an even better time with three." She sat up then, leaning forward slightly to display her generous breasts. "We did it that way the last time you were here as I recall."

His expression filling with fury, Diego took two steps forward and responded angrily, "This is not merely a woman but my wife, and you had no right to enter this room without an invitation, Carmela. Now put on your clothes and

311

get out!"

Carmela rose from the bed and saucily placed her hands upon the gentle swells of her hips. "Your wife?" She laughed with a throaty purr. "Why would a man as strong as you have married such a skinny, fair-haired child who can give him so few pleasures? Does she allow you in her bed more than once each week?"

As Carmela continued her insults in a brazenly enticing manner, Angelique inched back toward the door. She saw Diego take another step forward as he raised his hand and she knew he was going to slap the obnoxious woman, but the hostility of his reaction made no difference to Angelique. If Diego wanted to fight with whores, then she would get out of his way, for she knew she would certainly not stay with him in that room knowing he had shared the bed before with Heaven knew how many others. With Carmela's mocking laughter ringing in her ears, she sped along the corridor and dashed down the stairs to the bustling port. Only moments before it had seemed perched on the edge of paradise, but now it suddenly provided Angelique with a stark vision of hell.

Chapter XVIII

Unmindful of the astonished stares that followed her, Angelique darted swiftly through the throng of sailors milling about on the sidewalk in front of the hotel. She hurried on toward the *Diablo* at the most rapid pace she could manage after all the walking she had done that day. She would have preferred a more neutral destination, but as a stranger in Santa Cruz de Tenerife, she had no idea what other options might be available for a respectable woman. Therefore, returning to the ship seemed her only alternative.

The confusion upon the docks was not nearly as great as it had been in Barcelona, but she had to make her way carefully through the maze of carts and heaps of cargo awaiting loading. The stench of rotting produce pervaded the air and by the time she had at last reached her husband's ship, she felt dizzy and weak. She made her way up the gangplank, but wanting to remain out of doors rather than sit in Diego's cabin, she chose a barrel conveniently placed at a distance from all the activity going on on deck and sat down to rest.

The sea provided a serene view for contemplation, but the thoughts that swirled about in her mind produced nothing but turmoil. Carmela had been nothing like the courtesans she had seen in Paris. Those women were always beautifully

313

groomed and stylishly dressed. They behaved with manners as fine as the ladies they pretended to be, and never had she seen one as vulgar and coarse as Carmela had been. There was obviously a great deal of difference between being a wealthy man's mistress and being a common whore, but she was appalled to think that Diego had patronized such an ill-mannered woman.

He knew so many delightful techniques for making love. Had he learned them from a trollop like that? she wondered. Had he made love to a slut like Carmela in the same slow, tender way he made love to her? She was so sickened by that possibility that she did not even want to know the answer. When he did not soon appear, she began to wonder if she had not been foolish to leave him alone with a whore who had obviously expected he would be pleased to find her in his room. Carmela had appeared to be nearly Diego's age. They might have been lovers for years, and with her gone, would he continue to be angry, or would he simply take advantage of the commodity Carmela had been so eager to sell?

She continued to stare out at the vast expanse of water and her hands were clasped tightly in her lap as she tried to think of what she could possibly say to her husband when he arrived. More than two hours passed before he did.

Diego placed an elaborately designed bird cage upon the deck and gestured proudly. "I went all the way back to the home of the man we met to buy this for you. I know you've been miserable since we left Barcelona, and if a few canaries will help pass the hours, then I want you to have them."

Angelique's blue-violet gaze reflected her amazement as she looked up at her husband's engaging smile. Did he actually think the tiny yellow birds would distract her so completely that she would forget the dreadful scene at the hotel? "I don't want the birds now. Give them away, set them free, I don't care what you do with them, but I don't want anything around to remind me of this awful place." Lifting her chin proudly, she returned her gaze to the sea, avoiding his curious stare altogether.

Diego clasped his hands behind his back, attempting to keep his temper in check, since his lovely bride had lost hers so completely. Finally he knelt down in front of her, moving so close that the toe of her slipper brushed against the hard muscles of his thigh. "There was no reason for you to run off like a frightened child, Angelique. Carmela was the one who was unwelcome in that hotel room, not you. Now come back with me. Don't let her spoil the nice evening we'd planned." His voice was soft, inviting the intimacy he longed to share.

Angelique's pretty features were set in an angry mask as she replied, "I will not go back to that hotel where we would no doubt be disturbed repeatedly by Carmela or others like her. I could no more sleep in that bed now that she's been in it than I could swim from here to Vera Cruz! If Carmela is your usual companion here, then I suggest you'll be far happier with her tonight than you'll be with me."

Diego sighed wearily. "It makes no sense for you to blame me for Carmela's tactless eagerness to ply her trade. She has nothing to do with us, Angelique."

Angelique looked down at her foot, wondering how Diego had managed to maneuver his body into such an erotic position. She was seated with her legs crossed and could not move without the toe of her right foot brushing the crotch of his breeches, and she knew exactly what his body's reaction would be if she were so careless. She tried to edge back a bit upon the barrel, but he simply moved further forward, and while to the men on board he appeared only to be seeking a comfortable position in which to speak with his wife, she knew better. He was blatantly trying to arouse her in order to make her agree to return to the hotel, and she would not go back there for any reason.

Furious that he would attempt to manipulate her feelings in such a devious fashion, she lashed out at him. "How many other women like Carmela can I expect to meet? Are there

315

several more here, or will I have to wait until we get to Vera Cruz? Should I expect whores to sneak into your bed each time I leave it or do your other women possess enough manners to wait in their brothels for you to appear?"

"Since I can't accurately predict the reaction of my own wife to any given situation, how do you expect me to know what whores might do?" Diego asked with a confused shrug. "This conversation is ridiculous. Now I want you to come back to the hotel with me where we can enjoy a relaxing evening by ourselves. Are you coming with me or not?"

"You mean you'll go alone if I won't join you?" Angelique asked in an incredulous whisper.

Diego rose slowly, and stretching to his full height, he towered above her as he replied, "I have asked you to come with me. If you refuse, I'll go alone. I'm as tired of being cooped up in my cabin as you are. Why should we spend another night in that crowded bunk if we don't have to?"

"It would be most uncomfortable, trying to make love with three people in your bunk, wouldn't it?" Angelique asked in a vicious whisper, appalled to think that her husband had actually enjoyed such a bizarre diversion. "Tell me, who was with you and Carmela, another woman or another man?"

His expression reflecting dark fury, Diego turned on his heel and walked away. He strode down the gangplank and kept on going without once looking back. He cursed to himself as he thought what anguish Carmela's insatiable lust had caused him, but what concerned him most was the fact that there was at least one woman exactly like her in each port the *Diablo* frequented. Until he had met Angelique, his tastes in women had leaned toward the bawdy. Would other women come looking for him when they spotted the masts of the *Diablo* in port? He had no desire ever to repeat the ghastly scene through which he had suffered that afternoon. He had not expected Angelique to take such a belligerent stand though, and he knew he had been right to leave her

316

alone for the evening. She had made the choice herself, so she would just have to suffer the consequences.

When the hour grew late and there was still no sign of Diego, Eduardo Ortiz approached Angelique hesitantly. *"Señora,* I must begin the preparations for supper. When do you expect your husband to return?"

Angelique had grown chilled and rose to return to her cabin. "He's not coming back tonight, so don't bother to prepare anything for us. I don't feel like eating."

Confused, Eduardo peered at her troubled expression closely. "I do not understand. Where does the captain plan to eat if he is not dining with you?"

Exasperated by the impertinence of his question, Angelique grew blunt. "Apparently there are far more amusing pastimes available here than dining with me, and Diego has chosen to pursue them. Now, if you'll excuse me, I wish to return to our cabin." She walked around the pretty bird cage she had ignored all afternoon and did not give way to tears until she had reached the privacy of the cabin Diego had refused to share with her that night. She had never felt so alone and wept bitterly over the unfairness of her fate.

Beneath the sun's first rays, the *Diablo's* crew made ready to sail. Octavio had arranged for the men to enjoy liberty in shifts, so each had had the opportunity to go ashore for a few hours and their spirits were high this morning. When Diego appeared, he quickly gave the order to cast off the lines, and in a few minutes the sleek ship was again upon the open sea. He remained on deck all morning, and his mood was so dark that none save Octavio dared approach him, and that was only to discuss matters pertaining to the operation of the ship, not to chat, as was their habit. When Angelique had not appeared by noon, Diego went to the galley to see what Eduardo had prepared for their lunch, then he carried the tray to his cabin.

317

Angelique was seated at the table reading when Diego entered. Blushing deeply, she closed her book and set it aside. No one had thought to bring her any breakfast, and she was quite hungry, despite the blackness of her mood.

"Did you sleep well?" Diego asked politely.

Since she knew that faint purple circles marred the fair skin beneath her eyes, Angelique saw no point in lying. "No, I did not sleep at all."

Diego set the table and placed a bowl of freshly made fish chowder in front of her. He had not enjoyed their brief separation either, though he would not admit it. "That's unfortunate. I found the hotel bed very comfortable."

"I'll just bet you did!" Angelique leapt from her chair so rapidly she spilled her bowl of chowder, but once on her feet she realized she had nowhere to go. She turned her back on Diego and, crossing her arms over her chest, she dug her fingernails into her flesh to keep from crying in front of him.

Since he considered such tantrums childish, Diego sat down and began to eat as though she were a most charming companion. There was freshly baked bread and creamy yellow butter bought ashore only that morning, and he thought the meal unusually good. "I went to sea when I was sixteen, Angelique, but I was not a virgin even then. I cannot even count, let alone name, all the women I've known, but—"

Angelique put her hands over her ears to shut out the sound of his voice. She knew he wasn't boasting but merely explaining his past in a matter-of-fact fashion, yet she was thoroughly disgusted by his words. "I don't want to hear it!" she cried. "Can't you understand that? I don't want to hear anything about anyone else!"

Diego finished eating, hoping to give his bride sufficient time to regain her composure. Then he stood and tried to put his arms around her, but she moved away quickly, as if repulsed by his touch. "All I want you to understand is that whatever I did before I met you can't be changed. If I spent

318

my time gambling or drinking too heavily or with women who are not fit to polish your slippers, you must forgive me for it. It can be no other way, Angelique. You can't continue to punish me for the way I lived before we met. That's childish. It isn't fair to me, and you're only making yourself miserable by being so obstinate."

Wheeling around to face him, Angelique responded angrily, "Is it being obstinate to refuse to share my husband with whores? Is that not my right as your wife?"

"Angelique, do you honestly think I'd prefer to spend my time with a woman as crude as Carmela when I have you?" He studied her expression closely, astonished to find she had no such confidence in herself. He was shocked even more as he noted the changes the hardships of the voyage had made in her appearance. She had gone from being slender to thin, and where her features had been delicate, they were now fragile. But he would certainly never call such an exquisite beauty skinny, as Carmela had. She looked very young and dear, but the pain that filled her gaze was not in the least bit childlike and he longed to make her understand what he was trying so desperately to say. "There is an immense difference between being with a stranger for a few moments of pleasure and being with you. There is no comparison at all, really. If I have failed to make you understand that, then I am very sorry."

Angelique could not look at him without recalling Carmela's provocative stance. Nude, with her hips thrust forward, she had obviously been confident of his reaction to her charms. "Having made love to you, I cannot imagine how you could have displayed the same tenderness with other women if you cared nothing for them. If it was not love for you then, but no more than lust, how could you even bear to do it?"

Diego was amazed by her question. "The pleasure was enough in itself, Angelique," he said simply.

"Then there is no difference in being with me or in being

with Carmela, despite what you said? One woman is as good as another to you?" She felt sick that she was so naïve, yet terribly hurt that he did not understand how greatly Carmela's arrogant assumption that she would be welcome in his hotel room had shocked her. She could not bear to think of him being with other women, and now that she had met one, she could not erase the boisterous brunette's taunting image from her mind.

Since walking out on his bride had not produced the slightest improvement in her mood, Diego decided against choosing such a strategy again. "I will bring you another bowl of chowder, for I'm certain the portion you didn't spill has grown cold. Sit down and make yourself comfortable. We can talk after you finish eating."

As soon as he had left her, Angelique sat down to butter a piece of bread. She ate so hurriedly that she was embarrassed by her own hunger. When Diego returned with her lunch, she ate it all without uttering a word. He sat munching a banana slowly, as if greatly amused by her obvious appreciation of her meal.

"What did Eduardo serve you for supper last night?" he finally asked. "You look famished."

"I told him not to bother since I was alone, and I was too embarrassed by the way I'd spoken to him to fetch my own breakfast this morning," Angelique admitted reluctantly between bites.

Diego had enjoyed the best of meals ashore but did not taunt his bride by describing the menu. True to his word, he did not speak again until she had finished eating all her chowder and two bananas. "Well, I'm glad to see you've regained your appetite, no matter what the reason, but you mustn't skip meals in the future. I had not imagined the trip would be so difficult for you. Perhaps my decision to leave Barcelona was wrong. Would you like to return to Spain?"

Unable to understand his reasoning, Angelique simply stared at her husband for a long moment. She was shocked to see he was serious. "But how can we go back? You've a cargo of wine in the hold and men who expect to share in the profits of its sale. We have nothing to which to return anyway—no home to call our own, no relatives who'll even speak to us. Oh, perhaps that is not completely true of your father, but he's angry with us still. I doubt Ramon Ortega would let you go unchallenged after you cost him a large commission and nearly killed one of his men. Even if you aren't afraid of him, I certainly am. Why should we go back, when there is nothing in Barcelona for us but trouble?"

"If you've decided you don't want to be my wife, you'd be better off in Spain, that's all. I want you to be happy, and if my slightest touch disgusts you now, then—"

Angelique turned away, not knowing how to describe how she truly felt. "It is only that I thought we had something unique, but if you've been with so many women, had so many casual affairs, then perhaps it is only practice that makes your touch so wondrous."

Diego's throat closed in a painful knot. That he had not only badly disappointed her but also greatly disillusioned his innocent young bride caused him the worst anguish he had ever suffered. "You once thought my character admirable. If that unfortunate scene with Carmela has cost me your respect, then I'll simply have to try to regain it. You mustn't think that what we've shared isn't unique, for it most certainly is. Why do you think I wanted so desperately to find you? It was because we had something together that I couldn't bear to lose, something so special there seems to be no adequate word to describe it." When he could think of no suitable term to illustrate the emotion she created in his heart, he gave up the effort and continued. "Men don't truly make love to whores, Angelique. They don't kiss them, or caress them. They don't bother to arouse their passions. They simply use them to satisfy their own needs. Such women sell their bodies without sharing their souls. If you cannot forgive me for using countless women in such a selfish fashion, then life is going to be very difficult for both of us." Rising slowly to his feet, Diego stacked her dishes upon the tray and prepared to leave. "I'll not make any excuses for the way I've conducted my life, since it's no different from that of most men I know. I do want you to believe you're the only woman I'll ever want now though, and I hope you'll still want me."

Without speaking, Angelique watched him go. Too much had happened between them far too quickly. She barely knew the man who was her husband. He was idealistic but lived by his own code of ethics, a very convenient code, which apparently permitted him to do as he pleased. He had shown little respect for his father's far more conservative opinions, and none for her mother's feelings. The trust that existed between them was no more than a tenuous thread, and she was dreadfully worried that they would constantly be at odds as parents.

Far more frightening to her was the knowledge that there was a violent streak in him that hinted at a cruelty far more malevolent than that inspired by the revolution that had swept her homeland. Folding her arms upon the table, she rested her cheek upon them and tried to imagine what their life might have been if he had been introduced to her at a party or ball instead of meeting her as he had in a moonlit garden. The past could not be changed, as he had remarked. That chance encounter beneath the stars seemed to have sealed their fates in an instant, though she could see little in their future other than confusion.

Young women were supposed to be ignorant of the vices of young men and certainly never question them about them. But how could she have ignored Carmela's intrusion upon their lives? How could she have stood there while Diego threw her out of their room and then pretended such a hellish scene had never occurred? Had he hit the obnoxious whore, perhaps given her a severe beating, or had he merely raised his hand to send her hurrying on her way? She honestly did not know what he might have done, since he was fully capable of displaying any reaction between the coolest disdain and the blackest rage. She knew precious little about her husband, except that he was a handsome and virile young man, but she had seen he could behave as a gentleman if the occasion demanded it, and she could do no more than pray he continued to wish to do so with her.

Returning to the deck, Diego was uncertain what he had accomplished with Angelique. At least she had not asked to return to Spain, and he considered that to be a point in his favor. She had catalogued their problems there most expertly, but he was sorry she had not forgotten about Ramon Ortega, since he already had. The problem was that she was alone too much of the time, left to brood upon the unfortunate set of circumstances that had precipitated their departure from Barcelona, and he should have anticipated this and prevented it from happening. Noticing that the bird cage still sat where he had first placed it, he returned to his cabin to summon his bride.

Angelique sat up quickly as Diego came through the door, embarrassed to have been caught napping. "Did you forget something?"

"No, but you have. There are four pairs of canaries waiting for you to feed them. Birds eat an enormous amount each day and cannot be left untended. Their supply of water must be replenished as well."

His statement was delivered in a friendly fashion rather than a scolding tone, but Angelique did not understand why he had bothered to make it. "I told you the Canary Islands are the last place on earth about which I wish to be reminded. I don't want the little birds. Give them to one of the men."

Diego walked over to the table, took Angelique's upper arm in his firm grasp, and lifted her from her chair. "When I give you presents, I expect you to take proper care of them,

323

if for no other reason than to please me. Every man on board knows the birds belong to you, and the responsibility for their care is also yours. I have no extra men to whom I would assign such a task."

Her husband was angry now, and rather than argue with him again, Angelique walked quietly out on deck. The cage was a masterpiece and the tiny birds exquisite, but she felt not the slightest bit of pride in owning them. She knelt down to watch the canaries hop from perch to perch and asked, "Where is their food going to be kept?"

Diego swiftly returned with a decorative tin filled with a variety of seeds. "Keep this wherever you like. You can bring water from the galley, but you'll need to check on the birds' supplies at least twice a day. They are prisoners, you see, and will swiftly die without your attentions." He grimaced to himself then, thinking he might also expire if she should stop loving him, and he resolved not to allow such a tragedy to occur. "They can be tamed quite easily and will learn to sit upon your finger if you are patient with them."

After having been forced by her mother's demands to be patient for so many years, Angelique doubted she could now summon enough of that quality to accomplish such a task. She remained with the birds only long enough to see to their basic needs, then returned to the privacy of their cabin to rest for the remainder of the afternoon. Diego watched her depart with a thoughtful expression on his handsome countenance.

A short time later, when Diego replied with unmistakable annoyance to one of Octavio's routine questions, he caught himself and apologized. "I am sorry, my friend. This voyage has swiftly become the worst I ever recall making, and it is not because of the weather." Indeed, the late fall weather had been excellent in all respects.

Clearing his throat nervously, Octavio gathered his courage in order to give his captain some advice he thought the man might not have considered. "It is unfortunate your bride has no maid or suitable female companion with whom to spend her time. Women are very different from men you know, and some days are far more trying for them than others. Perhaps your wife's mood will soon improve."

Diego watched his mate's cheeks color with a bright blush and finally realized what it was Octavio was attempting to say. He had to chuckle then, for, in reality, Angelique had been pregnant the entire time he had known her, so the depression she had suffered of late could not be blamed upon her body's monthly cycle. He paused to wonder then if pregnancy could influence a woman's mood, but since Octavio had no wife and children, he doubted the man would know the answer to such a question. When he realized his mate was awkwardly shuffling his feet and waiting for him to make some reply, he gave the best one he could supply. "Yes, the cost of a maid would have been a worthwhile expense, though my wife has never had a personal attendant. But where could I have put such a female anyway? Could she have shared your cabin?"

"Sir!" Octavio was at first shocked, then seeing the familiar sparkle brighten Diego's eyes, he laughed with him. "I would have done my best to make her feel most welcome."

"Yes, I know you would have." Diego relaxed a moment longer, then, hoping to make his bride seem less temperamental, he told Octavio the truth. "When I took Angelique to the hotel yesterday, we found Carmela there in the bed waiting for me. Naturally, my bride was horrified by such a spectacle and it will take her a few days to recover. She is truly a delightful young woman, not a moody and difficult one."

Octavio gasped sharply. "Carmela has slept with every man on board this ship at one time or another, but that your wife should have met her is most unfortunate. I do not think it was wise to leave her alone after such a shock, however. She must have believed you preferred Carmela's sullied charms to her own."

Diego shook his head. He had not meant her to think that and doubted that she had. She had not accused him of being unfaithful and he thought the subject would be better left closed now. "She is far too intelligent to think me such a fool, Octavio. Now, I suggest you let me tend to my wife's needs while you give your attentions to the *Diablo.*" He winked slyly, certain the man knew exactly how he planned to improve his wife's mood.

Angelique bathed and dressed for supper as she did each evening, but she did not know what she could expect from her husband after their conversation at noon. She had not seen him since she had fed the canaries, and while she tried to think of topics they could discuss without arguing, she could think of no interesting ones. She sincerely hoped they could pass the evening agreeably.

When he appeared at last, she noted his questioning glance and realized that he had had the same concern. She smiled, a bit hesitantly, but it was a welcoming smile all the same.

"If we can maintain this same speed, we will be in Vera Cruz before you know it, my pet." Diego brushed her cheek with a light kiss, content to begin with conversation. He had brought their supper as usual and handed her the silverware to set the table while he arranged the dishes.

"I have never thought to inquire why you have no cabin boy. Is it considered proper for a captain to serve his own meals as you do?"

"Probably not." Diego had brought an extra jug of wine along that night, thinking that the intoxicating beverage might improve his chances with Angelique if his charm proved unequal to the task. "I have taken several lads on voyages. A few have grown up to be sailors, while others I've sent back for more schooling to enable them to work as clerks in our offices on land. We left so suddenly this time

326

that I simply had no opportunity to hire a cabin steward."

"It is like being an apprentice, isn't it?" Angelique swept her skirt aside to take her place at the table. They had fresh meat and vegetables that night, thanks to their stop at Santa Cruz de Tenerife, and although the aroma of the meal seemed most enticing to Diego, her stomach lurched slightly at the smell and she closed her eyes for a few seconds to force away her unease.

"Angelique, are you unwell?" Diego frowned impatiently, not understanding why it was her misfortune to be so sensitive to the gentle sway of the *Diablo* when it bothered him not at all.

"No, I am fine now." She smiled as best she could and quickly buttered a bite of bread to ease her queasiness. She swallowed deliberately and was pleased when she felt no further ill effects. "This looks delicious, doesn't it?" she commented brightly.

"Yes. Eduardo can actually prepare tasty meals when he has fresh goods with which to work. It is when we are forced to consume pickled cabbage and dried fish that he has to take the most abuse."

Angelique raised her hand rapidly to cover her mouth, for she had begun to gag. In a moment the feeling passed and she apologized. "Please, I will have to worry about the change in menu when it takes place, but I simply can't do it now."

Diego nodded curtly, sorry he had upset her so needlessly. It seemed that nothing he did was right, and he grew angrier by the minute thinking of how many more days they would have to endure aboard the *Diablo*. "I have always loved the sea with an unwavering passion, Angelique, right from the very moment my father carried me upon his shoulders down to the wharf, where one of his ships was docked. I was entranced by that handsome ship and sailed upon her at my first opportunity, and never, before tonight, have I regretted not having some other profession."

Angelique placed her fork upon the edge of her plate and

broke off another bite of bread and buttered it. "I'm sorry. I don't understand. You've said we're making good time. Why doesn't sailing please you if it always has?"

Surprised that she did not understand his meaning, Diego explained, "Because it makes you so miserable, that's why. How can I take pride in that?"

"You can't consider it your fault that I've been bothered by seasickness, Diego. You have pampered me so sweetly that I'll be dreadfully spoiled by the time we arrive in New Spain. Now tell me something more about these cabin boys you've sent to school. I've never heard of a captain doing that. Is it a common practice?"

Diego was so delighted by the warmth of his wife's gaze that for a moment he did not comprehend her question. He wanted only to crush her in a powerful embrace and carry her over to the bunk to begin a night he hoped to fill with several hours of loving, but he dared not be so brash. After taking a long swallow of wine to restrain such a burst of emotion, he explained calmly, "No, I've never heard of anyone else doing it, but some lads have a knack for figures and are better suited to keeping accounts in an office than looking after me. I simply saw that their natural talents weren't wasted, that's all. It is a smart way to run our business, really. Young employees are very loyal and hardworking. When they're given a task they enjoy doing, they prove superior in all respects to men we hire who have been trained elsewhere."

"Why are you being so modest, Diego? I think it is commendable that you'd provide for the future of another man's son as thoughtfully as you would for your own."

"I doubt any son of ours will be content to sit upon a tall stool all day with a ledger on his lap, Angelique. I'll not give him a ship though, until he earns the right to be a captain, as I did."

Raising a graceful brow quizzically, the pretty blonde inquired, "If you went to sea at sixteen, how many years did it take you to assume your own command?"

Diego chuckled as he admitted, "Two years is all, but I am exceptionally bright."

Angelique laughed with him, sorry now that everything had gone so wrong for them the previous evening. "It is possible for a man or woman to be too bright for his or her own good, Diego. My imagination is such a vivid one because of the many years I've spent solely in my own company that I'm afraid it gets away from me at times. I am sorry I ruined the night you had planned yesterday. Jealousy is not an easy emotion to control, it seems, and until I met you, I'd had no experience with it. Will you forgive me?"

When she reached across the table to take his hand, Diego readily laced his fingers in hers. "There is nothing to forgive. Just take good care of the canaries, that's all I ask."

Angelique pulled her hand shyly from his, pleased that he had accepted her apology so promptly. It was one of her mother's favorite techniques, she recalled with a sudden stab of guilt. But she had been sincere, not merely attempting to manipulate his emotions to her own advantage, she reflected bitterly. She gave her full attention to her dinner rather than dwelling on that thought, and she did not realize how her sudden withdrawal appeared to her husband.

While Diego usually considered observing his bride's expressions a fascinating pastime, he soon became puzzled by her abrupt change of mood. She was frowning slightly, contemplating some troubling matter she obviously did not wish to share, and he decided to leave well enough alone. He had never spent as much time conversing with a woman as he had spent with her, however, and suddenly he felt cheated by her silence. "I cannot make our marriage a happy one alone, Angelique. You'll have to make some effort to please me too."

Other than producing an intense stare, his remark brought little reaction. "I beg your pardon?" Angelique asked politely.

"Oh, forget it!" Diego poured himself another goblet of wine and noted that she had not touched hers. It appeared he was not going to be able to influence her mood either with charm or with spirits, and he sat back in his chair and regarded her with a sullen stare.

She had always thought Diego's vivid brown eyes remarkably handsome, with their thick fringe of long, black lashes, but the look Angelique saw in their depths conveyed such anguish and torment that she was nearly moved to tears. Pushing what was left of her supper aside, she rose from her chair and, going to him, she perched lightly upon his right knee. She rested her hands upon his shoulders and leaned forward to kiss his cheek. Her lips moved with exaggerated slowness first to his ear, then toward his mouth. She could feel his body growing tense and hear his breathing quicken, yet she continued to cover his face with light, teasing kisses and only occasionally stopped to let her lips touch his.

He kept his hands at his sides, allowing her to do as she pleased without restraint, until at last her tongue invaded his partially open mouth to tempt him with an unmistakable invitation. He then wrapped his left arm tightly around her waist to hold her close while he slid his right hand slowly up her leg, pushing her lingerie aside so he could touch the satin-smooth flesh of her thigh before reaching the tangle of blonde curls he longed to explore.

Moving gently against Diego, Angelique unbuttoned his shirt while continuing to kiss him. His bare chest was warm and seemed to invite her caress as she let her fingertips follow the trail of dark curls leading to his belt buckle. Unfastening that barrier, she slipped further down his leg, giving herself the room to slide her hand beneath the lightweight wool of his breeches while her new position allowed him complete access to the mysteries of her sweetly perfumed body that he sought. She let the rhythm of her fingertips match his, which aroused him to ever greater heights, even as her deep kisses plundered his mouth until he could no longer catch his breath.

Diego did not pause to inquire as to how he had managed to arouse his wife's passions to such a fevered pitch, for he knew she had a heart fully as wanton as his own. He put both hands upon her waist to place her upon her feet for an instant, then pulled her back down upon his lap so she was facing him this time. Her legs were now spread open upon his thighs so that he could enter her easily and he achieved that feat so expertly that she found herself impaled upon him before she could have uttered so much as a word of protest, if she had been inclined to do so.

She wrapped her arms around his neck and followed his deep thrusts with a slow, steady roll of her hips, which she knew would nearly drive him mad. Finally she increased her movements to bring about his release, and in that instant she recalled Carmela's provocative pose and knew she had won all that that bold temptress had hoped to gain. As the first wave of cresting ecstasy swelled within her own body, she wanted to shout with exultant joy, for she alone had won Diego's heart and she was more than content with such a magnificent prize.

Chapter XIX

There were days when Diego could think of nothing but the perfection of his wife's lithe figure, which still showed scant evidence of approaching motherhood. At other times it was the marvelous, vibrant hue of her eyes—the blue that flashed with purple sparks when he aroused her passions— that entranced him most. She spent her mornings on deck now and her pale golden skin was deepening to a delicious tan that shone with the soft blush of health. She let her thick curls flow loose in the breeze and that lustrous cascade was so tempting that he could not walk by her without pausing to reach out and wind a strand or two of her glossy tresses around his fingers. He adored her and yet could not describe himself as content, for though Angelique was a treasure more precious than gold, she was also a woman whose very nature defied possession.

He knew she had lived the usual life of a child of the French nobility. She had been cherished, protected, carefully guarded for the most part from all worldly influence, until the night they had met and he had swiftly taken her innocence. In spite of her sheltered upbringing, it had been her spirit that had enchanted him, even more than her beauty. But through bitter experience, he had learned that her behavior was impossible to predict. He knew she had not been teasing the day she had said he would not be able to control what she did when he was at sea. She might have agreed not to name a daughter Françoise, but what else would he have to forbid? he wondered.

The more he considered the possibilities of temptation that existed in Vera Cruz, the more convinced he was that he would have to give up the command of the *Diablo* if he wanted to keep Angelique for his wife. That he would soon be faced with such an impossible choice nearly tore his heart in two. But he knew if he were to be so foolish as to leave her alone for months at a time, there were many single men in the city who would swiftly begin to call upon so delectable a woman. Such men would introduce themselves as his friends to gain her confidence, but that would be the last time any of them would recall she had a husband. Angelique was a beauty, and so young. Would loneliness soon make her forget that adultery was a sin? While he feared that their future might be fraught with peril, Diego found himself surrounded with problems in the present as well.

When Angelique had first begun to remain on deck for an hour or two, she had chosen a place protected from the wind and had sat beside the ornate cage filled with constantly fluttering birds. The crew had not been pleased by the change in her routine for they had felt inhibited by her presence. They had had to govern their language and gestures with a restraint they found extremely difficult to maintain.

Then one morning one of the more bold of the men had stopped for a moment to admire the pretty little canaries she tended so sweetly. He had said no more than a word or two in passing, but when the others saw the delighted smile Angelique gave him, they too began to find excuses to speak with the charming young woman. Diego had not known how to discourage such a practice, when his wife clearly enjoyed

333

the brief conversations as much as his men did. He would wander by, curious to know what they were discussing, and always found that the topics encompassed home and loved ones, never the boastful flirting he had expected and would have swiftly forbidden. Angelique did little more than listen attentively to the sailors' melancholy memories without sharing any of her own, but he was jealous all the same.

He wanted to keep her sympathetic concern all to himself, yet he dared not forbid her to speak with his crew or order the men to avoid her. It was a torment he could not seem to resolve, and he grew increasingly restless and withdrawn as a result. He began to push the crew to the limit, citing the need to make haste as the reason, and no one realized that his sole purpose was to have his lovely bride all to himself again.

Once they had reached the West Indies, the icy gray-green of the Atlantic Ocean gave way to the clear blue of the Caribbean. The water was warm and the days fair, but Diego had no desire to stop to replenish their supplies in Havana. His goal was Vera Cruz, and he held the *Diablo*'s course steady toward that destination. After the disastrous way their brief stay in Santa Cruz de Tenerife had ended, he feared giving Angelique the opportunity for a confrontation with the many other whores he knew. He was a changed man now, a happily married man, and having seen the pain he had caused his wife, he had vowed not to allow his less-than-respectable past to catch up with him ever again.

"One day will make little difference, Diego," Octavio told him. "Why not put in at Havana for a night, at least? You would have the time to spend with your wife while the men would have the opportunity for some relaxation as well." Octavio thought his captain's decision to skirt Cuba without stopping unreasonable and stated his opinion clearly.

"I will provide a generous bonus for all hands once we reach Vera Cruz. That thought will have to be enough to keep them content until we reach there." Diego had deliberately made his manner stern, and he was surprised when Octavio continued to argue.

"You know what the men are saying, don't you?" Octavio lowered his voice to be as discreet as possible. "They think that it is because you have your wife with you that you will not agree to stop, for they know you already enjoy the amusement they crave."

Diego drew back his hand so quickly that Octavio lunged out of the way, not realizing the captain had not meant to actually throw a punch. He knew him to possess a vicious temper but had not wanted to arouse it, and he apologized effusively. "Forgive me if I have offended you. It was my intention only to mention their insignificant opinion, not to provoke a fight between us."

Taking a step backward, Diego let his hand fall to his side as he cursed under his breath. "Since every man on board seems to admire my wife so greatly, please remind them that it is for her comfort that I wish to complete this voyage as rapidly as possible. The women in Vera Cruz are well worth the wait, and the extra pay the men will have then will buy them far more amusing companions than they would have been able to purchase in Havana. Provide extra rations of ale if you must, but I don't want to hear another complaint from any man." He was so disgusted with himself for coming so close to striking Octavio that he walked straight to his cabin. Once there, however, he found it impossible to hide the bitterness of his mood from his perceptive bride.

Angelique had been sewing and looked up as Diego walked in. She had worn only a few of her new garments and was saving the others for Vera Cruz, but she had found her favorite dress growing too snug in the bodice and was letting out the seams. Embarrassed by the changes in her figure, she hoped Diego would not inquire about what she was doing, but when she saw his troubled expression, she realized he was too preoccupied to be concerned with her activities. "What's happened, Diego? I hope there's no trouble."

"None that concerns you, my pet." But as he spoke he

realized that quite the opposite was true and blurted out a brief explanation. "It seems the men have all enjoyed your company so greatly, and envy me so much, that they would like to make a stop in Havana so they might take their enjoyment of feminine companionship to its natural conclusion."

Her blush was plainly visible beneath her newly acquired tan as Angelique watched her husband pace their cabin with such a determined step that she doubted he would ever walk off his anger. "I am not as naïve as you believe, Diego. I know sailors like to visit prostitutes. Why don't you make a stop in Havana if it will make all the men happy?"

"Because I am the captain, and I've chosen not to deviate from our course, that's why." Diego turned then to face her, suddenly unable to contain his real frustration. "Perhaps if you weren't so eager to speak with the men, didn't give them so much of your attention, they wouldn't be thinking about women all the time!"

Angelique could not believe Diego was serious and began to laugh. "You can't mean that. You simply can't. This morning one fellow told me about his grandmother and another spoke about the aunt who'd raised him. A third said a little about his brother's children. Those are scarcely the types of conversations that would fill a man with lust!"

"Don't laugh at me, Angelique!" Diego cautioned her harshly, in no mood for such sport.

Laying aside the gown upon which she had been working, Angelique rose and went to him. "Do you now wish me to stay here in our cabin all day? As I recall, it was your suggestion that I spend my time on deck, because you thought the fresh air would help me feel better. Just tell me what it is you wish me to do, for I'm so confused now that I don't know what it is you expect of me."

Unfortunately, Diego was equally confused himself, though he knew it was wrong of him to blame his problems on Angelique. "You have always behaved in a ladylike fashion, and if the men are driven wild with desire by conversations about their grandmothers, then it is no fault of yours! I want only to reach Vera Cruz, where I can make a proper home for you, and I'll not tarry along the way for any reason."

Relieved to find that she was not at fault for his anger, Angelique smiled prettily. "As long as we are together we are at home, Diego. This cabin is adequate for the time being. You needn't deprive the men of their recreation on my account. A day or two in Havana will make no difference to me."

"Well it does to me!" Diego wanted no more of this controversy. "Our next port is Vera Cruz, and if any of the crew should be so daft as to complain about it to you, then just send them to me!" He slammed the door on his way out, not in the least bit angry with his bride but furious with himself for ever allowing his men to speak with her in the first place.

Angelique sat back down, distressed that Diego had not taken her suggestion more seriously. He seemed to regard their prompt arrival in Vera Cruz as more important than his crew's morale, but did he honestly believe the men would try to influence him through her? she wondered. How could they possibly approach her with such an indelicate request? The more she thought they might wish to take advantage of the friendships she had enjoyed making, the more depressed she became. She did not even want to go out on deck the next morning but knew she would have to make a brief appearance to feed the canaries at least. With the tin of birdseed firmly clutched in her hand, she left the cabin, expecting to step out into the warm sunshine, but instead she found the sky filled with an eerie red haze. Curious as to what caused the peculiar glow in the heavens, she went immediately to her husband to request an explanation.

Diego laughed at her question. "I am at a loss as to the truth about the phenomenon, but the superstition is that a

337

red sky at dawn means a storm is brewing."

"Have you found that to be true?" Angelique had thought the rose hue of the sky very pretty and was disappointed to hear it was considered a bad omen. "After your many years at sea, you must have some opinion of your own."

"We are probably in for a bit of bad weather, but the *Diablo* is a sturdy vessel and will be in no danger of sinking." Diego would welcome any challenge—even one provided by foul weather—to free his mind from its ever-present worries about his wife's welfare.

"This was why your father was so concerned about our making a voyage now, wasn't it? Wasn't he convinced that the trip would be too dangerous to risk because of the uncertainty of the weather?"

"Yes, but I am captain of this ship and he is not," Diego reminded her emphatically. "Feed the canaries and allow me to make the decisions regarding the safety of the *Diablo* and those aboard." He inclined his head in a mock bow, attempting to end their conversation, even if on a strained note.

"Perhaps a detour to Havana should be reconsidered," Angelique offered seriously, but she would not allow him to dismiss her as though her opinions had no value.

"The weather will be no better there than on the open seas," Diego explained through clenched teeth. "Now go and see to your pets!"

Why he had become so furious with her over such a small matter Angelique could not imagine, but she had no desire to fight with Diego in front of his men and so turned to go. She found the canaries anxiously flitting about their cage and, thinking they were merely hungry, she quickly replenished their food and water before returning to the cabin. She heard the raindrops when they began to fall but knew someone would cover the birds with the piece of canvas she tossed over the cage at night and did not worry over their comfort. If they were still living free on their island, they would get wet

338

whenever it rained, she realized, and she did not think water would harm them.

Diego did not join her at noon, but Eduardo brought her some bread and cheese and explained that the inclement weather made it too dangerous to light a cooking fire, which she readily understood. She had little appetite but tried to eat a few bites before lying down for a nap. When she awakened, the ship was still being pelted with rain and the wail of the wind had reached an almost deafening roar. It was impossible to walk about the cabin when the pitch of the floor changed constantly, and when Eduardo failed to bring her any supper, she was more relieved than disappointed. Attempting to read made her feel worse than merely resting, while embroidery proved impossible to do. She hoped Diego would have some time to spend with her that evening, but she had fallen asleep by the time he returned to the cabin.

When Diego finally came to bed, Angelique moved over to give him room to lie down, but he pulled her into his arms and nearly crushed her with the force of his embrace. His hair was damp and his body so chilled that she shivered as she wrapped her arms around him, but she did not complain of the discomfort. "Have you more blankets? I fear you'll fall ill you're so dreadfully cold."

Diego silenced her solicitous words of concern with a deep kiss he did not end until the flames of their shared passion had given his aching muscles all the warmth they required. His powerful body then swiftly conquered hers, savagely savoring her inner fire until his reason was consumed by that exotic heat. The force of his desire led him further still, plunging him ever deeper into the well of her love until, with a shattering climax, he found the dreamless peace he had sought so eagerly in her arms. He clung to her still, unwilling even then to release the lovely creature whose affection had pleased him so thoroughly that the narrow bunk seemed as comfortable as a bed of clouds.

"Diego?" Angelique whispered his name softly. "Please,

339

Diego, you must allow me the space in which to breathe."
Her fingertips moved over his shoulders in a smooth caress,
but when she realized he was sound asleep, she gave him a
brutal shove. He had been exhausted, but that was no excuse
to leave her a prisoner in his arms. By the time she had
struggled to claim a comfortable portion of the bunk for
herself, she was wide awake and, recalling that Diego had
not spoken even one word to her, she grew increasingly
offended.

It was obvious he had come to take her love for granted
and she wished she had not responded so hungrily to his first
kiss. While it was true that a man need not court his wife as
though he were still trying to win her favor, should he not
show her far more consideration than Diego had displayed
that night? she reflected bitterly. Was this all she could hope
for in the future—a few moments of passion at the close of
each day rather than the tender affection she enjoyed so
much and had come to expect? She let her hand wander over
his hip before it came to rest upon his waist and, snuggling
close, she prayed he had not already become bored with her
charms when she was certain she would never tire of his.

The storm continued to build in intensity during the few
brief hours Diego slept. The next day brought still heavier
torrents of rain and he cursed himself for being too great a
fool to have set a course for a safe harbor when he had had
the chance. Now they were at the mercy of the elements,
unable to do more than man the bilge pump and pray the
Diablo did not take on more water than they could pump
out. Since he worked twice as hard as any of his men, none
complained of his error in judgment, but he had no doubt
that they blamed him for the predicament they were all in
and were relying upon him to get them out safely.

When the rain showers tapered off in the afternoon, Diego
allowed Eduardo to light the cooking fires long enough to
prepare a nourishing soup, and he carried a small kettle to
his cabin to share with Angelique. Sinking down into his

chair, he apologized for his sorry appearance. He had not taken the time to shave that morning and his wet, rumpled clothing appeared to have been slept in. "You must forgive me. I've no time to change my clothes. This lull in the storm cannot last and I've only a short time in which to eat."

"A few minutes spent putting on dry clothing would scarcely be time wasted, Diego." Angelique regarded the damp puddle in which he was sitting and insisted, "Just tell me what to take out and I'll get it ready for you while you're eating."

Reaching out to catch her wrist, Diego pulled her back toward the table. "No. Sit down and eat. I want to talk with you."

"About what?" Angelique asked apprehensively.

"Whatever you like. I'm afraid I did no more than fall into bed last night, and I do not want you to be lonely." He winked as he took another spoonful of soup, hoping she would not be angry with him when he had little choice about where he spent his time.

"You did quite a bit more than simply 'fall into bed,' my dearest. Don't you remember?" Angelique could see by his confused expression that he obviously did not. "That's really not at all flattering," she continued. "I know some men become bored with their wives, but I didn't think it would happen to you so quickly."

Diego studied her petulant expression and tried to find some clever way to disprove her assumption. "If I live to be one hundred, I will never become bored with you. I'm so tired I can scarcely see straight, and if I disappointed you somehow last night, then—"

"Oh, it was certainly no disappointment. Far from it. I'm only sorry you don't recall what happened," Angelique replied flippantly. "In fact, it was one of your more passionate performances."

"Performances? Is that what you'd call it?" Diego rose to his feet, thoroughly disgusted with her choice of words. "I

341

don't perform like some whore who is paid to please those who share her bed, and I'm sorry to hear that you think I do!"

On his way out he slammed the door with a force that shook the sturdy table, and Angelique grabbed hold of her bowl to keep her soup from sloshing over the rim. "Damn!" she cried. "I've made a mess of everything—again!" Diego was worn out and so was she, but why had she been so spiteful when all she had truly wanted was some reassurance of his love? she mused miserably. Before she could finish eating, the storm had again begun to buffet the ship, and she glanced longingly at the bunk, though she knew she would probably now spend all of the night alone.

Diego had just taken over the wheel from Octavio and was straining to maintain their course through the downpour when a fierce streak of lightning shot through the sky. The resulting thunder was faint, but ensuing claps grew to threatening proportions as each new flash of lightning drew closer. Not an inch of canvas was unfurled and the tall masts of the elegant ship were stark, defiantly reaching up to the turbulent heavens like clenched fists daring the elements to strike. In reply to that proud taunt, the next burst of lightning lit the ship with a glow as bright as noon before an angry wave of thunder rolled over it with the force of a demon's curse. Diego gripped the wheel still more tightly and prayed the *Diablo* would escape the storm's latest fury, but in the next instant a fiery streak of lightning split the dense cloud cover with jagged precision and struck the ship with a ferocious blast, sheering off the mainmast. The violent roll of thunder that echoed over the badly damaged ship deafened the young man and sent him sprawling among the debris of the splintered mast. With no hand upon the wheel to guide the rudder, the *Diablo* lurched into the waves, its timbers shuddering mournfully as the storm continued its battle to the death.

The first sounds of thunder had frightened Angelique, but she knew she was safest in Diego's cabin and made no move to leave it. Though she prayed that the ship would prove equal to the task of surviving the gale, she also realized she would be foolish not to be prepared to take to the lifeboats if that command should have to be given. She searched through her new wardrobe for the most practical garment and, choosing a gray wool dress trimmed in black, she pulled it on, then added her cloak and tied it securely at her throat. She was aware that it would be a tragedy of immense proportions if Diego were to lose the *Diablo,* so she would certainly never complain about losing her new gowns, but nevertheless she hoped her precautions would prove unnecessary. Searching the room briefly, she picked up the ship's log and placed it upon the bunk. Not wanting to leave the Azteca gods behind, she took them from their drawer and, after wrapping them in a nightgown, she placed them with the log. Her jewelry was too expensive to lose and she rolled her sapphire necklace and matching earrings in a handkerchief and then jammed them into her pocket. Since her suitcase would be too cumbersome, she placed the little statues and the log in a pillowcase and sat down upon the bunk, once again hoping she was merely being foolish rather than clever. Each clap of thunder was progressively more deafening, but when the lightning struck the mast, it sounded to her as if Diego must have fired several cannons, for the ear-splitting report shook the whole ship with a dreadful shudder that left her stunned. She did not even realize what had happened until the *Diablo* began to drift into the waves and she knew instinctively that there was no longer a man at the helm to guide her.

She had to force herself to remain calm and stay in the cabin where Diego would be able to find her, for she knew if she were to go running out on deck, she might be swept overboard and he would never discover what had become of her. He had been wrong, she reflected, trying to keep her panic from increasing. She felt no worse now, when the weather was so rough, than she had when they had first sailed out of Barcelona's harbor. Perhaps it was only possible to be just so seasick and she had long ago reached her limit. She sat clutching the precious idols and prayed that Diego would soon come to tell her he had everything well under control, but she knew in her heart that this could not possibly be true. Though he was the best of captains, the storm was simply too strong to be overcome by a mere mortal, no matter how brave a man he might be.

In a heroic effort to reach the wheel, Octavio scrambled over the debris that littered the deck, but the waves were now cresting high above the bow and time and again he lost his footing and went sliding toward the rail. The fierce gale fought him savagely for possession of the *Diablo* and when he finally managed to grab the wheel, he no longer had the strength to control the rudder. The sleek ship was repeatedly swamped by the battering waves and after the hatch cover on the forward hold gave way, he knew all hope of riding out the storm was gone. The ship was taking on water so fast he feared it might go down with all hands unless he acted without another instant's delay. Sounding the alarm to abandon ship, he tied down the wheel and went to get Angelique while he ordered the men to see if Diego, or at least his body, could be found.

The fear in Octavio's dark eyes was sufficient to terrify Angelique, but she had to scream to be heard over the malevolent whine of the wind. "Where's Diego? Where is he?" The mate did not bother to answer but grabbed her arm and pulled her along beside him. One lifeboat had already been lowered to the water and he cursed the men who had put their own safety before that of a young woman. He shoved her into the next boat, but she leapt out the moment he released her.

Angelique searched the frantic expressions of the sailors who surrounded her, seeking some news of her husband. Octavio grabbed for her again, but she managed to escape his grasp only to be caught by another pair of hands. "Where's Diego? I won't leave without him!" She was again dropped into the lifeboat, but she clung to the man who had pushed her down upon the seat and refused to let him go. "Where is my husband!" she screamed, but she was even more horrified when she received only an agonized stare and no answer. Surely Diego would not refuse to leave his ship, but if he had chosen such a suicidal course, she was determined to remain with him. She still held the pillowcase and although she did not want to use the weight of the idols as a weapon, she would certainly do it before she would leave the *Diablo* without her husband.

As she attempted to rise, two men suddenly emerged from the heavy veil of rain. They were supporting Diego between them and, seeing that she was already in a lifeboat, they lowered the unconscious man into her arms and then scrambled aboard themselves. The *Diablo* was now listing severely and the lifeboats were lowered with frantic haste, taking the last of the men off with only seconds to spare before the gallant ship was drawn below the waves.

Angelique could not bear to watch the *Diablo* sink, for it was Diego's pride and she had loved it too. She knelt in the bottom of the lifeboat, shielding her husband from the constant spray of rain and waves while she tried to ascertain whether or not he was still alive. Placing her fingertips against his throat, she waited for what seemed an eternity before she felt the steady beat of his pulse. She vowed then that if he had lived to be taken off his ship, she would not allow him to die in her arms. She cradled his head in her lap and prayed that the Lord had not deserted them entirely. She

345

was oblivious to the men who struggled with the oars, their task simply to keep heading into the waves so they would not be swamped and sink. With the fear of death for inspiration, they desperately attempted to succeed in this crucial chore.

Lightning continued to streak across the sky, but it was moving eastward, and soon the thunder grew fainter until the rumbling and the bright flashes could no longer be detected. Water dripped off the hood of her cloak, but Angelique protected Diego from that additional discomfort and he soon began to stir. He moaned but did not open his eyes. She looked up at the others. They were as frightened as she was, but she tried to smile, for she could offer no other form of encouragement. The night stretched on endlessly and the punishment of the storm was brutal. By the time the weather finally cleared late the next day, exhaustion had overtaken them all and they fell asleep where they sat. None of them had had the strength or the foresight to realize that their adventure had just begun.

Angelique awakened late the next morning to find six pairs of eyes watching her with a mixture of curiosity and hatred, which was not at all reassuring. The sky was still gray and the threat of additional rain was not yet over, but it was the sailors' clear animosity that frightened her most. Were they all so superstitious that they blamed her for their misfortune? she wondered uncomfortably. If they were the types who considered it bad luck to have women on board, she knew she would have great difficulty disproving their theory. To make matters worse, Diego was now far too warm, and she had no idea how to care for a fever in an open boat. She scanned the horizon slowly, hoping to see some sign of land or another of the lifeboats, but they were totally alone on the clear blue sea. She hugged her husband more tightly, wishing he would awaken, since she was positive he would know exactly what to do.

With none of them having either the experience or the intelligence to claim authority over the others, the six sailors spent most of their time arguing over whose turn it was to row. They knew the Caribbean Sea was filled with islands and hoped to drift with the current toward one, but they had no fresh water or food and little energy left after what they had been through to man the oars and make their progress toward safety more swift. When on the third day the sun broke through the clouds, only four of the men awoke to see it while the other two had fallen victim to the same fever that still burned within Diego's unconscious body. Angelique bathed the men's faces with a handkerchief she kept dipping in the sea, but that measure did little to ease their pain.

"You might as well save your strength, *Señora*. None of us is likely to live to see another dawn."

"If you think I wish to sit in a boat with six dead men, you are sadly mistaken," Angelique responded hoarsely. Of all their problems, thirst was the worst, and her mouth was so dry she could barely move her tongue to speak.

"There are seven of us," the sailor reminded her.

"Diego is not going to die," Angelique insisted.

The man shook his head, certain she was wrong, but as Angelique again dipped the handkerchief in the water, she saw the flash of a fish's bright scales and asked excitedly, "Quickly, one of you, how can we fashion a net to catch some fish?"

The sailor who had just been arguing with her clearly thought her mad, but one of the others pulled a knife from his pocket and leaned over the side to see if any of the fish that filled the sea might be swimming close enough to stab. When none were, he slid back to his seat with a dejected frown.

"You've a knife. Let's tie it to an oar and use it as a spear," Angelique suggested, sorry she had not thought of the idea before they had all become so exhausted from exposure. The men were only slightly less eager to die than they were to follow her suggestion, but, by diligent effort, the man who owned the knife finally managed to spear a fish.

"It's a snapper," he announced proudly, but looking at his companions, he realized it was too small to feed them all.

"Let me have a try," the more surly of the men offered, but more than an hour passed before he had any success.

The two raw fish provided a meager meal, but Angelique saved every edible morsel and pressed out the liquid to pour down the throats of the unconscious men. "We'll have to keep trying to reach land. If we can spear two fish, then we can spear a hundred, and none of us need die."

Shamed into accepting the challenge she had offered, the four sailors took turns fishing when they could no longer row, but the raw fish provided only the barest amount of nutrition and moisture and they all grew steadily weaker. When another of the men fell ill, Angelique had no tears left to shed. She had worked so hard, but she could not keep four desperately ill men alive all by herself. She simply did not have the strength. With Diego clutched tightly in her arms, she fell into an exhausted sleep. Her last prayer had been a humble plea that she and her husband might be allowed to awaken together within the gates of paradise.

Chapter XX

The well-appointed cabin was illuminated by the last of the sun's rays. They produced a soft, golden haze that seemed to envelop the fair-haired man seated at the desk in a shimmering halo. Angelique sat up slowly, taking in every detail of her surroundings, but she could not imagine how she had come to be in the man's bed. From the gentle sway she felt, she knew she was on board a ship lying at anchor in shallow water rather than at sea and, no longer able to contain her curiosity, she called out to the finely dressed stranger. "Monsieur?"

Startled by the sound of her voice, Lucien threw down his pen and leapt to his feet, ecstatic as he replied in French, "I had feared you might never awaken." He crossed the short distance to the bunk and sat down at her feet, smiling with unrestrained delight as he reached out to touch her forehead with a hand that proved to be as soft as a woman's. "Your fever has finally broken. God has answered my prayers."

"I have been ill?" Angelique raised her left hand to brush away a stray curl and, noticing immediately that her wedding ring was missing, she asked anxiously, "I was wearing a sapphire ring. Do you have it?"

"Yes," the man responded with a chuckle, "but I am no thief. I merely placed it in my desk with your other jewelry for safekeeping. Allow me to introduce myself. I am Lucien Dangermond, captain of the *Marie Alise.*"

"I did not mean to accuse you of theft, Captain." Angelique swung her feet over the side of the bunk, intending to rise. "Where are the others? I want to see my husband."

"You have been delirious for the better part of a week, *chéri.* If you try to stand, you'll surely faint and perhaps again fall ill. I must insist that you remain in bed while I bring you something to eat. After you have taken some nourishment we will talk about the others."

"You are very kind, but no." Disregarding his warning, Angelique attempted to rise, but a sudden wave of dizziness forced her to sit down again quickly before she collapsed in a heap. She took a deep breath and apologized. "Forgive me. You were obviously correct. I am too weak to walk about just yet. I will have to take your advice, Captain Dangermond, but please hurry."

"I have cared for you myself since I have no women aboard. To find you are French is a most delightful surprise. Won't you please tell me your name before I go?" the man asked politely.

"It is Angelique. Was Diego unable to tell you that?" she asked nervously, dreadfully worried about him still.

"Diego is your husband?" Lucien inquired with an easy smile.

"Yes. He was the captain of *El Diablo del Mar,* the ship we were forced to abandon in the storm. Where is he?"

Lucien gave the distraught blonde's shoulder an affectionate pat as he rose to his feet. "First you must eat and then I will keep my promise and tell you about him and the others."

When he returned with a bowl of thick fish chowder, Angelique ate it all without really tasting a single bite. She was intrigued by the well-mannered young man, but not wanting to stare rudely, she stole glances at him through her

350

thick lashes. His appearance was quite pleasant, his hair a honey blond and his eyes more gray than blue. He seemed to be of no more than medium height, but his build was very muscular and his skin deeply tanned. He was obviously a robust individual and his keen gaze studied her with a rapt attention she found most disconcerting. He had been pleased to find she was also French, but she dared not ask about his politics. His manners were polished and his mode of dress elegant, so she doubted that he supported the revolution that had cost her so dearly, but she knew better than to assume she was safe with him when perhaps she was not. But if he had cared for her himself, then she had very few secrets left, she realized with a deep blush. "Is this your nightshirt I am wearing?"

"But of course. The nightgown in which you'd wrapped the small statues you had with you did not survive my efforts to wash it. I am sorry."

Angelique swallowed the last spoonful of chowder and handed him her empty bowl. "You need not apologize. I appreciate all you have done for me, but now that I am finished eating, please tell me about my husband and his men, for I am most anxious to see them."

Lucien carried the bowl over to his desk and poured two brandies into small silver goblets. "I must insist you take a sip of this before I begin."

His smile was charming, but Angelique was too exasperated with his constant delays to do more than toss down the fiery liquid in a single gulp, an action she regretted instantly.

Lucien paced up and down beside the bunk while he waited for Angelique to catch her breath and stop coughing. "Forgive me. I did not realize brandy was an unfamiliar beverage to you."

"No, it is not, but I had forgotten how much I dislike it." She handed him the goblet and sat forward clutching her knees, eager to hear his story.

351

When Angelique had regained her composure, Lucien finally began. "We were bound for Norfolk, Virginia, when the storm blew us way off course. We suffered some minor damage and were seeking an island with a protected harbor in which to make our repairs, when your lifeboat was sighted. I quite naturally lowered a boat and men to offer assistance."

Angelique interrupted then. "You sighted only our boat. None of the others?"

"Only yours." Lucien smiled sadly. "Perhaps the other survivors of your husband's ship were taken aboard by someone else, or they might have reached an island."

"I certainly hope so. They were all good men, dear friends." Angelique was disappointed they were not on board the *Marie Alise* too. "I did not mean to interrupt you. Please continue."

Lucien nodded slightly. "There were four men with you and—"

"No. There were seven men. You must be mistaken," Angelique insisted firmly.

Lucien stared down at her for a moment and then went to his desk to bring the *Diablo*'s log to her. "I cannot read this language. Can you?"

"It is Catalán," Angelique explained quickly. "But what is it you wish to know?"

"The last entry; what does it state?"

Angelique opened the leather-bound volume and flipped hurriedly through the pages. "It's gotten wet and the ink has run badly, but Diego wrote only one sentence. It appears to be about our encountering heavy rain."

"The date?" Lucien prompted.

"November twenty-first. Is that important for some reason?"

Lucien paused a moment to bring the chair from his desk so he could sit down by her side. "When did the . . . the *Diablo*, was it? When did it sink?"

352

"The storm began on the twenty-first, and it was late the night of the twenty-second that we had to abandon ship after we were struck by lightning. But I know there were seven men in the boat with me!" Angelique insisted once again.

"Chéri, you must try to think more calmly. How many days can you recall being adrift?" Lucien reached out to take her hand lightly in his and was enormously pleased when she did not draw away.

"It rained all day the twenty-third. The twenty-fourth was still cloudy, but it was sunny again on the twenty-fifth." Angelique tried to concentrate, but her memory grew hazy. "Diego was ill, then two of the sailors also became feverish. We caught fish and ate them raw. I remember one more man coming down with the fever too and then"—she bit her lower lip nervously—"I can't separate one day from the next after that. I guess you must have found us."

"So you remember perhaps the twenty-seventh or twenty-eighth?"

Angelique shrugged. "All I know for certain is that I want to see my husband. Can't we worry about what day it is later?"

"No, this is very important," Lucien stated firmly. "We did not take you aboard until the second of December. You say there were seven men with you and you know your husband and four others were ill. It is obvious that even if you don't recall it, three of the men must have died and their bodies would have been thrown overboard."

"Dear God!" Angelique felt as though every drop of blood had rushed from her body, and indeed her face grew deathly pale as she clutched his hand with both of hers. "Was Diego among those still alive when you found us?" she finally managed to whisper.

"Can you describe him to me? All five of you were ill and unable to supply your names," Lucien responded sympathetically.

Angelique found it impossible to draw a deep breath, and

when Lucien brought her another glass of brandy, she was careful to drink it more slowly. "Diego is easily half a head taller than the other men. Even with a week's growth of beard, he is by far the most handsome too. He has black hair with a slight curl, and brown eyes. Oh, surely you would be able to recognize him from that description if he had still been with me in the boat."

"Yes, he was among those we brought on board." Lucien sat back, carefully weighing his words before continuing. "You had all suffered terribly from exposure in addition to the fever you shared. This is now December seventh, Angelique. Five days have passed."

"I don't care how ill Diego is. Please take me to him now." Angelique's eyes filled with tears as she begged him to listen. "I know I am still weak, but I want to take care of my husband myself."

"That is impossible, chéri. We tried to give each of you the best of care, but your husband and the other men all died within hours of each other on the evening of December second. You are the only one to survive."

Angelique suddenly heard a woman's hysterical screams, and the piercing shrieks continued until they were hoarse, racking sobs, but she did not realize that the terrified wail was her own voice echoing inside her head. Lucien pulled her into his arms, muffling the sounds of her anguished cries in the soft folds of his velvet coat as he offered what comfort he could, but she was too heartbroken to do more than weep until what little strength she had was expended and she fell into an exhausted sleep.

The Frenchman then went back to his desk to make a notation in his log that his lovely patient had awakened and had provided him with her name. He dared not leave her for fear she would awaken to face her grief alone and so he continued to keep a vigil at her bedside throughout the night.

* * *

354

It was late the next morning before Angelique again awakened. She recalled her conversation with Lucien Dangermond with pristine clarity. Diego was dead, yet for a reason she could not comprehend, she had survived the ordeal that had claimed the lives of seven strong men. The only explanation was that the last to fall ill had cared for her more tenderly than he had the others, but she did not even know which man that might have been. She closed her eyes to offer a silent prayer for the repose of his soul and began to realize that spending the rest of her life without the man she loved would be a torment she did not believe she had the courage to face. Beatriz had never recovered from a similar tragedy, and she doubted she could either. It would be far better to be dead than to live the life of a bitter widow who could never forget what she had lost.

When she felt Lucien's lips touch her cheek, she opened her eyes quickly, shocked to find he had taken such a liberty.

"I cannot bear to watch you cry," Lucien explained, bending down to wipe away the tears that still streamed down Angelique's cheeks. "Can you sit up again? If so, I will bring you something more to eat."

"I am not hungry." Angelique closed her eyes again, lost in the pain of her memories.

"Angelique!" Lucien called loudly, speaking her name as a command.

With a weary sigh, Angelique opened her eyes and turned toward him. "It would be far more kind of you simply to let me die. I don't want to live another day without Diego."

Lucien frowned slightly, then sat down at her feet and gave her knee an affectionate pat. "Had God wished you dead, you would have died when the men did. Do not presume now to question His wisdom." When she did not respond, he chose a new approach. "Are you forgetting that I have bathed and dressed you myself? You are very slender, but the slight swell of your abdomen can mean only one thing. You are carrying your husband's child."

355

Angelique's pale complexion filled with color at his statement. How long had it been since she had thought of the child? She looked away, ashamed to think the babe was dependent upon her when she wanted only to join Diego in death.

"Think of the babe, Angelique. Perhaps that is why you have survived—to give him life. You must not be so selfish as to refuse to do so. You must not cheat your husband of his heir."

Angelique's lashes seemed so dreadfully heavy that she could no longer keep her eyes open, but as sleep overtook her again, she realized that Lucien was right. She could not fail Diego now, not when his child needed her.

Lucien leaned forward, ready to shake Angelique soundly, but he saw that she had fallen asleep again and left her alone. She was far too lovely to risk losing, and he kissed her brow tenderly before he went to make certain the cook would have something delicious prepared for her when next she awakened.

Though Angelique continued to sleep much of the time, Lucien was by her side at every waking moment. He was pleasant but persistent in his efforts to make her eat what he considered sufficient nourishment for a pregnant woman. "You must indulge me, Angelique. My wife was very frail and she gave me no children. Perhaps you will allow me to be godfather to yours."

"You are a widower, Lucien?" Angelique was pained by the thought, for he had treated her so sweetly that she had become quite fond of him. To please him now, she took the last two bites of her supper.

"Yes." Lucien's gray eyes grew smoky with sorrow. "Her name was Marie Alise, and the only comfort I have is that she did not live to see what has become of her beloved France."

His tone was too bitter to be insincere, and Angelique attempted to draw him out. "You are not in sympathy with the ideals of the revolution then?"

Astonished that she would not understand his feelings, Lucien leapt to his feet and shoved his chair aside with a forceful kick. "I was too great a fool to become involved in politics until it was too late, but men who would sentence to death a woman as lovely as our queen will never have my sympathy. Too many have died in the name of their cause for me to ever embrace it."

"I did not mean to upset you, Captain." Angelique sipped her tea slowly, hiding her keen interest in the answer to her next question. "You said you were bound for Virginia, but you did not come from France?"

Lucien swung around quickly and his glance appeared hostile at first, but then it softened as he realized she was merely curious. "No, I had been on the island of Martinique. I have no desire ever to return to France."

"Good, for neither do I." Angelique took a deep breath and let it out slowly. "I do not wish to be a burden to you, however. You have been so very kind. How will I ever be able to repay you?"

"There is nothing to be repaid, *chéri*. If you and your husband had found me adrift at sea, would you not have given me the same fine care I have given you?"

"Why yes, of course, but—"

"No, there is nothing more to be said. Those of us who depend upon the sea for our livelihoods must take care of each other whenever the opportunity arises, for if I help you, then one day you will be alive to help me."

"Lucien"—Angelique patted the edge of the bunk to draw him near—"Diego did not own only one ship, but many. His father's company has offices in Vera Cruz. If you'll take me there, I will see you are given a reward. You deserve a generous one, and the Aragons will want you to have it."

Puzzled, Lucien took her hand in his. "Aragon is your

357

name? I did not realize that Diego was from such a prominent family, but I require no more than a smile as my reward."

Angelique knew the frequent smiles she gave him were faint ones. "You are very gallant, Captain Dangermond, but I still think you should be provided with a more tangible reward."

"Do not tempt me, or I will name one." Lucien's eyes sparkled with mischief as he teased her.

Despite the considerable romantic experience her marriage to Diego had provided, Angelique was still far too innocent when it came to being able to recognize when a man was flirting with her and she failed to comprehend what it was Lucien wanted. "Since Spain and France are at war, I know you could not sail into Vera Cruz in broad daylight, but there must be a way you could put me ashore, and I could ask whoever is in charge of the business affairs of the Aragon Line to provide whatever it is you wish."

Lucien shook his head. "I require nothing they can provide. I would be happy if you would but try again to stand and take a step or two."

Since she had tried walking about on several occasions when he had not been with her, Angelique was confident she could please him. "If that is all you want, Captain, then I will be happy to try." She pushed back the covers and swung her bare feet to the floor. When he stood and offered his hand, she took it and, after a moment's hesitation, rose gracefully to her feet. She felt a bit light-headed but smiled as she took a step forward. Observing that Lucien was a scant three inches taller than she, Angelique perceived with a sudden stab of conscience that she had been comparing him to Diego and her eyes filled with tears.

Lucien quickly slipped his hand around her waist, "Do not overtire yourself, *chéri*. I do not want to make you feel ill."

Smiling as best she could, Angelique shook her head, "No, it was nothing. I'm fine. You needn't hold me so tightly. I can take a few steps on my own."

While Angelique was confident that she could, Lucien was not so certain, and now that he had her in his arms, he did not want to waste the opportunity for further intimacy. He pulled her around to face him as he lifted his left hand to the nape of her neck. Winding his fingers in her thick curls, he lowered his mouth to hers, but the instant their lips met, she pushed him away with a surprisingly forceful shove.

"Please, you mustn't!"

Lucien reached out to grab her waist again so she could not escape him. His touch was still light yet confining as he pulled her back into his arms. "Forgive me. I did not mean to frighten you with my affection or take advantage of your illness. Here, let me help you take a few steps and then I must insist you return to bed."

His mouth had been warm and his kiss gentle, but Angelique's cheeks were still stained with a deep blush. She had not expected him to kiss her, but now that his tone was so tender, she felt guilty for having reacted so rudely. She frowned with concentration as she took several steps with him at her side. He was in his shirt sleeves and the hard muscles of his arms were a vivid reminder to her of his superior strength, but as he had promised, he helped her back into the bunk and stepped away with a polite bow.

"I don't enjoy being an invalid. Tomorrow I will try to take a few more steps." Still embarrassed, Angelique focused her attention on her hands, which were folded tightly in her lap, rather than on her attractive companion.

Lucien leaned forward to place his fingertips beneath her chin to force her gaze up to his. "I am a very patient man, Angelique. You need not be afraid I will ask for more affection than you are ready to give," he assured her with a charming smile.

"I am not afraid of you," Angelique lied with a shy smile. "But I love my husband. It is so difficult for me to believe that he's dead. I really can't believe it."

"But you must." Lucien was clearly perturbed by her inability to accept the truth. "Unfortunately, he and the others had to be buried at sea, so I have no grave to show you. He wore no jewelry of any kind, so I have nothing of his to give you to offer as proof either, but you must accept the fact that he is dead."

Angelique's expression still reflected her determination as she attempted to describe her torment. "We were not as close as we should have been, but there were times when the distance between us vanished completely, when no separation existed between our souls, no space where the person who was Diego ended and I began. It was the precious times like those, when we were truly one, that I cannot forget." Her voice faded to a hushed whisper as she recalled that the last words she had spoken to her husband had been said in anger. "I loved him so, but if he had not married me, he never would have considered making another voyage to Vera Cruz so late in the year, and he would still be alive."

"Ah, now I understand." Lucien patted her curls fondly before he turned to go. "You must not feel guilty, *chéri*. Our lives are in God's hands, not our own."

When he left her alone, Angelique was again overwhelmed with grief, for she lacked the faith he possessed and was certain her husband's death had been entirely her fault and no one else's.

By the end of her second week on board the *Marie Alise,* Angelique was sufficiently strong to be awake most of the day and she grew extremely curious about Lucien Dangermond. He had told her he had been seeking an island with a protective harbor in which to make needed repairs, but she could not recall ever having heard the sounds of any sort of work. She had seen no one but him, although he mentioned others by name from time to time. He had moved his belongings to his mate's cabin and he mentioned Yves frequently, but she had never met the man. She had been able to discover little about Lucien and that disturbed her, since he was so very attentive to her needs. She was ashamed to think she had been so involved in her own tragic loss that she had forgotten his. "Forgive me if I remind you of things you'd rather not discuss, Captain, but did you lose your wife recently?"

They were seated at his table, sharing supper, but Lucien was so startled by her question that he needed a moment to reply. "No. She died five years ago. As I told you, she had never been strong, but our families had encouraged the marriage since we were children. Neither of us questioned the wisdom of such a match, but it was unfortunately a very brief one."

"You have named your ship in her memory then?"

"No, she christened the *Marie Alise* herself, but perhaps it is time I gave the ship another name, one that does not have such sad memories." Lucien swallowed the last of his ale and poured himself more. "Five years is a very long time."

Since she had clearly depressed him, Angelique was sorry she had asked about his wife and selected another topic quickly. "How are the repairs progressing? I must say your crew is extremely quiet. I have not once been disturbed by the sounds of their work."

"What?" Lucien sat up straight as he returned her curious look.

"You said you were bound for Virginia but had to make some sorts of repairs." Angelique was as confused as he seemed to be. "At least that's what I thought you told me."

"Oh yes, of course." Lucien broke into an easy grin. "I will proceed to America in a day or two, but there is no reason to hurry."

"It will soon be Christmas. Wouldn't your crew rather spend the holiday in port than wherever we are?" Angelique had only a view of the blue waters of the Caribbean from his cabin and was not at all certain where they were.

"But of course. I have been very selfish, *chéri*. I have left my crew to fish and lie about the beach while I have had the pleasure of entertaining you. Perhaps it is time we set sail for Norfolk. You will like Virginia. The state has both wealth and beauty."

Angelique looked down at the silk nightshirt she wore. Fortunately the man owned several, or she would have had no change of clothes at all. "My gray dress and cloak were ruined by the sea water. It will be difficult for me to enjoy much when I have nothing appropriate to wear."

After a moment's hesitation, Lucien got to his feet. "In the bottom of my trunk, I believe I still have a garment or two of my wife's. Let me look."

While the thought of dressing in his dear wife's clothes was a distressing one, Angelique could think of no better alternative. Lucien had an extensive wardrobe and his taste seemed far more flamboyant than Diego's had been. She wondered briefly if his wife had shared his passion for bright colors and expensive fabrics.

When he returned with a lovely suit in burgundy velvet, she reached out to touch the soft fabric with a fond caress. "This is very beautiful, Lucien, but are you certain you want me to wear it?"

"Yes. There is lingerie as well. There is no reason for me to keep Alise's clothes when she can no longer wear them. She was not as tall as you, but there is a generous hem. Can you alter the garment yourself?"

"Yes, if you have needle and thread I might use." Angelique stood and held the skirt up to her waist to judge the length. "Yes, I see what you mean, but I am tall for a woman."

"Nonsense. You are precisely the height you should be," Lucien remarked with a teasing grin. He laid out the other things that had belonged to his wife and then found a tin containing the thread and needles she would require. "You need not rush this project. It will be several days before we are ready to leave here."

"It will be nice to have something to occupy my time,"

Angelique responded truthfully.

"Have you been so very bored?" Lucien asked skeptically. "I have done my best to keep you amused."

Angelique found his admiring glance impossible to meet and looked away. He always behaved as a gentleman, polite in all respects, and after his one attempt to kiss her, he had not tried again, but nevertheless she felt uneasy around him, for there was always far more in his glance than in his words. Her figure was still slender enough to be alluring, and she knew he wanted her, but romance was the very last thing she needed. She was sorry he did not seem to understand that her reluctance to allow their friendship to become anything more was quite natural for a woman so newly widowed. "It is getting late. I'd like to prepare for bed."

"I will see you in the morning then." Lucien gathered up their supper dishes and excused himself without argument. After only a moment's hesitation Angelique went to the door with the intention of locking it, but she found that the key was missing from the ornate brass lock. She knew she had seen the key many times and wondered when Lucien had decided to remove it. Crossing to his desk, she hurriedly sorted through the contents of the drawers but found no keys. Her jewelry was still wrapped in her handkerchief, but she could not very well take out her ring without letting him know she had searched his desk, and that seemed somehow dishonest. Reminding herself to ask him for the ring when next she saw him, she got ready for bed, but on that night, as on all the others, she saw Diego's flashing smile the instant she closed her eyes. That enchanting sight always brought a fresh torrent of tears and she prayed they would never wash his memory from her heart.

Much to her disappointment, Angelique found Alise's clothing quite a bit too snug and what she had thought would only be simple alterations became major modifications. Lucien had returned her ring, but she knew she would have to sell the matching earrings and necklace as soon as they reached Norfolk so she would have some money to buy the additional clothes she would need and to pay for passage to Vera Cruz. She doubted she could find a buyer for the Azteca gods and she sincerely wanted to keep them anyway, for Diego had been so fond of them.

It had taken her the better part of two days to let out the seams in the burgundy suit, but Angelique was pleased with the results of her efforts. The folds of the full skirt hid her pregnancy while the rich color of the velvet made her fair complexion glow with the reflected hue. She had bathed and washed her hair and had styled it in an attractive upsweep of curls. She would have liked to have had a pretty bonnet but considered herself fortunate to have such an elegant outfit and did not complain that she lacked the necessary accessories to complete it. By some stroke of good fortune, Lucien had also kept a pair of Alise's slippers, which were surprisingly comfortable, and Angelique was quite pleased with herself when he joined her for supper that night.

"Well, what do you think?" she asked, turning slowly so he might admire her efforts more fully. "My condition may soon be difficult to disguise, but I do not think I will cause undo comment when we reach Virginia."

Lucien could not hide his pleasure, for Angelique was so beautiful he was completely enchanted by her. "You are stunning, and your face is so pretty that no one will notice your waistline. I will see to it that you have a dozen new gowns as soon as we arrive in Norfolk."

Angelique allowed him to seat her at the table before she began to argue. "You have done far too much for me already, Captain Dangermond. I can accept no more of your charity. When we reach Virginia, I will have to locate a buyer for my jewels and find a way to reach Vera Cruz. Diego's father must be sent word of his death, and because my husband was a wealthy man, I am certain his child and I will

364

be well provided for by his estate."

"I am a wealthy man too, Angelique," Lucien stated without boasting. "You need not sell any of your valuables. I will continue to provide for all your needs."

Angelique laid her fork aside, determined not to insult the man, since he had been so kind to her. "I appreciate all you have done for me. I have made it a point to tell you frequently how grateful I am for your help. However, I want to go to Vera Cruz, for that is the city Diego chose for our home and I know he would want me to live there. You know you can't take me there, so we will have to part company in America. It can be no other way. I want to raise our child on Spanish soil."

"Since the Spanish Crown has the peculiar habit of not fully recognizing the rights of Spanish citizens born in their colonies, you would be wise to return to Spain for the birth of your child. Did your husband not explain such things to you?" Lucien spoke in a nonchalant manner, seemingly unconcerned about the baby's fate.

"Yes, but he thought such distinctions among people with the same heritage absurd. He was far more liberal in his views than the Spanish Crown, and since he had the resources to provide for his children, I don't think my child's birthplace will really matter."

"You are mistaken, *chéri*. Where the child is born will matter a great deal. It is not a question that must be decided tonight, however. Now what do you think of this wine? You have hardly tasted it." Lucien replaced the drop she had sampled and sat back to observe her reaction.

Happy to change the subject of their conversation before it led to an unfortunate argument, Angelique took another sip and, after taking the time to savor it, she smiled. "This wine is French, isn't it? How delightful! Where did you get it?"

"I still have a bottle or two saved for a special occasion," Lucien explained as he raised his goblet in a silent toast.

"You seemed well enough at last to enjoy it, so I am happy to see that you do."

"Yes, it is delicious." Lucien was always a gracious host, but Angelique had no wish to impose upon him any longer. She could not bear to think of herself as Diego's widow but knew she could hide from that reality no longer. As they dined, she continued to think of Vera Cruz and wondered if she would have any trouble convincing the employees of the Aragon firm who she was. She could take the *Diablo*'s log as proof, she supposed, but she hoped they would not doubt her word.

Lucien watched Angelique toy with her food and while he made no comment upon her obvious lack of appetite, he made certain she drank the flavorful wine. While she was lovely in the deep red suit, he recalled each detail of her exquisite figure with a rush of emotion that he kept well in check until they had finished their supper. "Would you like to come out on deck with me for a minute or two? The fresh air will help you sleep."

She had not once been out of his cabin and accepted his invitation with enthusiasm, not realizing that Lucien would use the excuse of a stroll to slip his arm around her waist. The man was always finding ways to touch her that seemed completely innocent, but she was convinced they were thinly veiled attempts to lead her into accepting much more. She could tell little about the *Marie Alise* in the dark, but it seemed about the size of the *Diablo*. There were a few men lounging about, but she saw several fires lit upon the beach and the sound of singing drifted easily upon the night air. "Your men seem very content."

"Yes, but they are simple souls, not given to contemplating more than what is within their reach." Lucien stopped to lean against the rail and raised his eyes to the star-filled heavens. "It takes far more to satisfy me."

Angelique took a step away, but the slight distance that she put between them was not enough to make her feel comfortable. She could sense the tension within the handsome Frenchman and she knew she was the cause. He did not speak again and yet his desire was a tangible force that needed no words to be understood.

The night was lovely, he had again remarked upon her beauty, and he had been alone for five long years. He would be satisfied with nothing less than her love, she knew, but she had none to give. She took little comfort in the sea breeze he had brought her out to enjoy and prayed he would accept her excuse for wanting to return to his cabin. "The beauty of the night is delightful, but I still tire far too easily and really must bid you good night."

After a moment's hesitation, Lucien agreed sadly. "As you wish." He walked her back to the cabin, stacked their dishes upon a tray, and, after paying her another compliment upon the attractiveness of the burgundy gown, he took his leave.

Angelique had heard more anguish than flattery in his words and paced the confines of the cabin for half an hour before she began to undress. She was frightened but could not place the blame for her apprehension on anything Lucien had said. It was only that she had to rely upon him for everything—for each bite of food and sip of water, for the clothes she wore and for the bed in which she slept. It was not a comfortable feeling to be so dependent upon a man who had grown overly fond of her, and she vowed not to let herself fall into such a position ever again. She had to set an example for Diego's child, and she would not allow her husband's only son or daughter to grow up thinking she was a weakling who had to cling to a man for support. Her mother had lived that way after her husband's death, but she would not.

That matter decided to her satisfaction, she lay down upon the bunk, but, as always, Diego's haunting image brought tears to her eyes. How could Lucien Dangermond expect her to have forgotten so quickly the husband she adored? She would never forget Diego, never betray his memory by caring for another man. Since she had no other means to reach civilization, however, she could not be rude to Lucien, but she prayed he would not take advantage of her situation to press for affection she would never willingly give. That possibility filled her dreams with terror, and she greeted the new day with a dread she feared would be impossible to hide.

Chapter XXI

The next morning Angelique found her attempts at conversation with Lucien Dangermond filled with awkward silences, for he seemed preoccupied with concerns he did not care to share and was unusually quiet. His aloof manner did nothing to soothe her restlessness and she knew she could not abide remaining in his cabin all day. When they finished eating breakfast, she asked if she might not again go out on deck. "I won't be in the way. I promise. Your men will not even notice I'm there."

Lucien frowned slightly, then shook his head. "No, I cannot permit you to roam the ship at will. It is far too dangerous."

"Dangerous?" Angelique tossed her blonde curls, plainly believing his response preposterous. "How can it possibly be dangerous? Diego permitted me to—"

Outraged by her bold display of impertinence, Lucien interrupted with an emphatic gesture. "Angelique! It matters not at all what your late husband allowed you to do. You are on board my ship now, and you will follow my orders as promptly as all my men do."

Shocked as well as hurt by the arrogance of his tone, Angelique had great difficulty holding her tongue while she fought to regain control of her own temper. The gray of

Lucien's eyes had been so warm at times, but now she saw only ice reflected in their stormy depths. "I understand a captain's orders must be obeyed without question or he'll swiftly have a mutiny on his hands. You needn't shout to make me see the obvious."

Lucien slammed his fist down upon the table with a force that threatened to splinter the thick wood. "The obvious, is it? Should we not drop all pretense then?"

Angelique sat back in her chair, sorry now that she had said more than *bon jour* to the man, but she had not realized his mood would be so foul this morning. "What pretense has there been between us? I don't understand what you mean."

Lucien's piercing gaze swept over her slowly as he rose to his feet. As always, he was handsomely dressed. His coat was a pale, mint green wool, his waistcoat lemon yellow satin, his spotless breeches cool ivory, and his black boots shined with a high gloss. His white linen shirt made his tan appear even more deep, but his expression was one of pure disgust. "I have waited with what I believe to be admirable patience for you to regain your health. Since you're clearly strong enough to crave more excitement than I've provided, how much longer do you plan to send me to bed as you did last night with no more than a brief smile and a cool good night?"

Her cheeks burned with a bright blush at his question, and Angelique licked her lips nervously, hoping to think of some way to make him understand why her response could never be more than what he had already received. "Captain Dangermond, I think you are a very handsome man, an attractive and appealing companion in every way. I am not made of stone. I know how compelling the attraction between a man and woman can be, but it is too soon for me to feel any emotion save grief. You have treated me so sweetly. Can you not allow me the time to mourn my husband for a proper interval?" Angelique selected her words with care, seeking to buy the time to allow her to get away from him. Spain did not permit any other country to trade with her colonies, but there had to be some way for her to find a ship, Spanish or otherwise, that would take her to Vera Cruz. Not knowing precisely where they were was a great disadvantage however, but since Norfolk, Virginia, was nowhere near her final destination, she knew she would be foolish to go that far with a man who was so eager for her company. "Perhaps it would be best if you set me ashore on Cuba. Surely from there I'll be able to find a ship bound for Vera Cruz. I am so flattered you like me, but until after my child is born, I—"

Lucien swore an oath so vile, she knew it would have shocked Diego had he been there to hear it. "My patience has reached its limits now, Angelique. Now! I want you—here, today, not in six months' time! I am willing to give you exactly what you want: safe passage to Vera Cruz. I demand only what is rightfully mine in return." He made no effort to conceal his lust and it contorted his even features into a menacing mask.

"What is rightfully yours? Have you taken leave of your senses? I am a respectable widow you happened to rescue after a shipwreck, not some whore you plucked from a tavern along the docks!" Angelique's glance darted hastily around the immaculately kept cabin. The Azteca gods sat upon his desk, silently observing their argument, and she thought instantly how easy it would be to crush the arrogant swine's skull with the elegant little lady of death.

Seeing the threat of violence in the bright lavender hue of her gaze, Lucien went to the door and shouted for his mate. In a matter of seconds Yves appeared, and he quickly introduced him. "I have had no opportunity to present Yves Bernard to you, *Señora* Aragon, but I know you will be happy to meet him now."

Angelique had never before encountered such an enormous individual. Diego had been tall, but Yves Bernard was a giant. He seemed close to seven feet in height and she estimated that he must have weighed nearly three hundred

371

pounds. He wore a tattered red silk scarf over the greasy tendrils of his dark brown hair and a gold hoop earring in his left ear. His shirt and breeches were far from clean and it was obvious he never bothered to polish his boots. He had a dangerous-looking knife thrust under his wide leather belt, while he carried the cruel whip known as a cat-o'-nine-tails in his right hand. Most frightening of all was the fact that his tiny black eyes, which regarded her closely from between the tangled hair of his brows and beard, showed scarcely a glimmer of intelligence. He looked like no mate she would ever imagine serving aboard an honest ship and she could not find her voice to acknowledge Lucien's introduction. She simply stared up at the man, her eyes filled with a curious mixture of amazement and fright.

"That is all, Yves. Thank you for responding to my call so promptly." Lucien shut the door behind the mate and turned back to face Angelique. "He is a remarkable man, extremely loyal, like a pet. Have you ever owned a pet, *chéri?*"

Angelique had not once thought of her canaries until that very instant and was saddened to think they must have perished in the storm. "Yes," she admitted softly, "I have owned pets."

"Good. Then you know if you treat them well, they will serve you faithfully, even to the point of valuing your life above their own. If any harm were to come to me—even so slight an injury as a scratch from one of your pretty nails— Yves would react with the most ferocious anger imaginable. If you are foolish enough to believe you could survive even one minute of his abuse, let me assure you that you are badly mistaken. Now let me begin once again. I wish to offer you a bargain. I want you, but unfortunately you seem to be consumed only with the desire to reach Vera Cruz. I will take you there. You were right, you know. I can come and go as I please, and the Spanish authorities are neither clever nor swift enough to stop me." After pausing a moment to be certain his words would have the proper effect, Lucien

372

continued. "I am certain you know exactly what I want of you in exchange for passage to Vera Cruz."

Angelique raised her hand to her throat, thoroughly sickened by his crudely worded proposition. "I have trusted you, thanked you repeatedly for your kindness to me. Has it been your intention all along to offer a bargain as despicable as this? Has none of your affectionate attention been sincere?"

Lucien laughed out loud at the innocence of her question. "I am most sincere, *chéri*. I would prefer to keep you with me forever, but you care far more for your husband's memory than you do for me. Am I not a fine enough gentleman for you? I have told you I am rich, yet you want nothing my money can buy. You say I am handsome, but my touch obviously disgusts you. You have given me no choice, Angelique, but to have you the only way I can."

"So you have offered a bargain so vile you must know I will refuse it?"

Lucien took a threatening step closer. "I will see that you are well provided for. I'll not merely deposit you upon the docks of Vera Cruz at midnight. I will treat you very nicely. You already know how kind I have been to you. Nothing need change between us, except the intimacy of our relationship."

"Stop it!" Angelique leapt to her feet and turned her back on him. Diego had once promised to treat her well too. She bit her lip savagely to put the bitterness of that memory behind her. Since Lucien seemed obsessed with his wealth, she turned with the only counter offer she could make. "I'll give you my jewelry. The sapphires are worth a small fortune. They will pay for my passage with a great deal left over for you."

"But I had already planned to keep your sapphires, *chéri*. You will have to do much better than that," Lucien replied with a smug smile.

"You bastard!" Angelique lost her temper completely

then, but as she took a step forward, Lucien crossed to the door.

"Must I call Yves once again?" he asked with a quizzical expression on his features.

"You haven't the courage to beat me yourself?" Angelique taunted, clenching her fists at her sides. It was plain to her now that Lucien never lifted a finger to do any of the work sailing the *Marie Alise* entailed. He simply gave the orders and let his "pet," Yves, enforce them. But despite his threats, she was certain she would never change her mind about his offer. "Why would you have gone to such lengths to save my life if you valued it so little?"

"Oh, but you are mistaken, Angelique. I prize you very highly. The sea does not often provide such fabulous treasure, and I want only to appreciate that gift as fully as possible. Now what is your answer? Is it to be me or Yves?"

Since the thought of death was not in the least bit terrifying when she knew Diego would be waiting for her in the next world, Angelique smiled seductively. "Call your dog, Captain, because I'd sooner sleep with the devil than with you."

Lucien's light eyes filled with fury, but, rather than call his mate, he strode out the door and locked it securely behind him.

As soon as he had left her alone, Angelique began to search the cabin for a weapon. The knife she had used during breakfast would barely spread butter. It would never serve to slash a throat. The scissors he had provided for sewing were too small to inflict more than a shallow wound, but she hid them in her pocket, thinking they would be effective if she could somehow stab Yves in the eye. She found nothing else worth considering, though the Azteca gods drew her attention again and again. She felt they wished to tell her something important, but she could not imagine what it might be.

Once she had searched every drawer and closet, Angelique

paused to wonder if she might not be able to use the element of surprise, but she found it was impossible to hide in the confines of the compactly designed cabin. She could not even stand behind the door to leap out as someone entered. Pacing distractedly, she put her hand in her pocket to grip the shiny scissors while she prayed that Lucien was not truly the lunatic he had appeared to be that morning. But somehow she knew the odds were slight.

It was late afternoon when Lucien reappeared. He took the precaution of remaining at the door while he spoke. "You have had sufficient time to reflect upon my generous offer to escort you to Vera Cruz. What is your decision?"

Angelique looked the Frenchman up and down slowly, unable to comprehend how she could have misjudged his character so completely. Diego had thought her a master of deceit, but her talents paled in comparison to this man's guile. "Why have you not remarried, Lucien, or taken a mistress? Why are you so determined to have a woman who does not want you when there must be many who would be pleased to cater to your every whim."

Lucien was not amused by her question. "You are the woman I want, *chéri*. Now have you decided to be reasonable about my request or not? I told you, I am no longer willing to waste my time being patient with you."

Since his mood was merely belligerent now rather than angry, Angelique continued her attempts to play upon his sympathy. "I thought you were a gentleman and a very charming one, too. I'm greatly disappointed to find out now that I was mistaken. How can I agree to your bargain when I can no longer trust you to keep your word?"

"Is that a no?" Lucien's sardonic grin grew wider still. "There are some men who find violence far more satisfying than making love. I am not one of them, but Yves most certainly is. Do not make me give you to him."

"I am not making you do anything!" Angelique pointed out quickly. "You know what you should do. You should

375

behave as the gentleman you pretended to be and take me to Vera Cruz!"

Lucien shrugged. "I am flattered you believed me to be a gentleman, no matter how briefly. Perhaps it was a mistake not to tell you the truth about myself from the beginning. Well, no matter. It is time you saw for yourself exactly what sort of man I am. Then I will ask you once again to make your choice. Come with me. We must take a short walk."

Tightly clutching the small pair of scissors, Angelique kept her hand in her pocket as she walked along by Lucien's side. He held her left arm in a firm grip, but her right was free, and the thought that perhaps she should make an attempt to kill him crossed her mind swiftly, but she was too curious about what he wanted to show her to take that risk. Despite his threats, she doubted he would hand her over to Yves, when clearly he wanted her for himself. At least he appeared to want her, but perhaps that was merely a convenient lie too.

Lucien led her across the deck of the *Marie Alise* and down the gangplank. There was no one on the beach, but he crossed the white sands with a long stride and, taking hold of her left hand, he led her down a narrow path that wove its way through the lush tropical vegetation. He did not speak as they moved through the dense foliage, but after they had traversed a steep incline, he came to a halt at a small grove of palms that overlooked a wide clearing. Below them they had a clear view of a ring of more than two dozen thatched huts. Some were dilapidated and clearly many years old, while others appeared to have been constructed only recently. It was a miniature city with a small army of men lounging about in varying states of idleness. At one end of the camp there were pens containing goats and chickens, while at the other end stacks of wooden crates and barrels forming a cargo of some sort that waited to be loaded. Here and there a young woman was occupied with cooking or washing, and a few were at work drying fish. Lucien waited until

Angelique had had an ample opportunity to observe all there was to be seen before he spoke. "I find it convenient to make my home on an island that most consider deserted. The conditions are somewhat primitive, but the privacy more than makes up for that slight inconvenience."

Angelique could do little more than stare as, one by one, the men who were gathered below turned to look up at her. They were a tough-looking lot, and though none was as large as Yves Bernard, clearly all were very much like him. Most were barefoot, stripped to the waist, bearded, and grimy with sweat, but it did not appear that they had been doing any strenuous labor. How a man, who took the pride in his appearance Lucien did, could stand to surround himself with such filthy rabble, Angelique could not imagine, but she lifted her chin proudly, as if the sight of his mangy crew did not frighten her at all. "Then you were not bound from Martinique to Norfolk, as you told me?"

Lucien chuckled as if she were teasing. "I go wherever I please, *chéri*. I merely return here from time to time to, shall we say, recuperate between voyages."

What he was was suddenly so plain that Angelique could see no reason not to say it. "You're a pirate, aren't you? A sea-going bandit, that's all!"

Lucien pulled her close with an angry jerk and his fingers cut into the tender flesh of her upper arms cruelly. "I am no pirate, but a privateer. France is at war with Spain, and whatever booty I take as Spanish ships leave the Caribbean finances that cause!"

Though appalled by that information, Angelique was still not too stunned to question him. "But you said you were not in sympathy with the Revolution. Are you telling me now that you are? Or is the war merely a convenient excuse for your thievery?"

Lucien released her with a rude shove, then had to reach out to catch her when she stumbled. "I am no thief! I take only what should be taken, and that I do in the name

377

of France!"

Angelique turned away, convinced that nothing he said was the truth. "Since you twist the facts to suit yourself, I'll not bother to ask any other questions of you."

"Good. Perhaps you have finally learned that my wishes must be respected. I have only one more thing to show you before we return to the ship, and I am certain you will find it fascinating."

"I doubt it," Angelique responded sarcastically, and when he drew back his hand to slap her, she dodged out of the way. Swearing loudly, he reached out to grab her left hand once again and started down a trail leading to the clearing below. He pulled her along beside him as he circled the camp, then finally stopped in front of a hut that was under construction. Yves was supervising a small group of men who, at first glance, appeared no different from the others she had seen. Then Angelique noticed the iron shackles on their ankles. "You've taken prisoners?" she asked incredulously.

"I take a few, from time to time. But I have some others who will interest you more." He gestured for Yves to follow them as he yanked Angelique along beside him to the next hut. He whispered a brief command to the mate and then gripped Angelique's hand even more tightly. The brawny Yves had to bend down to enter the small dwelling, but he soon emerged with a scrawny prisoner under each arm. He tossed the men, who appeared to be blinded by the brightness of the sun, at Angelique's feet and then turned to reenter the hut.

Angelique stepped back, so startled she did not immediately recognize the disheveled pair as two of the men who had occupied her lifeboat. She tried to recall their names but could not. One was the man who had owned the knife they had used to fashion a spear, while the other was the fellow who had been so very disagreeable. They were bearded and dirty, but she was so happy to see them alive that tears came to her eyes. But before the men regained their vision well

378

enough to realize who she was, Lucien pulled her back into the shadows and clamped his hand over her mouth. He then whispered hoarsely in her ear. "I have that precious husband of yours, *ma chéri*. I've told Yves to bring him out and lash him to the pole in the center of the camp. You have never seen anyone flogged, have you? I'll warn you now that it is not a pleasant sight. A cat-o'-nine-tales tears the flesh from a man's back with such precision that the effect is the same as being flayed alive. Yves enjoys floggings so intensely that it is difficult to stop him once he has the scent of blood in his nostrils. There have been times I've instructed him to give no more than five lashes, but he has lost control of himself and killed men I'd simply wanted punished. I would hate to see such a tragedy occur to your husband, who has only this day risen from the dead."

Yves half dragged and half carried Diego and another man from the hut. He dumped the other sailor from the *Diablo* in the dust, then shoved Diego along in front of him. The leg irons Diego wore made his normal stride impossible, but he fought back at each of the mate's rude shoves and hostile blows. The burly man not only had an advantage in height but also outweighed the Spaniard by more than one hundred pounds, and he seemed amused by Diego's efforts to fight him as though they were equals. Finally growing bored with his prisoner's resistance, Yves manhandled Diego out into the open area in the center of the huts and swiftly placed his wrists in the iron cuffs attached to the pole. The slovenly mate then took hold of the back of Diego's collar and ripped off what was left of his shirt, exposing the powerful muscles of his back to full view.

"He has spirit," Lucien whispered softly. "I admire that. It is a pity he is to be beaten when he does not even know why."

The Frenchman had Angelique wrapped so tightly in his arms that she could scarcely draw a breath, but she struggled to get free with the same ceaseless defiance Diego had displayed. She had not realized that any man could be as cruel as Lucien had revealed himself to be that day, but she would not stand idle while her husband was tortured. As Yves began to flick his gruesome whip against his thigh, she bit down on Lucien's fingers until she tasted blood.

In the second it took Lucien to change hands, Angelique screamed Diego's name in a terrified shriek. He tried to turn toward her, but Yves struck him with the back of his hand, slamming his face into the pole with a force that split his left brow and nearly knocked him unconscious.

"Bitch!" Lucien shoved Angelique against the side of the hut. "There's only one way you can help that handsome husband of yours, and you know what it is, don't you?"

Angelique's eyes filled with a furious hatred, for she had quickly come to despise Lucien. She could no longer reach the scissors in her pocket, but she knew that attempting to kill him would solve none of her problems. Even if she could succeed, Yves would swiftly kill her, and Diego as well. She realized that Yves was the one who would have to die in order for them to gain the upper hand. When Lucien lowered his hand from her mouth, she knew what response she would have to give. "I will agree to your bargain. I will do whatever you wish. Just don't let that fiend touch Diego."

A slow smile spread across Lucien's lips. "So, you have decided you do want me after all. It is unfortunate you have waited so long to accept my offer, for now I am no longer able to provide the same generous terms."

"What do you mean?" Angelique dared not imagine what evil plan Lucien had devised, but the wicked gleam in his light eyes was not reassuring.

Lucien shook his injured hand, then turned Angelique around and shoved her out into the sunshine. Gripping her left arm tightly, he explained, "You'll keep still. You'll not try to speak to your husband ever again. You'll spend your time pleasing me, and if for even a moment I'm not delighted with your company, Diego will be the one to suffer. Do you understand me now? You shed one single tear, or speak one word of complaint to me, and I'll tell Yves to bring your husband out here again and whip him until he grows tired of the sport!"

Angelique was so sick to her stomach that she did not think she could walk back to the ship let alone make love to Lucien, for he had proven to be the worst of villains. "You'll have no reason to complain about my behavior as long as Diego is safe."

Lucien made no response until they had reached the plateau where he had first stopped to let her observe the camp. He then waved to Yves. "I told him to stop as soon as Diego screams. How many lashes of that whip do you think he can bear in silence?"

"What?" His treachery enraged Angelique so intensely that she tried to kick him. She clawed at his face with her nails, but Lucien was so strong that he promptly subdued the violence of her reaction without suffering any harm. She screamed at him then, using the most abusive words she could command in French before switching to Catalán to complete her insults. When he laughed at her furious outburst, she tried once again to make him understand the terrible mistake he had made. "Diego will never scream, you madman, and Yves will kill him!"

Lucien had grown very weary of Angelique's fiery temper and shook her soundly. "No man has the courage you describe, not even your beloved Diego Aragon! Just watch and you'll see!" He held her so tightly she could not turn away from the gruesome spectacle about to take place in the sailors' village. As bloodthirsty as their captain, the crew of the *Marie Alise* had gathered around the pole to shout rude insults that Angelique knew Diego could not even understand. The first time Yves's barbarous whip struck his back, it left nine long, bloody trails, but he did not even flinch. He did not utter so much as a moan, let alone a scream, and Angelique began to beg in hoarse sobs, "Stop Yves now! He's going to kill Diego, can't you see that!"

"That would be a small tragedy. You had already thought him dead. Perhaps by sundown he will be." But Lucien knew he would be a fool to risk losing the only weapon he had to control Angelique. He could feel her whole body shudder as the whip again tore across her husband's back, and he pulled her around to face him. "Kiss me and I will tell Yves to stop."

Angelique was certain she was going to be sick now, but she placed her hands upon the Frenchman's lapels, gently pulling his head down to hers. She slid her tongue between his lips to explore his mouth with a sensuous caress, forcing herself not to count the horrible sounds the vicious whip made each time it slashed Diego's already torn back.

Lucien did not pull away until he was certain Angelique could provide no more pleasure with her teasing kiss, but by then Yves had already dealt Diego five savage blows and he gave him the signal to stop. "There. You see how compassionate I am? Now do not make me whip Diego again!"

Angelique could barely focus her eyes upon her husband. The deep slashes inflicted by the cruel whip had torn the muscular planes of his back to shreds. His blood had dripped clear to his knees, staining his breeches with gore, but he had not made a single sound. Perhaps it was more a matter of stubborn pride than courage that had sealed his lips, but she could stand no more. She had always known what kind of man her husband was, but now she knew exactly what sort of man Lucien Dangermond was also, and she vowed she would beat him at his own game. He might lie every time he opened his mouth, but she knew how to do that too. If it was a beautiful mistress he wanted, then he would have one, but she would be the most demanding and difficult of women, and after her many years at her mother's side, she knew precisely how to do it.

Lucien watched as Angelique's expression reflected first horror, then determination and was puzzled. He had intended to march her back to his cabin and have his fill of her, but before he could take a step, she swayed slightly and fainted in his arms. He had no choice then but to carry her back to his bunk, where he left her to recover from an ordeal he knew had caused her as much pain as Diego had suffered, but that had been his intention all along.

Diego rested his head against the pole and wondered why the brute with the whip had stopped tormenting him. Blood from the gash in his left brow ran down into his eyes and he was certain the wound his father had inflicted had been reopened. He did not know how long they had been kept in the darkness of that tiny hut, for he had been too ill to notice his surroundings when they had first been brought ashore. He could see no better than a mole coming out into the sunlight after months underground, but he knew he had heard Angelique's voice. She had called his name, and that was all that mattered to him. The agony the massive beast with the cursed whip had caused him was bearable only because he knew Angelique was nearby. He had been told she had died of the fever that had nearly taken his life, and he had been too weak to question that lie. Was she being treated as a prisoner also? Was she being kept in another miserable hut and thrown only enough scraps to survive? When he straightened up, what was left of his back sent a jarring pain surging through his lean frame, but he knew that no matter what cruelty he had to suffer, he would have to survive it to save his bride.

Yves Bernard took a deep breath, then gave the end of his scraggly beard a savage tug, for he was annoyed by his captain's change in orders. The Spaniard had done him no wrong, but he had been told to beat him until the man screamed for mercy, so to stop before he had been successful in wringing a cry from his lips frustrated Yves greatly. He took his time walking up to the pole, then slowly unfastened the iron cuffs that held Diego's wrists, expecting his victim to slump to the ground unconscious from the pain.

"Where's my wife, you bastard? Where is she?" Diego shouted angrily as he was set free.

Understanding neither Catalán nor Castilian, Yves made no attempt to communicate but spat upon the ground, and, poking Diego in the ribs with the butt of his whip, he headed him back toward his hut. He enjoyed taunting his prisoners as much as he had enjoyed torturing cats when he had been a small child, and he gave the Spaniard a savage kick to send him sprawling as he moved through the door. Raising his whip with a menacing snarl, he saw the other three men returned to their quarters before he sealed the door of their temporary prison. He then walked back to the hut, where he was enraged to find that none of the prisoners he had been supervising had done a bit of work in his absence. He gave them all a taste of the whip to make certain they would not be so slothful ever again.

Diego stretched out upon the straw mat that served as his bed and rested his cheek upon his arm. "Did any of you see Angelique? I know I heard her call my name."

Andres wiped the tears from his eyes, for he was certain Diego would soon be dead from pain if they did not do something to treat his wounds, and they had nothing, not even fresh water, to wash away the blood. "I thought I heard her voice too. When we were first taken out, I could not see well enough to say if she was there or not, but I heard the sound a woman's skirt makes as it sweeps the ground when she moved out of our way."

Enrique shrugged. "I saw no more than her hem. I cannot say who she was, but there was a woman outside the hut."

The last of the sailors came close to whisper, "We are at the mercy of the woman who brings our food. Can we trust Teresa to tell us the truth now, when it was she who told us your wife was dead?"

Diego closed his eyes and clenched his teeth to fight the mounting waves of pain that throbbed down his back in ceaseless ripples of agony. "Is there not one among us who has the charm to entice the truth from her lips?" he asked.

Enrique peered at his two companions in the dim light that filtered in to the crudely fashioned dwelling. "She has little time for me, sir, or for Andres or Gustavo. You are clearly her favorite."

Diego had to consider that possibility for a long moment, since he had noticed little about the young woman. His thoughts had been too filled with memories of Angelique to consider Teresa's comings and goings as anything more than interruptions that signaled the times to eat. He did not even know what she had brought. He had simply eaten it in order to regain the strength he had lost while he had lain ill. His only thought had been to escape the villains who held them captive. "Why do you think she favors me?" he asked hoarsely.

"She serves you first each time she comes, and she gives you more food too," Gustavo responded. As always, his voice was touched with the sharp edge of complaint, but he spoke the truth.

"Perhaps she knows I was your captain."

"You are captain still," Enrique assured him. "They have a ship. We will bide our time and steal it."

"The four of us will steal these pirates' ship?" Gustavo asked sarcastically. "We would not get far."

"There may be other prisoners," Andres suggested hopefully. "If they are holding us, there may be others—perhaps our own companions from the *Diablo*."

While the others were contemplating that possibility, Diego began to shake as though chilled. He had never been in such excruciating pain and now he felt so cold he could not help but shiver. His sailors hovered around him without knowing what should be done, but their tears soon dripped upon him, mixing with the blood that still oozed from the long cuts covering his back.

As soon as it came time to distribute the meager meal the

prisoners were given each evening, Teresa lit a lantern and went first to Diego's hut. She was attractively dark, due to her mother's Indian blood, while her father had been Spanish. Since she was among the few who spoke the prisoners' tongue, Lucien had assigned her the responsibility for their care. While his decision had been a practical one, she had rebelled at the extra work until she had seen how handsome Diego was. The others were not ugly, but she had found their captain especially appealing, for his bronze skin and dark hair reminded her of her mother's people, whom she remembered from childhood. She had been sorely disappointed when he failed to notice her beauty, since all the other men in the camp found her attractive and showered her with compliments. When Dangermond had told her to inform Diego of his wife's death, she had been glad to deliver the message, thinking he would then have an eye for her, but he had taken the news very badly and she had grown tired of trying to make him notice her. She hoped tonight would be different, however, for he had been badly hurt, and if she could ease his pain, then he would surely be grateful to her.

Diego was barely conscious when Teresa arrived. She knelt down beside him and swept his hair back from his forehead as she spoke in a soothing whisper. "I have medicine for your back. I could not come before dark, but now that I am here, you will feel much better."

With the last of his strength, Diego reached out to grab her wrist. "My wife is not dead! Where is she?"

"How should I know?" Teresa replied flippantly. "Captain Dangermond said she was dead, so I told you. I know nothing more."

Knowing Diego was in no condition to question the young woman, Andres spoke for him. "Do not lie. She was here this afternoon. We all heard her shout Diego's name. You must

386

have seen her."

"There was a blonde, but she could not be your wife, Diego. She must be someone else." Since Lucien had kept the woman hidden until that day, Teresa had no idea who the fair-haired woman was. Yanking her hand away from Diego's feeble grasp, she removed the cover from a small clay pot. "Dangermond likes only fine ladies. He has nothing to do with us. We are not good enough for him. But where he got the blonde I do not know."

"She is my wife!" Diego insisted through the heavy veil of pain that threatened to suffocate him.

Teresa began to apply the cool herbal salve to his wounds as she argued, "No, she could not be your wife. She stood upon the bluff kissing Dangermond while you were being whipped. No wife would do that."

"You're lying!" Andres was ready to slap the girl for telling such a ridiculous lie, but she lifted her chin proudly, clearly insulted.

"You were watching your friend. I alone was watching Dangermond. The blonde was kissing him, and with passion too. I tell you she could not have been Diego's wife. She must have been one of your other passengers. Was there not another woman with you?"

Diego turned his face away to hide the tears he could no longer contain, for he could not understand why Angelique had chosen to desert him when he knew that the final word he would speak on earth would be her name.

Chapter XXII

When Angelique awakened to find herself lying nude in Lucien's bunk, she was dismayed for no more than an instant. He had made no secret of the fact that he had undressed and bathed her when she had been ill, but now she wondered if that was all that he had done. That was not a question she would ask him, however, since he would undoubtedly consider such an inquiry a complaint and threaten to whip Diego again. She did not care what the hateful man asked of her. She would do it if it would save her husband from further brutal beatings by the abusive Yves.

"The scissors!" she cried aloud, suddenly remembering her meager weapon. She got up to check the pocket of the burgundy velvet skirt and was not surprised to find that they were gone. Lucien would know exactly why she had taken them too, she thought miserably. Hearing the rattle as he inserted the key in the lock, she scrambled back into his bunk and pulled the covers up to her chin but made no pretense of being asleep.

Lucien wore a satisfied smirk as he entered his cabin. "No more foolish tantrums, Angelique. Let us begin our bargain in an agreeable fashion."

Leaning upon her elbow to be comfortable, the pretty blonde regarded the pirate with cool disdain. "I will have no

388

difficulty meeting the terms of our bargain if you abide by them."

"Good." Lucien shed his coat and then unbuttoned his satin waistcoat. "I will move my belongings back in here tomorrow so we can spend all our time together. I am the best of lovers. I'll not disappoint you."

Although her stomach lurched, Angelique smiled as though his boast were an immensely exciting promise. "I will give you my opinion later," she purred softly.

Lucien laughed as he continued to peel off his spotless attire. "I knew the moment I first saw you that you were a woman like no other. You were more dead than alive and still your allure was unmistakable."

Angelique's soft blue gaze swept over him with an appreciative glance. His body was well muscled, deeply tanned, but it inspired not the least bit of hunger for his touch. "I have always thought you handsome, Lucien," she managed to say convincingly, but she now knew his attractive façade hid a most malevolent character. His enjoyment of her flattery was a valuable weapon she would use against him.

As he joined her in the bunk, she thought only of Diego and how cruelly Lucien had treated him. When he pulled her into his arms, her glance fell upon the Azteca gods and she heard clearly the word their stone lips could not speak aloud. It echoed again and again in her mind like the piercing wail of a banshee: Death! Death! Death! Though an ugly word, it somehow gave her courage as he kissed her, for she knew there had to be a way to kill Lucien Dangermond and his evil pet, Yves, before they killed one or both of them. She relaxed in his embrace, accepting all the affection he wished to give without protest, but also without passion. He drew back, disappointed in her lack of response.

"You are as cold as ice!" he complained bitterly. "No woman at all but merely a shadow of what your beauty suggests."

Angelique could not argue that point, but she was grateful Diego had told her that whores shared only their bodies, not their souls. She had not expected to feel anything with Lucien and was glad that she had not. His lust could cloud his mind while hers remained clear. She would find a way to use that against him too. Lifting her hand to sift his fair hair through her fingers, she attempted to appear saddened by his insult. "If I have failed to please you, you must remember how much I have suffered in the last weeks—perhaps too much to ever again be the woman you desire."

Lucien frowned, confused by her solemn words. "Your nature is a delicate one, that is true, but—"

"You promised to treat me sweetly, as you always have." Angelique bit her lower lip as her eyes filled with tears, and she was pleased when his expression reflected remorse. His mouth returned to hers and his kiss was now so light she scarcely felt it. She raised her arms to encircle his neck as though grateful to be given this second chance to please him. He was gentle and very tender, and she supposed some women might consider him an expert at the art of love. Yet she could not forget what a hideous monster he truly was and gave him no more of herself than she had before, though he fell asleep in her arms with a contented sigh, as if they had shared the deepest pleasure.

The only pleasure Angelique derived was the knowledge she had succeeded in fooling him, and she vowed to continue to do so for as long as it took for Diego to regain his strength after the savage beating he had suffered. Perhaps by then she would be able to think of some way to do away with Yves and his detestable master. She smiled as Lucien slept, for he was now a prisoner in her embrace, and she vowed that if there was a way to kill the heartless villain, she would swiftly find it and not hesitate an instant to use it either.

The next morning the three sailors from the *Diablo* were

taken out of their makeshift prison to join the other prisoners, who were at work building the new hut. None of the men were strong enough to do much work, but Yves could not understand why they were not more industrious. They did only enough to avoid being lashed by his whip, but they noted that the other prisoners bore the scars of frequent encounters with the surly mate.

Diego had not been alone for more than a few minutes when Teresa again came to tend him. She saw that the bread and fish she had brought earlier for his breakfast had not been touched and scolded him as she applied more salve to his back. "If you do not eat, your wounds will not heal."

Once her medicine had dulled his pain sufficiently for him to think clearly, Diego began to question the young woman. "Where have my friends been taken?"

"They are helping to build another hut. Do not worry about them. They will be back with you tonight." Teresa slid her fingertips lightly over the deepest of his cuts. "Why did Yves do this to you? Did you refuse to work?"

"I was not even asked to work."

"Dangermond does not beat men for no reason." Teresa had left the door of the hut open to let in sunlight so she could see him clearly, and she shifted her position as she worked so as not to block the light. "The captain is a mean one, but he is not crazy."

"Where does this Dangermond stay?"

"He lives on his ship. I told you our company is not good enough for him."

Diego pressed his luck. "And the blonde?"

"Oh, she must be with him, for I had not seen her before yesterday. But if she is truly your wife, you should divorce her."

Ignoring her unwanted advice, Diego continued. "How did you come to be here, Teresa?" He turned to smile at the young woman in an attempt to draw her into further conversation, since he knew she had information that would

391

prove useful.

"The story is an old one. I met a handsome sailor who spun tales of an island paradise. When I got here, I found most of his words were lies."

"Isn't he jealous that you're taking care of me?"

"No. He was killed in a raid last spring, but since there are other men here who wanted me to stay, I did." Teresa was quite proud of the fact that she was the prettiest girl on the island. She had forgotten to consider that the blonde was also a beauty, however. "There, that is enough. I'll not answer any more of your questions until you give me something in return." Teresa replaced the lid upon the jar of salve and gave him her most dazzling smile as she waited for his response. Her teeth were even and very white, and they made her effort to charm quite effective.

"I have not a damn thing to give you, Teresa. You must know that," Diego replied brusquely, quickly losing patience with her flirtatious ways.

"I will have to be content with a kiss until your back has healed. Then I shall expect much more of you in payment for my kindness."

"What about all these men who want you to remain here? Am I going to have to fight a hundred men in order to keep you for myself?" Diego held his breath, hoping she would answer without realizing what he had asked, and she did.

"Oh no. There are no more than fifty men here. Some have their own women and others stay too drunk to care. You would have to fight no more than twenty," she replied with a lilting giggle.

"Those aren't such bad odds. Come here." When she bent down, Diego reached up and wound his fingers in her hair to hold her mouth to his as he gave her a kiss he knew she would not soon forget. "Now go before Yves or Dangermond becomes suspicious of why you spend so much time with me."

Breathless, Teresa leaned down again to kiss his cheek

before leaving, so delighted that he had kissed her that she did not stop to wonder why his manner toward her had changed so suddenly from indifference to passion.

The pain in his back having been dulled by the salve, Diego ate the fish and bread while deep in thought. He would string Teresa along for as long as he had to, but he was going to find out the truth about Angelique and the mysterious Captain Dangermond. He reflected that the enchanting blonde had had no suitors before they had met and perhaps she had actually fallen in love with the man, although he found that possibility difficult to accept. Even if she was with Dangermond by choice, he would not leave her behind when he escaped the pirate's stronghold. She was still his wife, no matter how faithless she had proven to be, and if such an important fact had somehow slipped her mind, he intended to see that she did not forget it again.

Angelique found Lucien surprisingly easy to manipulate once she channeled all her energies in that direction. When he brought her water for a bath, she invited him to share it, even though the tub was too small to permit such a diversion. He got into the habit of sitting down to talk, but he could not watch her bathe without becoming aroused, so she spent as long as possible bathing and cleansing her hair so he would be in an incoherent frenzy by the time she handed him her towel and asked him to pat her back dry. He would take her swiftly on those occasions and she preferred haste to the agonizing hours he spent making love to her in the evenings. The darkness hid the revulsion she could not keep from her expression, but in the daytime she had to use all her wits to keep him occupied with pastimes other than making love.

"Do you ever go to Martinique, Lucien?" Angelique was stretched out upon his bunk as he sat at his desk.

"Yes, why?"

"I need something more to wear, that's why. It is a pity you

393

had no more of Marie Alise's clothes for me to use. Aren't you tired of seeing me in this one suit?" Angelique frowned petulantly, as if the matter of her lack of wardrobe were one of her primary concerns. "I had such pretty clothes, and now I have next to nothing."

Lucien turned around to face her. "Why don't you simply wear my nightshirt and stay in bed. That will solve your problem as well as mine."

"What problem do you have?" Angelique asked sympathetically. "Why haven't you told me that something is bothering you?"

Lucien crossed the cabin quickly and sat down by her side. "You are as restless as I am, *chérie*. We should be surrounded by our own kind, not living here as though the rest of the world does not exist."

"You wish to return to France?" Angelique asked skeptically. "Life is not nearly as easy for pirates in the Mediterranean as it is here."

Lucien brought Angelique's hand to his lips, "I am no pirate, despite your insults, but no man of fine breeding is safe in our homeland now."

"That is certainly true." Although Angelique doubted Lucien had any real claim to being a member of the aristocracy, she did not taunt him with her suspicions. He liked to behave as a gentleman only when it suited him, she noted, though a true gentleman would behave with fine manners all the time. "It was not to France that you promised to take me, Lucien, but to Vera Cruz. And you have said nothing in the last few days about when we'll sail for New Spain."

"No, I have not," Lucien admitted frankly. "It will not be a long voyage, but you must not push me to begin before I am ready."

When he leaned down to kiss her, Angelique raised her hand to his nape until he was the first to draw away. Since his mood was so agreeable, she asked politely, "You first offered

394

your bargain before I knew Diego was alive. You plan to take him and the three sailors from the *Diablo* with us to Vera Cruz, don't you?"

Lucien laughed at her question, clearly thinking it ridiculous. "I may set them free; then again, I may not. It will all depend upon whether or not you continue to please me, *chérie*. See that you do." Rising to his feet, Lucien backed away with a courtly bow. "I do believe I have seen women's clothes about somewhere. You will excuse me while I conduct a search, won't you?"

Angelique did not trust herself to do more than nod, but the moment he was gone she cursed loudly. The bastard was only playing with her, exactly as she was toying with him, and it was getting her nowhere! She got up and paced the cabin with a vengeful stride. Somehow she had to get a message to Diego, to let him know she was trying desperately to gain their freedom, but she saw no one but Lucien each day and he certainly would not carry any such note to her husband. She considered possible alternatives until her head was aching from the effort, but she was no closer to escaping Lucien than she had been the day he had sighted their lifeboat and had brought her aboard the *Marie Alise*.

When he returned, Lucien carried three brightly colored silk gowns, which he shook out with a flourish. "I found these in a trunk I had forgotten."

The gowns were lovely, but Angelique hesitated to accept them. "Did these belong to your wife or to someone else?"

"Booty, you'd call them," Lucien admitted with a deep chuckle. "Go on. Try them on for me."

Angelique took the royal blue one first, for the color was as vivid as the Caribbean sea that surrounded them. "I am not certain I can wear a stolen gown, no matter how attractive it is."

"It is a small crime compared to mine, *chérie*. Do not worry over it. Now, should these not fit you well, you'll wish to alter them. You know where to find the needles and thread, but I believe you mislaid these." He removed the small pair of scissors from his pocket and placed them in her hand. His eyes glowed evilly as he lowered his voice to a menacing whisper. "Whom did you plan to kill that day, me or yourself?"

"Yves," Angelique replied with a defiant smile.

"Yves!" Lucien scoffed at her revelation. "You would not have been able even to scratch that brute's hide with those."

Angelique turned away, then replied flippantly as she looked back over her shoulder, "Did you expect me to go meekly if you gave me to him? Did you think I'd simply die of fright without trying to protect myself?" She slammed the scissors down upon the table, then tossed the blue silk gown aside as she began to disrobe. She knew she should not have spoken to him crossly, for he flew into rages so easily, but she hoped the sight of her unclothed figure would distract him from his anger.

Not placated by her graceful pose, Lucien grabbed Angelique's shoulders and spun her around to face him. His mouth bruised her lips cruelly as he kissed her with the fierce passion her defiance had aroused. He crushed all trace of her resistance by the strength of his embrace, then yanked away the last of her lingerie before forcing her down upon the bunk. Not taking the time to remove his own clothing, he simply unbuckled his belt and unfastened his breeches before he dropped between her legs. "Fight me now, Angelique. If anger is all you feel when we make love, then use it against me!" He grabbed her wrists and held her pressed firmly against the pillows. "If you won't give me the fires of your passion, then I will take the flames of your hatred gladly."

Angelique knew it was useless to utter curses, but the fury in her glance darkened to a smoldering hatred as she whispered, "I'll never fight you when Diego will be the one who is punished instead of me!"

Lucien found her insolence such a powerful aphrodisiac

that he could no longer argue and, stifling the retort he was about to make, he abandoned himself to the burning desire that raged within him. His hands moved over the tender flesh of her breasts with bruising force and his kisses were so demanding that he soon tasted the blood he had drawn from her swollen lips. When she refused to retaliate for his brutality, he quickly lost interest in the barbaric sport he had begun and, plunging deeply within her, satisfied himself after only a few quick thrusts.

He moved off the bed then with a hearty laugh, as if he thought he had truly beaten her in a game of wills. Straightening his clothing, he grinned as he boasted proudly, "I'll make a pet of you yet, *chérie*. You'll be my slave soon, exactly as Yves is."

"Never!" Angelique shouted back at him. She was too shaken to make any move to cover herself, but she knew he was the one who should be ashamed of his actions, not she.

"I think I will pay your husband a visit this afternoon. After all, we have never spoken together, and we have much in common now." Lucien let his glance wander down Angelique's lush curves, and was not surprised to find he wanted her again, but he forced himself to put off another encounter until later. "You will be interested to know that a pretty young woman has been caring for his wounds. I want him strong, you see. He is of no value to me dead. Her name is Teresa, and she is, unlike you, always hungry for a man's attentions. Your husband must be very bored, and Teresa can be most amusing, or so I've heard. She is scarcely my type, but my men like her."

While Angelique's defiant expression did not change, her heart lurched with the thought that another woman was with Diego. She knew all too well that he was no stranger to women like Teresa, and she wondered if he would remain faithful to their wedding vows. The pain of her doubt was far worse than the suffering she had endured from Lucien's insatiable lust, and it was all she could do not to cry in front of him. "You are a fool not to ask a ransom for us," she told him, trying to keep her voice steady. "Diego's father would pay any sum to set us free—more gold than you could obtain from raiding a dozen ships. Why don't you take us to Vera Cruz and hold us for ransom there?"

Lucien walked back to the bunk and dropped his hand to the tip of her breast. "What is it about Vera Cruz that makes you so eager to go there? Do you have a lover waiting there? Is that it?"

Angelique ignored the touch of his hand, for it disgusted her. "I wish to have a home, to be happy again with my husband. If you can grow even more rich in the bargain, why should you refuse?"

"A ransom?" Lucien scowled. "Too difficult to arrange, Angelique. You will have to think of something more to my liking while I am chatting with Diego. Is there anything you wish me to tell him?"

"You would actually do it?" Angelique asked incredulously.

"But of course. Don't you trust me?" Lucien spread his hands in a gesture of innocence.

"Then tell him my only thoughts are of him—that every minute of the day and night I am thinking only of him." Angelique watched anger transform Lucien's proud features and was happy to see she had hurt him as deeply as he had hurt her. As soon as he slammed the door on his way out, she rolled over on her stomach and began to sob, for she was so thoroughly miserable she could no longer stifle her tears.

Lucien seldom visited the sailors' camp, for he and his crew shared no common interests. He paused here and there to speak with men he knew were respected by the others, then walked to the hut where Diego was being confined. Taking the precaution of having Yves drag him out into the sunlight, he greeted him warmly, as if they were the best of friends. "I am Captain Dangermond, your host. I hope you have found your accommodations comfortable." He waited a moment for Diego to respond, then realized the man did not speak French and switched to Castilian.

When he saw that the Frenchman was handsome, if too much of a dandy for his taste, Diego worried all the more, for he knew how dearly Angelique regarded her homeland and countrymen. He still could not believe she would prefer this fop to him, however, and responded angrily. "You can go straight to hell!" He turned away, meaning to go back into the hut, but Yves blocked his way.

"Apparently you have some complaint about my hospitality." Disregarding his prisoner's clear dislike for him, Lucien walked around Diego slowly, pausing to note the condition of his back. "You look well enough to work." Then, in French, he spoke to Yves. "See that he joins the others tomorrow."

"That I will, sir." Yves grinned with pleasure, then flicked the whip that never left his hand. "I will see he works hard."

"Perhaps you would enjoy digging a new well." Lucien told Diego, crossing his arms over his chest and pursing his lips thoughtfully. When Diego made no comment, he turned again to Yves to give him directions in French. "Yes, give him a shovel and see that he digs a new well."

Yves nodded. As always, he was ready to do Lucien's bidding.

Lucien moved away, terminating the brief interview, but he suddenly turned back as though he had just had a casual thought. "Oh yes. Your wife wished me to give you a message."

Infuriated by his taunt, Diego went for him. "You bastard!" he screamed, but as he leapt forward, Yves grabbed him by the scruff of his neck and lifted him completely off the ground before he had gotten close enough to do Dangermond any harm.

Lucien pretended to be dismayed by the hostility of Diego's reaction. "Angelique will be disappointed to hear you refused to listen to her message, but no matter. I know how to lift her spirits." He smiled then, delighted with his own evil cunning. "She is a remarkable young woman, as you well know, and I enjoy her company as greatly as she does mine." He walked away then, not listening to the vile string of insults Diego continued to hurl until Yves had shoved him back into his hut.

Lucien was so pleased by the masterful way he had handled his first confrontation with Diego that he went for a stroll along the beach rather than return to his ship, for he wanted to give Angelique sufficient time to worry about what he might be doing to her precious husband. She was a most intriguing woman, unique but far more difficult to control than he had anticipated, and that bothered him, for he truly did want to make a pet of her, exactly as he had boasted.

The next morning, when Diego was taken out with the others and given a shovel, he found the work of digging in the soft sand as torturous as Lucien had meant it to be. Because he had not fully recovered from the effects of the fever or of the beating, his weakened muscles soon grew tired and began to ache painfully. Sweat poured out of him and stung the partially healed cuts on his back until he was in such agony he could no longer raise the shovel. When Yves shouted at him to keep working, he staggered toward him, collapsing in the sand at his feet. His performance was so convincing that the mate carried him back to his hut and left him in peace for the rest of the day. Diego had always been strong, but he knew that if he had not feigned the fainting spell, he really would have been unconscious soon. He was as furious with himself as he was with Dangermond, for he realized that unless he regained his strength, he could not beat him in any contest, let alone regain his wife's loyalty.

As Diego and his men ate their supper later that day, Andres whispered, "I have counted forty-five men. There are five other prisoners, and if we have a plan of escape, we should easily be able to convince them to join us."

Gustavo was quick to argue. "There may be more men on the ship. Who knows? Just because you have counted only forty-five men does not mean there are not many more."

"It does not matter whether there are forty-five or sixty," Diego interrupted. "With nine men, our best chance will be to sneak out of this camp and steal the ship. We needn't fight any men except those standing guard, and from what I've seen, Dangermond relies upon Yves's whip to keep everyone in line." He tore off another bite of the hard bread, for his appetite had finally returned and he felt ravenously hungry. "I am not well enough to go yet, and if the others are no stronger than us, then we must bide our time for awhile."

"Your wife is easily worth two men, Captain. Do not forget she will help us," Andres reminded him. "With you ill, she gave the orders in the lifeboat, and without her cleverness we would all have perished."

Although he did not doubt the truth of his statement, Diego cast Andres a wary glance, "We will leave Angelique out of this for the time being, and Teresa is not to be trusted either. We will pry out what information we can from her with flattery, but make her think we are too tired and ill to attempt an escape. She may be Dangermond's spy, regardless of how sympathetic her manner seems."

"You do not believe her tale about your wife then?" Gustavo dared ask.

"It could be a cunning lie, or it could be the truth. I will have to wait and see for myself. But for now, I am content just knowing Angelique is alive." After they finished their supper, Diego had each man relate what he had noticed about the camp, hoping to piece together the most accurate picture possible. "We will keep our eyes open and make friends with the other prisoners, but I'd like to be gone in less than two weeks."

The three sailors nodded in agreement, happy to see their captain was again well enough to assume command, for they admired both his intelligence and bravery tremendously. "Two weeks," they murmured softly, almost in unison, and their dark eyes were alight with hope. When Teresa again arrived to treat Diego's back, they were not shocked when he kissed her good night.

After having had the Azteca gods upon his desk for more than three weeks, Lucien finally grew curious enough to ask about them. "These small carvings are finely crafted if rather grotesque, but had your husband no other treasures on board his ship worth saving?"

They were eating breakfast and, while Angelique found it difficult to look the man in the eye after the fiendish way he had treated her the previous afternoon, she managed to reply nonchalantly. "Diego purchased those in Vera Cruz last summer. They were made by the Indians who met Cortés, and he valued them so highly that I couldn't leave them behind."

"They are deities of some sort, I suppose?"

Angelique related as much about the figures as she thought Lucien would appreciate, then mentioned quite casually, "Diego had planned to visit the man who had sold them to him, for he had also offered to sell a map to a gold mine and Diego was sorry he had not bought it also."

"A gold mine?" Lucien remarked skeptically. "Where was this mine supposedly located? Near Vera Cruz?"

"I really don't know. You'd have to ask Diego about that." Angelique took another bite and mused thoughtfully, "We planned to investigate the man's claims, for he was an expert in antiquities and would have known whether or not such a gold mine actually existed." Holding her breath, she prayed he would take her bait.

Lucien stared at Angelique as she continued to eat, then tossed his napkin aside. "I will send Yves for Diego now, for taking gold from a mine would be far easier than taking it off a Spanish ship."

"But he will be furious with me for telling you about the mine!" Angelique protested sharply. "Perhaps it was all a hoax."

"The little gods are obviously authentic." Lucien was enjoying Angelique's fright immensely. "I had no idea you were afraid of your husband, *chéri,* though I did find him to be an ill-tempered brute. Did he beat you?"

"No, of course not," Angelique told him readily, but she could see that he did not believe her.

"You must excuse me for a moment. I will send for Diego, but I think he would like to bathe and dress before he sees you again. I am certain Teresa will help him to look presentable." He smiled as if that thought pleased him considerably, but Angelique did not give him the satisfaction of allowing him to see how upsetting his words had made her.

Diego was again at work with the shovel when Teresa came for him and explained that he must change his clothing. He wiped the sweat from his brow as he stopped to rest. "Just give me the clothes. I can dress myself, Teresa."

"But you need to bathe. Captain Dangermond insisted upon it. You must come to my hut where I have everything ready." Her eyes flashed with a mischievous sparkle and she turned to the brawny overseer. "Yves, remove his chains. We do not want to make the captain wait."

The mate first took the shovel and tossed it aside before he

403

removed the chains from Diego's ankles. He laughed as he gave the Spaniard a rude shove to start him on his way, as if he knew that what was in store for him could not possibly be pleasant.

As he followed the pretty dark-haired girl to her hut, Diego used the opportunity to note the activity surrounding the huts nearest theirs and was pleased to see that several appeared to be unoccupied. These were in the older part of the village and he assumed that the former residents had moved into the newer dwellings when they had been completed. He was a skilled observer and missed nothing on the short walk, but Teresa was obviously using her time far differently, for as soon as they entered her hut, she threw her arms around his waist and reached up to kiss him.

Diego took the young woman's hands and pushed her away. "I don't want Dangermond to come looking for me, so that will have to wait until later." He smiled sadly, as if the thought of postponing her affection actually pained him.

"There is always time for a kiss," Teresa replied petulantly.

"But I want far more than that, Teresa, and I don't want to be hurried. We will have to wait for another time. Now since you have the water heated, I'll get in the tub." He had thought that one of the sailors had stolen his boots and was surprised to see them leaning against the table, upon which lay a pair of white breeches, stockings, and a coarse linen shirt. "Have you had my boots all this time?"

"Yes, but you have not needed them." Teresa's dwelling was furnished with no more than a mat for sleeping, a chest for her belongings, and a small table and two chairs. She pulled up one of the chairs in front of the tub and sat down to talk with Diego while he bathed. Her curious glance gave him no privacy at all, but she admired his masculine form too much to offer to step outside. "You do not mind if I stay, do you?"

"This is your house," Diego pointed out with a ready grin. He tossed the blood-stained breeches aside and stepped into the small copper tub. It was really too small for a man of his size to use effectively, but he knew it was probably all the camp had to offer and did not complain. He soaped his body thoroughly and washed his hair before standing up to rinse himself off with the bucket of water she had placed beside the tub. It was not the most enjoyable bath he had ever taken, but he felt clean again and was grateful for that. Running his hand over his beard, he asked for a razor but was promptly refused.

"The captain said your beard is too handsome to shave off. Just get dressed and we will go."

"You mean he does not trust me with a razor. Don't you?" Diego dried off quickly with the rough towel she provided, then picked up the breeches. "Just whose are these?"

"You ask too many questions, Diego. The captain provided breeches but no razor. That is all I can tell you." Teresa was disappointed he had not wanted to make love and pouted as she watched him dress. He was the most perfectly built man she had ever seen, with his broad shoulders tapering to a narrow waist and his limbs well muscled and tanned. She was angry that he did not seem to care for her, for she liked him so very much.

Diego found the breeches too snug for a comfortable fit but finally managed to fasten them. The legs were not long enough, though that fault was hidden by his boots, and when the sleeves of the shirt also proved to be too short, he simply rolled them up. "At least I am clean," he remarked wryly. "That will have to do."

Teresa tossed the breeches he had discarded into the bath water. "I will let these soak and try to wash them later. Now let us hurry."

"Have you a mirror?" Diego tried to comb his hair back

from his face with his fingers but swiftly gave up the effort.

Teresa brought a small mirror from the chest that held her clothes. "Here. Look at yourself quickly and then we must go."

Diego winced at his reflection, for he was not at all pleased with what he saw. His face was too thin and marred by the scar running through his left brow, and while his beard grew low upon his cheeks, he did not think it enhanced his appearance any. "I am sorry I asked."

"But why? You are very handsome!" Teresa took his arm to propel him out the door. "As good looking as Dangermond any day."

"That is a comforting thought." Diego expected some sort of guard to escort him to the ship and was surprised when none appeared. He followed Teresa around the clearing and up the bluff, then paused to look down at the camp. "Are there any children here? I've not seen them if there are."

"No. This is not a good place for families." Teresa took his hand again to encourage him to hurry. "Sometimes the men get so drunk they don't know what they are doing. I go and hide, but some of the other women are not as clever."

"Do you have to go far to hide?" Diego asked innocently. "I've no idea how large this island is."

"It is not large enough when the men are all drunk!" Teresa said seriously as she looked back over her shoulder at him. "You do not like to get drunk, do you?"

"Sometimes I do," Diego admitted with a charming grin. "Dangermond doesn't let his prisoners drink though, does he?"

"No, never. But here is the ship. You must be quiet."

Diego breathed a sigh of relief, for the *Marie Alise* was a bark, a near duplicate of his own *Diablo,* and he was confident he could sail her blindfolded on the darkest night. "Lead the way," he ordered politely and gestured with a gentlemanly bow.

Swinging her hips proudly as she walked in front of him, Teresa took him straight to Lucien's cabin and rapped lightly at the door.

Inside the cabin, Angelique was seated at the table. The new blue gown had proved to be close enough to her size to be flattering without alterations, and she had taken the time to coil her hair atop her head. She knew she looked pretty, but she was terrified, for she had no idea what Diego's reaction would be to her sharing Lucien's cabin. She knew he would be furious, of course, but she was frightened that he would think she had had some choice in the matter, when truly she had been given none. She clasped her hands tightly in her lap to keep them from trembling and prayed that by some miracle the visit would go well.

"Ah, there you are, Diego." Lucien ushered them into his quarters, but while he offered them both chairs, only Teresa took one. "You are looking considerably more fit than you were a few days ago. I knew the work would be good for you."

"You asked me here to inquire about my health?" Diego remarked with a sneer. He had glanced only briefly at Angelique, and finding her delicate beauty and wistful expression heartrending, he forced himself to ignore her. It seemed obvious to him that she had not been mistreated, while he could still feel each painful slash of the whip as though he had been beaten only this morning. Hearing a noise behind him, he turned to see two brawny sailors take up positions on either side of the door. Dangermond was not going to allow him to walk about without guards after all.

"But of course. You are my guest. Unfortunately, the disagreement between our countries makes complete freedom impossible to grant, but I do want you to survive your stay with us, even if you do not enjoy it." Lucien smiled in his most ingratiating manner, caring little that he was openly insincere.

Diego placed his hands behind his back and his feet apart in an alert stance. "Your concern is as phony as your smile. Just tell me what it is you really want."

Lucien had removed his coat and waistcoat and had left the top three buttons of his shirt open, for he knew such carelessness in his attire would imply he had been enjoying Angelique's favors at his leisure. He moved behind her and laid his hand upon her shoulder in a clear gesture of ownership as he replied, "I have just learned that you are acquainted with a man who knows the location of a gold mine. I am intrigued with the idea. If I take you to Vera Cruz, will you get the map for me?"

Diego took a step forward and his brown eyes reflected a vicious fury as he now looked directly at his wife. "Why in God's name did you tell him about that?"

She had wanted a smile, a glance, some sweet signal that he understood her suffering as she understood his, but this angry stranger reminded her not at all of the husband she loved so dearly. He was far too thin but no less handsome with his beard, and she could not help but notice that the tight fit of his breeches revealed more than she thought he would wish her to see. When at last she found her voice, she replied calmly, "To trade a map for our freedom seemed a fair exchange."

"That's clearly not all you're trading!" Diego shouted angrily.

Lucien cleared his throat before speaking. "I'll not let this discussion deteriorate into a domestic squabble. My proposal is a simple one. I am intrigued by the prospect of this mine and I wish to see the map. I want you to get it for me."

"No," Diego replied firmly. "If it is gold you want, then I'll get that for you, but I'll not bother an old man for a map that leads nowhere."

"If indeed it leads nowhere, then why would you mind giving it to me?" Lucien asked with a quizzical glance. "Need

I remind you how unpleasant I can make your stay here? Since France and Spain are at war, so are you and I. Your rations are not generous now. How long could you survive on half? Do you find the work I assign too difficult? Then you'll have more of it. Need I continue?" When Diego did not respond, he issued his demand. "I want that map and you are going to get it for me."

"If you want it so badly, then get it yourself, Dangermond. I'll not help you with anything!" Diego was tempted to spit on the floor to emphasize his point but thought better of it since there were women present.

Lucien began to remove the pins from Angelique's hair, spilling her fair curls upon her shoulders. "Angelique is such a pretty thing, isn't she? My men are very jealous of my good fortune and would like to share in it. I can chain her to that pole in the village as easily as I did you, Diego, but I'd never beat her. I'd simply leave her there for a day or two and let my crew entertain her in whatever manner they wish. I'd make certain you did not miss a minute of that spectacle either."

Only by the greatest force of will did Diego restrain himself from attacking the man for making such a vile threat. His eyes narrowed as his glance darkened with hatred. "My offer is the same. I'll buy our freedom but with my own gold, not with an old man's map."

Lucien laid the back of his hand against Angelique's cheek in a gentle caress. "Your husband is a stubborn man, isn't he? Well, no matter. I will give you one day to reflect upon your decision, Captain Aragon. Then I will either take you both to Vera Cruz and set you free in exchange for the map, or I will make a whore of your wife. The choice is yours."

"She is already your whore!" Diego pointed out with bitter irony.

As the two sailors moved forward to lead Diego away, Angelique called out to him. "Your mother always told me you were too stubborn for your own good, Diego. Do not

409

make such a mistake now."

Startled by her strange bit of advice, Diego strode out the door and Teresa ran along behind him. She was chattering so noisily that he did not immediately realize that Angelique had mentioned his mother, who was long dead and whom Angelique had never met.

Chapter XXIII

Teresa clutched at Diego's arm as they walked along the path to the village. "You'll take me with you, won't you? Promise me that you will, please!"

Scowling fiercely, Diego was only dimly aware of the dark-eyed young woman's incessant pleas. "Take you where? What are you talking about?" he finally turned to ask.

"To Vera Cruz! You're going, aren't you?" Teresa danced along beside him as they came to the clearing.

Diego walked straight to her hut, yanked off his boots and stockings and threw them inside before peeling off his shirt. He knew he would be expected to return to work, but it was not that tiresome prospect that was troubling him. "I'll not go to Vera Cruz with that bastard, Teresa, so you can stop your pleading now."

"But you must!" Teresa tagged along after him as he walked back toward the well he had been ordered to dig. "Dangermond was not bluffing! He'll give your wife to the men. He'll do it!"

Diego stopped in his tracks, certain the man had not been serious. "He'll no more do that than I'll take him to the man with the map."

Teresa's eyes widened in terror as she continued to plead

411

with him. "No! You are wrong! You must agree to go to Vera Cruz or your wife will be raped by every man in the camp! Dangermond never makes threats he does not carry out. I tell you he was not bluffing. You must go to Vera Cruz and I want to go with you!"

Diego stared down at the agitated young woman, but he was already so filled with rage that her frantic warning scarcely made an impression. "What makes you think I care what he does with Angelique?"

"But how can you not care? Is the woman not your wife?"

Diego did not know how to answer that question. If he had found Angelique huddled in the corner of Dangermond's cabin, bound hand and foot and sobbing pathetically, his opinion of her would have been different. As it was, she had been enjoying far more comfort than he had and he was furious about it. "The coward gave me until tomorrow to make my decision. I'll make it then."

As he walked away, Teresa called after him. "You would be a fool to do anything other than Dangermond's bidding!"

That night his companions found him strangely silent, but Diego was not accustomed to sharing his problems with anyone, most especially not with three members of his crew. A captain had to be in control at all times and that meant he did not share his worries with his men, no matter how dire the situation might be.

Not one damn thing had gone as he had planned it since the night he had met Angelique, he mused, yet this new dilemma tormented him so intensely that he finally had no choice but to confess it to the men who shared his hut or go mad. "Since you are all involved, let me tell you what has happened. I noticed today that the huts closest to ours are empty, so a fire would be an excellent diversion. We could dig our way out of this shack in a few hours' time, free the other prisoners, then, while the rest of us board the ship, one can remain behind to set a fire. The confusion should be so great that we'll be able to kill Dangermond and get under sail

412

before anyone notices we are not locked in our cages. I have already asked and there are no children about, so if the fire spreads over the whole camp, anyone who dies will deserve to meet such a gruesome end."

Andres and Enrique nodded, while Gustavo, as always, disagreed, "I do not see why a fire must be set. Couldn't we simply slip away in the dark of night? If we alert the whole camp with a fire, someone will tell Dangermond and then our plot will be discovered."

"Not if we wait until the last instant to start the blaze," Diego argued. "There is only one problem, however. We must make our escape tonight."

"Tonight!" the men gasped. "But we have not told the others, have not discussed the plan with them. We cannot leave them behind or risk the chance they might say no!"

"Why must it be tonight?" Enrique asked in a frantic whisper.

"For some reason I do not pretend to understand, Angelique told Dangermond about a man I know in Vera Cruz who has a map to a gold mine. He has threatened her with the worst of punishments if I do not agree to get him the map. He may be bluffing and he may not, but I must make my decision tonight."

"What sort of man would mistreat your wife?" Andres inquired with a pained expression. "She is a lady. We cannot allow any harm to befall her."

Diego's frown deepened, for he no longer knew what to think about his beautiful bride. "She said something to me; perhaps it was an attempt to warn me. She mentioned my mother, whom she has never met, as if they were close friends, but if she told that lie to warn me of something, I cannot imagine what it might be."

The four men sat in the darkness of the small hut, each giving the matter their deepest thought. "Could she mean that Dangermond is lying too?" Andres suggested.

"Yes, but about what—wanting the map or torturing

413

her?" Diego cried out in frustration.

Gustavo waited for someone else to voice an idea, but when no one did, he leaned forward. "Perhaps she meant only to warn you, to say something to you that would not make the Frenchman suspicious but would let you know he is not to be trusted."

"How could she possibly imagine that I would trust him?" Diego responded impatiently. "No, it was something more, something deeper, but what?"

Gathering all his courage, Andres suggested shyly, "Maybe she wanted to say 'I love you,' in a way only you would understand."

Diego rubbed his hand over his beard, still not pleased to have one, and let the truth of Andres' words flood his anguished mind. It was such a simple trick, so straightforward a deception, that he was appalled he had not seen the truth behind her parting advice himself. What had really happened between her and Dangermond? Was nothing as it seemed to be? Had the hand that had rested so gently upon her shoulder once held a knife to her throat? He cursed his own folly, for while he wanted to trust his wife, he knew he did not. If she were truly on Dangermond's side, then she would betray him again and again, until the Frenchman had the map he wanted. But what if the opposite were true? What if she truly loved him and had spoken only to share a secret, to tell him of her love? He had blamed her for enjoying her captivity, but if she were only striving to survive as he was, he could not let her suffer for his lack of understanding.

His choices were now more clearly defined, but he was worried about the fate of his men. "If we do not attempt an escape tonight but wait until tomorrow, there is a chance Dangermond will take me to Vera Cruz but leave you behind. Do you want to take that risk? Whether Angelique mentioned the map to inspire Dangermond to take us to Vera Cruz or simply to distract the villain, I don't know, but if I can get there, I should be able to get free and summon help."

"It is you who must make the decision, Diego, for it is your wife who is in danger." Enrique knew his companions would agree, and they murmured their assent.

Diego stretched out on his stomach, praying he would make the wisest choice. If their escape went as planned, it would be the best alternative, but since every decision he made lately seemed to lead to the worst of consequences, he thought it might be wiser to wait for Dangermond to make the next move. Finally he whispered, "We will wait and see what tomorrow brings."

He had completely forgotten Teresa with all his other problems, but the young woman entered their hut a short while later and, after placing the lantern in the center, went to his side. "Your back is nearly healed, but my medicine will keep the scars from being so ugly." She applied a light coating of the salve, beginning at his shoulders and moving slowly to his waist with a feather-light touch. She then let her fingertips stray down his arms as she leaned forward to whisper, "I will stay with you tonight. Your wife will never know."

Teresa was pretty and Diego had no doubt that her affection would be sweet, but she was the very last diversion he wanted that night. "I won't take advantage of you like that, Teresa. I will do my best to take you to Vera Cruz, but you needn't buy your passsage with your body."

"But I was not thinking of Vera Cruz, only of you!" The pretty young woman protested.

"No, it is because I am fond of you that I cannot let you do it, Teresa. Now go." Diego ignored her enticing descriptions of the delights she would give him and finally, with a stifled cry of frustration, she picked up the jar of salve and the lantern and left.

Gustavo covered his mouth with his hand so she would not hear his laugh, for he had been tremendously amused by their exchange. "I do not think she believed you, but I wish she had asked me to make love to her, for I would not

415

have refused."

Andres and Enrique would not have objected to her advances either, but they kept still rather than distract their captain, who clearly had far more important matters on his mind.

The usually supremely confident French captain was as troubled as Diego that night. He shifted his position slightly so he could look down into Angelique's eyes. "That husband of yours puzzles me, *chéri*. Either he is a fool and doubts my word, or he cares nothing for you. Which is it?"

"Perhaps both," Angelique admitted sadly. She had often recalled the last time she and Diego had made love. It had been the first night of the storm, and he had not spoken a word to her but had merely used the fire of her passion to warm his chilled body before he had fallen asleep. The memory of that night haunted her. His indifference had hurt her then and once again the next day, when they had argued about it. Now, as she lay pinned beneath Lucien's hard-muscled body, she could remember none of the many times when making love to her husband had filled her with joy.

Lucien's lips brushed her cheeks lightly. "Then the man is indeed a fool. He may doubt I'll give you to my crew, but you do not, do you?"

"I no longer care what you do to me," Angelique replied bitterly. Having to sleep with fifty men or a thousand could be no worse than having to sleep with Lucien, she believed. She despised the man, yet she lay placidly in his bunk as if she found his affection most pleasant. His lips covered hers again, and his tongue filled her mouth so that she could not scream aloud, but in her mind she shrieked at the outrages he had made her suffer, outrages that Diego seemed to have no desire to end.

Being cruel as well as devious, Lucien waited until late afternoon to summon Diego. He again sent Teresa with clean clothes for him and told her to provide him with another bath so that his appearance would not offend his wife. The girl had not looked pleased about the task, but he had sent her on her way with a hostile reminder of the torture she would soon suffer if she disobeyed him. He was pleased by the fear in her eyes, for he knew she would convince Diego that he never made idle threats.

Diego was too preoccupied to notice Teresa's mood as he bathed and dressed. She had not badgered him again about making love, and he hoped she had finally realized that he would not cater to her whims while his wife's life was in danger. He had decided to accept Dangermond's conditions—arguing a bit about it first, of course—but he would not trust the scoundrel to keep his word about any part of the deal. He would get the map. Hell, any map would do, he told himself, but he meant to get Angelique away from him as swiftly as possible. He would not forget his men either. If he could not free them now, he would come back for them.

He strode into the Frenchman's cabin and planted his feet firmly upon the bare planks of the floor, as if he expected a long and bitter argument. He cast a brief glance toward Angelique, who was now clad in a flowing lavender garment the lace trim of which complimented her delicate coloring superbly, but there was no recognition in her returning gaze. She appeared to be in a daze, and he wondered if Dangermond had drugged her or had simply beaten her into this stupor. Diego asked quickly, "I want to speak with my wife first—alone."

"Oh, really?" In contrast to his casual attire of the previous day, Lucien was wearing his powder blue velvet coat, a royal blue satin waistcoat, and pearl gray breeches. He had decided to dress in style for whatever the day would bring. "I doubt she wishes to speak with you, but no matter. Your request is denied. I have no time to waste with idle conversation. What is your decision to be?"

"State your terms for me again." Diego straightened up to

his full height, relieved to find that the muscles of his shoulders did not complain too painfully when he flexed them. The two guards were again at the doorway as a reminder that an attack on the Frenchman would be foolhardy, but his hands were clenched in tight fists at his sides, making his real desire readily apparent.

"My terms are so simple I doubt you could have forgotten them," Lucien snapped angrily. "I will take you to Vera Cruz, where you will secure this map that reveals the location of a gold mine. Once the map is in my possession, I will release you and Angelique. If you should refuse—"

"There is no reason to frighten my wife unnecessarily," Diego interrupted before the pirate could again describe what he had in mind for her. "There are three men from my crew here. I want to take them with me."

"Do you now?" Lucien began to smile, knowing he was going to get exactly what he wanted. "Is there anything else?"

"Yes. I want to take Teresa too," Diego responded calmly.

Lucien turned away for a moment to consider the matter fully before he agreed. "She will have to stay with you and your men. I have no separate accommodations for her. But perhaps that is what you wanted in the first place."

"Of course," Diego agreed with a chuckle. He dared not look at Angelique, however, but prayed she would not think the worst of him.

"We will sail in two days' time." Lucien paused to give Angelique a light kiss upon the cheek before he continued. "When we reach Vera Cruz, we will work out the rest of the details."

"No, we must work them out now," Diego insisted firmly. "My contact is an elderly gentleman. He will sell me the map, but only if I go alone to his place of business. If your bullies accompany me, he will be suspicious and pretend he has no idea what I'm talking about."

"But of course. I will want you to approach him as you always have. It is a simple errand and I will trust you to

418

complete it, for I will be holding Angelique to see that you do."

Diego nodded, but he was certain the man could not be trusted to report the time of day accurately, let alone carry out his side of the bargain. "No harm must come to Angelique—absolutely none."

"How can you imagine that I would harm her?" Lucien asked in amazement. "She means a great deal to me, and I am as relieved as you are that she will not have to be given to my men tonight."

Not convinced by his ridiculous declaration, Diego looked again at his wife. It was not until he called her name, however, that she focused her attention upon his face. "You see, Angelique. My mother brought me up well. I am not nearly as stubborn as you feared I would be."

Angelique had spent the most wretched day, for she had been unable to avoid listening to Lucien's endless recitation of the cruelties she would suffer if her husband did not agree to his demands. Now she could scarcely believe that Diego had given in so easily. And she did not really comprehend why he had agreed if indeed he had grown so fond of Teresa that he could not stand to leave her behind on the island when they left. The girl was very pretty and the bronze of her skin was only a shade lighter than Diego's. She could not help but think that they made a handsome pair, perhaps a far better pair than she and Diego. But despite her misery and confusion, she let Diego know that his message had been received, if not necessarily understood completely. Finding her voice, she said softly, "I will write to your mother at my first opportunity to let her know how mistaken she was."

Relieved to find that Angelique was far more coherent than she appeared, Diego turned to go, but Lucien called after him.

"Be certain you have the well completed, for we cannot sail unless it is."

"You'll have your well, Dangermond. Don't worry over

it." Diego shook his head as he walked ahead of the sailors. The village did not need another well. The man was merely playing with him, making him work on a strenuous project just to punish him. "I'll see him in hell yet," he promised himself, and with a satisfied grin, he walked back to the camp without giving his guards any problems.

True to his word, Lucien refused to weigh anchor until Diego had dug a hole of sufficient depth to tap the underground spring that provided the camp with fresh water. That a new well would be unnecessary because the few women left behind would be able to use the present well or carry water from the source of the spring on the far side of the island seemed irrelevant to the French pirate. Diego did not waste his breath arguing the matter but worked as swiftly as possible to complete the project.

The labor exhausted his body but did not fatigue his mind. With each shovelful of damp sand that he tossed over his shoulder, he cursed the man for keeping Angelique from him. She was his wife, not Dangermond's concubine! He now understood clearly that the man had no respect for anything—not love, or marriage, and certainly not for truth—and this knowledge brought with it a warning he would not ignore. He knew he could expect Dangermond to trick him at every possible turn and that was a chilling prospect, for it was Angelique's life that was at risk. As soon as he had her safely settled in Vera Cruz, he planned to outfit a ship and pursue the French demon to the gates of hell if necessary. He would search relentlessly from one end of the Caribbean to the other, but he would find him and put a swift end to his contemptible life. That one thought sustained him when he found sleep impossible.

Teresa no longer came to his hut, so he was saved the bother of making excuses to her at least, but he would see she was put ashore in Vera Cruz. She had helped him and he wanted to repay her kindness in the only way he could. He would keep his word, even if Dangermond could be counted

420

upon to go back on his.

Once his ship had set sail, Lucien's mood became one of exhilaration. He took great pride in his skill as a captain. He had long held the belief that his navigation was more than merely proficient; it was extraordinary. And he felt that he was so expert at forecasting the changes in the weather that he was without peer. It amused him immensely to think he had escaped the storm that had sent Diego's ship to the bottom. In his opinion, he was clearly the superior man in every way, and he did not want to miss an opportunity to prove that point to his stunning captive.

The second morning of their voyage, he drew Angelique down upon his lap and gave her a warm hug. "Can that oaf of a husband of yours fence with any real skill?"

"Fence?" Angelique never knew what to expect from Lucien, but this question struck her as being one of his most absurd. "I have no idea. He has had no occasion to engage in the sport since I have been with him."

"Then I think you might enjoy what I have planned for this morning's entertainment. Let's go out on deck."

"Oh, Lucien, no!" Angelique hurriedly scrambled off his knee. "You can't challenge Diego to a duel. That's totally senseless! He's promised to get the map for you, and he will. You said that was all you wanted."

Lucien grabbed Angelique's shoulders and gave her a forceful shake. "Hush! I mean only to have a bit of sport, not to kill the man. Now do you wish to witness this contest, or not?"

Angelique was so thoroughly sickened by his idea that she wanted only to remain by herself, but she had so few opportunities to see Diego that she dared not miss this one. "Of course I want to watch. I imagine you're very good."

"Oh, I am much better than that, chéri, much better. I am superb!" he boasted proudly.

421

This time Lucien did not bother to see that Diego was given the opportunity to improve his appearance before he was brought up on deck. Teresa had washed most of the blood from his own pair of breeches, but they were now stained and dirty from his efforts to dig the well. The shirt he had been given had belonged to several men before him and was tattered and frayed. Barefoot, he waited for Yves to unlock the leg irons and forced himself not to strike the burly man in the nose with a quick jerk of his knee. He planned to remain calm, no matter what the provocation, for he knew that if he did not, none of those who depended upon him to win their freedom would ever set foot in Vera Cruz. When Lucien tossed him a fencing foil, he was surprised the man had not removed the small button at the tip, which prevented injury during practice. He gripped the handle of the finely crafted French weapon and took a step forward. "What do you expect of me now, Dangermond, mere sport?"

Happy to see that Diego presented a far from admirable appearance, Lucien smiled slyly. "Yes, that is all. I enjoy a bit of exercise, don't you?" Before the tall Spaniard had the chance to respond, Lucien went after him, suddenly lunging across the deck to begin the play with a savagery that shocked Diego into taking up a vigorous defense.

Angelique kept to the rail, staying out of the men's way, but she had been as surprised as Diego by Lucien's un-announced assault. She knew exactly what he was doing. He wanted to defeat her husband, humiliate him if at all possible, and she had to admit that it looked as if he could do it handily. She knew Diego to have remarkable grace as well as agility, but he was displaying neither of these qualities this day. Lucien was not only quick but vicious, and Diego was kept so busy parrying his brutal thrusts that he had no time to mount an attack of his own. Then as quickly as he had begun, the pirate signaled to Yves, who came up from behind Diego and ripped the slender foil from his hand.

"That will do for today. I can see I've exhausted you. Shall we give it another try tomorrow?" Lucien was not even breathing hard, Angelique noted, while Diego was drenched with sweat. "You may refuse if you like. I'll understand. No one enjoys being overmatched."

Diego wiped the sweat from his eyes with his shirt-sleeve and shook his head. "Nonsense. You barely gave me time to get the feel of the foil. I'll gladly take you on again tomorrow." He smiled then, as if the prospect of facing him again were a very amusing one.

"Take him below!" Lucien ordered Yves. He turned away then and gripped the two foils in one hand before reaching for Angelique's arm to pull her along beside him. He was angry he had not been able to wring the confession from Diego's lips that he had clearly won. "Your husband does not appear to have ever held a foil, let alone been taught how to use it properly," he snarled at Angelique.

"You were magnificent," she responded readily, her praise bringing a smile to his lips. "I was most impressed with your skill."

"I am very good at all things, *chéri,* or have you forgotten?" He let his gaze travel slowly down her figure. While the changes were slight, they were there. He suddenly pulled her close. "Let's not waste another minute talking, for I will have your company for only another week or two longer. You know which sport is my favorite."

Angelique preceded him into his cabin and, knowing he could not see her face, she grimaced as she reached for the hooks on her bodice. Perhaps Diego could not fence well, but what did that matter, she reflected. At least he had had enough cleverness with a saber to avoid being hurt, and she was proud of him for that. Lucien had stopped to toss the foils into Yves's cabin, but if she had had one handy, she would not have used it for sport but for a far more deadly game. "Aren't you afraid of injuring Diego so seriously that he won't be able to secure the map for you?"

"No, of course not. With the buttons attached, the foils are

423

safe, but if I had removed them, I do believe you'd be a widow by now. I am disappointed in Diego. I thought better of him, but you will take my mind off him, won't you, *chéri?*" Lucien pulled her close and was pleased to find her kiss sweet. She was worth the lives of a dozen men, and he laughed inwardly as he wondered just how many he would have to kill to keep her.

Chapter XXIV

Watching the daily fencing matches was almost more than Angelique could endure, but she attended every one. Lucien displayed a graceful style combined with brutal strength, though Diego continually exhibited no more than the most elementary knowledge of the sport. He was able to fend off the Frenchman's attacks by sheer determination, and she admired him for that, yet she had the persistent suspicion that he was far more skilled than he let Dangermond suspect. For what purpose he would conduct such a ruse, she did not know, and she would have much preferred seeing him beat the villain at his own game, but that never even came close to happening.

Each day the two men would fence until Lucien grew bored with Diego's clumsiness, and then he would swiftly end the match. It would be Yves's task to refasten the leg irons to Diego's ankles and the brute would often use that opportunity to cuff the Spaniard smartly or otherwise do him harm, but Lucien made no move to put an end to his mate's underhanded tricks and Diego could only try to avoid them. The entire spectacle sickened Angelique, for she was in constant fear that her husband would be badly hurt, and though she was grateful he never was, she became miserable whenever she watched him being led away with Teresa tagging along after him. The vivacious brunette genuinely seemed to care for her husband, but that only made the knowledge that they were together both day and night all the more painful to her. She could not speak with Diego—could not even reach out to touch him—and the sight of lively little Teresa dancing about as they left the deck was almost more than she could bear. There had been days when she had regretted coming out to watch the men—days when seeing her beloved brought so much more pain than pleasure—but then the next morning she would again find herself at the rail, eager for the only glimpse she would have of her husband that day.

It was all Diego could do to ward off Lucien's barrage of vicious thrusts. He had no opportunity to do more than glance at Angelique to see if she looked well. Sadly, he feared the strain she was under had begun to take its toll. She clung to the rail, letting her hair blow wildly about in the breeze, and seemed to care little about the near hysterical impression she conveyed. Her expression always reflected the tension she was feeling and he found himself wishing she would stay in Lucien's cabin rather than torment him with her presence when she remained beyond his reach. He longed to go to her, to wrap his arms around her and tell her he would set everything right as soon as he possibly could, but he knew that if he were to take one step toward her, Yves would undoubtedly haul him off for another whipping and he would not be allowed on deck for the rest of the voyage.

His wife's mental state was not his only worry, however, for Teresa continued to be a troublesome burden. Since she had only a few meager articles of clothing, she took up little of the space they had been assigned below deck, but he was tired of waking up to find her arms wrapped around him. Any of the other men on board the *Marie Alise* would have taken advantage of her favors gladly, and he did not understand why she persisted in pestering him with her affection when it was so unwanted. When his subtle hints got him nowhere, he finally told her to her face that he wanted her to keep away from him.

"But Diego, I want only to be safe. You and your men are far more kind than the rogues who serve Dangermond. Don't make me leave you. I've nowhere to go." Teresa's dark eyes filled with tears as she whispered her plea. He and his men were filthy and were always kept in chains below deck, but she did not dare leave them, for she knew only too well how Dangermond's crew would treat her. Diego turned away, exasperated by her tears. "I did not mean that you should leap over the side, Teresa, just sit somewhere else for awhile."

Finally deciding to take part in the argument he could not help but overhear, Gustavo spoke up. "Come here and sit beside me, Teresa, for I do not have a lovely wife whose presence on board this ship gives me no peace. Come over here to me."

Teresa brushed away her tears and decided to go where she was wanted. She sat down beside him and crossed her legs to get comfortable, since there was nothing but the hardness of the deck upon which to sit. "I have forgotten your name. Is it Gaspar?" she asked.

"No, it is Gustavo," the man replied with a chuckle, "but if you like the name Gaspar, then call me that. I am a most agreeable man."

Andres and Enrique could not let him speak that lie without argument and soon the three men were all talking with Teresa.

Diego was left to his own thoughts at last. He tried to recall each detail of the walk through Vera Cruz to the small shop where Eduardo Marquez sold his precious antiquities. He wanted to be familiar with courtyards, alleyways, the dark doorways of impressive homes—all the places in which he might have an opportunity to jump anyone Dangermond sent to follow him, and he was positive the Frenchman would send someone. Once he had assured himself that he was not being followed, he would go straight to the authorities for help. He was certain that with merely a handful of trustworthy men he could seize control of the *Marie Alise*. It was either that or return to the ship with some sort of map and hope Dangermond would set Angelique free as he had promised. He had absolutely no faith in the Frenchman to do that, however, and Diego planned to kill him before he could harm them any further. He knew that if he could kill Dangermond quickly, the Frenchman's crew would show themselves to be cowards and would swiftly surrender. If only his men could somehow kill Yves while he was away. Then taking the ship would not be half as difficult. It was Yves who worried him most, for the giant would not be easy to kill and they had not one weapon among them. He looked over at Teresa then and wondered out loud, "Does Yves like women, Teresa?"

Though surprised to hear him speak to her after his cold dismissal, Teresa was clever enough to understand what he was thinking. "You wish to use me again, Diego? It is too late for that. I have other friends now."

Diego shook his head. "It is a simple question. Please answer yes or no. Does the man like women?"

"There was a woman on the island last year, one who drank like the men until she did not even know her own name. I saw him take her down to the beach late one night and no one ever saw her again. Does that sound like he enjoys women?"

Chilled by her gruesome tale, Diego went back to plotting their escape without asking for more help from Teresa. He had merely wanted her to distract the man for a second or two, long enough to rip his knife from his belt and use it on him, but the risk was too great. Angelique could do it, he thought suddenly. She had more wiles than any woman alive. But he did not want his wife to have to do anything

428

more than survive. She was all he could think about now. He had to get her away from Dangermond! He was sorry he had not been able to attempt the escape he had devised on the island. Dangermond had brought the other prisoners along on the voyage and Diego had seen that they were in worse health than he had feared. It vexed him considerably to know that if his plan had gone smoothly, it would have saved them all the agony of making the voyage to Vera Cruz in chains.

While Diego continued to perfect his new plan, Angelique paced Lucien's cabin slowly. "What is Diego to wear tomorrow? He can't go anywhere in the filthy rags you've kept him in."

"That is certainly true. I can find something that will fit him. You need not worry he will be embarrassed by his appearance," Lucien replied with even more smugness than was his usual style.

"Clothes you've stolen from someone else? I doubt they'd fit him." Angelique used every opportunity she had to complain about the way Diego was being treated. She had seen no improvement in his situation, but at least she knew her constant attempts to help him annoyed Lucien and that pleased her.

Lucien walked over to her and his look was not at all pleasant. "You are right, of course. He has to be well dressed. Perhaps it would be a mistake to wait until tomorrow night to try to fit him. You are handy with a needle. I'll get what I'd planned for him to wear now, and you can tell me how it looks on him."

Angelique lifted her chin proudly, not about to refuse his request. "I shall be happy to help in any way I can. The sooner you have that map, the sooner Diego and I will be free."

"You mustn't forget Teresa, *chéri*. Then you and

Teresa and your precious husband will be free," he pointed out with a malicious grin.

Angelique turned away rather than allow him to see how much that thought upset her. "Just bring the clothes and let's see what needs to be done with them." To her absolute horror, however, Lucien returned not only with stylish apparel but with Diego, whom he had quickly drenched with sea water rather than allowing him the time to bathe properly. With his hair dripping wet, barefoot, and clad only in a ragged pair of damp breeches, he looked as startled as she to be there.

"I have clothes for you to wear tomorrow, Aragon, but Angelique is so worried they will not fit you handsomely that I want you to try them on now. Just toss those breeches in the corner and put these on."

Angelique knew Lucien was trying to embarrass them both, but she would not give him that satisfaction. "Go on, Diego. You're far too handsome to be so shy." She gave him a dazzling smile, then winked slyly before sitting down upon the bunk where she busied herself unbuttoning the shirt he was to wear.

Lucien's expression darkened when he saw that her teasing remark had made her husband smile. "Just be quick about it," he commanded sharply.

Since he had no choice, Diego dropped his breeches with a nonchalance he thought quite admirable. This time the pair Lucien handed him were too large and he had to grip the waistband to keep them from falling. "As you can see, the tailor had someone far heavier in mind when he made these," Diego remarked with a touch of humor.

"Yes." Lucien gestured impatiently to Angelique. "Well, hurry with the pins. I want him out of here."

Angelique brought the pins and stepped around behind Diego, laying her hand upon his side as she moved. His skin was so warm to her touch and her mind flooded with blissful memories she had thought forgotten. "I'll take in the back

430

seam. It won't be difficult," she remarked softly, but she made the mistake of looking up then and the sight of the long, red scars that crisscrossed Diego's back brought tears to her eyes. It made her sick to recall how horribly he had suffered and she felt so dizzy she had to clutch his arm to steady herself. "Just a moment. I'm nearly finished," she managed to say, but then the floor seemed to lurch out from under her feet and she heard the pins falling all around her. Diego made a grab for her and caught her around the waist, but it was too late. She had already fainted.

When Angelique came to, she saw that Teresa had taken her place and was adjusting the fit of the red satin waistcoat Lucien had provided. Still feeling unwell, she closed her eyes rather than watch the dark beauty fondle her husband with a touch the intimacy of which spoke far more than her few words.

"Can you not stand still?" Teresa asked impatiently. "I will poke you with the pins if you do not hold still!"

"I would not even feel that pain!" Diego snarled in reply. "Does my wife faint often, Dangermond?"

"Only with pleasure," Lucien assured him, but he held a pistol pointed at his prisoner's heart to inspire him to keep his temper in check. "Undoubtedly she was overcome by the sight of you. She will be well tomorrow."

"She'd better be."

Angelique stole a glance at her husband, pleased to hear he was still concerned for her health. He was not looking her way but still at Lucien, and she did not want to give away the fact that she was awake when it might save her from the pirate's attentions for an hour or two. Resting comfortably, she listened to the two men as they completed their plans for the mission in Vera Cruz.

The ship had been flying the Spanish flag for several days but had not been sighted by any other ship. Lucien meant to wait up the coast from Vera Cruz and put Diego ashore after dark. Diego did not argue with the plan since the old gentleman who had sold him the idols lived in back of his shop and could be visited at any time. She was counting the hours on her fingers, adding them up over and over again. By midnight the next night she would be free. If, she thought suddenly, Diego was able to get the map and Lucien were to keep his word. At least she had gotten them as far as Vera Cruz. Now it would be up to Diego to make the most of that opportunity. She had tremendous faith in her husband and did not doubt his cleverness, but she also knew what a treacherous liar Lucien was, and she continued to pray that all would go well.

After Teresa and Diego had gone, Lucien laid the clothes that needed attention upon a chair at the table, then turned to Angelique. "You may stop your pretense now, *chéri*. I have but a few scant hours to enjoy the delights of your company and I'll not miss what will be my last opportunity to touch your heart with my devotion."

"Devotion!" Angelique sat up to face him, her eyes blazing with a furious light. "You're devoted to no one but yourself and you know it!"

"Ah, how you wound me with your hatred, *Señora* Aragon. Your words cut me as deeply as the knife you'd like to thrust through my throat each time I have you."

"It's not your throat I'd slit first, Lucien," Angelique informed him, knowing he could not harm Diego now, for he needed him to fetch the map he had come to prize so highly. That thought gave her the confidence to be far more bold than she had previously dared to be. "Have you ever had a woman you didn't have to rape?"

"Stand up!" Lucien shouted, insulted by her taunts. He decided he would have to teach her again that he still had to be obeyed. She had no sooner risen to her feet than he hit her across the face with the back of his hand and his stunning blow knocked her to her knees. "There are many ways for a man to take his pleasure from a woman, Angelique, and I have neglected to show you some of the most diverting." He grabbed a handful of her hair to yank her to her feet, then ripped the blue silk gown from her shoulders. His teeth left angry red crescents upon the tender flesh of her breasts, but she did not cry out. She did no more than thank God she would soon escape the detestable creature she now considered more animal than human.

When he was not taken up on deck for a fencing match the next morning, Diego used the time to tell the other prisoners he hoped to set them free that night. He gave no details of his plans, for he had never trusted Teresa and did not intend to give her any information he knew Dangermond would swiftly use against him. All the men were restless, afraid to hope that the agonizing days of their imprisonment would finally be over, but he encouraged them to believe they would soon be off the *Marie Alise* and able to enjoy life as free men once again. In the late afternoon he was taken to Yves's cabin, where he was permitted to shave, but the vicious mate stood behind him to make certain he did not attempt to use the razor for any other purpose. He had been allowed to bathe in a tub he doubted had ever before been placed in the mate's quarters, then he was given the clothing Lucien had told him Angelique had been well enough to alter. He had to admit he looked respectable, if a bit thin, but his appearance was the least of his worries. His plan was fraught with danger, but his greatest fear was that Yves would be sent to stalk him. He would have no choice then but to elude the monster, enter Señor Marquez's shop by the front door, then slip out the back and go for help. He would then have to return to the *Marie Alise* before Yves discovered he had been fooled and could report that fact to Dangermond. Diego knew that if Lucien believed he had been tricked, the pirate would be gone by the time he could bring troops to capture his ship.

Angelique was seated at the table and her eyes were alight

with excitement as Yves brought Diego into the cabin. She thought he looked splendid and so much more like himself with the dark blue coat and white breeches, which now fit his lean physique perfectly, thanks to her efforts. She doubted he had ever owned a red waistcoat, but it was elegant nevertheless and the bright color gave her spirits a much-needed lift. As always, his boots shone with his efforts to polish them. She was as proud to be his wife as she had ever been not only because she admired his handsome appearance but because of his abundant courage as well.

She smiled warmly, unable to put her emotions into words but praying he understood her delight that they would soon be together again. The hours since she had last seen him were a merciful blur, and while she knew exactly what would be in store for her while he was gone, she no longer cared. Her thoughts were focused solely upon freedom and therefore she felt immune to all fear and pain that Lucien might still try to inflict.

Rather than her loving glance, Diego saw the deep purple bruise on Angelique's right cheek and turned to the Frenchman. "How dare you abuse my wife? Can you not honor the agreement you insisted upon yourself? I have promised to bring you the map and still you have beaten Angelique!" He was furious with the man, but as he had the previous day, Lucien held a pistol firmly in his grip and Yves stood at his back, making any protest other than a verbal one futile.

"Angelique and I have a different set of terms than I have with you, Aragon. They are not open for discussion, however. Now, as soon as darkness falls, we will proceed down the coast. I've decided to go along with you, for I don't trust you to keep your part of our bargain if I'm not there to make certain you do."

"You don't trust me?" Diego scoffed. His thoughts were a frantic whirl. Once they were in Vera Cruz, he was certain he could kill Dangermond swiftly, then sneak back on board the *Marie Alise* with enough troops to crush whatever resistance the pirates might mount. In so many ways, Lucien had fallen right into his hands and he could scarcely keep from laughing out loud over it. "My word is far better than that of a ruthless pirate!"

"I will ignore that insult for the moment." Lucien's eyes narrowed as his glance swept over the still-arrogant Spaniard. He knew that none of his cruelty had inflicted the slightest wound upon the man's proud spirit and he was infuriated that he had not been able to break him. "My men will row us ashore in one of the lifeboats and wait for us until midnight. Yves will stay here with Angelique, and I have already explained to him that if we do not return before midnight, he has my permission to do as he pleases with her before passing whatever is left of her along to the rest of the crew."

"I've told you before that it is unnecessary to frighten my wife with your vile threats. We will return long before midnight and he'll never have the opportunity to do more than kiss her hem." Diego was livid at the man for leaving such instructions with the barbarian he called a mate. "Can the brute even tell time?"

Lucien chuckled. "But of course. He will not make the mistake of beginning before the last stroke of midnight. Since it is nearly sunset, you are to return to his cabin to wait until we are ready to leave the ship." He gestured with his pistol. "Take him away, Yves, and see that he is bound hand and foot without ruining the clothes his dear wife worked so diligently to prepare for him. I'm sure you can amuse yourself for an hour or two by thinking about what Angelique and I will be doing to pass the time."

Diego's stare was murderous, but he turned away and strode out of Lucien's cabin rather than listen to any more of the man's crude attempts at humor. That he had beaten Angelique enraged him and he vowed to do far worse to him before he killed him in the slowest, most painful manner he

435

could invent.

Angelique calmly sat waiting for whatever Lucien cared to suggest, but her mind was far too busy to worry over what the pirate might demand, for she was thinking of what she would say to her husband when they finally had the opportunity to be alone together. She had done whatever he had requested without a trace of guilt, for she had had no choice in becoming his mistress. And although she had shared his bed for more than a month, the revulsion she felt at his touch had not lessened by a single degree. She loathed him, and the glance she turned upon him now showed the depth of her hatred with stunning clarity.

"Well, *chéri*, must I tell you to disrobe and get into my bed, or would you prefer that I helped you to remove your gown as I did yesterday?" Lucien started to lay his pistol aside, then, seeing her glance follow his action, he left his cabin for a moment to give the weapon to Yves to hold. "You would shoot me, wouldn't you, Angelique?" he inquired casually as he moved back through the door.

"Yes," the delicate blonde agreed without emotion. She would have done it cheerfully.

Lucien chuckled as he began to unbutton his waistcoat. "Perhaps I should have given you to your husband for an hour. Do you think he would have liked that? Unfortunately Spaniards are very proud. I doubt he'll want you after you've spent so much time with me. Then, of course, there is Teresa. Her figure is very attractive, and, quite frankly, yours is beginning to look a bit too maternal to inspire passion."

"If you had had any respect for my condition, Lucien, you would not have made me your mistress. Do not try to torment me with insults now. It is far too late." Yet Angelique knew that her once shapely figure had undergone several changes, and while Diego would not complain that her breasts had become more ample, she felt that her swollen waistline would not please him. It was a problem she would gladly face, however. Since he knew the child she was

436

carrying was his, she would not allow him to make fun of her. If he spoke so much as one word of complaint or ridicule, she would simply not allow him in her bed until she had regained the figure he had once admired. That ought to teach him how a man should treat a pregnant wife. Even as she decided that, she knew she was being foolish to be angry with Diego about something he might never say, but the idea was surely preferable to thinking about Lucien's lust.

"If you do not get into my bunk, *chéri,* I shall take you in that chair!" Lucien commanded sharply.

Hoping he would swiftly fall asleep if he took her in the bed, Angelique complied with his demand, but only for that reason. She kept telling herself that this would be the final time she would have to bear the fiend's attentions, and despite his tender attempts to arouse her passion, she remained, as always, indifferent to his touch.

Lucien kept Diego's hands tied behind his back as they walked the short distance into Vera Cruz. He then freed him but kept the muzzle of his pistol pressed into the small of his back. "Do not make the mistake of trying to escape me, Aragon, for few women raped by Yves survive the experience. I shudder to think what a pregnant woman would suffer at his hands."

Ignoring his conversation since it consisted mostly of threats of the lowest nature, Diego walked swiftly through the deserted streets. Lucien had insisted upon waiting until quite late to enter the town, then had made him walk ahead of him in the center of the street so he could not dart into a doorway as he had planned. He had not given the pirate that much credit, but, clearly, escaping him was going to be much more difficult than he had anticipated. He did not change his plans, however, but only shifted them back slightly. He would wait until they left Eduardo's shop, for once Lucien had the map tucked away in his pocket, he would undoubtedly relax his guard, and the instant he grew careless, Diego meant to wrestle the pistol from his hands and shoot him with it. He planned to aim for his belly, so he would linger in agony for several hours before death finally overtook him. It was what the bastard deserved. When finally they reached the small square upon which Eduardo's shop faced, he whispered a question. "What name shall I give him? We must make him think you are a Spaniard, if a very fair one."

"Gonzales is a common name. Tell him I am Luis Gonzales, another captain with your father's line. He will believe whatever you tell him if you are convincing, and I will do as little talking as possible. But I warn you again to be careful. Do not try to trick me, or Yves will split your charming wife in two with the first thrust of his gigantic—"

Diego interrupted his lurid description with a bitter snarl. "Don't worry. You'll have the map when we leave." You'll not have it for long though, Diego swore to himself.

Eduardo Marquez was still in his shop polishing a bit of jade he had just bought, and, seeing Diego at the window, he hastened to unlock his door and bid him enter. "Captain Aragon. I had not expected to see you again until the spring."

Diego had not thought of the date until that very instant and realized that the quiet in the streets meant the holiday season was entirely over. Christmas had come and gone without any observance in the pirates' camp, and he reasoned that it was probably the middle of January by now. He tried to smile as he introduced Lucien as a fellow captain, Luis Gonzales by name. He noted the old gentleman's inquisitive glance and was relieved when he did not remark upon Lucien's fair hair and dapper appearance. Hoping to distract him from any such questions, he began to speak in an enthusiastic tone. "I married as soon as I returned to

Barcelona, and I've brought my wife here to make our home. She was so taken with the three Azteca gods I bought from you that I was hoping you had another I might purchase as a gift for her."

Lucien cast a critical glance at Diego but followed him over to the counter at the far end of the shop and took the seat next to his. Although Diego had told him that the shopkeeper was elderly, he had not imagined him to be as old as this man appeared to be. Eduardo Marquez was nearly bald, stoop shouldered, and so thin that his clothing seemed to be suspended in air rather than resting upon the firm contours of a human body. Like many old men, he was a talkative soul, and he continued to question Diego about his bride until Lucien was tempted to turn the conversation to the real purpose of their visit. But he knew that good manners required this exchange of irrelevant pleasantries and kept still.

"I am so pleased to hear your wife admires the idols you purchased from me, but unfortunately I have none of their quality at the moment. Perhaps if you were to give me your address, I could call upon you when I have something worth showing you." Eduardo took up the polishing cloth he had been using and continued to work upon the small piece of jade. "Treasures such as those do not appear often. I cannot say when one will come my way again."

Diego frowned sadly. "That is most unfortunate. I was hoping to surprise Angelique with something special. I don't suppose you still have that map you told me about, do you? Surely she would be pleased with gold."

Eduardo looked over at Lucien, obviously alarmed by Diego's question. "You have told your friend about my map?"

Diego shrugged. "Why not? You told me it was for sale. I did not think its existence was a secret."

Eduardo nodded. "Then that was my mistake, for I have offered the map to no one else." After a long pause, the old

439

gentleman continued. "If you have some interest in the map, perhaps we can discuss it again."

"Yes, I am interested in it. In fact, I've thought about it quite often in the last months. I think I may have been very foolish not to buy it when I purchased the idols." Diego leaned back in his chair, hoping to appear relaxed, even though he had never been more on edge. "I know it is late, but could we see the map tonight?"

Eduardo looked over at Lucien, who was smiling pleasantly, and, deciding that the two men were both honest souls, he reached under the counter for a map of New Spain. "I keep this map to show my customers from where my treasures come." His breath wheezed through his chest as he spoke, and, shivering slightly with the chill of the night, he drew his gray woolen shawl tightly around his shoulders. "I need little sleep at my age. If you two do not mind the lateness of the hour, I will tell you something about the map. Then, if you think you might want to buy it, we will discuss the price."

"We are not tired," Diego assured him. "Please tell us about this map of yours."

"Do you know Campeche?" Eduardo pointed to the coast that curved up toward the Yucatán.

"Yes, I've been there," Diego replied with a pleasant smile, and Lucien nodded as if he had been there too.

"A fascinating city," Eduardo remarked absently. "It was fortified in the sixteenth century to withstand the attacks of the pirates who pillaged the coast. Filthy rabble," he added as an aside.

Diego had a difficult time suppressing a burst of raucous laughter in response to his comment. "Ah yes, detestable villains," he managed to agree with a straight face, but he dared not glance over at Lucien as he said it. "The coast will be sufficiently safe for an armed ship to sail now, however. How close to Campeche is the gold?"

"It is not in Campeche." Marquez squinted at the worn

map. "You must continue up the coast, following it closely, then go on to the Yucatán. The end of the peninsula is flat and you must drop anchor here at Lago de Lagartos. Leave your ship there and proceed inland to what was the land of the Maya," he declared with admiration. The rasp in his voice mellowed to a warm resonance as he explained, "They constructed fabulous cities with the aid of remarkably skilled stonemasons and decorated them with intricate carvings of their gods, but they were all abandoned after the Spanish Conquest—a great loss. Since you own a Quetzal-cóatl, Captain Aragon, you will be interested to know that the Maya worshipped him too, but as Kukulcán. I will try to get their rain god Chac, for you. He was their principal god because severe droughts plagued the region and sacrifices to him were thought to bring the much needed rain."

"Human sacrifices?" Diego asked with clear distaste for the topic.

"Unfortunately, yes," Eduardo responded with a sigh of regret. "We cannot expect the Maya to have lived as we do. Heathens often have vengeful and bloodthirsty gods."

Lucien turned the map around so he could see it more easily. "Other than for the growing of *henequen* to make rope, the Yucatán is considered worthless. Gold has been found in the central portion of New Spain but has never been reported in the Yucatán," he scoffed in Castilian with an accent so close to Diego's that Eduardo mistook him for a native of Barcelona, as was his companion.

The old gentleman chuckled slyly, then was convulsed by a fit of coughing from which it took him several minutes to recover. "If your friend is certain there is no gold in the Yucatán, perhaps he would like to leave and we can complete our business alone."

"Please do not insult Luis." Diego slapped Lucien upon the back as though they were the best of friends. "He will be consumed with envy when he sees the first nugget I take from this mine."

441

"Did I say the gold was in a mine?" Eduardo asked with a startled gasp.

Diego leaned forward, alarmed by his question, for he wanted nothing to go wrong now. "It was so many months ago that you offered to sell me the map that I can't recall. Perhaps when you spoke of a map and gold, I just assumed it was in a mine."

Eduardo shivered again. "No, it is not in a mine."

Lucien spoke softly in a tone that masked his anger. "Then just where is it?"

After a long pause during which he again polished the jade, Eduardo began to explain. "The Yucatán is built of limestone. Often the currents of underground rivers erode the rock and caves are formed. The ground above them can sink, thereby causing deep depressions. These holes, *cenotes*, fill with water. They were considered sacred by the Maya. They used them as sites for sacrifices of all manners of objects, even those made of gold." He paused for a moment in his explanation, purposely letting the men's anticipation mount. "I have a map that leads to a *cenote* filled with the most fabulous of treasures. I alone know of its location now that the Indian who sold me the map is dead." As a twinkle of excitement lit his wrinkled face, he explained, "I must get the other map out to show you the rest, but I am afraid the price has gone up since we last spoke."

Diego shrugged. "You know I am good for whatever price you require. Show us the map."

"I know you to be honest as well as wealthy, Captain Aragon. That is why I offered to sell you the map, for I knew you would not cheat me." Eduardo eased off his stool slowly and, pushing aside a gray- and red-striped serape that hung over the doorway to the adjacent room, he shuffled away to get the map.

Diego turned to Lucien and spoke in a low whisper. "Have you enough to cover whatever figure he might name?"

"Of course." Lucien patted the bulge in his waistcoat

pocket. "I would not have let so important a detail slip my mind, though it obviously did yours." Placing his hand upon the pistol at his belt, he reminded him again, "Do not forget that I am in charge here. The night is far from over, Aragon. Be careful not to upset me."

Before Diego could respond to his unwanted advice, Eduardo Marquez returned carrying a battered tin box. "The Indian who gave me this map was a Maya. These people still live in the Yucatán, guarding their secrets as they always have. Only a few of their once magnificent cities are known today. The others lie hidden beneath the jungle, which has reclaimed their sites. It is to one of these lost cities that you must go." He placed the box on the counter but did not open it. "I think now it is time for payment. Then I will show you the map and explain its details."

"Since I owe Diego some money, I will buy him the map to settle my debt," Lucien announced. Withdrawing a leather pouch from his pocket, Lucien loosened the drawstring. "See if these don't more than cover your price."

Diego was as amazed as the old gentleman by the jewels that spilled forth upon the counter. There were two magnificent ruby rings, an unset emerald of flawless beauty, and the vivid blue sapphire necklace and earrings that he had given Angelique as a birthday present. That the pirate had stolen her jewelry should not have surprised Diego, but it did.

While both Diego and Eduardo were focusing their attention on the sparkling jewels, Lucien rose with practiced stealth. Pulling the pistol from his belt, he brought it down upon the old man's head with a crushing blow, spattering his venerable blood upon the precious jewels he had been examining so closely.

"Mother of God!" Diego screamed as he leapt to his feet. "You've killed the old man!"

"You did not expect me to actually part with those jewels, did you?" Lucien laughed at the idea, then pointed the gun at

443

Diego. "This is where we part company, Aragon. You see, Angelique is as precious to me as she is to you." As Diego came toward him in a flying leap, the pirate jumped back and fired. The loud report of the pistol echoed against the walls of the small shop and the sound seemed deafening in the stillness of the night. Severely wounded, Diego fell and lay sprawled in a widening pool of blood that seeped from the wound in his head.

Satisfied that the handsome Spaniard was dead, Lucien did not bother to reload and fire again. After he shoved the pistol under his belt, he pushed the dead shopkeeper's head and arm off the counter, then gathered up the blood-drenched jewels in his handkerchief. He replaced them in the leather pouch and, picking up the tin box, he rushed out the door. His actions had taken no more than a few second's time, and he was on his way back to his ship before curious neighbors looked out their windows to see who had fired a shot. Discovering no one in the street, all went back to their beds.

Angelique paced the cabin anxiously the entire time Lucien was gone. She had no idea of the hour, but she prayed that Diego had dispatched the rogue in time to return to her before midnight. She could not believe he would have trusted Lucien to keep his part of their bargain, so, she reflected, that would leave him with only one option: to kill him. And realizing that such a deed might not be accomplished before midnight, she had devised her own plan. Lucien had forgotten to take the small sewing scissors away from her again, and she now had them firmly in her grasp. Yves would expect her to fight him, but she would pretend to faint and then, when he bent over her she would lunge for the artery in his throat. It was a gruesome plan, but she would carry it out without hesitation. Visions of blood filled her thoughts, but when Lucien returned to his cabin

444

alone, she could do no more than ask excitedly, "Where is Diego? Didn't you get the map?"

Lucien's smile seemed a devilish grin. "Oh yes, I have the map. I am tempted to tell you that Diego has taken Teresa and gone, but that is a bit too cruel a trick even for me to play. Actually, I have just sent her and the prisoners ashore, for they were becoming too great a bother to keep."

"Where is my husband?" Angelique demanded with an anguished cry. "Where is he?"

"I killed him," Lucien replied with remarkable calm. "I shot him in the head and left him for dead. Now you really are a widow, Angelique, and I'll never let you go."

His words hit her with the brutal force of a savage blow, though with all her strength she refuted his words. "You're lying, you miserable bastard. You're lying again!" She lunged for him and the scissors sliced through the air with deadly intent, but he was too agile to be caught by her surprise attack and grabbed her wrist in a grasp so painful that the scissors slipped from her fingers.

"I should have known you would be angry with me. Well, no matter." Lucien yanked her to him and tightened his hold upon the delicate bones of her wrist as he watched her eyes fill with tears. "If it is proof you need, then I have it." Pulling her along beside him, he went to the table, then emptied out the contents of the leather pouch. Within the stained handkerchief, the sparkling jewels were still sticky with fresh blood, and Lucien laughed as he saw Angelique's eyes widen in horror. "Now do you believe me? You are indeed a widow. As soon as I've recovered a lost treasure in gold, I will chart a course for Martinique so we can have a doctor attend you at the birth of your child. Then we will be married."

Angelique could not take her eyes from the sapphires. Their brilliant blue was dulled beneath the rapidly congealing blood and she tried to back away, but Lucien kept her by his side. "That you've murdered someone is clear, but I know it wasn't Diego," she persisted. "You couldn't tell the truth if your wretched life depended upon it and I'll never marry you! *Never!*" she vowed hoarsely.

Lucien gave an evil chuckle. "Do you expect to be able to raise your late husband's babe yourself? I suggest you reconsider such a decision, *chéri,* or the moment he is born I shall give him away and you'll never see him again."

Angelique finally wrenched her eyes from the gory jewels and tossed her curls with a defiant flip. "You'll burn in hell forever for your crimes, but you'll not threaten me again! I'd rather you gave my child away. Then he'd never have to suffer the revulsion of knowing you!"

Enraged by her fiery burst of temper, Lucien pressed her against him in a savage embrace and his mouth hungrily silenced her protests. As always, her hatred fed his passion and so consumed was he by his need for her that his lust dispelled his last ounce of sanity. He lifted her into his arms and carried her to his bunk, delighting in the fury of her resistance. More than an hour passed before he fell into an exhausted stupor with her still imprisoned in his crushing embrace. But she was wide awake, plotting his doom by methods of such evil cunning that they would have horrified even the most unprincipled pirate.

Chapter XXV

Angelique leaned over Lucien's shoulder as he studied the map. Her golden curls brushed his cheek, yet he did not seem to notice the distraction. Drawn upon parchment, the map was stained in the deep creases where it had been folded since the day in the distant past when it had first been placed in the shallow tin box. The detail was superb and yet nearly incomprehensible to a man accustomed to the precise notations of nautical charts. There were fanciful drawings of Mayan gods decorating the border, while the numerous buildings of the lost city to which they were to travel were shown in crude perspective in the center. As soon as he had opened the map, Lucien had realized he had been a fool to kill the previous owner before he had revealed all his secrets. He would not admit such a grave error to his lovely companion, however, and continued to study the map with rapt attention, certain that once he reached the Laga de Lagartos all would become clear to him. "Lake of the Lizards! Is that not a ridiculous name?" he asked sarcastically. "Lizards do not swim!"

"Perhaps there are many nearby, Lucien, or the shape of the lake could have reminded someone of a lizard. I doubt that they meant the water was full of them." Angelique was paying little attention to the skillfully drawn map for she was busy memorizing the coastline. There were cities noted: Progreso, Sisal, and Merida, which was slightly inland. She meant to escape Lucien's grasp as soon as he left to search for the treasure in gold. No matter what the risks, she was determined to elude whomever he selected as her guard and swiftly return to Vera Cruz and Diego. She had obstinately refused to accept the arrogant Frenchman's repeated boasts that he had killed her husband, for she knew that the pirate was a complete stranger to the truth and had lied about Diego's being dead once before. Not wanting to arouse his suspicions by any further display of curiosity in the remarkable map, she turned away and resumed the restless pacing that occupied most of her waking hours.

Lucien refolded the delicate map and replaced it in the tin box. They had sailed out into the Gulf and were approaching the Yucatán from the Caribbean to minimize the possibility of hostile encounters with Spanish ships, but thus far his luck had held and they had sighted none. "El Lago de Lagartos is not really a lake but a long, narrow inlet, so it appears to be misnamed in all respects. If we sailed deep within it, we would have to fight our way out if anyone should wish to blockade the entrance." He paused a moment. "I do not like traps, *chéri,* but in this instance I think we would be safe within this so-called lake."

Angelique made no reply, since the man knew she did not care whether or not he and his band of cutthroats were safe. He walked up behind her and, as his hands encircled her breasts, she grew tense, dreading his touch, but his lips were soft as they caressed her throat. She would not fight him, for her anger only aroused him all the more. It was her cool indifference that crushed his pride, so she offered neither acceptance nor rejection. Their relationship had changed considerably since Diego was no longer on board, but thoughts of her husband were still all that occupied her mind. Diego was vibrantly alive in her heart and she would never cease her efforts to return to him, just as she knew he would make every attempt to rescue her. Someday they would be together again and she prayed with each breath she drew that the day would come soon.

Lucien dropped his hands with a frustrated sigh. "That you tolerate my touch is not enough, *chéri,* when the mere sight of you makes my whole body ache with its need of you. Why does my kiss still not give you the slighest thrill?"

Angelique turned toward him slowly. "I don't enjoy the attentions of a man whose actions I consider beneath contempt, but then, why would I? Vermin of any sort simply disgust me," she sneered, caring little if he struck her again.

Her taunts had turned so vicious that he was sickened by them, and he left her alone for the remainder of the afternoon.

It was not until Lucien brought her a lightweight cotton shirt and trousers that Angelique realized he would not be leaving her on board the ship but taking her with him when he began his trek through the jungles of the Yucatán. "You cannot expect me to accompany you on this expedition!" she exclaimed as she tossed the clothes aside. After announcing that such an idea was preposterous, she let Lucien know that she had no intention of donning the baggy cotton garments. She had become so impossible to please that she knew she now made her mother seem the soul of kindness by comparison and that thought brought a satisfied smile to her lips.

Thoroughly bored with her tantrums, Lucien reached out to catch a handful of Angelique's glossy curls and yanked her around to face him. "You will walk by my side. I'll not leave you here when you'd swiftly run away. How can you believe me to be as foolish as that? Now put on these clothes quickly, for there is no time to waste. Each minute I am on Spanish soil is a minute too long!"

"Exactly like each moment I spend with you!" Angelique

retorted with a defiant laugh.

The look in his gray eyes was colder than the chill of arctic winds as Lucien drew back his hand, then suddenly dropped it to his side. "There's no time for me to beat you senseless for that insult, as you deserve. Just dress and we will be on our way. The sooner this adventure is begun, the sooner it will be over."

He had already put on simple peasant garb himself. Though he knew it would fool no one at close range, he had found all manner of disguises to come in handy and so used them whenever possible. More than one captain had made the foolish mistake of thinking he was being approached by a ship of the Royal Spanish Navy, only to realize as he was hit broadside that he had allowed the most cunning band of pirates on the high seas to come within easy firing distance. Lucien was nervous all the same, however, for forays upon land were definitely not his specialty.

The coarse cotton fabric was scratchy to the touch, but Angelique slipped on the shirt and trousers without further complaint. The drawstring waistband allowed for a comfortable fit, but she dared not ask how she looked in such unbecoming garb. She soon realized, however, that such attire might actually help her escape him, since she knew that dragging a skirt through the sand was not easy. Wearing trousers, therefore, would have to be an improvement. He had even provided leather sandals that were close enough to her size to be comfortable. She fastened them around her ankles, then wiggled her toes before straightening up and turning to face him. "With my hair I'll not pass for a peasant, Lucien, not even from a distance."

Handing her a frayed straw hat, Lucien took her arm and started her toward the door. "Stuff those fair locks of yours into the hat or I'll cut them off as short as mine."

Angelique gave him a withering glance, but she knew he was not teasing and quickly coiled her hair atop her head and covered it with the hat. "There. Does that please you?"

"Everything about you pleases me, *chéri,* but you already know that," Lucien responded with a devilish grin. "Now let us go."

Angelique followed him out on deck and stood by the rail as they navigated the entrance to the inlet known as Lago de Lagartos. She was fascinated by the lush foliage that grew in such abundance at the water's edge. She had heard that parts of the country resembled Spain's arid landscape, but this primeval world reminded her not at all of the terrain surrounding Barcelona. The vegetation here was so thick that she wondered how any trails could possibly exist through its tangled depths.

Lucien, however, did not seem surprised by what they found and scanned the shore, searching for the precise spot indicated by the map so that he could drop anchor. When at last he sighted a steep wall of rock jutting out into the water, he issued a series of loud commands to his crew. Each man performed his task with a precision that amazed her and in less than half an hour she stood beside Lucien on the shore. He had everything ready: food, water, and weapons for the dozen men he had chosen to accompany them. Angelique was sorry to see that Yves would be making the trek overland, since his presence alone constituted a threat to her survival, but she dared not speak a word in protest, even when he took the place in line directly behind hers. Satisfied that the men he had left on board the *Marie Alise* would follow his orders until his return, Lucien led the small party of explorers past the rocks to a narrow opening in the underbrush where an old trail began. Though once paved with stones, the path was now partially hidden by grass that had grown between the rocks, making it uneven, but to a man intent upon following the ancient road, its direction was clear.

Lucien held the map in one hand and a razor-sharp machete in the other. The once-straight trail now twisted and turned through the tangled shrubs and vines, and after an hour they had succeeded in moving no more than a hundred yards through the untamed forest. The Frenchman then had to call a halt for a much-needed rest. "I estimated the distance as no more than a day's walk, but I can see now that I was overly optimistic."

While it was still early morning, the heat and humidity were so oppressive that Angelique doubted she could walk much farther. "I think I should go back to the ship, Lucien. I'll just slow you down."

Her fair skin had grown quite pale and tiny beads of perspiration dotted her upper lip, and it was obvious that she was not faking fatigue, but Lucien shook his head. "I'll carry you on my back if I must, but you're staying with me." When she sat down upon the path, he knelt beside her and waited until he thought she could safely continue, but he took the precaution of stopping more frequently so none of them would get overtired. The map had many useful reference points, and when they finally stopped for the night, he was certain they had covered at least a third of the distance toward the lost city.

Three men busied themselves hacking out a clearing, but Angelique considered the proportions of the camp far too confining to guarantee her any privacy and she said so. "Do you really expect me to sleep with all these men no more than a few inches from my side?" she whispered petulantly to Lucien.

Disappointed in the slowness of their progress, Lucien was in no mood to listen to Angelique's complaints, but since he wanted privacy for a far different reason than she did, he insisted upon it. Taking up his machete, he cleared a place for the two of them that was several yards down the trail from the men. "There. You now have your own apartment where you can enjoy the sight of the stars without worry that you'll be disturbed by any man save me."

Exhausted, Angelique stretched out on her side on the blanket he had tossed her and fell sound asleep before he could return with her supper. He sat down and ate the dried fish and hard biscuits before he shook her shoulder. "Wake up, Angelique. You'll need to eat something to keep up your strength."

Opening one eye, Angelique looked at the meager fare he had provided and shook her head. "No, thank you. I'll just get sick if I eat that tonight."

Lucien knew she had had a far more difficult time that day than the rest of them, but that realization did not dampen his romantic mood. He wanted her as he always did and reached for the drawstring on her cotton trousers. "Perhaps later then," he replied softly. "Much later."

Angelique sat up quickly, but there was no place for her to run. The underbrush was too thick to be pushed aside easily and the path Lucien had cleared led straight back to his men. She felt trapped. "Do you really want to be bothered with carrying me tomorrow? That's exactly what's going to happen if you don't let me get some sleep."

Lucien chuckled at her threat. "So I will carry you. You do not weigh all that much, and it would be most pleasant to feel your arms around my neck for the whole day."

Disgusted by the mere thought, Angelique shook her head, sending her bright curls flying. "Can't you allow me to sleep in peace for even one night?" she asked caustically.

"No." Lucien pulled her into his arms and ended her resistance with practiced ease. He was too strong to be more than merely annoyed by her attempts to avoid his caresses, and he subdued her defiance with a deep kiss. Swiftly satisfying his craving for her then, he lay back to gaze up at the stars. "There will be at least one more day, perhaps two, before we reach our destination. I hope to spend no more than a day dragging the bottom of the *cenote* for gold, and then we'll return to the ship. Now that we've cut a trail, I'll wager we can traverse the distance in half a day."

Paying scant attention to his remarks, Angelique struggled to pull her clothing back into place in the darkness. She was thinking that when the men were occupied with their attempts to get the gold, she could slip away if she had not made good her escape before then. The idea of spending even one more day in Lucien's company revolted her so thoroughly that she lay down with her back toward him, not interested in hearing his plans. He fell asleep quickly, and she noted that he had left the machete with Yves so she would not be able to use it on him. She found it amusing that he was afraid to leave anything within her reach that could be used as a weapon. In her opinion, it was probably the wisest thing he had ever done to safeguard his own life.

When swarms of mosquitoes overtook them the next morning, the men began to curse loudly, but Lucien swiftly put a stop to their complaints by reminding them that they would all share in the treasure he was about to find. So intent was he upon keeping them eager to reach their destination that he missed a curve in the stone path and led them several yards astray before realizing his mistake. He then called a halt and sat down to rest.

Angelique leaned back against the trunk of a *ramon* tree, wiped the perspiration from her brow, and fanned her face with her hat. "I have never been so uncomfortable in all my life, Lucien. Why did you have to insist on bringing me along to share your misery?"

"Shall I have Yves carry you this afternoon, *chéri?* Would you prefer his company to mine?" Lucien leaned over to give her a kiss upon the cheek, but when she turned her head to avoid him, he grabbed her chin to force her lips back to his.

Angelique hated Lucien's kisses, for he seemed determined to win her affection in the same brutal manner a horseman breaks a wild mount to the saddle. And, like a wild horse, she bit him, and her teeth drew blood before he struck her and she had to let go. Wiping her mouth on the back of her hand, she stared at him coldly.

Lucien massaged his swollen lip, sorry he had no way to punish her here in the wild. "Why would you wish to wound me when I have been so good to you?" he inquired bitterly. "I want only to make you happy, to make you my wife."

"I am already the wife of Juan Diego Aragon!" Angelique argued defiantly. "One husband is all any woman is allowed, even on Martinique!"

Enraged by her taunt, Lucien rose to his feet, grabbed Angelique's arm, and jerked her up beside him. "I wish now I had scalped the bastard; then maybe you would have accepted the truth!"

"I doubt you could force yourself to speak it!" Angelique spat, then darted away as he swung his fist at her. But Yves caught her in his arms and spun her around to face Lucien.

"Take her back to the end of the line, Yves. I'm sick of looking at her." Lucien called down the line that the rest stop was over and, taking up his machete, he began to swing the long knife in broad arcs to slice through the vines that blocked the ancient roadway. He swore to himself as he continued to move forward at an agonizingly slow pace and thought about what he would do with Angelique that night, for while he could not deny that her defiance aroused his passion, he did not want her insolence to inspire rebellion among his crew. No, he had to make her understand her place—to understand it and accept it—for he would never let her go.

Disgusted that he had been made responsible for her, Yves muttered a vile string of curses and kept giving Angelique rude shoves as they moved down the path Lucien and his men had cleared. Every two steps she would feel the brute's hand in the center of her back, pushing her on. As usual he was mean, striking her for no reason and forcing her to keep walking at a pace far more brisk than she could easily manage, but she balked so often at this mistreatment that they soon fell far behind the others. Coming upon a wide place in the trail, she pretended to need to remove a pebble from her sandal, simply to gain a few seconds rest. As she bent down she noticed that the foliage leading off to the right and left was scant enough for her to push through and she realized that the trail Lucien had cut must have intersected another. It looked to her like a recently cut path, and one still in use, as opposed to the forgotten trail they were having such difficulty following. As she rose to her feet, her decision was made and, without a moment's hesitation, she chose the path to the right and darted off into the underbrush. Yves made a grab for her sleeve, but she was too swift for him and plunged down the trail, gathering speed with each quick stride. She was glad then to be wearing trousers, since they did not impede her movement as the long skirt of a gown would have. She knew the dusty path had to lead somewhere and prayed it circled back to the coast or went directly to a village the inhabitants of which would be friendly. She could hear Yves breathing heavily, for the effort to chase her was a strain with the heavy pack he was carrying on his back, and she forced herself to expend the last of her strength in a frantic dash to escape him. The way was narrow and allowed her to flee, while the overhanging vines and branches snagged Yves's clothes and pack, making the trail nearly impassable for him. He kept coming, however, the heavy thud of his footsteps echoing like the roll of thunder in the humid air.

Angelique's slight store of energy had nearly been spent and Yves was gaining on her with each lumbering stride when suddenly the path branched off in two directions. Instantly she chose the less traveled, hoping the density of the underbrush would allow her to elude the brute and find cover to hide but all too quickly the way became clear on each side of the trail and a sob escaped her lips as she felt the fiend's fingertips slip down her spine as he made another grab for the back of her shirt. She sprang forward, scrambling up a steep incline, and the soft limestone came away at her touch, showering Yves with thick white dust as

456

he continued his close pursuit. Blinded momentarily, he stopped to curse her again as he rubbed his eyes, but she did not pause for an instant in her frantic bid for freedom.

Nearly exhausted, Angelique tripped, but as she got up, she saw someone just ahead. The Indian boy looked about ten or twelve years old and his black eyes widened in astonishment as he saw her dashing headlong toward him. Then he saw Yves rapidly advancing and understood her terror. Wasting no time in shouting directions, he ran forward, grabbed Angelique's hand, and pulled her along behind him through the maze of trails that crisscrossed his homeland. Then, as suddenly as he had entered the chase, he slowed and drew Angelique to his side as he walked stealthily around the edge of a mosquito-infested clearing. They had just reached the far side as Yves appeared at the end of the trail. He stopped to adjust the heavy pack he still carried, then pressed on across the clearing. He had taken three long strides when the earth began to crumble beneath his feet. With a whoosh of dank air the limestone gave way and he plunged into the depths of a subterranean cave, leaving behind no more than an eerie shriek, which hung on the air for an instant, then abruptly ceased.

Angelique stared first at the gaping hole in the center of the clearing, then at the boy by her side. He nodded excitedly with a mischievous grin and she knew he had deliberately led Yves to his death. Shaken, she sank to her knees, grateful and yet horrified by what he had done. He began to pat her head lightly and his attempts at comfort were so surprisingly soothing that Angelique quickly wiped away her tears. "There are others. Can you take me someplace to hide?" she asked in Spanish, but the lad shook his head, not understanding her question. She pointed down the trail then and took his hand, hoping he would see that the danger had not yet passed. He nodded quickly. Putting his fingertip to his lips, he led her carefully through the underbrush to another trail, which curved back toward the coast.

457

When they were certain no one was pursuing them, they sat down to rest and Angelique had time to wonder how long it would take Lucien to notice that she and Yves were missing. He had been occupied in slashing away the verdant foliage at the very front of the line of men, while she and the mate had trailed several yards behind the steadily advancing column. She had not heard Yves call out before he had started after her, so perhaps it would not be until Lucien stopped to rest that their absence would be noted. She had no doubt he would go back to search for them and she was certain that the trail of broken branches and trampled vines Yves had left in the wake of his hasty pursuit would be easy to follow. The question was whether or not he would notice that her footprints led around the hole where Yves had fallen to his death. If he did not, then he would believe her dead too, but if he were clever enough to realize she had not been killed, then he would continue his search.

Rising to her feet, she gestured impatiently, for the more distance she put between herself and the pirates, the safer she would feel. The boy sprang to his feet, bowed slightly, then reached out to again touch her golden curls as innocent wonder lit his dark eyes. Angelique had no idea what had become of her hat. It had fallen off when she had first left Lucien's trail, but the oppressive heat made her sorry she had lost it. Apparently, the lad had never before seen a blond woman; nor did he speak Spanish. This indicated that his tribe would be an isolated one, and she hoped all his people would be equally friendly when she arrived at his home. They walked for nearly an hour before the Indian motioned for her to remain where she was standing while he went on ahead. He was gone only a few minutes, but that was more than enough time to frighten Angelique, for she knew that if he failed to return, she would be lost deep within the dense jungle with no machete to help her blaze her own trail out.

The friendly boy returned with another young man who seemed slightly older but was no taller than he. They continued down the path for several yards, then turned left into a clearing where half a dozen thatched huts stood amid the ruins of what had once been the courtyard of a magnificent Mayan temple. Small children scampered up and down the steps leading to the two-story building, which had long ago fallen victim to the tangle of vines that grew into and around the delicate stone filigree that decorated the facade of the second floor. The twisted roots of the elmlike *alamo* trees surrounding the building had distorted the angles of the walls and given the massive stone structure the haphazard appearance of a house of cards. There were large, rectangular openings in the walls of the first floor. Whether they had been doors or windows, Angelique could not determine, but the interior of the large temple was dark and forbidding.

She was amazed that the once proud people who had built such an imposing edifice of stone could now reside in its gloomy shadow in simple thatched huts, and she wondered how the Spanish could have conquered a people who had left such remarkable monuments to their existence. She dared not move closer, yet she yearned to examine the carvings above the windows, for they reminded her of the intricate designs that covered Diego's three idols. The thought of those treasures remaining in Lucien's hands angered her, but she knew there was no way she could sneak back aboard the *Marie Alise* to get them.

As Angelique stood entranced with the sight before her, the residents of the village had slowly emerged from their homes and had gathered together to stare at her. The Indians were small and lithe and quick, and they were as curious about the blond stranger in their midst as she was about them. The boy who had been so helpful began immediately to describe how he had found her being chased by a brute of monstrous proportions. He danced around gesturing wildly as he revealed how he had tricked the villain into straying over land all knew to be unsafe. The small crowd listened with rapt attention, then a woman came forward to observe Angelique more closely. She walked around her three times, then touched her blond hair with a timid caress.

Angelique tried to smile as she prayed these friendly Indians were not Aztecas who might have habits of a nature far too gruesome to contemplate. When the woman gestured for her to follow, she did, though hesitantly, but they walked only a short distance to a large, clear pool surrounded by a steep limestone formation on one side and a dense stand of palms and ferns on the other. After several minutes of coaxing, the woman finally made Angelique understand that she wanted her to discard her garments, which had become soiled and torn on her flight through the forest, and bathe. She nearly wept with the sweetness of that thought and, when another woman joined them carrying a clean shift of lightweight cotton, Angelique quickly cast the coarsely woven shirt and trousers aside.

She did not know which the women found more amusing, her lace-trimmed camisole and bloomers or her figure, but she peeled off the fine linen garments and, after scrubbing them furiously to wash them clean, lay them upon the rocks to dry while she bathed and washed her hair. Since she'd been given no soap and had no way to ask for some, she did the best she could to remove the layers of powdery limestone dust that had accumulated on her fair skin and hair. The women had provided no towel either, so she had no choice but to stand in the sun for a few minutes after leaving the refreshing pool. The air was so humid that she soon realized she would never get dry and, after picking up her still-damp lingerie, she pulled the loose-fitting shift over her head.

The arrival of such an unusual visitor was quite naturally considered reason enough for a celebration and, by the time Angelique and her two companions returned to the cluster of huts, the party was well underway. One man was playing a drum that had been fashioned by stretching a hide over one end of a hollow log. He held the instrument under his left arm and tapped upon it lightly with his right hand. Though it provided a lively rhythm, Angelique prayed its sound would not carry far enough to alert Lucien to the presence of these Indians.

She strolled around as the women busied themselves making *tortillas*, and she used the time to note in which directions pathways left the village. She had no idea how far she had come, but she did not think it was nearly far enough to make her safe from the pirates' grasp. Stopping to observe the women cook the flat corn cakes, Angelique sat down upon a block of stone that had tumbled down from the elaborate cornice that decorated the temple. Weeds had grown up around it, but still it made a passable stool. Her glance strayed over the smaller fragments of stone that lay scattered about, and she reached down to pluck one from the weeds. She found that it contained a figure carved in high relief. The body was adorned with lavish plumage, but the head was clearly that of a serpent. "Quetzalcóatl," she mused softly, recognizing the fearsome god at first glance. She found it difficult to swallow as she looked up at the smiling Indians who surrounded her. Dear Lord, who are these people, she wondered silently, and how will I ever be able to escape them if I find that I am no safer in this forgotten village than I would have been with Lucien?

Chapter XXVI

Diego awoke with a start. His heart was pounding wildly in his chest and his head throbbed with a pain so intense that he could not make out the faces of the three men who stood at the foot of his bed. The room was filled with the brilliance of the noonday sun and he knew instantly that Lucien Dangermond would be well on his way to the Yucatán. He threw back the covers then froze, impaled by a blinding pain that tore through his skull as he attempted to sit up. He had no time to be ill, not when every second Lucien gained put him that much further out of reach. "Where are my clothes?" he heard himself ask, but his words sounded garbled even in his own ears.

One of the men came forward to grip Diego's shoulders firmly. "Do not try to rise. You have lost too much blood and will surely faint. You must rest."

The stranger's voice was kind, but Diego had no time to waste in listening to sympathy. "No, I must leave at once. Bring me my clothes!" he commanded in the stern voice that usually made men rush to obey him.

The pleasant stranger was pushed aside then by a tall, gaunt man who spoke with clipped precision. "You are under arrest for the murder of Eduardo Marquez and will go nowhere. Now tell us your name and be quick about it. I have waited three days for you to come to your senses, and I am not a patient man under the best of circumstances, least of all when there has been a brutal murder."

"Three days? It has been three days?" Diego asked incredulously. He closed his eyes tightly, trying to find the missing hours, but his mind was a merciful blank, having shut out the pain he had suffered as well as suppressing his usually excellent memory.

"Please, Colonel Muñoz. There is no reason to suspect my patient of murder. There is absolutely no evidence to support that accusation." Stepping forward again, the sympathetic man introduced himself. Gray haired and slight of build, he had a gentle, courtly manner. "I am a physician, Dr. Armando Flores. I was called to treat your head wound by Jaime Ortiz, this gentleman here." He drew the embarrassed Jaime closer to the bed so Diego could meet him. "Jaime lives just up the street from Señor Marquez's shop. He happened to call upon Eduardo quite late the other evening, and when he discovered his good friend dead and you severely injured, he came for me. Had he not found you when he did, I am certain you would have soon bled to death."

Diego found it difficult to concentrate upon the doctor's words, for his voice was so soft that it nearly lulled him back to sleep, but he resisted that temptation. "I must reward you both then, for I am most grateful to you for saving my life."

Jaime laughed nervously, too embarrassed to accept any such credit or praise. "You misunderstand. I am no hero. My wife and I fight each time I drink too much *tequila* with my friends. I have spent many a night with Eduardo. It was my bad habits, or fate perhaps, that led me to his door the night of the tragedy."

"Then I am grateful, to your wife as well, Señor Ortiz, but you could not have been too drunk or you would not have had the presence of mind to summon a doctor." Diego thought the situation very amusing, for clearly he owed his life to a drunkard's nagging wife.

Colonel Muñoz cared little for Jaime Ortiz's domestic problems and interrupted to repeat his question. "Your name, what is it?"

"Juan Diego Aragon. If you'll send someone to the offices of the Aragon Line, they will tell you I am no murderer." Diego tried again to sit up and this time had more success. He found that if he moved slowly, the pain in his head was not unbearable, and he was able to swing his feet over the side of the bed. He turned to the doctor and said, "My clothes, please."

"You are Captain Aragon?" Colonel Muñoz asked with a startled gasp. "Of the ship *El Diablo Del Mar?*"

"My ship is no more, but I am still Captain Aragon. Now must I leave here clad only in these sheets?"

The colonel drew Jaime aside. "Go down to the docks and bring whomever you can find to identify this man. He could be anyone, for all I know."

"Yes, Colonel." Jaime was a simple man who frequently ran errands for others, and he left immediately to see to the officer's request.

"I have sent for someone to identify you. Until that time, you will remain under arrest, and in that bed." Ignacio Muñoz pulled up a chair and, after sitting down, folded his arms across his chest to wait.

Diego took a deep breath, still not understanding why he had been accused of the old man's murder. "I was shot by the same man who killed Señor Marquez. How can you think me a murderer?" he asked caustically. "Do you actually believe I killed Eduardo, then shot myself in the head? Isn't it obvious there was someone else present?"

"Oh, I agree. There were obviously two of you in the shop."

"Well, that's a step toward the truth at least. Tell me something, Colonel. Was there a pistol in my hand?" Diego had found the man impossible to respect, for he had recognized him instantly by his hostile attitude as the type who cared more for his own glory than for justice.

"No, there was no pistol anywhere about, but you could have killed Marquez, then fallen victim to your accomplice's treachery. It has happened often in the past. Two men will plan a robbery, then one will become greedy and want to keep everything for himself."

That was surprisingly close to what had happened, Diego realized, but the man had his facts all wrong. "Since you recognized my name, how is it you do not also know I am an honest man?"

"You are the prisoner here, not I, and I'll answer no more questions. If you truly are Aragon, then you'll learn everything soon enough." Colonel Muñoz's glance became an intense stare. He was not about to be tricked by anyone, least of all a murderer.

Dr. Flores excused himself for a moment, then returned with the clothes Diego had been wearing when he had found him. "I will not have my infirmary turned into a prison, Colonel Muñoz. If my patient feels up to getting dressed, I will be happy to help him. My wife laundered his shirt, so I think I can make him look presentable."

Muñoz rose to his feet and drew his pistol. "Help him dress if you must, Dr. Flores, but if he attempts to escape, I will shoot to kill."

"Escape? I doubt the man can stand unassisted. He will not escape!" Armando scoffed at that unlikely possibility. He knew he was wasting his breath arguing with the officer, however, and turned to Diego. "You will need warm water to wash. Let me bring that first and then some soup. My wife has a pot of *albóndigas* simmering. What you need now is plenty of rest and good food."

Diego was grateful for the physician's kindness, but he kept his eye on the colonel, not wanting to arouse his suspicions, for the last time a pistol had been pointed at him the result had been disastrous. He doubted he could hold a razor steady enough to shave, but at least he was able to wash his face. "I seem to be compelled to grow a beard again, Colonel, but I'm certain I'm still recognizable." As he reached up to touch the bandage that covered his wound, Dr. Flores caught his hand.

"I would not do that if I were you. The gash was deep, creasing the bone, and very nearly fatal. You must not remove the bandage yet. As for your back, those scars are recent ones. I have seldom seen a man who has been so brutally whipped. For what were you punished?"

Diego found the incident difficult to explain. "The story is too long to recount, but the man responsible for Eduardo Marquez's murder is to blame, and it's only one of the many crimes for which I intend to make the bastard pay."

"You'll have to clear yourself of murder first, or you'll not live long enough to extract revenge from anyone. I can guarantee that," Muñoz vowed boastfully.

Diego ignored his threat, for dressing required his full concentration. His head ached so intensely that he wanted only to lie down and go back to sleep, but he knew such weakness would allow Lucien to lengthen his lead. By the time Jaime Ortiz returned, he had eaten two bowls of the rich vegetable soup filled with meat balls and was fully dressed, but only because Dr. Flores had helped him.

Colonel Muñoz had expected one man, perhaps two, to accompany Jaime. He was not prepared for the flood of visitors that crowded into the small infirmary. He recognized one man as an executive with the Aragon Line, but the other men were sailors, who whooped excitedly and danced about hugging each other and the man he now had to admit was Juan Diego Aragon. This fact made his task not only difficult but extremely delicate, for the citizens of Vera Cruz depended heavily upon trade with Spain for all manner of goods, and he could not prosecute a man with the influence Diego Aragon possessed. Vera Cruz would cease to exist as a city if all the Aragon ships boycotted the port, and he would then find himself out of a job, his wife would undoubtedly leave him, and his children would curse his name. He pulled out his handkerchief and wiped his brow, uncertain what action he could possibly take to solve Eduardo Marquez's murder without bringing an abrupt end to his own career.

Diego raised his hands, needing more space in which to breathe. "I am more pleased to see that so many of you made it safely to Vera Cruz than I have words to express. There is no time for a celebration now, however. I'm going after the pirate who still holds Angelique captive. Who'll go with me?"

Gustavo was the first to volunteer, his voice an eager one. "I have been waiting for just that opportunity."

"We all have!" Octavio Blanco exclaimed as he slapped Gustavo on the back. "Most of us were picked up the day after the storm by a ship bound from Cuba to Vera Cruz. We have been going to the Aragon offices each day, hoping for word of you. When Gustavo, Enrique, and Andres appeared there this week, we pried every detail of your ordeal from their lips. None of us will rest until Dangermond is hanged."

"You know the whereabouts of the pirate Lucien Dangermond?" Colonel Muñoz shouted, hastily putting away his pistol and pushing through the crowd surrounding Diego's bed. The murder of one elderly man was tragic but of slight consequence when compared to the barbarous piracy of Dangermond. "There is a large reward for his capture. If you wish to pursue him, I will gladly gather troops to assist you."

Diego stared at the arrogant colonel for a long moment. "Does that mean I am no longer under arrest for murder?"

Flustered by his question, Ignacio tried to avoid it. "Dangermond has been the scourge of our coast, and none have been able to stop him. If you can capture him, then you'll be able to prove your own innocence."

"Of whose murder is he accused?" Teresa asked from the sidelines where she had been standing, hoping Diego would

467

notice her. Though disappointed that he had not, she nonetheless had been too curious to remain silent any longer.

"That is no business of yours," Muñoz responded impatiently. "We have important plans to make, but nothing can be accomplished here. Let us go down to the port where arrangements can be made for a ship."

"I must command that ship, Colonel. I'll not involve the Royal Navy in this." He recognized the man from his firm. A skilled accountant, he looked very ill at ease among the gathering of rowdy sailors as Diego addressed him. "Señor Torres, any vessel that is afloat will do. Can you furnish one on such short notice?"

Emilio Torres had suffered through nearly a month in which he had been surrounded each day by Diego's lively band of men. He had found them all lodgings, bought them new clothes, paid for their meals. He would have done anything within his power to restore the rambunctious crew to Diego's command. "The *Coronado,* a bark just newly reconditioned, is in port. She is without a captain at present, but if the *Diablo* is lost—"

"Precisely. Assign the *Coronado* to me," Diego requested confidently, then he had to pause a moment to catch his breath, before whispering to Octavio, "Have you a carriage? I can't walk any farther than the door."

Octavio nodded and turned to the men. "Well, you heard the captain. We'll be sailing on the *Coronado.* Pack up what few belongings you've managed to gather in the last weeks and get on board as quickly as you can."

Eager to depart, the men bid Diego good-bye, then left in twos and threes to attend to their errands before going down to the port to locate the *Coronado.* Teresa walked to the door with Gustavo, then turned back. Emilio had taken Dr. Flores aside to settle Diego's bill, while Jaime Ortiz and Colonel Muñoz were standing outside talking. Seizing the only opportunity she would have to speak with Diego, she ran back to his side.

"Take me with you. Your wife should have a woman to serve her, and I was once a ladies' maid."

Though startled by her request, Diego promptly refused it. "When we come back to Vera Cruz, I will see that you find honest employment, Teresa, but my wife will have no need of a maid on board ship. You will have to remain here."

Insulted, Teresa's eyes darkened. "I saw her figure clearly when you fenced with Dangermond, but a pregnant woman should not be made to travel alone. She will need a maid, even if you do not think so."

Diego readily understood Octavio's startled glance, for he knew that his mate was aware that he and Angelique had been married not quite four months. Had Angelique gotten pregnant on their wedding night, she still would have been able to hide her condition. He had thought that once they reached Vera Cruz he could keep the scandal from her name, but he had forgotten that every man in his crew knew the date of their wedding. "I don't want you on board. It is as simple as that, Teresa. I'll have Emilio give you money— whatever you need—but you'll not come with us. Don't ask Gustavo to try to change my mind, either."

"It is not your money I wanted!" Teresa responded with tear-filled eyes. She ran to the door and, taking Gustavo's hand, pulled him along down the walk.

"You are going to become a father soon?" Octavio inquired skeptically. "After all your bride has suffered, I did not think—"

Wanting to end their discussion quickly, Diego told the mate the truth, then added, "I do not want Angelique's name sullied for any reason, and the fact that she's been Dangermond's prisoner will cause more than enough gossip. It is true that her pregnancy is advanced enough to be noticeable, but I'll not have the men, or anyone for that matter, speculating about her virtue. Is that clear?"

Octavio nodded slightly. "Your men will do nothing to

469

bring dishonor to her name. Need I remind you of that? The three who were with you regard her as highly as they would a saint."

"Good." Diego struggled to his feet. "Just help me to the carriage. I can do nothing for Angelique until after I've killed Dangermond."

"You do not plan to hand him over to the authorities to hang?" Octavio slipped his arm around Diego's waist and was shocked to see how thin the once powerfully built young man had become. "I think the colonel expects to see justice done where the citizens of Vera Cruz can witness it."

"And congratulate him," Diego agreed. "No, I will kill that madman myself. Dangermond is mine." Yet how he would manage that feat when walking from the bed to the door was so difficult, Diego was not certain. "You'll have to help me, Octavio. You'll all have to help me. But if any man ever deserved to die for his crimes, it is that one."

"He is a dead man already," Octavio vowed as he helped Diego into the carriage. Colonel Muñoz followed, along with Emilio Torres. After Diego had again thanked Dr. Flores and Jaime Ortiz and had promised them a generous reward, the group made their way to the docks, where they found the decks of the *Coronado* already filled with men making ready to sail.

By a supreme effort of will, Diego walked up the gangplank alone and into the captain's cabin, but he quickly sat down at the table and rested his head upon his arms. He listened to Emilio Torres's description of the ship and its history, then asked him to arrange for supplies to be loaded immediately.

Once he was gone, Diego sat back and tried to focus his eyes on Ignacio Muñoz. "I think I know where Dangermond has gone, but I'll need a few days to recuperate more fully before we set sail. I can't lead you to him until I'm certain I won't faint just strolling across the deck. Give me three days. That way you'll have time to assemble your troops. Two dozen men should be plenty."

"Two dozen?" Muñoz scoffed at so slight a number. "I will bring twice that. I do not want Dangermond to escape us." He paced the cabin nervously as his excitement continued to mount. He was pleased that Diego had no wish to involve the navy, for it would be to his advantage as well. "Yes, three days will be sufficient time to make my preparations. I will return tomorrow afternoon. Perhaps you will be feeling better by then and we can discuss a specific plan of attack."

"Yes. Until tomorrow afternoon then." Diego returned the colonel's salute with a nonchalant wave, but as soon as the man had closed the door on his way out, he motioned for Octavio to come close and whispered, "Get everything loaded as swiftly as possible. I want to sail before dawn."

Octavio broke into a broad grin. "Colonel Muñoz will be greatly disappointed, but I for one do not think we will miss him. Do you truly know where Dangermond might be?"

"I know exactly where the bastard is, and luckily he believes I'm in my grave." Diego took a deep breath and rose unsteadily to his feet. "Rest and good food was all Dr. Flores could prescribe, so wake me when supper is ready."

"That I will, Captain." Octavio waited to make certain Diego could reach the bunk safely, then knelt to pull off his boots without having to be asked. "The *Coronado* looks like a trustworthy ship, but she'll have to go a long way to surpass the *Diablo* in my heart."

"As long as she'll make it to El Lago de Lagartos, I will not complain. I mean to take Dangermond's ship for my own then."

"A pirate ship?" Octavio asked in surprise.

"The *Marie Alise* by name, but I'll have Angelique rechristen her *Lord of the Wind.*"

Octavio watched Diego stretch out upon the bunk and close his eyes. "*Lord of the Wind?* Who might that be, sir?"

"The Aztecas called him Quetzalcóatl; the Maya, Kukulcán. By either name, he's the fierce Indian god who's going to help me rip out Dangermond's heart while it's still beating."

Appalled by his grisly description, Octavio quickly left to attend to his chores, certain his captain had not fully recovered from his injuries, for he had never known him to be such a bloodthirsty individual in the past.

Diego relied upon Octavio to plot their course and take command of the *Coronado*. The ship slipped smoothly out of port under the cover of the dense gray mist of early dawn, and when Colonel Muñoz arrived at the empty dock and realized he had been tricked, he was infuriated to think he had not even asked Diego in which direction Dangermond had gone, thus making any effort at pursuit impossible. He was able to contain his rage only by reminding himself that Diego would soon return to Vera Cruz with Lucien Dangermond in chains. Then it would be he who would oversee the arrangements for the pirate's trial and swift hanging. Pleased by the thought of the promotion such an accomplishment would surely bring, he turned back to his carriage whistling merrily.

Caring not at all for Colonel Muñoz's pride, Diego forgot him completely as he focused his attention upon getting well. He left his bunk each day only long enough to share meals and plot strategy with his mate. By the time they reached the mouth of El Lago de Lagartos, his efforts to regain his strength had proven very successful. While he had only a small portion of his customary vigor, he could stand without growing dizzy and walk about the cabin without tiring. He had removed the bandages from his head to find that Dr. Flores's neat stitches extended slightly past his hairline to touch his forehead. The scar that had formed after Yves's repeated blows to his left brow disgusted him too. "Lord help me, Octavio, but Angelique is likely to run screaming when she first sees me."

The jovial mate shook his head in disagreement. "As I recall, she was extremely fond of you. I doubt a few scars will change her mind. Besides, your hair will cover the slight mark on your forehead and the scar through your brow is hardly disfiguring."

"You're forgetting my back. That's the worst of it." Diego responded, not accepting his mate's kind encouragement as the truth.

"Your bride did not strike me as the fickle sort, so I doubt she married you solely for your handsome appearance."

Diego turned away quickly, not about to discuss the reason for their hasty marriage. "I hope you are right, but so much has happened to each of us that perhaps nothing will be as it once was between us."

Octavio disagreed. "I lack your experience with women, Captain, but I know I'd do whatever I could to make my wife happy if I were fortunate enough to be married to a woman like Angelique." Seeking to distract the young man from his worries, he quickly changed the subject. "Now let us again go over our plans to set her free."

The *Coronado* lay at anchor, waiting for the report of the scouting party they had sent to skirt the shore of El Lago de Lagartos. "I didn't see the map, so I have no idea how many days' journey the Mayan city is from here. If Dangermond's ship is still anchored within the inlet, then we'll strike just before dawn, capture whatever men are on board, and hope Angelique can be rescued without any casualties to our crew. I told you the only man who concerns me is the mate. Yves is a brute who'll be about as easy to kill as an enraged bull. We'll have to face him sooner or later though, and I'd prefer to take him by surprise. I'm betting Lucien left him behind to command the ship and guard my wife."

Octavio nodded thoughtfully. "Yes, that is logical, but he would have to leave her from time to time, perhaps to bring meals or to attend to his other duties."

"Let us hope so." Diego sat down upon the edge of the bunk, but his tension was still readily visible in his alert pose. "He'll be stationed outside her door, not inside. Dangermond is too jealous to leave Angelique in his mate's lap."

"Let me handle Yves," Octavio volunteered. "I know a trick or two I'll wager he does not."

"You're wagering your life, you realize," Diego cautioned him sternly.

Octavio shrugged. "If just before dawn we were to slip aboard the *Marie Alise,* I could call out to Yves, lure him out on deck, and the moment he appears, I will lunge at him. The men will back me up."

Diego chuckled at his mate's confident grin. "We've never fought pirates in hand-to-hand combat. This encounter may not go as well as your usual brawls in waterfront taverns."

Octavio chuckled as he rose and walked to the door. "The *Marie Alise* is within our grasp. I can feel it. Go to sleep. I will wake you when the scouts return."

Though he did not argue, Diego was sick of sleeping alone. When the mate left he stretched out on the bunk, propped his head upon his hands, and prayed that Angelique loved him still. Perhaps he should have brought a woman along, though certainly not Teresa. He would hire a mature woman to serve his wife, a kindly, gray-haired Frenchwoman, if he could find such a person in Vera Cruz. He could not hire Teresa, for every move she made was calculated simply to arouse him. She would just make Angelique jealous when there was no cause, and he would not permit that. There was so much he wanted to do for his lovely wife, and the thought that she would soon be in his arms was a torment he could scarcely bear. Giving up all attempt to rest, he went up on deck to talk with Octavio while they waited for the scouts to return.

Since they knew the *Marie Alise,* Gustavo, Enrique, and Andres had volunteered to go with the small scouting party, and Andres was the one chosen to brief Diego on what they had found. "The ship lies well within the inlet, but so near the shore we can walk out to it. There were men with rifles posted in the bow and stern, but they were paying little attention and did not see us. Most of the crew seems to be on board, and from the amount of noise they were making, I'd say they were all drunk."

"Did you see Yves, or any sign of Angelique?" Diego asked anxiously.

"No sir, and we waited more than an hour, hoping to catch a glimpse of your wife."

"Thank you." Diego dismissed Andres before turning to Octavio. "I don't like the sound of this. Dangermond is no fool, so why would he be so lax with his crew?"

"When it will work to our advantage, why should we question what sort of captain he is?"

Diego frowned. "Damn it! If Yves were on board, there would be discipline aplenty. Since he obviously isn't there, then who can be guarding Angelique?"

"It is nearly sunset. We have only the hours of darkness to wait to learn the answer to that question," Octavio offered as encouragement.

Diego walked to the rail and his dark glance slowly swept over the verdant forest of the Yucatán, which stretched out before him. As far as the eye could see, the vivid shades of green extended in a vast sea of endless vegetation. It would have been a soothing scene at a less troubled time, but not now. "We'll not wait until dawn but strike at midnight. If the crew of the *Marie Alise* is drunk now, they'll be unconscious by then. We'll eat supper as soon as the cook can prepare it, then assign men to four boats in groups of eight. Other than the three who died of fever in my lifeboat, how many others did you say were lost?" He rubbed his hand across his forehead, upset that he could not recall that bit of information as readily as he knew he should.

"Five more, sir. We are shorthanded, but the men are so thirsty for vengeance that it won't matter."

"Are the five known to be dead? If not, I'll have a try at finding them when this is finished. I don't want them living out their lives on some tiny island in the Caribbean if I can prevent it."

"They were unaccounted for the night of the storm, Captain. They are lost." Octavio did not want Diego to dwell on such painful thoughts, for he knew the man felt responsible for the loss of the *Diablo* and its five crew members. "We can do no more than say prayers for them when we return to Vera Cruz."

"We will do that then," Diego promised. "As soon as it is dark, we can enter El Lago de Lagartos, lower the boats, and move as close as we dare until it is time to strike."

Diego had forced himself to rest until it was time to begin their raid, but the gentle rocking of the lifeboat made him ill nevertheless. That discomfort was so slight an annoyance however, that he scarcely noticed it. Andres' report had been most accurate. The sounds of merriment aboard the *Marie Alise* carried over the water so clearly that they could make out individual voices in the boisterous singing. While he could not understand the French lyrics, Diego assumed that sea chanteys in any language would have similar themes, mainly the perils of life at sea and the joys of beautiful women of easy virtue.

In the last half hour the activity and noise had diminished markedly, and Diego now whispered to the man at his side. "Our wait is nearly over. Remind the others that I want no one killed if it can be avoided." No one but Yves, and he meant to take care of that hateful barbarian himself, he reflected inwardly. Diego had never consciously plotted a murder before he had had the misfortune to fall into Lucien Dangermond's hands, but that he could now do it so easily did not strike him as the least bit extraordinary. He had fought his share of fights in foreign ports and more than he cared to count at home in Barcelona, but his motive had always been to beat his opponent into submission, never to slaughter him.

He turned to look back over his shoulder again. He was in the first boat and Octavio in the second, and two more boatloads of men lay in reserve at the rear of their line. In such warm weather, the pirates would be asleep on the deck. He planned to sneak aboard, disarm the sentry in the stern himself, then make his way to Lucien's cabin. Either he would meet Yves on the way or he would not, but Angelique would be in his arms before the sun rose to greet the new day, he vowed. He had forced himself to breathe deeply and again go over the actions he would have to take so he could make them without conscious effort when the time came. But at the thought of Angelique, the calm discipline of his thinking erupted in a storm of anguish that flooded his lean frame with a longing so intense he had to fight back his tears. Grasping the hilt of his knife more tightly he strained to hear the last of the pirates' conversation. There was an occasional groan, as if to protest a misplaced step, and then, finally, the silence was broken only by the echo of one man's deep snoring.

Diego counted to one thousand slowly, then tapped the shoulder of the man beside him to send the signal to the men at the oars. The boat sliced through the still waters of the lake silently and swiftly reached the *Marie Alise*. The pirates had carelessly left their rope ladders hanging over the side of the ship and Diego was the first to scramble up and board. He stepped over the men sprawled upon the deck, cautiously making his way to the stern. The man on guard was facing the far shore and dozing. Diego grabbed his rifle at the same instant he struck him a crushing blow across the back of the neck. He caught the unconscious sentry as he fell, slipped a gag over his mouth, tied his hands behind his back, then shoved his limp body out of the way. He could hear his men creeping up the ladder one by one and sat down for a moment to catch his breath. That he had so little stamina disgusted him, but he was too close to setting Angelique free to take the time to rest and he soon pushed himself back up to his feet. It was then he realized it was only excitement that had caused him to be short of breath, not physical exertion. He was again strong enough to carry out any action he might attempt. The secret, he had discovered, was to remain calm, even though he found the anticipation of his reunion with Angelique almost unbearable. Octavio soon came to his side to report that each of the pirates had been gagged, tied, and placed in neat rows upon the deck. Most had not even awakened from the depths of their drunken stupors when they had been bound, and there had been no casualties of any kind.

His knife drawn, Diego now turned toward the captain's quarters. There was no light showing beneath the mate's door and when he tried the latch, the door swung open easily. He hesitated at the doorway, every muscle tensed as he readied himself to spring, but he heard no trace of the heavy breathing noises he had assumed Yves would make while he slept. With Octavio close behind him, he turned to Lucien's door and gently eased it open. "Angelique?" he called breathlessly, but his voice echoed eerily in the empty cabin.

Octavio moved past Diego, fumbled around for a lantern, and swiftly lit it. "Is this her dress here on the bed?" He held up the silk gown for Diego to identify.

"It must be." Diego's gaze darted restlessly about the neatly kept cabin, for he was devastated to find it empty. "Bring me the first man you can sober up enough to question," he ordered, then paced up and down anxiously, ready to slit as many throats as he might have to to learn the truth, but the terrified man who was brought to him took one look at the knife in his hand and fell to his knees, sobbing incoherently.

"Where is my wife?" Diego screamed as he yanked the

478

pirate to his feet. He repeated his question, but he could not understand a word of the wretched captive's high-pitched French. "Angelique, where is she?" he tried again, this time waving the discarded dress for emphasis.

The pirate nodded eagerly as he again attempted to tell Diego what he wished to know.

Realizing his mistake, Octavio apologized hurriedly. "I'll find a man who speaks Spanish, Captain. There must be at least one."

"Take this coward with you!" Diego gave the badly frightened man a shove to send him on his way, then thrust the blade of his knife into the table top simply to avoid the temptation to use it. Left alone, he raised the silk gown to his lips where its softness was too painful a reminder of the beauty who eluded him still. Tossing the garment aside with a bitter oath, he swiftly searched the cabin for others. Finding her clothes still there, he knew she had to be with Lucien and despaired that it would be hours until dawn brought the light he would need to follow their trail.

It took Octavio the better part of an hour, but at last he found a man who could answer Diego's question in an understandable manner. "As always, the blonde is with Dangermond." Seeing the hatred glowing brightly in Diego's eyes, the pirate offered more, hoping to win some concession in return. "I know where their trail begins. I will take you there at dawn."

Diego was not surprised that the man was so eager to cooperate, since he had little choice in the matter, but he did not trust his report until he saw the newly cut trail with his own eyes. Leaving Octavio in charge of their prisoners, he took Octavio, Enrique, and Andres, then chose ten others from the many volunteers to go with them. None had slept since the previous night and the humidity hampered their progress greatly, but they did not slacken their pace or stop to rest until late afternoon. The trail Lucien had cut was so fresh that it was easy to follow, but Diego knew that if they met the pirates returning to the *Marie Alise,* they would have too little room to fight them effectively. "We'll make camp here. Dangermond won't be any more eager to move through this forest at night than we are."

They ate some of the dried beef, cheese, and tortillas they had brought along and washed it down with generous amounts of ale. Too tired to complain about the hardness of the ground, the men then stretched out in the dusty trail to sleep, but Diego took the precaution of posting sentries at each end of their column. He took one of the first shifts himself, for he had no intention of falling victim to a surprise attack as the pirates had. He had so much nervous energy churning inside him that he paced up and down the narrow path with a ceaseless stride, and then, when he was relieved, he slept so poorly he was awake to rouse his small army from their slumber at the first glimmer of dawn.

"We may reach the lost city today or perhaps not, but we must approach it in silence. It is my hope we'll find Dangermond and his men at the *cenote,* intent upon bringing up the treasure from the depths of the pool, and Angelique resting off by herself. If she's in the midst of them, we'll just have to wait in hiding, for I'll not jeopardize her safety for any reason." The men all nodded, easily understanding why Diego would not risk his wife's life with unnecessary heroics.

Intent upon maintaining stealth, Diego came upon the Mayan city so suddenly that morning that he barely had time to raise his hand to halt the column before they stumbled out into the clearing. One moment the trees and vines shrouded their view and in the next they were bathed in bright sunlight. The buildings, which faced a central square, were all overgrown, hidden beneath three centuries of vegetation, but the uniqueness of their form was still visible through the tangled vines. Lucien had not bothered to clear the trail any further but had simply trampled down the brush in his eagerness to reach the *cenote*. Diego and his men stepped carefully along the twisting path the pirates had left, straining for the sounds of human voices to guide them. Then, with the same abruptness with which they had reached the clearing, they came upon the pool.

Lucien was kneeling at the water's edge, staring into the clear pool with a fascination so deep he did not notice that the birds that had filled the surrounding trees had suddenly taken wing. He had used nets affixed to poles his men had fashioned from long branches to drag the sacred waters and had brought up a steadily growing mound of objects. None had proved to be of gold, but he was certain the precious substance was there, just waiting for him to retrieve it. Calling to the man at his right, he urged him to again lower his net. "Try nearer to the edge. That's it. Go more slowly this time. Gently. It is a priceless treasure we're after, and we must coax it to the surface. Yes, that's it."

Diego instructed the others to circle the pirates' camp. He moved carefully to remain concealed while he kept Lucien always in sight. He counted eight pirates and, making certain none were on guard, he edged closer. From the animated conversation and occasional burst of excited laughter, he knew they had been successful in their efforts to dredge the pool, but where was Angelique? He found the pit they had dug to build a cooking fire and the area they had cleared in which to sleep, but he saw no sign of his dear wife. Or Yves, he suddenly realized with a sharp stab of terror.

Returning quickly to his men, he whispered his commands. "We'll move in close, but only watch their actions for now. If Angelique does not appear within the hour, then we'll attack. But leave Dangermond to me. He is the blond, and he's mine." Exhaling slowly, he warned them to be cautious, then made his way back through the dense underbrush, posting his men every few yards. He took the place nearest to the *cenote* himself and, crouching in the shade of an ancient *alamo* tree, he observed the pirates' efforts to rob the Mayan gods of their treasures.

Sweat poured down his back and the muscles of his legs soon began to throb with painful cramps, but he waited as patiently as he could until he was certain Angelique was not being kept nearby. Rising, he lifted his rifle to his shoulder and, pointing it at the back of Lucien's head, he stepped out into the clearing.

"Stand up very slowly, Dangermond, with your hands in the air," he called with a menacing snarl.

Lucien leapt to his feet, meaning to dart into the underbrush until he saw rifles aimed at his heart from every direction. Having no choice consequently, he complied with Diego's command and turned to face him. "Captain Aragon. Did my attempt upon your life fail, or have you merely risen from the dead to haunt me?"

Not taken in by the pirate's charming smile, Diego took a step closer. "We had a bargain: our freedom for the map that brought you here. I mean only to see that you keep your word. Where is my wife?"

Lucien shrugged. "That I do not know. She and Yves decided to take a walk and unfortunately neither returned. What perils exist in this forest I can only imagine. I am sorry you have come so far for nothing."

Dissatisfied with his sorry response, Diego lowered his rifle. He swung the butt in a wide arc and struck Lucien such a vicious blow to the stomach that the pirate fell to his knees gasping for breath. Without taking his eyes from the villain, he called to Gustavo, "Bind the others' hands behind their backs and lead them to the side one at a time, but leave this bastard here with me."

Hoping to bribe his captor, Lucien staggered to his feet and began to describe the objects they had recovered from the sacred waters. "We have found several stone idols of

482

exquisite craftsmanship if hideous design, many pieces of pottery, beads, and surely there is gold here too. Would you care to see what we've found?"

Diego shook his head and waited until Lucien's men had all been led away before he spoke again to Gustavo. "I want his hands tied now. Very firmly, please."

Fear crossed Lucien's countenance only briefly as Gustavo wrapped the cord so tightly around his wrists that it cut into his flesh painfully. "We've not gotten the gold yet, Aragon! We can't stop now when there will most certainly be great wealth for both of us to share!"

"How you can imagine I would consent to being your partner in any venture is beyond belief." Diego handed his rifle to Gustavo to hold and, making a fist, struck Lucien on the chin with all the force he could put behind the savage blow. The pirate's head snapped back and, as he staggered, Diego grabbed his shoulders to spin him around and forced him to his knees. Holding him at the water's edge, he asked again, "Where is my wife?" Without waiting for a reply, he pushed Lucien's face into the *cenote* and held him there until the drowning man's efforts to pull free had grown quite feeble. He then yanked him away from the pool and waited while he coughed and retched, fighting to clear the water from his lungs and fill them again with air.

"Where is Angelique? Where is she?" He asked once again and, as Lucien's gray eyes grew pale with terror, he shoved his face back into the *cenote* and held him under again.

When Lucien was pulled from the *cenote* a second time, he began to scream hysterically. He choked, gagging, as he began to sob, "She's dead! Both she and Yves are dead!"

"The hell they are!" Diego left the pirate's head underwater until his body was limp before he yanked him out the third time. When Lucien could finally draw enough breath to speak, he shrieked hoarsely, "I swear it! She is dead!"

"The Maya sacrificed slaves, Dangermond—men they'd captured in battle, just as I have captured you. I wonder if they slit their throats first and then tossed their bodies into the *cenote* or if—"

"Angelique is dead!" Lucien screamed once again, squirming in a pathetic attempt to escape Diego's firm grasp.

Disgusted, Diego rose to his feet and turned his back on the sniveling pirate. Retrieving his rifle, he turned to the line of men they had captured and asked the first, "If you'd like to live to see another dawn, I suggest you speak the truth, even though this miserable coward finds it impossible. Where is Angelique?"

Though he recognized the sound of the pretty blonde's name, the man had no way to reply to his question and looked toward a man standing farther down the line with a silent plea for help. After a brief hesitation, that man replied in broken Spanish, "It is true. She fell."

Diego held his breath as he clenched his fist at his side, ready to beat to death every one of this cowardly band if he had to in order to finally gain the truth. Turning back to Lucien, he explained tersely, "I'm taking only this man with me. If he does not lead me to her grave, I am coming back to finish with you. If by some chance he does show me her body, then you will beg me to kill you before I'm finished, do you understand? If you can remember any prayers, recite them while I'm gone." He placed three guards around Lucien and, forcing the other prisoners to sit in a tight circle, he left the rest of his men to watch them. "If anyone moves, shoot him. It will be no loss." Taking the talkative captive, he pushed him toward the path that led back the way they had come.

"Do not blame me! She fell!" the frightened man exclaimed.

Diego ignored his words and forced him to keep up a brisk pace as they followed the trail. When they reached the wide clearing the pirates had cut to spend their first night, the man turned around. "We must go back. We have come too far."

"No more mistakes!" Diego cautioned sternly. "I want the truth, not more lies!" He refused to believe that Angelique was dead. He had heard that tale before and he would not fall for it again.

"Help me. It is where two trails cross. You will see."

They traversed the path more slowly this time and Diego saw where it widened slightly at the same time his prisoner did.

"She ran away. Yves followed. Come and see." The man's eyes were alight with hope now that he had found the right trail.

Diego pushed the man ahead of him, for the haphazard path was easy to follow still. He stopped several times, searching for evidence that his wife had come this way, but he found nothing he could identify. When at last they reached the small clearing where Yves had fallen to his death, he stopped well away from the hole. The ground was trampled with the pirates' countless footprints, but he tried to imagine what could have happened.

"So she ran away, did she? With Yves running after her?" He shoved his captive toward the gaping hole. "Try the ground for me. Jump up and down. I want to see what force is required to cause it to break away as it did."

"Captain Aragon, I beg you . . ." the horrified man began to plead as he gazed into the jaws of the seemingly bottomless pit.

"Go on." Diego raised his rifle to his shoulder, taking careful aim. "Just walk toward the hole. If you start to fall, I'll catch you. Now move!"

Terrified that death faced him with every step, the man inched toward the opening in the sandy limestone. He took steps so tiny that he seemed not to be moving at all until Diego reached out to give him a forceful shove. He fell then, sprawled at the edge of the yawning opening, but the ground

485

supported his weight and held without more limestone crumbling away.

Satisfied with the results of his experiment, Diego motioned for the trembling man to rise. He then skirted the edge of the clearing, searching for the tracks he hoped the careless pirates had not obscured. Finally he found what he was searching for: one set of prints of bare feet followed by another small enough to have been his wife's. The tracks kept to the edge of the clearing and headed off down the trail at the far end. A smile of relief graced his handsome features as Diego turned back to his prisoner. "All right. I know where to find her now. Let's go back."

"Find her? But the woman is dead!"

Diego did not bother to argue. He marched the man back to the overgrown city and walked up to Lucien, who still sat huddled where Diego had left him. "Angelique is no more dead than I am, you miserable liar. Now get on your feet. You're going back to the *Marie Alise.* I want you to have the night to repent for your crimes. Then, when I return with my wife, I'll decide your fate."

Confused by the Spaniard's astonishing news, Lucien rose slowly. "But surely Angelique is dead. She must be."

Diego smiled with real satisfaction as he shook his head, not about to reveal why he held a different view. "Where are the artifacts you found?" he asked instead.

"They're over here, Captain," Enrique called. "They have a bag of things here."

Diego walked over to the heavy canvas bag and, without even glancing at its contents, he picked it up and hurled it into the center of the *cenote,* where it floated a few seconds, then filled with water and sank slowly out of sight. "Robbing a sacred well is the same as desecrating a church, Dangermond. I'll not disturb gods so long asleep. Let them keep their treasures. Angelique is all I need."

Shoving the disheveled pirate into the line of prisoners, Diego told his men to gather up every item that lay spread

486

about the camp and, after instructing them to load that equipment upon the captives' backs, he gave the order to march. As the line began to move, he looked back at the sparkling blue water of the sacred pool and crossed himself quickly, praying for the blessing of the Lord as well as that of the mighty Kukulcán.

Chapter XXVII

Diego circled the village slowly, watching the daily routine of the Indians with scant interest as he searched for Angelique. There was a new hut standing with the others. Could that have been built especially for her? he wondered. Intrigued by that possibility, he edged even closer and, taking cover behind the dense foliage, he knelt and waited for his wife to appear. He had gotten such an early start that he knew it was possible she was not even awake yet. He rubbed his hand down his cheek and over his chin, glad he had been able to shave before seeing her. He had never been so concerned about his appearance before he had met her, but now it was of vital importance to him to look his best. The best that he still could, he thought ruefully, but in the next instant his spirits soared as he saw his lovely bride leave the new hut.

Taking a deep breath, Diego rose slowly. He wanted to call her name but hesitated as he saw that, unlike the other women's simple homespun shifts, she was wearing a flowing white gown with a delicately embroidered border. They had dressed her like a princess, he thought and, as he watched her move about the small village, he saw that the Indians treated her with great respect, as if she truly were one, or perhaps even a goddess. These people would be descendants of the

Maya, a once proud and powerful race. They would have little left but their gods, he realized, and seeing a tall, slender, blue-eyed blonde, they would quite naturally assume her origins to be divine. They would scarcely welcome him then, when his intention would clearly be to take her away.

He swore under his breath at this new complication to his plans and crouched down again to wait. He would remain hidden until dark if he had to, but he meant to get Angelique away without causing a bloodbath in which she might easily be injured.

Fortunately, he did not have the entire day to wait, for Angelique soon left the others. Diego moved stealthily through the vines to the path she had taken and, after making certain she had not been followed, he rushed down the trail after her.

Angelique removed her garments and folded them neatly before stepping into the cool waters of the *cenote*. She had become very spoiled by the Indians who had befriended her, but as she splashed the water about, taking her morning bath, she knew she was now rested enough to undertake the walk to the coast. She would need the boy, or some other competent guide to accompany her, and as she dipped her long, blonde curls into the water, she wondered how she could make such a request when she still had no effective way to communicate.

In the next instant she heard a branch snap beneath a careless footstep and spun around to see who had followed her. The unexpected sight of her husband was a great shock. "Diego!" she called excitedly, but then she moved out toward the center of the pool, embarrassed that he had found her nude.

Diego laughed as he knelt by the side of the *cenote*. "You have never been so shy with me, Angelique, and this is no time to begin such displays of modesty. You must come out and dress quickly. I want to be gone before your presence is missed."

Angelique swallowed nervously. She was overjoyed to see Diego but did not understand his request. "I cannot simply leave without telling the Indians good-bye. They have been so good to me and I cannot allow them to think me ungrateful."

"I can see they have been extremely good to you. Undoubtedly they are simple folk who believe you to be a goddess. They have certainly dressed you as one." He picked up her gown to examine the intricate design decorating the hem. "Loving you so dearly, what do you think they would do to me if they were to discover I am taking you away?"

Frightened by that thought, Angelique looked up the path with an anxious glance, but no one was coming. "Turn around please, and then I'll come out."

Diego frowned as he rose to his feet. "Turn around? Did Lucien ever bother to show you such courtesy?"

Angelique blushed deeply at his taunt, for Lucien Dangermond was the very last person on earth she wanted to discuss with her husband. She remained where she was, however, until Diego finally realized she would not move until he turned his back. The glance that he gave her then was a most unsympathetic one, and she was near tears as she patted herself dry and hurried to dress. Hoping to improve his mood, she explained her plan. "I meant to leave here in a day or two, Diego. I thought that if I walked to the coast I could find someone who would be willing to take me to Vera Cruz. I didn't mean to remain here forever."

Angelique's expression was so very contrite that Diego was ashamed he had spoken sharply to her. He had wanted her to leap into his arms, to cover his face with kisses, and she did not even seem to be happy to see him. He was hurt and confused but knew they had no time to discuss anything now, when each second of delay increased the risk that someone would come along and try to stop him from taking her away. "Well, I have come to escort you to Vera Cruz myself, and since I'd rather not fight any sort of battle with your Indian friends, let's hurry."

He grabbed her hand and started off in the direction of the village but swiftly chose a path that led to the south instead. He was rushing now, he knew, but he did not stop to allow her a chance to rest until he was certain they were not being followed.

Breathless, Angelique clung to Diego's arm as she looked back over her shoulder. "How did you find me?"

"One of Lucien's men led me to the spot where Yves had fallen to his death. I saw that your trail continued, even though the pirates did not."

Angelique was amazed by so logical an explanation. "But there are so many trails, paths that intersect and double back, that—"

Diego sighed impatiently, thinking that surely she had rested long enough if she had the breath to argue. "Do you think I am like a fish out of water when I leave the sea, unable to accomplish even so simple a task as tracking my own wife?"

She had not meant to insult him again as clearly she had, and she reached up to kiss his cheek lightly. "Please do not misunderstand me. I know you are endlessly clever. Now let us hurry before the Indians realize I am gone." She did her best to keep up with his long strides, but she was exhausted by the time they reached the edge of the forest where the trail ended at the lake.

Diego did not bother to explain where he had gotten a ship or his plans for the *Marie Alise* as he whisked Angelique aboard the *Coronado*. Amid the cheers of his men, he lifted her into his arms and carried her quickly into his cabin, where, despite her initial shyness, he hoped to have a far more lavish reunion. "I have brought all your things here. Perhaps you would like to bathe again and change your clothes later." He pulled her into his arms then, nearly crushing her with the enthusiasm of his embrace.

Angelique bit her lower lip savagely to keep from crying, but that was what she truly wished to do—simply to weep—for the horror of what they had each suffered at Lucien's hands weighed heavily upon her mind. "What has happened to Dangermond and his band of rogues? Have you captured them?"

"Ask me no questions now, Angelique, not when you are at last mine again. I don't want to waste another moment when I've missed you so desperately," Diego responded hoarsely, his expression filled with longing.

Angelique tried to relax against him, but the joy radiating from his sparkling eyes did not allay her anxiety. She dared ask no more questions when she had no way to answer any he might pose. She stood on her tiptoes to touch his lips lightly with hers, that hesitant kiss her only show of affection.

Misunderstanding the cause of her reticence, Diego gripped her shoulders firmly and pushed her away. "I know I am no longer handsome, but does the mere sight of me repel you now?"

"Not handsome?" Angelique asked in wonder, her pretty blue-violet gaze filled with confusion. "I have always thought you far more than merely handsome, and you still are," she attempted to reassure him, but she saw by the grim set of his jaw that she had failed.

"If it is not the difference in my appearance that disturbs you so greatly, then what is it?"

Angelique was so distracted that she barely understood his question. "I am not disturbed, only surprised by your sudden appearance this morning. Dangermond told me you were dead, but I believed you to be in Vera Cruz and—"

Diego pulled her back into his arms, muffling her rambling explanation with his lips. He kissed her hungrily, wanting to arouse the wildness of the passion he knew she possessed. Her long gown had a gathered neckline and he quickly loosened the bow so the soft garment would slide to the floor. He had not expected her to be wearing her own lace-trimmed lingerie underneath and swore as he reached for the ribbon ties on her chemise. "I have done little but live for this moment, and now I am so clumsy that—"

"You have never been clumsy," Angelique assured him in a breathless whisper. This is Diego, she kept reminding herself, my own dear husband, and there is no reason to be afraid of him. And yet, unaccountably, fear filled her throat with a strangling terror. No questions, he had insisted, but suddenly she wanted to talk, to discuss anything rather than join him in making love, when she was so very frightened and did not even understand why. "Please tell me what has happened," she begged.

"Later," Diego responded impatiently, at last succeeding in freeing her from the lacy undergarments. He carried her to his bunk and, after placing her upon it, gently struggled to shake off his own clothing. He then stretched out beside her and pulled her into his arms. Her soft curls framed her face with a sunlit halo, and he kissed her sweet features again and again, longing to make their reunion an unforgettable feast of love. But, to his amazement, Angelique's response was still so cool that he drew back. "Since you ran away from Dangermond, I know it's not him you want. Now tell me, what is wrong?"

Angelique did not even know where to begin to describe the emotions that tore at her soul, for they seemed so very inappropriate. "I have missed you terribly. Truly I have. The days since the storm have been an endless nightmare. Perhaps I just need some time to be certain the worst is now over." When she laid her hands upon his shoulders, her fingertips brushed the scars made by Yves's vicious beating and she quickly lowered her palms to her sides, sickened by the memory of that day.

"Time?" Diego asked incredulously. He attempted unsuccessfully to quell the deep anger that her bizarre request aroused. "No. Tomorrow may never come. There is only now, only this very moment, and I'll not waste it." He knew how to lead a woman from hesitant kisses to the heights of passion, and he wanted no less from his beautiful bride. His need was simply too great to allow him to grant the favor she had requested and he kissed her very gently, praying such tenderness would show her all the consideration she desired. But while she did not resist his affection, she was so different from the loving creature he had first met in a moonlit garden that he could not have been more deeply disappointed. "If it is Teresa who has made you so angry with me, I did not even touch her!" he finally exclaimed.

Startled by the loud announcement, Angelique could at first not even recall the woman. "Who?" she asked curiously.

"If you've somehow managed to forget the silly wench, I'll not remind you." He sat up then and reached for his clothes, disgusted that he could not interest her in making love. But to his surprise, Angelique reached out to catch his arm.

"No, please don't go. Please don't leave me."

Touched by the note of desperation in her voice, Diego returned to her side, again drawing her into his arms. "Can't you make up your mind? I will not go since you asked me to stay so sweetly, but—"

Angelique slipped her fingers through the curls at his nape, pulling his mouth down to hers to silence his complaint. She knew exactly what he wanted in exchange for staying and she drew him near to attempt to comply. But she could not raise the curtain of ice she had wrapped around her heart to protect herself from Lucien's evil lust. She realized that Diego deserved her trust and a true expression of the love she felt for him, but there, on board his ship, the surroundings were too similar to those of Lucien's cabin. The horrid memories of the hours she had spent in the pirate's bunk gave her no peace, and the sweetness of Diego's gentle loving did not touch her.

Perplexed as well as hurt by his wife's withdrawn mood,

Diego vowed to wipe the memory of Lucien Dangermond from her mind. He wanted to possess the delightful creature who had once filled his heart with love and his bed with endless joy. How much time would she require to be his wife again—a few weeks, several years, a lifetime? The scars he bore were clearly visible, but perhaps hers, though unseen, were far deeper, he reflected. He combed her curls softly with his fingertips as she rested quietly in his arms, content for the moment simply to hold her until finally sleep overtook him, but it brought none of the visions of pleasure he had recalled so fondly while they had been apart.

Angelique was the first to awaken and, in the slanted rays of the afternoon sun, she looked down at her husband, sorry he had suffered so greatly for loving her. The scar through his brow would not fade this time and when she brushed his hair away from his forehead, she saw the line of sutures Dr. Flores had yet to remove. She leaned down to kiss his temple lightly, ashamed she had only added to his pain. "I love you," she whispered softly. "I love you more dearly than you will ever know."

A tear splashed upon his cheek and Diego awoke abruptly, startled to find his wife still in so downcast a mood. He pulled her close to his heart to comfort her anew, but she soon drew away.

"It is not simply the fact that I adore you that makes you so handsome to me, Diego. Any woman would think your looks appealing. Any woman would."

Diego was mystified by her praise and did not understand why she would be in tears if what she said were really true. "Thank you. But now it is time I got up and finished what must be done. I'll bring water for your bath, and then I want you to come up on deck."

"But why?" Angelique asked suspiciously, for there was something in the abruptness of his manner that warned her to be wary.

Diego leaned down to kiss her lips gently. "You'll have to

wait and see, but don't keep me waiting."

Lucien had been allowed to bathe and dress in clean clothes that morning, but then he had been left alone to agonize for hours over what punishment Diego would wish to inflict. He had paced up and down his cabin without ceasing—walked miles it had seemed—until finally Octavio came to escort him from the *Marie Alise* to the *Coronado*. When Diego greeted him briefly, then handed him a fencing foil, he thought the Spaniard must be joking. "Have you missed our sport so greatly?" he asked sarcastically, and then, finally noticing Angelique standing off to one side, his arrogance vanished. "My God, you are alive!" he exclaimed hoarsely, his eyes wide with surprise.

Angelique did not bother to reply. She returned his rapt stare without any show of emotion, but her indifference as always only inspired him to increase his efforts to impress her favorably.

"My wife is indeed alive and well, no thanks to you, Dangermond, and there is something I'd like her to see this afternoon. I've removed the buttons from your foils, so this time we can have a decisive match, our final competition."

Angelique watched Lucien's smile grow to a vicious smirk, for he was now certain he was in no danger of being hurt. She wanted to call out to her husband to stop such deadly sport before it began, but rather than give Lucien the pleasure of seeing them argue, she remained silent. She watched the two men touch the tips of their foils in a brief salute to show that each was ready to begin, but what she observed then came as only a partial surprise.

Diego's usual clumsiness was gone, replaced by both skill and a cunning grace. His form was superb and his talent clearly superior to that of the Frenchman. Her suspicions had been correct all along, she realized instantly, for Diego did indeed know how to fence with the effortless agility of a

496

fully trained master. He had learned each of Lucien's weaknesses and played upon them now, thrusting the wicked point of his foil ever nearer the villain's heart. What she was watching was not a fair contest or a duel to the death, but an execution. Growing faint with revulsion, she moved further away, keeping her hands clutched tightly to the rail for support.

Clearly Diego meant to kill Lucien—she was positive of it—and he had wanted her to be there to see the man die. He struck at will, first drawing blood from the Frenchman's right thigh, then his shoulder. Lucien did not beg for mercy, though blood stained his shirt-sleeve and dripped down his arm, making his grip slippery and his parries weak. He fought for his life more bravely than she would have thought possible, despite the look of terror in his eyes, but Diego was able to cut him at will, while he could not inflict the smallest wound in his own defense.

Diego might have insisted she come up on deck, but Angelique had no intention of remaining there to see any more of the gruesome spectacle he had planned. Though she hurried back to his cabin, she could still hear the sounds of the men's footsteps as they moved across the deck. Their motions had a smooth rhythm with a staccato beat, which echoed that of her wildly beating heart. She covered her ears in a vain attempt to shut out the sounds of the horrible sport taking place under the clear afternoon sky, but her imagination supplied the scene in far too realistic detail. She heard Lucien's anguished cry as Diego's blade pierced his chest, then the dull thud when his body slipped to the deck and lay still.

It was not until that very instant that she realized how truly violent her husband could be. There was a side to his nature that allowed him to be every bit as cruel as Lucien. He could be just as arrogant and demanding, every bit as proud and dangerous, as the pirate had ever been and she sank down upon his bunk, shivering as though chilled despite the uncomfortable warmth of the Yucatán.

It was not until he was certain Lucien was dead that Diego turned and discovered Angelique had fled the scene he had prepared especially for her benefit. He had wanted to show her which of them was truly the better man. Did she no longer care? he wondered with building anger. Infuriated that she had not even cared enough about him to wait to see which of them won, he hurled the foil he had used over the side into the lake and shouted angrily to Octavio. "Wrap his body in canvas and take it below. I'll give that much to Muñoz, at least."

Octavio acknowledged his command and, after seeing to the task, had the deck scrubbed clean of the villain's blood. He then approached Diego cautiously, seeing that his mood was far from good. "We are ready to sail. I will take half the men over to the *Marie Alise* and follow your course to Vera Cruz."

Diego hesitated a long moment before speaking, but then he made his decision quickly. "No. You stay aboard the *Coronado*. I want to command the *Marie Alise* myself."

"But I thought that since you moved your wife's belongings here, you—"

"Angelique will remain where she is," Diego interrupted brusquely. "I am the one who's leaving. Since the afternoon breeze is a strong one, let's make a race of it. The first ship back to port wins, and its crew must be treated to dinner and all the ale they can drink by the other." Without further explanation of his challenge, Diego assembled the crew and, taking half their number, left promptly for the pirate ship.

Angelique heard the sound of the anchor's being raised and tried to wipe away her tears so Diego would not know she had been crying. The Azteca gods were sitting upon the desk, their carved smiles wide, and she thought it remarkable that they had survived to be returned to Diego in such perfect condition. "You little creatures are going to find your lives very dull now, I'm afraid." She spoke softly to them, not

498

wanting her husband to walk in and discover her conversing with the idols as though they were expected to respond. "At least I pray our lives will now be placid ones." She closed her eyes again and sighed softly, worried still that she and Diego had found the horrors of their separation so difficult to forget. In a few moments she again drifted off to sleep, lulled by the gentle rocking motion of the *Coronado* as it moved out into the open sea.

Octavio juggled the supper tray as he knocked lightly upon the cabin door. When Angelique attempted to cover a wide yawn as she greeted him, he apologized for waking her. "I am so sorry. It did not occur to me that you would be napping. Your supper is ready and I did not want it to grow cold."

Angelique stepped aside to allow the mate to carry the tray to the table. "The Indians with whom I've been staying all slept in hammocks. I found it impossible to sleep in one though, for I worried constantly about falling out. I guess I'm just overtired still," she explained. "Sailors sleep in hammocks quite comfortably, don't they?"

"Oh yes, but it takes some getting used to at first." Octavio glanced around the cabin, stalling for time, but he decided it would be best just to blurt out the truth, and so he did. "Your husband is aboard the *Marie Alise*. We're having a race, you see, and—"

"What?" It was then Angelique noticed that the tray held dinner for only one. She had to gasp for breath, so shaken was she to learn Diego would leave her after they had just been reunited. Perhaps she had not reacted with the warmth he had expected, but she would have soon. Had he no patience at all with her—no consideration for her feelings? She slumped down upon the edge of the bunk, making no effort to hide the hot rush of tears that welled up in her eyes and spilled over her thick lashes.

"*Señora* Aragon, you must not upset yourself." Ashamed now that he had been so tactless, Octavio knelt at her side and reached for her hands. She was such a delicate young woman, so blond and pretty, and he could not bear to see her unhappy after all he knew she had suffered. "We will be in Vera Cruz in a few days. Then you will be with your husband again. Do not despair, I beg of you."

The mate was so sincere in his plea that Angelique was sorry she had not been able to hide her disappointment in her husband, and she attempted to smile. "I am sorry to be so silly. It is only that I wish Diego had told me what he planned to do before he left me here alone. That is all."

"But you are not alone!" Octavio protested. "I will see you lack for nothing," he promised.

"Thank you. I'm certain I will be fine." Straightening her shoulders proudly, Angelique patted his hands and then stood up. "I don't want my supper to grow cold. If you have the time to join me for a meal, please do."

It was such an unexpected invitation that Octavio blushed deeply as he scrambled to his feet. "Oh no. That would not be proper, *Señora* Aragon. I am no more than the mate. I cannot share your table."

"With Diego gone, you are the captain of this ship, are you not?" Angelique pointed out logically.

"Well, yes, that is true. However—"

"The captain is supposed to dine with his passengers, Octavio. Now you needn't apologize if you are too busy to entertain me tonight, but I shall look forward to your company whenever you have the time to dine with me." She walked with him the short distance to the door and did her best to smile again as she bid him good night, but the moment she was alone her expression became a determined one.

By the time she had finished her supper, she was extremely angry with the husband who had insulted her so rudely. "It is not your appearance that has changed for the worse, Diego. It is simply your manners!" she exclaimed to the idols who seemed to smile in agreement. "Do you think I'll let the man neglect me like this? Well, you're certainly wrong if you do!" Then, realizing that the little stone creatures had never been alive, she laughed at her own foolishness. They would soon reach Vera Cruz, as Octavio had promised, and there was no point in brooding over being left alone, when she could be using her time far more wisely to make plans for the future.

Though Angelique, who was grateful to again have a bed, slept soundly that night, Diego was no more comfortable than he had been the night before, when he had attempted to sleep on the narrow trail he had followed through the forest of the Yucatán. That Angelique had shared with Dangermond the bed he now occupied revolted him so intensely that he was certain he would become physically ill. He got up, dressed, and went up on deck to contemplate the view of the stars rather than recall what had taken place in the cabin he had chosen to occupy alone. The sails of the *Coronado* could be seen in the distance. She was running only slightly behind the *Marie Alise* and, giving his full attention to the race, Diego soon increased his lead to a commanding one. The satisfaction he derived was slight, but it was enough to exhaust him sufficiently to enable him to find sleep at last, regardless of whose bed he had chosen to occupy.

The port of Vera Cruz was busy in early spring. With so many ships in the harbor, Diego's actions were not only foolhardy but dangerous as well, but the *Marie Alise* swept through the crowded harbor in full sail before finally coming to rest at one of the docks owned by the Aragon Line. His crew gave a wild cheer, ecstatic to have won their race with the *Coronado,* but Diego found the victory a hollow one. It was only Angelique he wanted to hear cheering for him and she was not even there, but by the time he had bathed and dressed, Colonel Muñoz was.

501

Not ashamed of his actions, Diego wasted no time making excuses to the obnoxious officer. "It was a matter of honor," he explained. "It was a fair fight, and I won. I will turn over Dangermond's body to you the moment the *Coronado* appears. If you wish to arrest me for the pirate's death, then do so, but you know that no jury will convict me of murder."

Not pleased to see the evaporation of the chance for glory he had been certain would be his, Ignacio found it difficult to find his voice for a few seconds. He would not be so foolish as to threaten to try Diego Aragon for a pirate's murder, especially not when the circumstances indicated that his actions had been those that any other gentleman would also have taken. "Let me say only that I regret that the villain did not live to be executed here, Captain, but I will see that the reward offered for the man is given to you immediately."

Diego raised a brow quizzically, surprised the officer had given him no problems whatsoever. "That is very kind of you, Colonel. I will place the money in the fund my father maintains to aid the widows and orphans of our men lost at sea."

"But it is a most generous reward," Ignacio protested with a frown, sorry he had not earned a portion of it himself as he had hoped to do.

Disgusted by the man's greed, Diego merely shook his head. "Then that is all the more reason why it should go to those who will appreciate it the most. Now, if you have no further questions, I'll turn over the prisoners we have aboard. Then I'd like to make arrangements for my wife's lodgings, so she is not kept waiting once the *Coronado* arrives."

"Of course. I have brought men to escort the pirates to jail. If you will notify me when your other ship arrives, I will see to it that Dangermond's body is collected promptly." With a crisp salute, the colonel returned to his office, where he took out the bottle of brandy he kept for just such emergencies and poured himself a stiff drink to assuage the bitterness of his disappointment. Unfortunately, he got drunk long before he forgot how close he had come to the promotion he had been certain would be his when he personally captured Lucien Dangermond.

Diego had not bothered to ask Colonel Muñoz if he were still under suspicion for the murder of Eduardo Marquez, but since the officer had not mentioned it himself, he felt no desire to remind him of the ridiculous charge. Once alone, he made his way quickly to the villa where he usually stayed when in Vera Cruz and, after satisfying himself that it would be comfortable for his wife, he returned to the harbor where he paced the deck of the *Marie Alise,* impatienty waiting for Octavio's vessel to arrive. He had done his best to set a brisk pace, but he had not realized he had gained more than an hour's advantage. When he saw Teresa coming toward him, he cursed softly, not caring if she heard him or not.

"Good morning, Captain Aragon." The dark-eyed beauty greeted him warmly despite the abruptness of his dismissal the last time they had spoken together. "I hope you have not forgotten your promise to find me a good job. While I can be a very fine maid, there are many other things I do better." She came even closer to look up at him with a seductive gaze.

Exasperated with her for disturbing him before he had even had time to welcome his wife to Vera Cruz, Diego frowned angrily. "I never go back on my word, Teresa, but surely you did not expect me to find you work at a moment's notice. I will need a few days to secure a position for you."

Casting a flirtatious glance at the men lounging about the deck, Teresa licked her lips slowly before she asked coyly, "Where is your wife?"

"Unfortunately, she is aboard the same ship as Gustavo. I will tell him you came here to look for him. He knows where to find you, doesn't he?" Diego inclined his head in a mock bow, hoping she would recognize his dismissal for what it was.

"Yes, he does, but I think I will wait for him here." Teresa tossed her long hair as she turned and took up a position by the rail, her pose most provocative.

"I'd rather you waited elsewhere," Diego informed her coldly.

"Why? Will your wife be jealous?" Teresa laughed at the possibility as though it were most amusing. "Surely she does not expect you to be faithful to her now. Why don't we wait in your cabin? I promise to please you, and neither your wife nor Gustavo need ever know."

Diego was so shocked by her crude invitation that he scarcely knew how to reply. His first impulse was to wipe the wide smile from Teresa's lips with the back of his hand, but she was, after all, a woman, if a brazen one, and he did no more than speak sharply to her. "You will leave now. Don't make the mistake of ever coming to look for me again either. I will tell Gustavo where you might apply for work and it will be up to you to impress your prospective employers more favorably than you have impressed me."

Disappointed that her charms had again failed to sway him, Teresa backed away slowly. "Why are you so angry, Captain, if what I say doesn't tempt you?"

"The only thing you tempt me to do, Teresa, is to beat some sense into you. Now be gone before I lose what little hold I still have on my temper!"

Diego was so involved in his argument with the sultry brunette that he did not notice that the *Coronado* had finally entered the harbor. As the ship approached the dock next to the *Marie Alise,* Angelique had come out on deck, but she found the sight of her husband speaking with Teresa most disconcerting. She saw only the pretty girl's wide smile and seductive gestures and wondered why Diego had insisted there was nothing between them when there so obviously was. She turned away, having no wish to spy upon her husband. She would not call him a liar or ever mention Teresa's name, but she was hurt to think he had not told her the truth about what had happened when they had been Lucien's prisoners. He knew exactly what had happened to her. Why did he think she would blame him for anything he had done?

"*Señora* Aragon?" Octavio did not understand Angelique's pained expression when only moments before she had seemed so anxious to meet her husband. He took her arm and again led her to the rail. He waved to Diego, who was now standing alone on the deck of the *Marie Alise*. "He will come aboard the moment I have lowered the gangplank. I should have known I had no chance to beat him, but still I gave it my best try."

Angelique made a sympathetic response as she continued to stare at her husband. He seemed to be in no better mood than he had been when they had parted and she had hoped his greeting would be a most enthusiastic one. She lifted her hand to wave, her gesture hesitant, and he returned the salute before turning away. "I have not packed anything. I did not know whether or not we would be staying aboard." With that excuse, Angelique returned to the cabin she had occupied alone and, sitting down upon the bunk, she waited for Diego to come for her, assuming that he would want to meet where they would not have to pretend emotions they did not feel just for his crew's benefit.

Diego paused only an instant to tease Octavio about their bet, then he made his way hurriedly to the captain's cabin. Angelique had left the door ajar and he stepped inside without knocking. "Are you ready to go?" he asked after giving her no more than the briefest smile.

"Yes, I suppose I am. That is, I really don't want the clothes Lucien gave me to wear. This gown the Indians made

505

for me is far prettier anyway. So there's nothing to pack really." She knew she was barely coherent and was sorry, but she could not seem to hide her anger any other way.

"It is a pity you lost all the pretty clothes I had made for you, but we'll simply order more. There are fine seamstresses here in Vera Cruz too. Now, do not give your lack of wardrobe another thought, my pet. Let me take you home." Diego extended his hand and breathed a sigh of relief when she rose to take it. He drew her near and gave her a warm hug, afraid she would pull away if he attempted a more demonstrative show of affection.

"Where is home to be?" Angelique finally thought to ask as they left the ship.

"A villa I have rented." Since she actually seemed interested in where they would live, he described the house in detail as they rode there in a hired carriage. "The houses here look very much like those of Barcelona, don't you agree? Perhaps it is only the whitewashed walls and red tile roofs, but it looks like home to me."

While they traveled away from the docks toward the residential part of the city, Angelique was curious as always, though she tried to sit back and relax as she looked out at the passing scenery. "Why yes, this does look remarkably like Spain, only everything is of more recent construction. It's very pretty."

Diego kept her hand tucked against his side as they traveled. Her fingers were cool and suddenly he remembered her wedding ring. "I forgot to bring your jewelry. Well, no matter. It will be safe until I can return to fetch it."

Recalling that the beauty of the sparkling sapphires had been marred with blood the last time she had seen them, Angelique could not suppress a shudder. "Yes, I shall be happy to have them returned to me, but until I have more suitable gowns, I shall not need to wear precious gems. They would look foolish with this simple dress."

Diego had to agree, but while they seemed to be talking easily, it was about nothing of any importance, and he could see that Angelique was no happier than he. He could feel her tension and feared he was the cause. He had already sent a message to Dr. Flores asking him to meet them at the villa, for he wanted to be certain Angelique had the best possible care in the coming months. "I have sent for the physician who treated me after Lucien shot me and left me for dead. I want him to remove the stitches from my scalp so I no longer feel like a stuffed doll, and then I'd like him to see you, too."

"Oh, Diego, not again." Angelique pulled her hand from his and sat up straight as she began to argue. "I am well. I have no need of a physician's attentions. Besides, there are so many things I still do not understand. I know what happened to me but not all that has happened to you, and I am very curious still. Couldn't we simply talk this afternoon?" Talk until he was at least willing to tell her the truth about Teresa, she said to herself, though she dared not say the words aloud.

Diego reached for her hand again, this time bringing it to his lips. "Of course we can talk all afternoon, and into the night as well, if that is your desire, but first I want Dr. Flores's assurance that you are well."

"Those are your terms?" Angelique's blue eyes smoldered with a dark fury, not pleased to be presented with such an awkward choice. "Either I see this Dr. Flores, or you won't talk with me?"

"Angelique!" Diego gave an exasperated sigh, not understanding how he had managed to begin an argument when his motive was merely concern. "I want only the assurance that you are well. Is that too great a favor to ask? Dr. Flores is a responsible physician, and a gentleman. He will not torture you!"

Stung by his taunt, Angelique looked away. Diego thought she was simply being silly, when, in fact, she dreaded the thought of another man's touch. Surely this Dr. Flores would wish to examine her, ask her to remove her clothes, and . . . Suddenly she grew so short of breath she could not force herself to think what might occur next. "I will do no more than speak with him, Diego. No more than that!"

Shocked that she was so upset, Diego quickly agreed, but he was all the more frightened that there truly was something seriously wrong with his bride.

Chapter XXVIII

Diego found it nearly impossible to sit still while Dr. Flores hovered over him. "I will apologize for my wife's attitude now. She had a very sheltered upbringing and quite naturally has found these last weeks extremely difficult to endure."

Sighing sympathetically, the physician responded with a smile. "My own wife is high-strung, Captain Aragon. You need not worry I will upset yours needlessly, for I have had many years of practice at being both diplomatic and patient. Her problem could well be only exhaustion, and then rest will be all she requires." Flores removed the last of his tiny sutures from Diego's scalp and lay his tweezers and scissors aside. "There now. Your hair is so dark and thick that the scar will never be seen."

That possibility scarcely concerned him and Diego leapt to his feet as he tried to make the kindly physician understand just what horrors Angelique had suffered. "Lucien Dangermond was a most despicable villain. He used my wife as his whore. There is simply no other way to describe what he did. She is a beauty, and a proud one—as well she should be—and I would do anything to protect her from the vicious gossip that is bound to circulate throughout Vera Cruz."

Alarmed by the young man's agitated mood, the soft-spoken physician offered some sensible advice. "I know you have also been under a great deal of strain, Captain, and you will do your wife little good if you cannot achieve peace within yourself and provide her with a calm companion. I think what you need is a long rest too."

Diego found that advice absurd. "There is nothing wrong with me. It is only Angelique who needs your attention. She is pregnant, you see, and—"

"*Madre de Dios!*" Dr. Flores exclaimed with a sudden burst of insight. "I understand your concern now and you need say no more. I know how upset your wife must be. I will see that she is given the best care possible. While she may have served as a pirate's mistress, I can assure you that in time that tragedy will be forgotten. Now let me go up and see her without any further delay." He gathered up his instruments and replaced them in his black bag, his attitude now completely professional.

Grateful that the doctor had finally seen the urgency in his request, Diego relaxed considerably. "Yes, the sooner Angelique meets you, the sooner she'll see that her fears have been unfounded." He led the way up the stairs to the master bedroom, which extended across the front of the elegantly furnished villa. He knocked lightly at the door and, finding Angelique seated at the window seat looking out over the city, he promptly ushered Dr. Flores into the room and introduced him. Since she had no alternative as yet, the pretty young woman was still wearing the flowing white gown the Indians had given her. Curled up on the thick cushions at the open window, with her hair softly curling about her shoulders, she looked very much like the child he had once believed her to be. Seeing the physician's startled glance, Diego realized that the man was shocked to find such a young woman, but it had been months since he had given Angelique's age any thought.

"I will leave you two alone. Please just come to the door

and call for me if there is anything you require, Dr. Flores, and I will provide it immediately." With one last reassuring smile directed at his bride, Diego closed the door and walked back down the stairs. He had no idea how much time the man might wish to spend with Angelique, but with her being so reluctant to confide in a physician, it might take him hours just to begin a conversation, let alone discuss her health. With that thought in mind, Diego poured himself a generous drink and sat down to wait for the doctor's report. He was tired and soon dozed off, but he awakened immediately when the doctor touched his shoulder.

"I had not expected your wife to be either so young or so uncooperative, Captain, but by simply talking with her about Vera Cruz for awhile I was finally able to win her trust. I thought it best not to mention the child. I told her the medicine I had prescribed was only to help her regain her usual composure. Fortunately she believed me."

Diego rose to question the doctor, for he did not understand his meaning. "I'm sorry. Just what sort of medicine did you give Angelique if it was not simply a soothing tonic?"

Flores reached out to take Diego's arm in a reassuring grasp. "It is exactly what you wished, a mixture of several herbs, quite potent, which should cause a miscarriage before dawn."

Diego could not even catch his breath to scream for what seemed like an eternity. He grabbed the slender doctor's shoulders with both hands and lifted him clear off his feet. "The child is mine, not Dangermond's!" he explained in a tortured sob. "What have you done to my wife? My God, what you have done to her!"

His eyes wide with terror, the silver-haired physician tried to struggle free. "But when you said she was pregnant, I assumed—"

Dropping the man in a startled heap, Diego tore up the stairs and sped into the bedroom he had planned to share

511

with his wife. She was still seated at the window and smiled until she realized by his frantic expression that something was terribly wrong.

"What's happened, Diego? What's the matter?" Angelique asked quickly.

Not wanting to frighten her as severely as Dr. Flores had frightened him, Diego walked toward her slowly as he attempted to explain what had to be done. "The medicine the physician gave you was the wrong one. We'll have to get it out of you as best we can. Come over to the washbasin and put your fingers down your throat, or I'll do it for you, but there is no time to lose."

Despite the obvious urgency of her husband's request, Angelique shook her head. "There's no need for that, Diego. When he handed me that vile-smelling liquid, I just pretended to drink it. I poured it into the flowerpot on the balcony when he wasn't looking and he didn't realize I hadn't taken it."

Instead of being overjoyed with such wonderful news, Diego responded in a furious fit of temper. "Of course. I should have known. As always, whenever you're presented with a choice, you prefer to lie rather than tell the truth! You're an actress through and through, aren't you?" He raked his fingers through his tangled locks, not recalling the new scar until he felt it. "Why I bothered to worry about you I'll never know. You're the most devious female ever born. You delight in fooling men and I should have known it wouldn't occur to you to tell the doctor the truth!" He turned away to wipe the tears from his eyes before she could see them. He had never been so badly frightened as he had been when he had thought she had swallowed the poison that would kill their child. He was afraid he was the one who was going to be sick and, seeing that the doctor had followed him up the stairs, he kicked the bedroom door shut in the terrified man's face.

Horrified by his string of unwarranted insults, Angelique

512

left her comfortable perch by the open window and ran to her husband's side. "How dare you shout at me for telling lies! How dare you! Were I not such an accomplished actress, as you call it, we would both be dead! Why do you think Lucien had you whipped? It wasn't because he hated you. It was because he wanted to teach me a lesson, to show me exactly what would happen to you again and again if I failed to please him. Do you think I enjoyed sleeping with that snake? Do you? I despised the man and yet I made him believe he was as wonderful a lover as he claimed to be. I played my part well. I told him so damn many lies I can't even remember them all, and I'd do it all over again to save your life!" She turned her back on him then. "While we're discussing lies, I don't want to hear any from you either. Just leave me and go to Teresa, if that's what you really want to do. You don't need to start some ridiculous argument by calling me a liar! I'm not nearly as stupid as you seem to think. Just go!"

Angelique had her arms crossed over her breasts and stood tapping her foot impatiently as though she could not wait for him to leave, but Diego was astonished and absolutely fascinated by her fiery response to his remarks about her inability to tell the truth. It was obvious that the sharpness of her wit had not been diminished, no matter how physically degrading her time with Lucien had been. He realized then, with a deep stab of regret, that Dr. Flores had been right about him. He was as worn out by their ordeal as she was. Unfortunately, he had lost his temper as a result and had taunted her with an argument from their past. Such action had been senseless and cruel.

"No, I am the one who is stupid," he finally replied. "You have suffered far more than I had imagined and I was not even gentleman enough to thank you for valuing my life above your own. Teresa is an obnoxious nuisance and, while I think you'd prefer to be alone, I want to assure you that I'm not going to see her, not ever."

Diego left the room so quietly that Angelique did not even realize he had gone until she turned to look up at him and found the large bedroom empty. His apology had cost him too much of his pride, perhaps, but she had never felt more miserable and knew that if their argument had had any winner, it certainly had not been her.

The housekeeper was a pleasant woman who wanted only to please Angelique in every way she could, but the young woman remained so distant in her responses to offers of refreshment and service that Consuelo soon left her undisturbed. She knew Diego only slightly and his new bride not at all, but they seemed to her to be a most unhappy couple from what she observed of their first day in the villa. She waited for instructions for the preparation of supper, but when Diego had failed to return by sundown, she carried a simple meal to Angelique along with the new nightgown Diego had sent her out to purchase.

"*Señora* Aragon? Your husband asked me to find you a pretty nightgown and I hope you will be pleased with this one. I do not know his plans for the evening, but I thought you might be hungry, so I've brought you something to eat. Is there anything else I might do for you?"

Angelique was surprised when Consuelo entered the room, for she had not realized the hour had grown so late. "I would like to bathe if that's possible." She rose to take the nightgown and thought the delicate, pink, lace-trimmed garment very beautiful. "This is exquisite. Thank you."

"I will have your bath ready in a moment." Consuelo beamed with pride, and, delighted she had at least pleased her new mistress, she hurried to attend to her needs.

After a leisurely bath, Angelique finally looked at her supper tray, but she ate only the slices of fresh fruit before returning to the window seat where she had spent the day. The windows of most of the homes nearby were aglow with light and she wondered who the residents might be and how she could meet them and make friends. The night air was clear, and from somewhere there came the strains of music and an occasional burst of laughter.

Feeling very alone, she wondered where Diego had gone and if he would ever bother to return. She had found no pleasure in assigning the blame to him for their latest argument, but truly she felt not the slightest bit of remorse for anything she had said. Perhaps they simply viewed life from two perspectives that were so entirely different they would never enjoy the accord she had hoped they would find. She relaxed her pose as she watched the homes nearby grow dark, but she had no wish to go to bed when she would again have to sleep all alone.

Diego fumbled with the buttons on his waistcoat, then removed it with an easy shrug as he climbed the stairs. Other than the handsome outfit Angelique had tailored to fit him, he had few articles of apparel and reminded himself that he was in need of clothing as much as his wife. When he saw the light under her door, he attempted to be more quiet as he turned toward the smaller bedroom located adjacent to hers, but before he could open the door, Angelique stepped out into the hall. Knowing she deserved some explanation for the lateness of the hour, he cleared his throat and began one. "I had a bet with Octavio. He and his crew had to treat my crew to dinner tonight, since we won the race from the Yucatán." He felt very foolish and was afraid she would not believe that story even though it was the truth. "We were all in the mood to celebrate, and I neglected to note the time." Opening the door of the bedroom, he tossed his coat and waistcoat inside, not bothering to note where they landed.

Angelique began to smile, for Diego had obviously had far too much to drink and was trying his best to appear sober. Walking up to meet him, she took his hand to lead him back into the master bedroom. "I recall another night when you came home after attending a party, and had I not helped you to undress, you would have been forced to sleep in your clothes." Just the memory of that night made her laugh. "Do you remember that?"

Diego was not nearly as drunk as Angelique seemed to think and he was amazed to find her in a sympathetic mood. Since she seemed so determined to take care of him, he decided to enjoy her attentions and sat down upon the bed while she knelt to pull off his boots. "That night is no more than a blur, I'm afraid. What I do recall though is asking you about it the next day," he said without thinking what her response would be.

Angelique tossed his boots aside and rose slowly to face him. She remembered that occasion as well as he did, apparently. "Well, go on and say it. I know what you're thinking. I lied to you."

Rather than agree with her, Diego reached out to catch her hand and pulled her down beside him. "Now let's not start arguing again. I don't want to do that. Do you?" When he saw by her wistful expression that she did not either, he continued. "While we're on the subject of memories, let's think back to the night we met. What I did was take advantage of a beautiful young girl's innocence and rather than make me pay for that offense as she had every right to do, that dear girl created a string of the most intriguing illusions." He leaned forward to kiss his bride's lips lightly. "Why you are so devoted to me when I constantly behave like a fool I'll never know, but I'll never stop thanking God that you are."

Angelique's gaze softened from blue to the lovely violet Diego found so attractive as she replied, "You don't behave in a foolish manner. Whatever are you talking about?"

With an enthusiastic hug, Diego pulled Angelique across his chest as he lay back upon the bed. "You are the perfect wife for me, my pet, but how you can be so blind to my faults

516

I will never understand."

His dark eyes held such an enticing gleam that Angelique cuddled close as she replied, "Are you referring to your terrible temper, or to your excessive pride perhaps, or to your vanity, which leads you to believe that a few slight scars have ruined your looks?"

"Slight scars?" Diego scoffed loudly, for he could not help but object to that description of his battered appearance.

Angelique rose upon her elbow to kiss his left brow sweetly before pushing his shiny dark hair back from his forehead. "You have yet to tell me how Lucien managed to shoot you in the head. How could that have happened? I can understand how he might have shot you in the back, but—"

A wicked grin curved across Diego's lips as he watched Angelique reach for the buttons on his shirt. He made no protest as her slender fingers moved down his chest, but he untied the pink satin bow at her neckline without her noticing what he had done. He then slid his hand slowly up the creamy-smooth flesh of her thigh and laughed when she began to giggle. "He shot me because I'm not nearly as clever as you, my beauty. Now let's not waste any more of the night in recalling my many mistakes."

What he wanted was so plain in his loving caress, but there was still something Angelique needed to settle. "Diego, I think what happened when we were apart is better left forgotten too. I'd never willingly be unfaithful to you, but I can understand why you'd want Teresa. You needn't deny what happened between you two, but I hope it won't ever happen again."

For an instant Diego was furious with the enchanting blonde who fit so snugly in his embrace, but then he realized that her vivid imagination, while only a meager example of her many charms, was one of her most endearing qualities. "I want you to try your hand at writing poetry, my dear, or inventing plays and games to amuse our children, but do not ever use that fertile imagination of yours to convince yourself that I have been unfaithful to you. Should you ever insult me so rudely again, I will not even bother to deny it!" With that sincerely voiced promise, Diego captured his lovely bride in a tight embrace and held her locked in his arms until the passion of her kisses forced him to rise to cast off the last of his clothing.

Left alone for that moment, Angelique dimmed the light and slipped off the pink gown. She lay back upon the pillows as Diego returned to her and this time she moved her fingertips slowly down the scars that crisscrossed his back. His skin still held its usual luscious warmth and she drew him near, delighted to again be in his arms. She might have disappointed him when last they were together, but she had no intention of missing any opportunities to please him this night. Her caress was light, teasing, as it moved down over his hip and then across the taut planes of his flat stomach. "You are still perfect, Diego, perfect in every way," she assured him in a throaty whisper.

While discounting her praise, Diego considered the changes in Angelique's figure most appealing. He moved his hand lightly down her belly and thought the slight swell his child had caused was the most marvelous of mysteries. His kisses moved slowly over the fullness of one breast, then lingered at the delicately flushed peak. "I loved you the first moment I saw you, my angel. I loved you even then."

Thrilled by his confession, Angelique was too tactful to remind him that he had not been at all pleased by her laughter when he had landed in the flower bed. Instead she purred sweetly in his ear, "Surely my regard for you was no secret." She slipped from his grasp with a fluid grace and spread sweet kisses along his broad shoulders and then down the length of his spine, her tongue lingering upon the pattern of scars he now bore. Her fingertips teased the firm muscles of his inner thigh as he turned upon his back, but her touch was so pleasant that he did not object.

Her lavish affection was an endless delight and, as she

trailed her tender kisses over his broad chest, Diego tried once again to apologize, but his voice was no more than a hoarse whisper. "I should not have left you alone, not for the voyage, not today—"

"Not ever!" Angelique replied breathlessly before she sought to give him the deepest joy her exotic kisses could bestow. Her bright curls spilled across his stomach to tease his senses as she slid down by his side. She had no desire in her heart other than pleasing him, and as she felt the ripples of excitement sweeping through his lean frame, she considered their pleasure shared equally. She was alive again, as she had not been since the night the savage storm had destroyed the *Diablo,* and she wanted to savor the splendor of the moment forever.

Diego let the waves of pleasure wash over him until he could no longer hold back the crest. He moved quickly then, pulling Angelique up beside him so he could finish what she had begun. As it had so many memorable times before, her lithe body welcomed his with fiery warmth and fluid grace, but he held her in a tender embrace, believing her to be far more fragile now.

She soon proved him wrong. The passion of her deep kiss swiftly drove all thoughts of caution from his mind and he enveloped her in ecstasy, letting the rapture their love had again created bind their hearts anew. The past was forgotten in that instant and all pain was swept from their memories by the swift torrent of wondrous emotion they shared. They lingered together on that splendid plateau until the tide of their passion ebbed to a gentle warmth and the peace of sleep gradually carried them to the bright world of dreams.

It was nearly noon when Angelique finally awakened. She stretched lazily and yawned as she turned to look for her husband. He was standing at the window, dressed only in his breeches, and she watched him for a long while before he noticed she was awake. How she could have thought him like Lucien for even an instant she didn't know. Truly, he was nothing like that monster. His pride was not arrogance, nor was his great courage a threat to others. She was ashamed she had ever had the audacity to compare the two men and was thankful Diego would never learn she had done so.

"Are you hungry?" Diego asked with a ready grin. "Consuelo is a fine cook and—"

Angelique shook her head and her sly smile was so inviting that Diego came quickly to her side. "The harbor is interesting to view, isn't it?" she asked sweetly. "This seems like a fine house for you."

"For us," Diego corrected promptly. He stretched out beside her and then pulled her into his arms, cradling her head gently upon his chest. "I have just been watching the ships and thinking about what I want to do. I told you once that the spirit of revolution will reach here soon. For some reason, that no longer seems an exciting possibility but merely the inevitable tide of change. I cannot help but think of your father. Because I am a Spaniard, it will be assumed that I'll support the crown, just as it was assumed that he supported his king."

"But you won't?" Angelique wondered aloud.

Diego gave her temple a soft kiss. "Need you ask such a question? Of course not. I want to see all people enjoy the freedom they deserve."

Angelique studied her husband's expression closely, for she had seldom seen him in such a serious mood. "What is it you wish to do then, Diego? I want to hear your plans, but I insist they include me."

"How could you think they might not?" Diego leaned down to kiss her lips lightly but was soon lost in the sweetness of her kiss and had great difficulty drawing away. He lifted his hand to caress her bright curls and, taking a deep breath, he forced himself to continue. "I think the Viceroy will want to honor me for ridding the Gulf of at least one band of pirates. I plan to ask him for a land grant, but not here. In California."

Angelique sat up quickly, then remembered to draw the sheet across her bare bosom. Though blushing at her show of modesty, she could not hide her curiosity. "California, Diego? Won't that take many weeks at sea? I am so tired of living in a cramped little cabin. Must we go so far away?"

Diego brushed aside her complaints easily. "We needn't leave until after our baby is born. Besides, I can have Octavio sail the *Lord of the Wind* around Cape Horn and we can go over land to meet him at the Gulf of Tehuantepec. It is then only a brief cruise up the Pacific coast to California."

"The *Lord of the Wind?* You have replaced the *Diablo* already?"

Diego thought better of telling her just how he had managed to accomplish such a feat so swiftly. "Yes, indeed I have."

"You have this all well thought out, it seems," Angelique remarked dryly. "Your plans are all made?"

Seeing the fiery sparkle in her eyes, Diego attempted to smile in his most charming manner. "I think trade on the Pacific coast is going to be brisk in a few years' time. The choices are to remain here and manage my father's business interests—even though he forbid me to do so—or to begin to build a line of my own. I don't want to offer him any competition, or to be away for the extended periods that voyages to Spain require. And then, as I said, it is only a matter of time before Spain loses its hold upon this land. California is so distant that it has never been under firm control. I believe the opportunities there are unlimited. We needn't decide today, however, for I don't want you to travel until you are fully recovered from childbirth."

Angelique considered his explanation plausible, but still she thought there might be some other consideration he had not revealed. "Your reasons sound very sensible, Diego, but if you're thinking primarily of saving me from having to face what is certain to be the most tantalizing scandal to come to Vera Cruz in years, then I can't agree."

"What scandal?" Diego asked with all the innocence he could muster.

"I know that sailors love to spin tales. Doesn't half the town already know I was a pirate's mistress until you rescued me and killed him?"

Diego shrugged. "Who would be interested in such a story, Angelique?"

"Everyone, as you well know!" Diego was a very poor actor, she realized. His thoughts were as obvious as the deep golden tan that covered his well-defined features. Laughing, she kissed him once again. "You can't stop the gossip here any more than you could in Barcelona, but if what you really wish to do is remain here, then we shall do it and not give my reputation another thought."

As always, he admired her courage and, when Diego responded, his deep voice was hoarse with emotion, "Truly, I want to go to California for the reasons I described. That it will also serve to shield you from wicked tales is merely an additional advantage."

"Wicked?" Angelique asked pointedly. "They will be true, Diego. Unfortunate, perhaps, but certainly true."

Leaning forward so much that Angelique was forced to lie back upon the pillows, Diego disagreed. "There is only one truth, and that is this one," he whispered hungrily, peeling away the soft linen sheet so he could caress the lush curve of her breast.

Angelique's hand instantly covered his as she remarked, "I had no opportunity to ask. What did Dr. Flores wish to give me yesterday? He seemed like a competent man. How could he have made a mistake with his medicines?"

Diego tightened his embrace, refusing to allow the question to distract him from his quest to possess his delectable wife once again. "A potion for headaches, I

522

believe. A simple mistake he'll not make again, I can assure you."

Angelique began to smile, radiating an impish light that added further sparkle to her lovely blue-violet gaze. She would never call Diego a liar, not ever—not even when his lies were as transparent as this one. "Don't you see what you're doing? You're trying to protect me from a truth you can't reveal. That is all I ever did with you. Can't you appreciate my motives now and forgive me?"

All Diego saw was the luscious golden glow that the bright sunlight streaming through the open windows gave her fair skin. The ordeal through which she had suffered had not touched her beauty, and had she actually been the golden goddess the Maya had thought her to be, he could not have been more enchanted. "I have not told you often enough how dearly I love you. Can you forgive me for that mistake?" he whispered as his lips brushed hers.

"Yes, but until last night you had never spoken those words to me and I feared you never would," Angelique replied wistfully.

"Last night?" Diego asked in astonishment. "But surely I told you before then."

"Never." With a smile that grew slowly from shy to radiant, Angelique drew him into her arms and enfolded him in a seductive embrace. "I have been just as foolish," she confessed, "for I too kept silent about the love that fills my heart."

Diego flashed the wolfish grin his father found so objectionable, but he was far too happy to keep his joy from showing in his expression. "Then we must each remember to say the words." He paused for a moment, then queried softly, "But even if I failed to speak of the love you inspire, could you not feel it in the devotion of my kiss, or in the tenderness of my touch?"

As he moved with teasing slowness to carry their passion

523

for each other to new heights, Angelique found scant need for words. The depth of Diego's love had always been plain in his overwhelming affection, just as her love for him had been reflected in her enticing smile and seductive caress. "I will always love you," she whispered softly as the glorious splendor of his loving filled her heart to overflowing once again.

Diego drew her closer still, savoring her kiss until he was so filled with desire that he could barely breathe. "And I will always love you," he vowed, for he knew he had found the greatest of life's treasures in her arms, one far more precious than gold. He would never again fail to speak the words she had longed to hear, but, for now, the love that filled his heart with ecstasy needed no voice to be understood.

If you enjoyed this book we have a special offer for you. Become a charter member of the **ZEBRA HISTORICAL ROMANCE HOME SUBSCRIPTION SERVICE** and...

Get a
FREE
Zebra Historical Romance
(A $3.95 value) No Obligation

Now that you have read a Zebra Historical Romance we're sure you'll want more of the passion and sensuality, the desire and dreams and fascinating historical settings that make these novels the favorites of so many women. So we have made arrangements for you to receive a *FREE* book ($3.95 value) and preview 4 brand new Zebra Historical Romances each month.

Join the Zebra
Home Subscription Service—
Free Home Delivery

By joining our Home Subscription Service you'll never have to worry about missing a title. You'll automatically get the romance, the allure, the attraction, that make Zebra Historical Romances so special.

Each month you'll receive 4 brand new Zebra Historical Romance novels as soon as they are published. Look them over *Free* for 10 days. If you're not delighted simply return them and owe nothing. But if you enjoy them as much as we think you will, you'll pay *only* $3.50 each and save 45¢ over the cover price. (You save a total of $1.80 each month.) *There is no shipping and handling charge or other hidden charges.*

———— *Fill Out the Coupon* ————

Start your subscription now and start saving. Fill out the coupon and mail it *today*. You'll get your **FREE** book along with your first month's books to preview.